D0966353

MOURNERS
BELOW

JAMES PURDY

MOURNERS BELOW

THE VIKING PRESS   NEW YORK

LIBRARY OF CONGRESS CATALOGING IN PUBLICATION DATA
Purdy, James.
Mourners below.
I. Title.
PS3531.U426M6   813'.54   80-24995
ISBN 0-670-49142-X

Printed in the United States of America
Set in CRT Garamond

PART I

"**D**id you ever see a boy likes ice cream so much?"

Eugene Bledsoe spoke these words concerning his youngest son Duane in Moe's Villa and Sweet Shop, pretending to address some imaginary passerby on the very day he had received the notice from the War Department informing him that his two oldest sons, Justin and Douglas, had died in battle.

Eugene had summoned Duane into his den and without a word of warning had handed him the telegram, and when the boy had finished reading it, and weakly handed the fluttering yellow paper back to his Dad, the father had said only in a stern reprimand kind of voice "Duane!" as if he saw Duane about to overturn some expensive imported vase.

Mourners Below

(3)

"I thought we would go to Moe's Villa." Eugene then spoke in his everyday humdrum tone, and picking up his straw boater, took Duane by the arm and led him out of the house.

"Anybody who can ice-skate as beautiful as you can, Benjy ..." Eugene said after they were seated in the sweetshop, lapsing into the use of his youngest son's baby name, and then Eugene stopped for a moment in the face of his son's growing turbulent grief and incipient tears, but went on and finished with, "Any skater that good can't help liking ice cream. Do you want another dish?"

Duane Bledsoe did not respond to this question. In actual fact, he didn't like ice cream as well as his father made out, but it gave Eugene such pleasure to watch him eating a sweet, both on that horrible day of the War Department telegram and forever afterward, that Duane ate ice cream as a kind of duty to please his old Dad (actually he was only fifty-five, and it had been his birthday just the day before, June 11).

Duane blushed as his father first smiled and then broke into a grin at the sight of the boy's mouth covered with the vanilla treat, and Eugene unfolded a napkin and handed it to him to wipe his lips on.

"Yes, sir," the father said, "an ice skater has to eat plenty of ice cream."

Duane was touching his lips with the thick linen of the napkin which Moe's Villa alone perhaps of all the world's remaining ice-cream parlors still supplied. Because Moe's belonged to a vanished age. Ladies of incredible wealth still came here for an ice, Viennese coffee, and the like. It was hardly a place for a young man and his Dad any day in the year, and scarcely the site to choose after the kind of news they were recipients of. But then, Duane sat studying his Dad, he was always so out of touch with things.

Even though they were at Moe's Villa, Duane waited for his father to say something about his dead brothers. He put his spoon down on the plate. The last of the ice cream had been tasted and swallowed. They had died after all, Justin and Douglas, in the same division, on the same day, and their bodies, according to the wording of the telegram, would not be able to be recovered. Why didn't Eugene say anything more, then? Why did he only talk about Duane's ice skating and then apologize for his having once decided in the presence of Duane's skating coach that he did not think it was advisable just now that Duane think of competing in the next Olympics after the war?

"I don't think he's ready for any such ordeal as training for the

James Purdy

(4)

Olympics." Eugene had spoken with Pete Foulke, the figure-skating coach, who had already sent one boy from our town to the Olympics. "Duane is, you have to admit, a very immature boy."

"But not so far as his ice skating is concerned," the coach had replied.

"Oh, but in everything else, you know, he is." Eugene spoke omnisciently.

The coach had bitten his lip and, capitulating, retired.

Yes, the only thing his Dad wanted to talk about was ice cream.

Justin and Douglas had been considerably older than Duane, and they had been gone from our town for several years before they had been . . . killed, so that the sense of loss was diminished slightly by their previous absence. They had been Annapolis graduates, both of them. In some ways they were more like two additional fathers than brothers; but they had been closer to Duane than any father. Like Eugene, they had also, especially when he was little, taken him to Moe's Villa, where they would watch him eat ice cream, as Eugene did today, and would laugh at him and then take him riding in their fast roadster.

At this moment, as he sat in the cool parlor, having tasted the ice cream, their deaths seemed more and more improbable. He wondered if another telegram would not arrive canceling out the news of the first one. Perhaps his father expected this also and that was why no grief was in evidence, no outward sorrow.

But that night, as he lay wide awake in bed, Duane heard a strange noise. At first he thought one of the wild lynxes had broken into the house, or some other nocturnal predator. He picked up a hockey stick which stood in the corner of his bedroom and walked to the stairwell which directly faced his father's bedroom. It was his father making the sound. Duane listened at the door for what seemed a long time, but back in his room the clock told him it had been only a few minutes. The sound had been like that of a pump which had been primed with difficulty and was grudgingly giving out its stream. There were choking sounds and even perhaps hiccups, and some whispering. Duane went back to bed. He threw off the bedclothes after a while. He saw his exposed calves, bulging with muscles and veins testifying to his incessant and almost only occupation, ice skating. Ice cream and ice skating, he remembered his father's words. Poor old Dad, he said. He felt better, though, that his father made the sounds of grief, since he would not speak of Justin and Douglas directly.

Up until the day of his brothers' deaths, his Dad, Eugene Bledsoe, had always left the bathroom door open wide while he shaved. Almost invariably, too, Duane had entered the spacious room and sat unbidden but welcome on the edge of the bathtub, which a visitor once had described as big enough to bathe a horse in. His Dad shaved with a straight razor which he sharpened daily on a strop which looked in its way as ample as the bathtub. He also, Duane thought, used enough lather to bathe a grown man in from the leftover suds, and Eugene's facility at shaving was both perfect and frightening. Duane sometimes believed the reason he had taken up ice skating was from observing his father shave. Also, up until the time of their deaths, Eugene had worn only his undershorts and house slippers for this operation. For a man who sat so much and seemed never to lift a finger at anything around the house, his arms were thick with sinews and brawn, his waist as narrow almost as Duane's.

But from the time directly after the War Department telegram, Eugene wore trousers while shaving, an undershirt (mended by himself), and a kind of apron to prevent the suds coming off on his trousers, and he half closed the door now.

"Can I come in, Dad?" Duane inquired on seeing the door half closed, the day after the news.

"I'll be through in just a moment. . . . Do you have to go, Duane?" he had added.

Duane could not say, "I'd like to watch."

He shaved only about once a week himself, and over his cheeks and upper lip more down than beard was scattering.

Eugene opened the door and looked at him.

"Nearly finished," he said, looking into Duane's eyes for the first time since their lives had changed.

Up until the time "their house fell" (the phrase came from his father long after the event) Duane had made some efforts to prepare himself for college by faithfully studying with his tutor and doing his lessons properly, but with the death of his two hero brothers, he felt as if everything holding him together was loosening. He saw that he had been able to go on up until that time only because of his brothers, who had enshrouded him with their strength, their expectations, their stern loving-kindness. They had written him very few letters, but the ones they had written had made a deep impression upon Duane. Justin had written him a letter once whose words he had never forgotten, words near the end of the second page just before the signature: *"I know you will make me proud of you, Benj, and I don't need to say more than this."*

But with both Justin and Douglas gone, and his father shutting the door to him during his morning shaving, Duane had the sensation of being in an ascending balloon, his moorings cut, and yet not able to rise very high either.

His father's closing the door on him while shaving upset him almost more than his brothers' deaths, which still seemed unconvincing.

For some years now, Mrs. Newsom had been doing the cooking and the housework for the Bledsoes, and the first supper after the deaths of Justin and Douglas she behaved, Duane thought, in a peculiar manner. As she brought the roast of beef in for Eugene to carve (she usually refused to eat with them but partook of the supper in the kitchen, which, to tell the truth, was a handsomer and pleasanter room than the rather gloomy and immensely long dining hall), Mrs. Newsom looked especially sharply at Duane to see, he supposed, if he was showing any grief; when all the time, he felt like saying, his grief was that Eugene closed the door of the bathroom on him now. It finally—his hurt at the closed door—brought tears of rage to his eyes, and Mrs. Newsom all at once looked satisfied, mistaking these tears for his grief over his brothers' passing.

"Would you like to learn how to box?" Eugene inquired abruptly while helping Duane to some mashed potatoes almost swimming in sweet butter and fresh cream, with tiny flakes of fresh parsley and paprika.

Duane put down his fork. He felt this offer was to make up for Eugene's not letting him watch him shave.

"Lyle Hawkins used to be middleweight champion in Chicago," Eugene went on, pretending to chew with enjoyment a piece of the beef. "I spoke to him about you the other day when he came into the law office."

Mrs. Newsom was standing in the doorway which led from the kitchen to the dining hall. Neither she nor Duane believed that Eugene actually conducted any business of any consequence at his law office. Once Duane had gone by and peeked through the glass door and found his father asleep at ten o'clock in the morning.

"Well?" Eugene wondered, watching Duane cut his meat.

"Could you bring him a little sharp knife, Mrs. Newsom?" Eugene spoke somewhat irritably. "Here, let me, Benj," the father said when Mrs. Newsom did not come back with a knife sufficiently quickly enough. "That cut is none too tender now, is it?"

"Do you want me to be a boxer, too?" Duane thanked his father for cutting his beef.

"Too?" Eugene wondered. Then: "Ice skating is no substitute for self-defense!" He shook his fork at Duane.

"Do I know Lyle . what's-his-name?"

"I could bring him round if you like," Eugene explained. "But you'd better go to his residence. He has just fixed up his barn for teaching . . . pugilism."

"Mr. Bledsoe," Mrs. Newsom began unexpectedly, as she handed Duane the sharp knife.

"What is it?" Eugene looked up at her.

"Nothing. . . . It can wait," she said.

Duane was sure she had wanted to broach the subject of the two boys' deaths.

"If it's important . . ." Eugene looked obliquely at her.

"Never mind now." She gave Duane a sidelong glance and then looked at his father as much as to say it could not be said in front of a boy.

"I suppose *they* would have wanted me to learn to box," Duane got out somewhat testily when he saw Mrs. Newsom and Eugene exchanging private looks.

Eugene flushed at the word "they." He cut himself another piece of the beef and put it down with a *plump* on his plate. Then, instead of cutting it even finer with his knife and fork, which he had raised for this purpose, he put these instruments down noisily.

"I will tell him to expect you, then." Eugene spoke loftily, as he probably did in his law office.

"What have you got for our dessert, Mrs. Newsom?" Eugene's voice boomed louder than either she or Duane had heard it in some time.

"We have a choice tonight, Mr. Bledsoe." Mrs. Newsom advanced into the dining hall and took up and away the two dinner plates from the table. "Custard pie or yesterday's devil's food cake."

"I'll bet I know who'll have the custard pie." However, Eugene's voice was so loud again that Mrs. Newsom and Duane stared at one another with almost terrified glances.

James Purdy

"He could never turn down a piece of custard pie to wind up with," Eugene said.

"I thought it was ice cream I couldn't turn down," Duane said in an almost surly voice.

Eugene looked at him. He had wounded his father and he was glad on account of the shutting of the door on him: How could he explain his anger over that to anybody, even to himself? Well, yes, all right, he would learn to box!

Lyle Hawkins spent most of the two or three hours with Duane recalling his career in the ring. One would have thought that the boy was a reporter and Lyle was trying to remember everything about his meteoric rise—and fall—as a boxer. He had brought out all the old boxing magazines and an album of photographs. Duane leafed through the photos somewhat dispiritedly. Lyle wore only a torn pair of blue jeans, an unmended sweat shirt, and a pair of extremely dilapidated huaraches. His curly black hair gave off an odor of cheap pomade.

Duane did not know which pained and embarrassed him more, looking at Mr. Hawkins's vanished fame and glory or having to answer the questions which came after every few pauses about the deaths of his brothers.

"You were all so close together," Lyle kept saying. "Bad for your father . . ."

He acted as if their deaths could not have any meaning for Duane, which made him feel even more at sea because, to tell the truth, they were already not as real as they should be, and their deaths were made more unreal when Lyle went on saying, *"They were your half brothers, weren't they?"*

"Yes, but we were . . . as close-knit as full blood brothers," he brought out awkwardly.

"I've been talking to the people at the skating rink," Lyle began after he had put away his picture albums, old magazines, and a framed photograph of him shaking hands with the President of the United States. "Duane, I don't think boxing and ice skating mix so good." He looked down at the boy's legs, perhaps studying what bulging calf muscles he had; well, after all, he couldn't help it if he didn't have a boxer's build.

"I don't think rope jumping, which, as you know, Benj, is the daily routine of a boxer, and running to boot . . ." He stopped and sneezed four or five times in succession. "This damned air," he cried, "goes right to the bottom of a man's lungs."

Duane brightened at the thought that Mr. Hawkins might not want to give him lessons in the art of self-defense, for he stared a long time at the boy.

"Let me show you my actual gym."

Duane wondered why he said "actual." It was like some of the words his father occasionally employed, common words but put before another word so that one wasn't precisely sure what he meant, but then his father was a lawyer, after all. . . .

The back part of the structure was considerably larger than it looked from the front living room. There was a small track which one could practice running on, two punching bags, a barbell set, a "horse," rings, and a number of pairs of deeply soiled boxing gloves.

"I will explain to your Dad about the conflict in being a skater and a boxer, you see," Mr. Hawkins said.

Duane studied the boxer's broken nose, the many little red lines over the whites of his eyes, his missing lower teeth, his mouth, which looked almost attached in its battered quality to his gums.

"You know, Justin and Douglas thought you had a career ahead of you as a . . . fancy ice-skating star. Too bad your Dad felt . . . it was too soon for the Olympics." He stopped.

Duane blushed furiously. Mr. Hawkins's statement of praise made up for all his unpleasantness, and for the dreadful odor of perspiration which came from his sweat shirt.

"I will explain the conflict to your Dad, Benj," he told him at the door.

"What's wrong with that man?" Eugene said, throwing his napkin down at the end of the evening meal. He was referring to Lyle Hawkins "He could have taught you self-defense. Of course he could. I have a notion to give him a piece of my mind. I'll teach him some self-defense!"

Eugene rose and went to his study.

Mrs. Newsom came in and shrugged her shoulders and lifted her eyebrows over her black-rimmed glasses. Mrs. Newsom and Duane often had little secret comments on Eugene's behavior. She was the only one who, in fact, admitted his two brothers were dead.

James Purdy

(10)

"He never mentions them," Duane almost sobbed a few days after the news. Mrs. Newsom's silence chided Eugene more than had she chimed in with Duane.

"Do you think I will ever grow as tall as them?" Duane asked, going out and watching Mrs. Newsom scald and dry the evening dishes. He picked up the tea towel and began drying the dishes for her.

"Duane, don't," she said, though she was pleased by his offer. "If your Dad saw you helping me again, he'd have a fit."

"Oh, he don't notice anything," Duane said and went on drying the dishes. "You didn't answer my question, Mrs. Newsom."

"Well, you're seventeen now. . . . My oldest boy, Laird, grew until he was twenty-five. His father measured him at that time. We couldn't believe it."

"I'm afraid I won't ever be as tall as them," Duane said.

"He ought to talk to you about their loss," Mrs. Newsom said finally. "It would make you both feel better. Total silence ain't right."

Duane stood at the space between the sliding doors which separated Eugene's study from the living room.

Without preparation or clearing his throat he got the same question out for Eugene as he had put to the housekeeper.

". . . Ever grow as tall as you and them?"

Eugene put down some long yellow sheets of paper.

"I wouldn't be at all surprised." He smiled.

"But what do you think?"

"Well, at your age . . ." Eugene thought back, and locked his hands behind his head. "Come to think of it, I was already six foot three, and I think I grew maybe another inch after that, but not much."

Duane could see Eugene was thinking hard about those years and showed no care or interest in whether he grew more or not.

"I don't think I'll make it, then." Duane turned to leave.

"Where are you going to now?"

"I thought you were busy."

"So old Lyle won't teach you self-defense." Eugene brought up the subject again. "Doubt anyhow he'd be much of a teacher, come to think of it."

"He thought it wouldn't do with my skating," Duane mumbled. He looked around the room, thinking there would be something there to remind both of them of the deaths of Justin and Douglas. Eugene's eyes

Mourners Below

followed where his son was looking, saw nothing, and came back to rest on the yellow papers.

"If you want me to insist," Eugene began again, "I can make Lyle take you for a student. He owes me many favors."

"I didn't much like him, Dad."

Eugene studied him curiously.

"May I ask what put you off?"

"I don't think he's taken a bath in a while, for one thing."

Eugene broke into a grin.

Duane sighed loudly, but Eugene did not appear to hear it, and Duane also knew that his father would never see Lyle, and, if he did run into him by chance, he would never ask about why he wouldn't give Duane self-defense instruction.

"Everything all right otherwise?" Eugene spoke in a tone that meant Duane should leave the room now.

Both Eugene and Duane had one physical discomfort in common: they were both frequently awakened at night by cramps in their legs. Eugene had even gone to the bother of purchasing a rather expensive medical book on cramps. It seemed that every time Eugene lectured on cramps, the night after his talk Duane would be mercilessly tormented by a series of charley horses which made all the flesh in his right leg rise up like ropes being hauled in by sailors. He felt he was being tormented by professional torturers in a dungeon. In a way he sort of enjoyed the torment; it was less boring than the rest of his life with Mrs. Newsom and Eugene.

But the same night, *it* happened, the thing which was to set him apart from everybody. The thing that was never to let him go, even after the actual manifestations were to cease, for the fear it would return, *they* would return, never left him. He blamed the cramps on his fancy ice skating. He blamed his seeing the things he saw that night on Eugene's icy reticence.

Worn out from the torment of his cramps, he had closed his eyes and, though not beginning to slumber (the courthouse clock had just struck three), he knew something was wrong, something was changing. At first he pretended his father had stolen into the room to help him with his cramps, but he knew better. He had to force himself to open his eyes.

James Purdy
(12)

They were sitting at the foot of his bed; he could almost feel their weight, even their breath. Yes, they had a weight, insubstantial as they were now, and they had a faint aroma too, though what it was he could never say or remember, except it was a bit like lily-of-the-valley. Douglas sat on his left side, and Justin on his right. They looked at him eagerly, imploringly, understandingly. His spine felt electrocuted, his mouth as dry as sand, his arms pinioned to his sides as if by steel thongs. They were liquid, or smokelike, yes like blue and pink smoke, their eyes like beautiful light violet pools in which water lilies grow. Then, like smoke **from** incense cones, they were gone!

He screamed; he called his father's name. Eugene came almost immediately to the door.

"Cramps," Duane said when Eugene sat down on the bed beside him.

"These old feather beds don't give a fellow enough support," Eugene commented, patting the bed again and again. "By golly, Duane, your hair is as wet with sweat as if you'd been playing football all day."

He heard more than a faint note of worry in his father's voice.

"I thought I saw ... something," Duane explained. "At the foot right there." He pointed.

Eugene pulled down the bedclothes and stared at his son's legs. He made a kind of whistling sound. He had discovered, Duane supposed, the exaggerated development of his calf muscles. Duane thanked God, though, that he had said nothing about his "vision." And he knew he would keep the secret of the ghosts to himself. He knew Eugene would never have tolerated such a thing. And Duane also knew that if he began by mentioning just the ghosts he might begin babbling about his brothers' deaths, finally screaming their names from the housetop and perhaps falling down from the high roof as he called on them not to be dead, not to leave him unlooked-after like this.

Mr. Bledsoe had repeatedly asked Duane not to dry the dishes for Mrs. Newsom as "it didn't look right, especially now he was getting on to being a young man," and going further he had pronounced: "But I don't need to give a reason, do I? You must stop it." Duane obeyed him only to the letter, for he continued to visit Mrs. Newsom in the kitchen after supper was finished, and she often thought he might as well have dried the dishes too for all his hovering over the dishpans and observing her every step and motion.

Duane had done so poorly in his senior year in high school that he would not be eligible for college this coming fall until he had made up a great deal of his work. His tutor, Duke La Roche, had gone off on a hiking trip, and nearly all his school chums were off at camp or visiting faraway places, or had in many cases joined the army. He was thus left with nobody to talk to, it often seemed to him, but Mrs. Newsom, who had not been unaware of his condition. Duane had been very pale the last few days, although usually he had a good high color, and his right hand shook markedly when he picked up his knife and fork or put his napkin back in its napkin ring.

Mrs. Newsom had called Eugene's attention to the change in his son, but the father had merely knitted his brows and remarked, "He's just going through that stage, you know. And without his tutor to keep him occupied, too!" As he said this he tossed what looked like a blank piece of foolscap into the wastepaper basket.

After his warning about not drying the dishes, Eugene frequently appeared surreptitiously in the kitchen, observed that Duane was not helping but was still—in his phrase—"waiting attendance" on the housekeeper, and scowled his disapproval of that; but then, pretending he was hunting for some twine in the kitchen cupboard, he would cut off the required length and walk huffily out of the room without a word.

"I'll walk Mrs. Newsom home tonight, Dad." Duane stepped into the parlor to announce his decision when all the dishes were washed and put away.

"Go ahead, why don't you," Eugene replied without looking up from his book, a history of the Battle of Antietam in the Civil War.

"I think maybe you should have a checkup." Mrs. Newsom broached the subject without warning once they were out of sight of the house with its great hanging green shutters which always seemed to follow them as if they were cameras.

"You've looked terribly peaked and drawn these past few days," the housekeeper went on, "but especially, Duane, today." She shot a glance at him with rapid-fire quickness. His only reply was to relieve her of the heavy market basket she had insisted on carrying, which contained some uprooted flowers from the Bledsoe garden that she was planning to transplant in her own plot, with Eugene's indifferent permission having been, of course, granted in advance.

When they reached the first big crossroad beyond which one saw the rolling countryside and not too far ahead Mrs. Newsom's own rather spacious house—with both a sprawling front and back porch anchoring the house like a ship in all that sea of green grass and shrubbery—they both came to an abrupt halt as if this was the acknowledged place to part.

"If I tell you why I'm peaked, Mrs. Newsom, will you promise to keep it a secret?" he wondered, not offering to hand her back the market basket.

She nodded gravely. Neither made any effort to continue walking.

"You won't tell Eugene, then?" In their unguarded moments together, they both called his father Eugene.

"You surely know me better than that!" Mrs. Newsom exclaimed, but without too much conviction.

"But you won't tell him even for my own good, as you did once before, remember?" he cautioned her.

"When did I do such a thing, Duane?" She spoke with injured pride. Then without waiting for him to answer, she said brusquely, "Come on with me to the backyard, why don't you? We can talk there undisturbed."

"Isn't your husband to home?" Duane wondered. He had never felt that Ab Newsom much cared for him.

"No one is around at all," she assured him.

They took a shortcut to the backyard, whose lush green grass sloped down to the flower garden in which countless varieties of roses, lilies, and hyacinths assailed their eyes and nostrils. Bending down, Mrs. Newsom was already busy transplanting the purple flowers taken from the Bledsoe garden. Neither she nor Duane knew the name of the plant, but he promised her to look it up in Eugene's bulky flower dictionary.

The transplanting over with, Mrs. Newsom urged Duane to be seated in a big oval-shaped wicker chair, and she sat down nearby in a tall green wooden chair.

"I can't bring it out," Duane said desperately. "So excuse me."

"Oh come now," she chided him, and began removing some of the soft earth that clung to her hands. She had raised four boys and two girls, she reminded him. She was fifty, and some days felt eighty. Nothing would appall or offend her, she assured him.

"I know I am not crazy, Mrs. Newsom," he began, and touched her arm as if to stop her from interrupting him. "But two nights ago, and last night also, though less distinctly, I saw them." He moved his head so that his eyes looked directly into hers.

"Who?" she said with the half-audible tone of a prompter who knows the next line.

"Justin and Douglas," he mumbled, and his hand touched her arm again.

"Oh," Mrs. Newsom said in a slightly louder voice.

"I don't know what to do, you see. Do you think"—he looked around the broad expanse of the yard—"that they will make . . . a practice of it?"

She shook her head, but she merely meant by this gesture that she did not know.

"We could move you downstairs," Mrs. Newsom said after a considerable silence. "The air might be better there, and there's a plain view of the trees and sky."

"I know it's them," he defended himself. "Mrs. Newsom," he went on, seeing he had got this far and she had not stopped him, "what do you think it means?"

"Well, Duane," she began now, as reasonably as if they were discussing a broken lock in the storeroom or repairing the lawnmower; and he could have gone down on his knees and thanked and blessed her for her calm. "If, Duane, you promise yourself not to be too afraid . . . I think it will stop. Eventually, of course."

He nodded his head almost with frenzy.

"I mean, Duane," she continued, and looked off to where she had transplanted the purple flowers, "they will want to stop coming to you also, you see. . . . In my opinion, you see them because . . . your father, well, is so close-mouthed and distant. He's held back too much, I believe."

"Oh, I don't disagree." Duane spoke with strained affability. "But not to contradict you, Mrs. Newsom . . ."

"Go ahead," she encouraged him, smiling faintly.

"I think," he confided to her in a low voice, "they would have come to me even if he had howled his head off in grief from the rooftops."

She smiled. "I'm sure he's doing the equivalent of that, Duane, in his silence. . . . Do you *want* to see them?" she asked after they had been quiet for some time.

"I don't believe so," he said huskily.

James Purdy

(16)

"Then the best thing for the moment, I feel, is to do nothing at all. . . . Just wait here, will you, Duane?" She rose quickly and walked rapidly toward the house. While she was gone, he dug his heels into the soft earth and muttered, "Damn Eugene Bledsoe anyhow!"

She brought back with her something rather large wrapped in a heavy cloth with red stripes on it. Slowly removing a quart-sized bottle from the cloth after she had seated herself beside him, she said, "It's an old family remedy I always keep handy." She put the bottle in his hand. "Beef, blood and iron, and some herbs . . . Take a tablespoon before bedtime, or better, two. Don't mind the taste."

"Thank you." He grinned and looked a long time at the bottle. "I promise to try it," he said, under her rather fierce scrutiny.

"But think about this," she said, putting the bottle back in its cloth wrapping. "It's not as uncommon as you may believe, Duane." She looked him full in the face. "Seeing the departed . . . My mother saw Papa after he passed on, and I saw, later, Mother, at her death. I've seen several . . . apparitions, matter of fact. I don't know that I liked it any better than you. But you must not think there's anything wrong with you merely because . . . they come to you. Understand?"

He flushed and half closed his eyes and nodded his thanks.

"Just so Eugene don't hear of it," he mumbled.

"He never will from me, and you know that."

She dropped her hands to her lap, and he knew from that and from the general lapse in the conversation that he should rise and take his leave, but he kept her sitting for a while longer. He tapped the bottle through the cloth. "I'm sure this will help," he raised his voice in parting. "I'm much obliged to you, I can tell you."

"If it happens to go on," Mrs. Newsom said, rising, "we have other alternatives we can turn to." For the first time ever she kissed him on the lips as he drew near her.

"Eugene should have let it all out when he got that telegram," Mrs. Newsom said out loud to herself as she saw him passing from view down the decline in the greensward.

For over a year Eugene Bledsoe had been "keeping company" with an attractive widow, Cora Bayliss, who lived a half mile or so from the Bledsoe house. Instead of walking directly, however, to Cora's, Eugene always made a long detour through an open meadow, which took him at least a mile out of his way, a stratagem he believed would prevent Duane and Mrs. Newsom from learning of his secret rendezvous. But since Duane had followed his father several times all the way to Cora's, and had shared this discovery with Mrs. Newsom, the detour, which spattered Eugene's high shoes with mud and cow dung, was a useless precaution. Whether he knew it or not, his relationship with Mrs. Bayliss was as much an established fact as was the location of his law office.

Cora was dressed in a hastily remade black silk dress in deference to Eugene's loss, and she wore both a diamond necklace and diamond earrings, perhaps for fear that the dark dress alone might not enhance her appearance for him tonight.

She had rehearsed how she would stand, what she would say as he came into her living room, whether she should kiss him on the lips or merely take his hand, whether she would sigh or perhaps weep (she had loathed both the older two Bledsoe boys and despised young Duane).

Whatever she had planned, however, Eugene's coldness, his unbending stiff greeting of her dashed all her plans. When he apprised her that he would not be remaining with her tonight, she knew there would be no exchange of kisses or intimacy of any kind. He had come at her bidding, would exchange mere civilities, and would leave. She might as well have worn a housedress and an apron, for all he cared. Nonetheless, she wept furiously for him, and pressed his hand, and wondered what God meant by taking the young and brave.

Eugene asked for some newspaper to wipe off his shoes, and after she had brought this to him, and had thrown away the stained paper, they found that since Eugene's "loss" would not be a topic for discussion or even comment, the only other subject with which they could deal at all was that of Duane.

Cora immediately expressed her regret that Duane detested her and had rebuffed every offer of affection or friendship which she had offered him. She then cited chapter and verse of the boy's deliberate unkindness and rudeness toward her.

Angry that Eugene would not stay even to sip tea tonight, Cora walked up and down the thick green carpet of her living room, which faced the meadow so deleterious to shoes.

"What I have done to Duane to be so slighted I would give anything to know!" she cried. Her entire fury now was directed toward the youngest son. "Eugene, do you know he deliberately overturned my glass of water at the drugstore yesterday where I sat munching on a roll and butter?"

Eugene shook his head gravely and reminded her that Duane was always very awkward with his hands when flustered in a social situation.

"I beg to differ with you there. He put his hand with extreme concentration on my water glass and then overturned it so that my skirt was sopping wet!"

To her added outrage she now saw that Eugene was smiling furtively, as if Duane's prank gave him considerable relief and pleasure; and indeed this act of his son's made him feel more kindly disposed to the boy, for what reason he himself could not begin to fathom.

"Eugene, he must know we are close. Some weeks ago when you and I were . . . standing here pressed together, I would have sworn I saw him outside by the old walnut trees."

He exchanged a look of pitying contempt with her. "He knows nothing, that boy," Eugene Bledsoe informed her. "He's entirely wrapped up . . . in his remedial lessons . . . and his ice skating. I don't think he knows there are two sexes."

"Oh, please don't feed me that," Cora sneered at him. "Even if it is a season of sorrow."

"When I've told you he knows nothing about such matters, the topic is closed," he said in his severest tone. "And I do not know what you mean by a season of sorrow. . . . Routine, discipline go ahead, no matter what the day brings."

She stared at him briefly, then, arranging her diamond necklace so that it fell a bit more evenly across her bosom, she returned to their only topic: "Couldn't you persuade him to be more civil, or at least decent, to me!"

It was perhaps at this very moment that Eugene realized that his feelings toward Cora were moribund, indeed dead as cold ashes. He had come here tonight against his will to see her, and her mention first of his "loss" and second of his intractable son had curiously enough finished all attachment and affection where she was concerned. He also found her black dress most unbecoming, and her diamonds in poor taste.

"Your interference in my domestic affairs I find quite intolerable," he began, and this statement caught her unprepared so that she sat or almost fell down on the ottoman which she had just had reupholstered at an outrageous price, the work having been done in New York.

"You know," he went on, "as who does not, that I have completely failed with Duane." He stopped as if amazed at the meaning and, indeed, at the extreme volume of his own words, for until he said it aloud, he had perhaps not realized how much he had failed with Duane.

"But I always thought you were close." She spoke between sobs, daubing her cheeks with a tiny perfumed handkerchief which gave off a strong scent of violets. "I've seen you in late fall days going hunting together. Another time, in the spring, I passed you in Catlett's Grove, where obviously just the two of you were going picnicking." She was still angry a year later that she had not been invited to share any of their outings.

Getting no response to this charge of his dereliction to her, Cora rose now and with her back to Eugene looked out another broad window which faced an expanse of wild nodding grass interspersed with thousands of dandelions all gone to seed.

"I am afraid Duane is very much like his mother, if you ask me," she said in a throaty, scolding voice. Not being able to see his face prevented her, perhaps luckily, from seeing the thunderstorm of anger which had come over him as a result of this observation of hers.

"I think I've told you a hundred times, Cora, never to mention that woman in my presence!" Eugene roared.

Wheeling about, Cora cried, "It seems to me that I am forbidden to mention quite a few subjects in your presence! In fact the only subject permitted me in your company is your youngest son! Whom you have spoiled, spoiled, spoiled, if not ruined! And don't look at me like that, for I mean every word of it!"

"Yes, you mean every word of whatever you say, for all there is to you is your tongue which wags at both ends from sunup to sundown, though what it wags about, you haven't the faintest notion. Mentioning my wife Aileen, for example!" he thundered on and, having risen, came directly up to her with such a fierce expression she thought for a second he meant to strike her.

"Poor Aileen!" she defied him. "I can imagine what she went through with you—with a Bledsoe." She looked up at the ceiling like one who appeals to a higher tribunal for corroboration of her statement.

"Since you believe yourself omniscient, supposin' you tell me what Aileen did suffer, why don't you?"

James Purdy

(20)

Striding up and down hard on the green carpet as if it were a trackless part of the meadow facing her, Cora began before he had finished speaking: "Silence, my dear Eugene, is one of the most terrible weapons human beings are capable of. When anguish and confusion bear down upon a person, when one longs to hear any word from those closest to us—for even an oath or downright obscenity is preferable to silence! To say nothing! God, I know what poor Duane must be going through!"

"So it's 'poor Duane' now, is it? You are as changeable as a damned weather vane in a thundershower. What would you have me harp on in front of you, will you tell me?"

"Not to mention his hero sons!" Cora went on speaking as if to an empty room. "Not to let Duane hear them mentioned!"

"How in frozen hell do you know who and what I mention to him, will you tell me?" He almost spat these words at her.

"I know how you treat him by the way you have treated me. A dead man could say more on any subject than you, once you have decided your lips are sealed!"

"So Duane has been here complaining about me!" he cried in his best prosecutor's tone.

"You must know better than that, Eugene Bledsoe. For I've told you till I'm black in the face that he hates me, that it is his very existence that has prevented you and I from marrying. I know it, and you know it."

"Well, if he's as desperate as you make out, he might pay a call even on a woman he hates, mightn't he?"

"Much as I dislike Duane," Cora was going hastily along, "and he is in many ways the most despicable boy I know . . ."

"Thank you, Mrs. Bayliss!" he scoffed, and then picked up his straw boater.

"I can see," she continued, not having paused even to hear his rejoinder, "and can of course understand that living with a man as incommunicative, as wrapped up in himself as you are, cut off from his son's mother, who, no matter what she is or has done, has some right to communicate with her only son . . . There is a kind of cruelty practiced which no law can reach to punish, or even uncover."

As she finished speaking, she extended her right arm, a gesture so striking that perhaps it was the reason he put his hat on while still indoors and headed for the door.

"Eugene," Cora cried, hastening after him, her long diamond necklace rising and striking her against the face, "Eugene, listen to me!" She stood now on the edge of the meadow calling to him. "I implore you! For your own good! Listen to what I am saying!"

"Good-bye, Mrs. Bayliss," he called to her over one shoulder.

"You will come back, Eugene," she said after walking a few steps into the grass. "You'll have to!" she shouted. "Who else will tell you which way the wind blows, you conceited prig? I ask you! Who? Who?"

She burst into tears and hurried back into her living room and threw herself on the ottoman.

Eugene Bledsoe had a certain proclivity which put both Duane's and Mrs. Newsom's nerves on edge. He had a habit when confronting a problem of pacing up and down, usually in his bedroom, and at the same time furiously jingling the coins in his pants pocket. His pacing, which often drove Duane out of the house and Mrs. Newsom to the farthest reaches of the very ample pantry and buttery, was followed inevitably by his pretending he had no appetite for supper and needed a breath of air. On such occasions, after his father had left the house, Duane would follow him down the street (as he had frequently followed him over the meadow and grazing land when his father was about to pay a call on Cora Bayliss) and would watch him go into our town's one expensive restaurant where he would dine in solitary grandeur.

It would be difficult to say which of the two, Duane or Mrs. Newsom, was more provoked by these charades. It was his father's hypocrisy which annoyed Duane, and it was the inconvenience of having gone to so much trouble for evening supper only to have it spurned which kindled Mrs. Newsom's wrath. Very often, in pique, she would take Eugene's serving home to her husband.

After his disagreeable row with Cora Bayliss, Eugene, who was in the worst temper anybody had seen him in in months, slammed all the doors of the upstairs of the house and then, changing his shoes (still stained from cow dung) to an even heavier pair, began a pacing which recalled the sound of a retreating army. Both son and housekeeper realized that something other than the news of Eugene's "sorrow" had prompted him to resume his old habit. (Actually, the War Department telegram had caused him to sit in stunned silence, hardly even moving hands or feet.) They dared not, of course, ask him what ailed him.

James Purdy
(22)

First he paced throughout the hallway upstairs, then in his own ample bedroom, then in the splendid empty guest room; then he repeated his march of duty and inspection. From downstairs they could not hear the jingling of the coins in Eugene's pants pocket, but the pacing shook the house tonight despite its solid frame.

"*He* should take up boxing, he ain't all that old," Duane observed to Mrs. Newsom in the kitchen, where the pacing sounds were less audible. "All that unused energy!"

"You don't think it is . . . his sorrow?" she said as she put the fresh green peas in boiling water.

"Not that kind of pacing, Mrs. Newsom. That's fury!"

"He will have a poor appetite tonight, no question about that, and just when I have gone to the trouble of surprising him with a crown roast of lamb."

With a movement of her head, Mrs. Newsom advised Duane to go into the dining room and stand in front of his chair, and she rang the heavy dinner bell (a practice which had been enjoined on her by the late Mrs. Bledsoe, Eugene's mother).

The pacing came to an end upstairs, and they could hear him descending.

Now all three sat down at the table.

"You may ask the blessing tonight," Eugene informed Mrs. Newsom.

For the past year Duane had refused to say grace on the grounds that as a result of his studying certain books lent him by his tutor, Mr. Duke La Roche, he was an agnostic. His father had been too astonished at such impudence to take it seriously at the time, but had nonetheless acquiesced in the boy's refusal to pray at the table.

"We thank Thee, Father, for what we are about to receive," Mrs. Newsom mumbled. Eugene closed his eyes tightly like a man who has suddenly got both eyes filled with hot cinders.

During the blessing, Duane stared with open eyes at the squirrels racing up and down the sassafras trees.

Grace over, both Mrs. Newsom and Duane watched Mr. Bledsoe over their soup bowls with almost diabolical curiosity. He must have sensed their scrutiny, for he went to the useless bother of taking his napkin out of his napkin ring and examining it punctiliously.

"I hope your napkin is perfectly clean." Mrs. Newsom spoke in a tone which bordered on sarcasm.

"I should have informed you earlier," Eugene Bledsoe commenced in a loud voice, and then fell to near inaudibility, "had it been . . . soiled." Eugene could not help noticing an exchange of glances which suggested complicity between his son and the woman whom he sometimes referred to as the "hired girl."

Eugene pushed his soup plate away from him.

"You're not going to pass up the crown of lamb, Mr. Bledsoe?"

Eugene Bledsoe's eyes assumed a very strange, soft, even liquid expression. "That is a real pity," he said, looking Mrs. Newsom full in the face. "Had I known earlier, I would have partaken . . ."

"The butcher only knew this morning," she explained, "that he would have the crown for our supper."

"I couldn't touch anything," Eugene began in a kind of weeping voice. "I've had a touch of dyspepsia again. And I'm expected in town concerning a business matter that has just arisen." He gave the same excuse he usually offered prior to leaving them alone together at the table.

He placed his napkin in the ring and was about to leave when he caught sight of Duane's face, which was changing color from rose to pale almost like the sky during heat lightning.

"Everything shipshape with you, Duane?" Mr. Bledsoe managed to get out these few words.

Duane barely nodded.

Unaccountably, Mr. Bledsoe tarried in the doorway separating the dining room from the living room.

"Need anything from up the street, either of you?" he inquired as he looked brightly in no particular direction.

Mrs. Newsom's voice broke the silence. "Duane should soak his feet in Epsom salts, I've told him, Mr. Bledsoe. I've warned him he is punishing his feet with so much skating. If you could pick up a package of that, sir."

Mr. Bledsoe looked considerably taken aback at the mention of feet and Epsom salts at the table, but his own guilt at deserting them without prior notification left him bereft of the will to say something corrective and cutting to the housekeeper. Therefore he merely nodded.

When he had got beyond earshot, Duane said, "He knows I would never soak my feet in Epsom salts even if my feet were hanging in blisters."

Mrs. Newsom was already entering the dining room, bearing the platter with the crown of lamb. She had decorated it with tiny little red, white, and blue paper festoons. It was as festive as Easter. And she was sure its exquisite aroma must be reaching Eugene's nostrils as he prepared himself to leave the house for his important business engagement.

Mrs. Newsom was laughing over Eugene Bledsoe's barefaced lies, but at the expression on Duane's face, she checked herself. He looked suddenly like a small boy who has had ice water thrown in his face by a prankster.

"Don't tell me you have lost *your* appetite!" she cried.

"No, Mrs. Newsom. Matter of fact, I'm famished."

Her face relaxed.

"Well, don't you go and follow him up the street and spy on him," she whispered. "After all, remember, he has had a heavy loss."

"He's had a loss!" Duane retorted irately, and without warning he burst into tears. He wept violently before her, convulsively, and pressed the napkin against his mouth to muffle the choking sounds coming from his breast.

On hearing the commotion, Eugene hurried down from upstairs and took a seat at the far end of the dining table.

"Duane! Look here, what is it?"

When the boy did not reply, Eugene rose and took hold of his son's shoulder with his hand. Duane winced under the heavy, iron pressure, but did not try to wriggle out of this embrace.

"Is it anything in particular this time, Mrs. Newsom?" the father wondered.

Mrs. Newsom was occupied with holding back her own tears, and her voice was therefore not steady enough for her to answer.

"I declare!" Eugene cried. He looked helplessly about the room.

"If I were you, Mr. Bledsoe, I believe I'd stay." She spoke in a whisper.

But Duane suddenly leaped up from the table and ran upstairs to his room.

"A fine how-do-you-do," Mr. Bledsoe remarked. He rose now with military stiffness and followed his son. Mrs. Newsom could hear his resounding knock on the closed door.

"Duane, oh Duane! Come on out, come on now. I am going to stay for supper. Duane, stop that infernal sobbing, do you hear? No man should carry on like that, God damn it! If I've offended you in any way ..." His voice trailed off.

After a long silence, during which Mrs. Newsom wondered just where Mr. Bledsoe was upstairs, she heard his steps descending the stairs. Eugene sat down again at the head of the table as if he had only heard the bell summoning him to dine.

He nodded to Mrs. Newsom, removed his napkin from the napkin ring, and indicated with a bow that she might serve him the lamb.

Her hand shook badly as she cut him a generous pink portion, poured some mint sauce over it, and helped him to some garden-fresh green peas and mashed potatoes.

"I think he'll have a piece of the lamb, cold, later on." Mr. Bledsoe spoke in his usual lofty, cool manner.

"Oh it'll be no trouble to keep it hot for him, sir," she replied in a manner nearly as lofty as his.

Mrs. Newsom had been more than vaguely aware of Eugene Bledsoe's prejudice against anything Roman Catholic. She had once absentmindedly left her missal and rosary behind in the front parlor, and he had handed them back to her the next day with a look of such contempt, even loathing, that she had found herself turning scarlet as she received them from his hands. But, she reminded herself, Eugene Bledsoe's prejudices were rather evenhanded, and in addition to running down the pope and the local bishop, he poured contempt on Negroes, Jews, Italians, and above all the beet-honkies (Mexicans) who nevertheless, as he pointed out, were only a temporary blight on the community, arriving in August at about the same time as the cicadas and vanishing like those green-winged droning insects at the coming of the first killing frost.

After the disaster of tonight's crown of lamb supper, she was preparing to go to evening service at St. Michael's Church when Duane came into the kitchen. After eating two helpings of the crown, his Dad had finally gone off up the street. She had her missal and rosary in her hand as Duane faced her, and she said somewhat coldly, "I am going to special services tonight, Duane ... at my church."

"Let me go along," he said with strange effusiveness.

James Purdy

(26)

"Without having had a bite to eat?" she scolded.

Mrs. Newsom all at once thought back to her scene with Eugene over her rosary.

"You told me once," Duane coaxed her, "that you often burned a candle for my mother. So I've been thinking, if you did it for her, who's still alive, maybe ... the two of us could burn candles for ... the departed ... if you get my drift."

"But your mother was very fond of ... the Church." Mrs. Newsom felt suddenly hemmed in. "I'll tell you what," she said. "I'll prepare you your dinner, and I'll not go to church tonight." She put down the missal.

"No, Mrs. Newsom," he was firm, "I couldn't taste a bite now. I want to come to church with you." He picked up the missal and handed it to her. "I tell you," he hesitated and fumbled, "I want to come with you tonight and have you burn candles ... for them ... for Justin and Douglas, do you hear? I mean, something should be done for them somewhere!"

"But the boys were not ... members!" The thought of Eugene's anger blotted out for the moment any other consideration in her mind.

"But, Mrs. Newsom, some ceremony of some kind ... Please ... When," he said in rising anger, "he won't so much as mention their names aloud! It's as though he never knew them! Let me accompany you."

"Grief takes many shapes, Duane." She hesitated.

"Or no shape at all?"

"I don't think he would approve of my lighting a candle for them. I know for a fact he would not approve of your accompanying me to church." As if it were happening all over again, she saw Mr. Bledsoe hand her rosary back to her as if it were a serpent covered with slime.

"Please," Duane began again. She looked him full in the face.

"It would never do, Benjy." She used his baby name suddenly. "If he found out—"

"But how will he find out?"

"Our town is a whispering gallery, Duane. Of course he'll find out."

"But then I'll tell him I went on my own account."

A sudden anger at Mr. Bledsoe, a remembrance again of his having insulted her religion in the manner in which he returned her rosary, made her say, "Very well, Duane, accompany me then if you will." Mrs.

Newsom spoke from a facade of cold impartiality, if not indifference. "But remember, I didn't ask you. And I'm not trying to influence or convert you, as God is my witness!"

"Convert me! Mrs. Newsom, for crying out loud, please!" But he stopped for a moment as if he took in review his father's position and prejudice. "Oh hang it all!" he said, and took her arm. "I'm going with you, and that's all there is to it."

The first shadows of evening were falling as they set out for St. Michael's. They said little on the way, and Duane began to feel that after all he was doing something, if not reprehensible, perhaps not quite admirable. He kept staring sideways at Mrs. Newsom. He wondered if she dyed her hair, it was so coal-black, but he was pretty certain she did not. She didn't care enough about what people thought to dye it.

Then all at once he smelled the incense, indeed he presently saw puffs of it floating out toward them before the sprawling Romanesque structure they were about to enter.

He felt a bit queasy, and faint also, from hunger.

"The candles are right here." The housekeeper drew his attention to a small altar which resembled a field aglow with countless flickering tapers.

"Duane!" she tried to bring his attention again to the candles, but his gaze was directed toward the congregation who, young and old, were all kneeling and looking raptly ahead of them.

"Duane"—she tugged at his sleeve—"shall I light a candle for you then?"

She saw to her anxiety that he was quite overcome by the atmosphere, which must be awfully strange to him. A little silver bell rang somewhere. Two priests were approaching the main altar. Their cassocks and the crucifixes which hung from their necks caught the reflections of countless shafts of illumination.

"Duane," she whispered, "are you going to be all right?"

He nodded.

'Then, see here," she instructed him. "Here are two candles," and she gave them to him and pointed to the host of burning lights before the image of Christ Jesus holding a lamb. "Light them for your brothers."

"Can I?" He turned to her in a kind of beatific idiocy.

"Duane, if you are uncomfortable, or unwilling, you had best leave. At once. Do you hear me? Light them or leave." She studied his terrible pallor.

James Purdy

(28)

"I will not leave," he informed her. His hands shaking convulsively, he took the candles from her and lit them from the flame of another candle burning in the center of the conflagration of light.

"Shall you not kneel and pray?" she wondered aloud. "You believe in the Lord, I am sure."

"Yes, yes, I think I do," he mumbled. He glanced furtively again about the church.

His knees appeared to buckle involuntarily. He held on to the effulgent solid brass railing and kept his eyes feverishly on the two candles which he had placed amidst the many other burning tapers, lit, he supposed, by other wretched, discouraged, and bewildered persons like himself.

"God, God," he muttered, as some saliva slipped from his lips and descended to his lapel, "touch his cold heart."

He rose and, taking her by the sleeve, said, "I feel desperately . . . dizzy," and rushed from the church.

He stood outside by the stone carvings of the Twelve Apostles, who appeared to transfix him with gimlet eyes.

"Duane, are you able to go home by yourself? I will miss service if you cannot. Do you hear what I am saying to you?" Mrs. Newsom spoke from the doorway of the church.

Just then they caught sight of Eugene Bledsoe coming along the walk.

He stared at both of them with a glance of lightning. His mouth had come open with amazement, and then it closed firmly with angry disapproval.

"Good evening, Mrs. Newsom." Eugene spoke without stopping. "Good evening to you, Duane," he gave his son a backward look of bitter reproach.

"Well, I don't give a damn if he saw us come out of the church or not." Duane almost spat out the words.

"Please, please," Mrs. Newsom began, "it's best for you to go home immediately, Duane, before his wrath explodes any further against us. Go on at once. I am returning to evening service—unless you need me, that is."

"I need nobody," he snapped. "Go on back in there. Go ahead! But, for your information, I'm not going home to face him alone."

"Where are you going then, dear boy?"

He stared at her eyes full of tears.

"We should . . . never have come here together." She spoke falteringly, with resignation as to what now would follow. "I am an old fool."

"No, I am the fool, Mrs. Newsom. Go on back in the church. Do you hear, Mrs. Newsom? Go back to your church."

"Don't scold me that way, Duane. I can't bear to hear that terrible tone to your voice, so like his! You, after all, requested to come."

"So I did." He shrugged his shoulders and wiped his mouth with his clean linen pocket handkerchief. "Go on back to service, Mrs. Newsom. It's quite beautiful and restful in there. . . . Thank you for the candles," he called after her retreating figure.

He saw her just then out of the corner of his eye deposit two dollars in the offertory box before the altar of burning candles.

No actor ever rehearsed a part more thoroughly than Eugene Bledsoe, as he went over in word and gesture the rebuke and reprimand he intended to give Mrs. Newsom for having taken his son to a service at the local Roman Catholic church. His all-around rage, which had been kindled by his meeting with Cora Bayliss and, more remotely, by the loss of his sons, somehow found its target in the benevolent, magnanimous Mrs. Newsom.

"I was aghast and, yes, thunderstruck to see you guiltily hurrying out of the Church of Rome together!" He had thought of using this declamation to begin his dressing-down of her. But he could not think of words stern enough to bring her to judgment.

He had sent Duane out of doors for the remainder of the morning prior to his calling Mrs. Newsom onto the carpet, and Duane now sat in the environs of the summerhouse watching the ladybugs light occasionally on his cotton shirt and open their inner wings.

His father's brass voice, however, soon reached him from behind the green shutters and muslin curtains of the house, and he fancied he heard from time to time the rather firm contralto of poor Mrs. Newsom.

"How dared you do such a thing?" Mr. Bledsoe had begun almost the moment she had entered his study, with its tables of pile after pile of legal papers. He had turned his back on her after leveling this rhetorical question at her.

Mrs. Newsom, unbidden to sit down, stood before him unmoved.

"I am left with no other conjecture"—he now half turned toward her—

James Purdy

(30)

"than that you are deliberately attempting to proselytize him with your faith!" He thundered out the word "Proselytize!" again.

"If your mother were here, Mr. Bledsoe, she would soon put such a charge to rout. I think you also know me better than that."

"Did you not suggest, then," he went on in his prosecutor's fashion, "that Duane accompany you to church?"

"I did no such thing!"

"He, in other words, asked to be taken?" Scorn and disbelief were written across his face and curled lip.

"Your son is extremely lonely, Mr. Bledsoe, and in addition," she paused a moment before bringing out the words, "very badly shaken by the loss of his brothers."

"That is a subject, as you know, we shall not go into."

"It is, just the same, in my opinion, behind his considerable unhappiness," she went on with quiet stubbornness.

"You have not replied to my question, Mrs. Newsom." His voice now shook the room. "Did he ask to be taken to your church without suggestion of any kind on your part?"

"What do you think of me? I declare!" she almost thundered back at him. "Of course he asked to be taken, and of course I opposed his coming. But see here, Mr. Bledsoe, and let us examine what is actually behind all this, if you will. If your son had boys his own age for company, or girls"—here Eugene snorted with contempt—"or if he were with companions of equal background, he would not dream of spending ten minutes with an old woman like myself. Yes, he wanted to go to *my* church, as you call it. I did not encourage him. He seemed so forlorn, after the to-do at the supper table. I could not very well refuse him."

"Forlorn, indeed. A boy his age is never forlorn."

"What did you think his weeping meant, then, at the table, pray tell?"

Eugene Bledsoe let out a great rush of air from his mouth as if to blow out of the room all excuses and all petitions for clemency or understanding.

"I will be perfectly frank with you, Mrs. Newsom," he began then. "My son . . . is not too bright. He has been a great and bitter disappointment to me, especially in view of the fact that the other lads are . . . were, that is, of such sterner stuff."

Here, whether he had fallen into the trap he so constantly avoided of mentioning his dead sons, or whether he felt suddenly ashamed at so downgrading his youngest boy, his anger rose and descended again on Duane.

"I mean," Mr. Bledsoe fulminated, "what future has such a young man? He has failed in everything!"

"I cannot really agree with you, Mr. Bledsoe, if you will allow me to say so. Duane is a bright boy, a charming boy."

"He is a fine figure skater, I am told," he scoffed.

"Yes," she agreed. "I saw him at the exhibition gala, and he was splendid."

"What exhibition gala?" Mr. Bledsoe was even more severe now, if possible, than he had been on finding the rosary. "I say, Mrs. Newsom," he cried, coming up directly to her now, "*what* exhibition?"

"Why, the one a year or so ago," she replied coolly. "I think it was shortly after you had told his coach he must not try for competition in the Olympics. . . ." She waited, perhaps for this to take its effect, and then continued: "He did so beautifully, and got an ovation. It was, after all," she observed, "in the newspaper, with his photo. . . . Mr. Bledsoe, I declare!" She took in his air of being totally at sea.

He turned away from her, and as he did so, his already thin lips became a barely perceptible line.

"He keeps his life a secret from me, that is true," he muttered.

"Duane feels"—she was surprised now at her own boldness—"that you have closed yourself off from . . ." She stopped, but then looking toward him, she saw with partial relief that he seemed not to have heard her last words.

Without having been invited to do so, Mrs. Newsom abruptly sat down. She felt, she would realize later, too reluctant, as well as too unsteady, to stand as a suppliant before such a pillar of arrogance.

"Evidently," Mr. Bledsoe went on, without appearing to have noticed she had seated herself, "indeed, quite obviously, he has found in you a confidante he never had in those who have his interests closest to heart."

He brought his pocket handkerchief out and wiped his forehead, though it was as dry as sand, as were his cheeks. He said something through his teeth, and then going up to the window, rested his right hand on the high sill and shook his head. She did not know whether he was cursing or praying or both.

James Purdy
(32)

"After what has occurred," he began, having left the window and come into the center of the room, "I do not see how I can continue to allow you to serve us."

He walked over to his untidy desk, seated himself, and after some fumbling found his checkbook.

"I am sure you must agree with me on this point." He turned to her, noted she was seated, and then began writing the check.

"Do you not agree with me?" he cried as he affixed his signature.

"The matter is entirely in your hands, Mr. Bledsoe." She spoke with such frigid dignity that he stared at her for a full sixty seconds.

Rising, he brought the check to her. "Therefore," he said, "will you kindly accept this?"

She had now risen also. "No, thank you, Mr. Bledsoe," she replied, and clasped her hands before her. "I don't want money from you under these circumstances."

"But you have earned it!"

"I will not accept money from someone who has accused me of deceit and underhanded dealings. Proselytism indeed! I will never take one penny from you until you have apologized for what you have said here. You may ask Duane whether I have at any time ever breathed a word to him about what you call 'my' church and its doctrine."

"This money is yours, and by God you shall accept it!"

"And as I have free will and my own self-respect, I will not take a cent from one who has so unjustly accused *and* condemned me. Is that clear? Your mother would weep to think how you have misjudged me. There was a fine and noble woman for you!"

She turned her back on him and touched the catch to open the sliding door.

"Mrs. Newsom, I am warning you, you must not leave this house under these circumstances. Do you hear me?"

He advanced to the sliding door and touched her sleeve. She recoiled as violently from him now as he had from her the day he had handed back her rosary.

"I have remained here after the death of your mother and your separation from your wife," Mrs. Newsom now spoke harshly, "only through my gratitude and devotion to those two ladies, and because of my feeling of responsibility and affection toward your youngest son. As for you yourself, Mr. Bledsoe, you need nobody. You are sufficient unto yourself, and do not require human companionship or warmth. Good day, sir."

She quickly opened the sliding door, a procedure which appeared to astound him almost as much as her speech, for he had somehow thought that only his hand was capable of operating the mechanism, and after a bit he found himself alone and staring at the fresh signature on his check.

At first he was tempted to tear the check to bits, but then spying a little oblong box sent to him from overseas by Douglas, or perhaps Justin, he opened its mysterious-looking lid and put the check inside.

"Damn such a belligerent conniving female!" he muttered as he heard her close the front door against him and her years of service there.

"I'm afraid we will be keeping bachelor's hall, Duane, for some considerable time to come."

Eugene Bledsoe addressed these words to his son from the threshold of the boy's room late that night after his blowup with Mrs. Newsom. Hearing the fracas and the voices raised in anger—all, he felt, over him—Duane had sped off on his wheel to spend the entire afternoon and evening at the skating rink, and had taken supper at his instructor's house.

Duane stood motionless now, unresponsive as a wax figure, on hearing his father's words.

"I have had to let Mrs. Newsom go," he explained in lavishly loud tones, like a sports announcer on the radio.

"Well," Duane countered sullenly, ignoring the announcement, "I only just learned *all* the details of your talk with Pete Foulke about how you didn't think I was Olympic material."

"Who's Pete Foulke?" Mr. Bledsoe was nonplussed at such a statement coming on the heels of his having broken the news of Mrs. Newsom's being dismissed.

"Pete Foulke is my skating instructor," Duane mumbled.

Actually, Duane was expecting a real dressing-down from his father now, even perhaps a razor-strapping, and to tell the truth, he had not quite taken in the fact also that Mrs. Newsom would no longer be with them.

"What is that cut over your left eye, Duane?" Eugene advanced to within a few inches of his son, a note of genuine concern in his voice.

Instead of replying, Duane half turned his back on his father.

"Here, let me see." Eugene turned his son toward him. "Let me have a look." And he brought Duane over to the window and stared at his wound.

"I slipped and fell on the ice, that's all," the boy explained in a surly, thick voice.

"That's a nasty little cut, though, Duane. Oughtn't it to be looked at by somebody?"

"It already has been. Pete put something on it."

"You see, I was right to want you not to go into competitive ice skating. It's a dangerous sport."

"Not as dangerous surely as soldiering!" Duane cried passionately.

"Duane!" His father stepped back from him with considerable trepidation. "I'm dumbfounded you could even compare the two!" He spoke brokenly.

In the face of Duane's overwhelming silence, Eugene went on, "After all, I did not exactly forbid Mr. Foulke, I guess that's his name, from training you for the Olympics that day a year or so ago. I merely told him that in my opinion you were too—"

"Too what?" Duane shouted, the spit flying from his distended lips.

"You seemed, and seem, for God's sake, too . . . unready!"

The whole disruption of their way of life as a result of Mrs. Newsom's leaving was suddenly shelved in the wake of this old sore-spot of Eugene's having spoiled Duane's chance at the Olympics. Even the deaths of Justin and Douglas appeared remote by reason of the spoiling of Duane's ice-skating career a year ago.

"As I say, Duane," Eugene Bledsoe commenced again like an orator who had unsuccessfully tried five or six times to memorize an upcoming speech, "I have been compelled to let Mrs. Newsom go."

"I'm not surprised, considering the way you were screaming at one another." Duane spoke with open contempt. "I had nowhere to go but to the skating rink. But I'm surprised Pete Foulke even speaks to me after what you've done."

Eugene tried several times to say something, and each time he made the attempt he would raise both hands, a mannerism familiar to those in our town who had observed him in the courtroom.

Duane took a seat in the big easy chair which his mother had had reupholstered shortly before she had left them (about four years earlier), and looked attentively if contemptuously at his extended fingers, which had also been slightly injured in his spill at the rink this afternoon. They were still flecked with dried blood.

"So Mrs. Newsom has been let go." Duane spoke these words in a voice which seemed ready to explode in laughter.

Taking his cue from his son, Eugene seated himself on a stiff wooden chair, which was as uncomfortable a seat for a man of his height as it was possible to find.

"We will have to get along without her as best we can," Eugene went on lamely.

Duane and his father were now both surprised that instead of Eugene giving his son a scolding, or even a razor-strapping, for having visited a Roman Catholic church, it was the son who acted like the injured party who might at any moment reprimand his Dad and possibly send him to stand in the dunce's corner.

"People will say I have been too hasty," Eugene went on in his new apologetic manner, and then, as if suddenly remembering at last that after all he had been the aggrieved one, his anger forced out the words: "I was incensed and indeed outraged that she should have taken you to her church, when she knows full well we are Protestants and—"

"But we can hardly call ourselves that anymore, can we, since we never attend our own service?" Duane spoke without sarcasm and indeed with no expression whatsoever.

"But we will attend service, if you wish, Duane." Eugene was suddenly eloquent and hopeful. "Reverend McKee has asked about you from time to time, you know."

"That's good of him," Duane retorted, glorying a bit in having the upper hand at last.

"I'm afraid I will be a very poor cook." Eugene now turned to the practical consequences of Mrs. Newsom's departure. "You'll have to bear with me for a while, Duane, until we can find somebody else. . . . But"—he studied his son worriedly—"that will not be the easiest thing in the world to do."

Eugene stood up, having delivered himself of all he had the strength for.

"Shall I go get the razor strop now?" Duane spoke in a voice that though shaky was of a taunting unpleasantness that made his father turn pale.

James Purdy

(36)

"Aren't you too big a boy for that, Duane?" Mr. Bledsoe observed, turning away toward the open door.

"Rather than blame an old woman and dismiss her"—Duane found his anger breaking out now—"it's me you should punish. I think you should strap me, and order her to come back. Especially if you cannot cook."

Eugene smiled in spite of himself.

"I can cook, Benjy. Enough to keep us from starving, at any rate."

"Don't call me Benjy anymore," Duane whispered. He covered his face with his hands.

"Any other orders while you're at it?" Eugene said.

Duane removed his hands from his face and smiled. He was glad he had aroused his father's anger at last, and he hoped he would strap him. It would be better than this insipid exchange of words.

"Well, and what did you think of their service?" Eugene found himself returning to this subject when he knew he should have followed his intuition and simply left the room.

"Oh, the service," Duane sighed, and shook his head. "Yes," he wondered, looking out at the streetlight shining down on the row of old walnut trees. "What did I think of it? Oh, outlandish, I guess." He had searched for a better word, but was unable to find one.

"In what way, outlandish?" Eugene wondered coolly.

"Well, the incense, you know, the little bells that rang from time to time, the way the priests were dressed up . . . like actors, you see." He gave his father an eloquent look of appeal. "After the plainness of our church, it was sort of like watching a pageant, or even a parade of some kind."

Eugene, however, barely heard his son's description of the forbidden spectacle.

"I wish you would promise me never to go again." The father spoke now with some anguish. "Could you promise me now you won't?"

Duane stared at Eugene in amazement. He could see that his having gone to a church which meant absolutely nothing to him personally had some strong and painful significance for his father, and that his father's rage and anger were connected with their own painful relationship, with Eugene's vague but very powerful feeling of dominion over him. And this dominion had been threatened by an old woman and by a religion which meant nothing to Duane beyond passing curiosity.

Mourners Below

(37)

"To tell the truth," Duane got out huskily, "I'm not much interested in ... religion of any kind."

Eugene moved again toward the door and indicated they would not pursue this topic further. But unable to leave the room on this note either, he turned anxiously back to Duane and said, "It's not, Benjy— or Duane, if that's what I must call you—that I oppose your going on with your skating lessons—and I'm told you have even made some little stir in public as a figure skater—it's only I didn't feel you were ready for anything competitive."

"You mean after my failing so miserably, I guess, in my senior year in high school?"

"Oh, Duane, Duane, this had all better be left for another time. To tell you the truth, I feel like somebody had taken the razor strap to me!"

Duane looked down at the carpet, which had also belonged to his mother.

"Your studies will all get straightened out in time." Eugene was saying this perhaps, they both felt, in order to have something to say.

"But it hurt me to hear you talk about using the strap on you, Duane. I'd hate to think you might remember me only by my having ... punished you occasionally."

Duane bit his lip, but was too exhausted by now to think of anything more to say, and his father bade him an inaudible good-night and went out, closing the door behind him.

The more Eugene tried to be a cook, the worse he failed. He purchased a Boston Cooking School manual for beginners and this replaced for a while his study of the Battle of Antietam and other Civil War studies.

His first breakfast for Duane and himself was a considerable, even memorable disaster. He burned the Irish oatmeal in the granite pan, ruining the pan itself in the process, and it had to be thrown out. The scrambled eggs were overcooked and dry as powder, and he had forgotten to purchase butter for the toast. Defeated, he had finally given Duane all his spare change to go to a nearby lunchroom for breakfast, while he spent the rest of the morning cleaning up the dishes, carrying out the untasted breakfast victuals to the refuse dump a half mile from their house, and hunting in the pantry for another pan to cook eggs in.

The evening meal, which in Mrs. Newsom's capable hands and smiled upon by her cheerful disposition had always in times past made up for many of the disappointments of the day, was now a ceremony of disagreeableness, poor appetite, and disgust. Nothing tasted right, there was either too much salt or not enough, dishes which should have been sweet were bitter, and those which should have had at least a neutral flavor reeked of incorrectly chosen condiments.

On Sunday Eugene attempted a roast of beef. It came out dry as string, with parts of it unaccountably bloody raw. There was no gravy, and the potatoes were burnt black. The parsnips had been cooked to mush, and the dressing on the salad tasted almost like coal oil.

In his pique and shame at having deprived Duane of proper fare by his dismissal of Mrs. Newsom, Eugene had attempted to bake a custard pie for dessert. By some unheard-of feat of culinary ineptitude, the bottom of the pie had moved up during its stay in the oven and become the top. When Eugene brought it in, after the disappointment of the roast of beef, Duane mistook it for cake, since the top was firm browned crust. To Eugene's partial relief, however, Duane found this recently invented recipe for dessert the most appetizing thing his father had yet brought out of the kitchen. Duane asked for a second helping, while his father, who had barely tasted a mouthful of anything, gazed at him with a kind of wounded gratitude.

After a week of experiments (one evening the entire kitchen caught fire and was put out by throwing pails of sand on the blazing oven) and with a growing feeling of famine on the part of both of them, Eugene threw down his stained napkin and bellowed: "A man has to admit when he is licked, Duane, or he is a blasted fool. I admit I am. I throw in the towel. I'll never learn to prepare grub so that either of us can eat it, and you know it."

Duane's resentment and rage against his father were somewhat mollified, and he put in a compliment here and there for one dish or another which had been partially palatable, but Eugene would allow no compliments or excuses.

"Tomorrow, I will go hat in hand," he told his son, "and see our housekeeper. Maybe she'll reconsider for *your* sake, Duane."

Eugene's failure as a cook, if anything, made the boy more sympathetic toward his Dad. Even his father's jealousy that a strange church service might vie with his own jurisdiction and dominion over his son began to seem not too terrible a failing on the part of a parent.

But a new awareness of his father's situation became clear to Duane as a result of Eugene's stint as a cook. Up until Mrs. Newsom's departure, Duane had assumed that Eugene, though not very successful as a lawyer, had at least some clients, some business. But with Mrs. Newsom's leaving, Eugene's devoting himself day and night to what he called household chores came as an eye-opener to Duane. His Dad evidently had no real present occupation or business, and was more or less doing nothing when he went to his office. Yes, his stint as a cook had proved pretty clearly that his old man was, if not in deep trouble, at some terrible impasse of enforced idleness and was marking time.

Mrs. Newsom was in her garden bending low over her marigolds and nasturtiums, and gathering from the latter their shiny black seeds which she would plant come the propitious phase of the moon. As she looked up from her work in order to avoid getting dizzy, who should swim into her line of vision but the rather outlandishly tall and lean figure of Eugene Bledsoe, who was advancing doggedly toward her front door.

She dropped the nasturtium seeds and did not stoop to pick them up. Could she, she was wondering, bear even to look at him again, let alone exchange ten words with him? But where could she hide? If he roused nobody at the front door, she knew him well enough to realize he would come to the back and see her among her hollyhocks and sunflowers. No, she would go forth and meet the enemy, for Duane's sake, if for nobody else's, and for the memory of Mother Bledsoe.

So she advanced through her own rather spacious house and opened the door as Eugene was pressing the bell with imperious energy.

He removed his straw hat and held it across his heart, smiled a crooked though somewhat sweet smile, which contrasted queerly with the tenor of their last meeting, and got out a hoarse "Good morning."

"Come in, Mr. Bledsoe. . . . Why don't you sit over here away from that strong sunlight?" Mrs. Newsom suggested after he had followed her silently into the front parlor. She had reached for a small bottle of camphor and dropped some of the liquid on her handkerchief and inhaled (a remedy against nerves which she had learned from Eugene's mother).

"See here," he began in a manner as awkward and callow as one might have expected from Duane, "I don't want to take much of your time." He stared at her apron stained with fresh earth from her gardening. "Fact is, Mrs. Newsom, I feel I have been over-hasty in doing what I have done." He looked down at the brim of his hat and, having gazed at it, his eye shifted to a raveling resting on the crease of his trousers, and he gingerly removed the stray thread and held it for a moment in his palm.

"How is Duane getting on?" she helped him.

"Duane?" he echoed her as if she had mentioned someone who belonged to some distant past. "I sometimes wonder that myself, Mrs. Newsom. I wish to God I knew how he was!" He put his hat down on the floor, and she rose, offering to hang it up.

"No, no, I won't be here that long."

There was a sudden and great silence.

"We have not done so well without you, Mrs. Newsom," Eugene Bledsoe finally began, like an actor who has memorized at least part of a long speech, though perhaps not the beginning. "I don't think our difficulties, though, will come as any surprise to you. You know our family pretty well by now."

Despite the solemn tone in which these words were delivered, Mrs. Newsom laughed, and Eugene joined in somewhat bashfully and tunelessly.

"I have been chief cook and bottle-washer since you left us," he now sang out in a more relaxed manner, and they both laughed over this picture, and Mrs. Newsom sprinkled her handkerchief with a few more drops from the camphor bottle.

As if the reserve of many months had broken, Eugene now went into some details about the parsnips, the scrambled eggs, and above all, of course, the custard pie which had risen from bottom to top, ending up as a cake. Much as this amused Mrs. Newsom, she was puzzled—being as she was such an adept pastry cook—as to just how he had accomplished this feat. Her questions as to his procedure began to border on the technical, finally, and therefore, out of mercy, she abandoned the inquiry.

He picked up his hat. He waited. He cleared his throat twice.

"I must apologize here and now," he began in an altered and old-sounding voice, "for the unkind intimation I made that you ... attempted ... to influence my son ... in matters of ..."

"It is of no consequence," Mrs. Newsom exclaimed almost in horror lest the subject of her church be raised again, even in the context of his seeking pardon. "Mr. Bledsoe, I erred also. I should have known better."

"I realize that you were entirely blameless," he said, although he did not totally believe this. He launched then, haltingly and still with a hoarse voice, into a brief chronicle of his Scottish Presbyterian origins, an account to which, it was rather clear, she did not give her undivided attention.

Mrs. Newsom put away her handkerchief and looked out the window. She found herself in the inexplicable frame of mind of being disappointed in Mr. Bledsoe's backing down. Despite her dislike of him (she had never warmed up to him in all the years she had served the family), his Rock-of-Gibraltar stubbornness, coldness, and lack of compromise had become as much a part of her general landscape and bedrock of reality as her church and her rosary. To suddenly see Troy fall, so to speak (her familiarity with this antique event came from her having attempted to help Duane with his Latin lessons over the years), or Gibraltar turn to silt and soft sand, denied her much of the pleasure to be derived from learning she could, if she wished, have her old position back.

"Don't say you won't come now!" he beseeched her, and in even hoarser tones made promise of a better salary.

She smiled and tried to enjoy her triumph.

"I'll have to consult with my husband, of course, Mr. Bledsoe. We thought we would go up to the north of Michigan on a fishing trip, you see, owing . . . to my having lately only ourselves to take care of."

As he scowled in his old bellicose manner, it was clear that Mr. Bledsoe disapproved of the fishing trip.

"But you do see your way clear to coming back . . . eventually?"

At first she thought she was going to consent to return because Duane needed her so desperately. But she knew better. In fact, as she glanced at him rapidly and then let her eye go out to rest on the red buckeye tree in full flower, she knew she would be coming back as much for Eugene as for Duane, or indeed more for the father than for the last remaining son. After all, Duane had his future before him, whatever it might offer. Mr. Bledsoe himself, she felt at that moment, had very little that could be called a future of any kind. She also knew better than Duane did that his father was more tormented by the loss of his sons than if a hundred ghosts had paid him midnight calls.

"I will return, Mr. Bledsoe"—she sealed the bargain now—"if for no other reason than that I still owe something to your mother's memory."

He bowed his head in embarrassed gratitude.

"Supposing we say, then, next week," she promised him. He kept his head bowed, this time in disappointment, for he could not tell her that next week sounded as distant as next year.

"Next week, then, it shall be." He smiled and, rising, moved toward the door.

They both paused a moment as if awestruck at how their roles were reversed, for now she stood as the mistress of her own house dismissing him until "later," and he was the suppliant and she the author and final signer of agreements.

"Duane will be in high spirits, Mrs. Newsom, when I bring home the good news," he told her, going out the door and then stopping to nod good-bye to her before putting on his hat.

Yes, it was true, she thought, staring after him. The old Eugene Bledsoe was no more. The man who had been a lady-killer, racehorse enthusiast, baseball authority, speculator in stocks and bonds, once a rather wealthy young man, and more currently father to two war heroes was little more, she realized as he walked gingerly but somehow a bit limpingly away, in the westerly direction to his house, little more than a shadow. She would be returning to his home almost like the true proprietress of those many, mostly vacant, rooms.

"You are one damned fool to go back to them!" her husband called to her from the ironing room situated immediately beside the ample kitchen where he was required to go when he smoked his pipe or chewed his Bull Durham tobacco.

She gazed at him absentmindedly through the veil of tobacco smoke. There was no way she could tell Ab Newsom what a victory she had won without arousing in him all kinds of suspicions and misdoubt, of which he already had more than a share.

"Will you tell me what makes that son of a bitch think he is better than us—or other folk? What has he ever accomplished—or any of his breed—will you tell me? Outside of sitting on his ass all day and spending his family's money like water. And those two whelps of his that got themselves blown to bits would have been no better than their old man had they come home, if you ask me. And now he can boast about them as war heroes for the rest of his no-account life, that's about the size of it."

As if to taunt her the more for her rash decision to return, Ab now tore off a piece of the plug of his tobacco and chewed and munched loudly.

Mrs. Newsom looked at him with mingled expressions on her face: pain, even shame at hearing him bespatter the Bledsoe clan. And she had a momentary feeling of guilt and remorse that she neglected her spouse, who even more than Eugene could hardly be called a shining example of achievement and a pillar of economic security.

But bending over him, she merely kissed him on his bald spot and pressed his arm.

"You've always done just as you pleased," he said in a softer tone.

"If money grew on trees, Ab," Mrs. Newsom said, reminding him of their shipwrecked financial situation, "I could maybe say no without a qualm."

Eugene Bledsoe's having eaten humble pie before someone whom he secretly regarded as little better than a scrubwoman, despite his awareness of Mrs. Newsom's worth and upright character, had an almost cataclysmic effect as he walked on home from his capitulation and her rather grand condescension to and acceptance of his plea to return. The anger which overtook him as he took the shortcut through the pastureland caused him to stop beside an elm which had been split in two by lightning the year before. His heart pounded so violently that he felt he heard his rib cage creak. He touched the thick bark of the tree. He had a passionate wish to return and insult her and tell her the agreement was off, that he wanted none of her charity, and that it would be better that he and Duane eat charred bread for the rest of their lives rather than accept her pity and her Good Samaritan self-sacrifice to their needs.

Gnashing his teeth, and digging his nails into his palms until he looked down at his hands in astonishment that he had brought blood to the surface, he changed direction and walked toward the flickering orange and yellow lights of the town itself. He looked in on Moe's Villa and then saw that the Acme Tobacco and Magazine Store was still open. He had meant to buy some chewing tobacco, which occasionally appeased his frequent attacks of fury, but the clerk informed him they were totally out of stock. As he turned away angrily, his eye caught at the back of the store a row of magazines devoted entirely, to judge by their sepia covers, to the female figure completely undraped. Hardly

James Purdy

(44)

knowing he was doing so, he purchased four of the more scandalous issues, of "art studies," threw his money down on the counter, and went out. It was raining, and he held the magazines to his chest. Whether to protect himself or the pictures was perhaps not clear to him.

Coming into the house, he called, "Duane!" a number of times, and getting no answer went into his den and without bothering to close the sliding door slumped down in an easy chair and began going through the magazines with a rapidity, even rapacity, which suggested a man looking for a lost thousand-dollar bill.

In his day, he could not help reminding himself, even the possession of such pictures would have landed a man in jail. But his memory of what past times had allowed was soon forgotten in his absorption at the display of the female figure in every pose, illumination of every inch, declivity, and rounded temptation of flesh, presented to the viewer in almost hallowed near-completeness, and Eugene had to admit he was seeing more in these pictures than he had in even the most abandoned of his sessions with his wives and his sweethearts. To his regret, he found that the genitalia were carefully hidden behind a fan, a vase, or tantalizing shadows.

His rage and humiliation at the hands of a "scrubwoman" were replaced by an equally burning and uncontrollable feeling of desire, and he stirred uncomfortably in his soft easy chair by reason of the stings his own flesh felt under the voluptuous banquet of naked femininity.

In his extreme agitation he looked up as if to ask for relief, respite, when his eye fell on Duane, who had come noiselessly in, surprised to see the sliding doors left open, and was in the process of closing them, thinking his father had left the house without remembering to do so.

They both exclaimed out loud at the same moment on becoming aware of the other's presence.

Duane's glance instantly took in the kind of magazine his father was absorbed in and the expression on Eugene's face was not lost on him.

"Well, what can I say, Duane?" Eugene began, his face flushed scarlet. "Even an old guy past his prime has to have a little ... entertainment from time to time."

He threw the magazine to the floor where it joined its other companions in fleshly opulence and invitation.

Eugene let his head fall into his open palms for a few seconds, then, looking up at his son with red eyes and lips as wet as if he had swallowed a whole glass of straight whiskey, he almost shouted, "I have been to Mrs. Newsom's, Duane, and I have persuaded her to come back to us."

Duane picked up one of the magazines, looked through it hastily, almost desperately, and let it slip to the floor with its companions, a kind of queer obeisance and awe written on his countenance, as if he had been granted permission to look ever so briefly at the scars of a soldier's battle wounds.

"You don't seem . . . glad"—Eugene watched his son—"that she will be coming home to you. It was not an agreeable task, to go there hat in hand . . . to beg her—that is, to admit," he said, some of the rage coming back, "I was in the wrong."

"Oh, Dad," Duane mumbled.

"Yes, 'oh, Dad,' " Eugene sassed him, though not energetically.

"As to these"—his father then waved his left arm in the direction of the glorious smut—"Duane, a fellow has to have a change once in a blue moon. . . ."

Duane only shrugged his shoulders, and then nodded almost imperceptibly.

He did not want to look at his father because he was aware that Eugene was still in a state of violent erection, recalling the day not too long ago when he had opened the bathroom door left unlocked and seen his father on the toilet.

But it was not disapproval or embarrassment which created the expression on his son's face, which Eugene took for coldness and even contempt. Duane's feelings at that moment had nothing to do with his father's devouring of gorgeous smut. Duane was disappointed in more ways than one that Mrs. Newsom was returning, and what Eugene would never have appreciated was that Duane had enjoyed their keeping "bachelor's hall," had delighted in his Dad's having been, however ineptly, chief cook and bottle-washer, and that Mrs. Newsom's imminent return, although providing them immediately with more comfort and well-being, would deprive Duane at least of some feeling of adventure, perhaps even danger, and he did not look forward to life settling down once again to routine and humdrum regularity. He had, in fact, enjoyed their bachelor escapade almost as much as when, in the old days, Eugene had taken Duane camping.

His father left the room abruptly.

James Purdy

Duane stealthily picked up the magazine his father had been leafing through. One of the pages was moist, probably from his father's perspiration. But as his fingers leafed through the publication and touched one stripped and seemingly invulnerable embodiment of fleshly delight after another, something rushed in upon his memory with such unexpected immediacy, even violence, that he found himself sucking in his breath as he did when he overexerted himself skating and leaned against the boards gasping for breath like someone about to suffer an attack.

His memory was carrying him back to a time three or four years earlier when he had stood outside Justin and Douglas's room (they had always shared the same bedroom, a room which was now locked tight and forbidden even to Mrs. Newsom to enter), and he heard again Justin's voice going on about how they had seen *him* naked in the arms of Molly Ferrand, and he had heard Douglas's tepid defense of the *him* on the grounds that "he's not too old for it, and, after all, he has no wife at present, and the need in him is strong." At that moment in their conversation Duane had rapped on the door. Justin had opened it—after a long pause—majestically. For a moment the oldest of the Bledsoe boys had looked scowlingly at his youngest brother, then his outward scorn and ill-humor had broken, and after inquiring, "Shall we admit the snot, Doug?" he had pulled him in, and then Douglas had mussed up Duane's hair, and both the older brothers pretended they were beating up on Duane, giving him mock punches in the belly, and finally Justin had lifted him up with one hand and held him over his head to Duane's squealing delight. Their horseplay had stopped the discussion of whomever they were discussing as not being "too old for it."

And until just now, leafing through this paper garden of blooming flesh, as ripe for the tasting as fresh fruit, Duane had never connected the *him* who had embraced Molly Ferrand naked as anybody in particular when suddenly he knew, of course, it had to be Eugene. His father. Their father.

Without even knowing he was about to do so, Duane hurled the magazine across the room against the lower wall, just as his father entered the room. So great was the force of his throw that the thing fell with broken spine and almost every page became detached from the whole; that entire side of the room became spread and littered with the bodies of sylphs.

"That's no way to treat printed matter!" Eugene protested in a loud whisper.

"Printed matter?" Duane repeated, rolling his eyes until only the whites were visible. Going over to the window and putting his right hand on the sill, he said vehemently, "Did you ever know a Molly Ferrand?"

His father was so completely taken aback by this question, coming as it did on the heels of Duane's throwing a magazine across the room with such violence, that he slumped down on the little settee.

"Turn and face me, Duane." When Duane reluctantly obeyed, he went on, "What is wrong ... Benjy? What is it?"

"I once heard my brothers speak of her." Duane's clear, fresh tenor voice rose as loud as a cornet.

"Oh, Duane, for God's sake," his father gasped. "Will you let up on me!"

Duane stared at him. He felt dimly and imprecisely at that moment something of his Dad's anguish as he had to hear the names of his sons mingled with, and in the same breath with, that of a woman like Molly.

"They should never have mentioned her to a young boy." Eugene spoke as if talking to himself alone in the room. "I'm truly surprised at them. Indeed, I am."

Duane bowed his head, and then hurriedly went over to the door, where he stopped.

"You'll feel like a different boy when Mrs. Newsom starts serving us with some decent grub. See if I'm not right, Duane. There's nothing like decent grub to help a man's disposition."

His son turned around and gave his father a faint smile, though not looking him directly in the eye, but it illuminated the room in a way that was better for Eugene than any words that could have been pronounced just then.

A few days after Mrs. Newsom had returned from "exile" and life had settled down to a more normal and, if possible, even more humdrum routine, Duane, as he had before her dismissal, kept circling about the dishpan, wanting to help dry the plates and not daring to (Mrs. Newsom gave him an occasional warning glance not to push their luck), when Eugene suddenly called out to him to come on the double to the parlor.

Duane rather expected another dressing down owing to his Dad's sullen disposition since Mrs. Newsom's return.

James Purdy

(48)

Without asking Duane to sit down, or even acknowledging his presence, Eugene went on reading from a battered ledger, and then finally looking up, he said stiffly, "Duane, I haven't measured your height in well over a year."

His son stared at him, if not dumbfounded, at least at sea as to what to say in reply. For Eugene certainly must have been aware that "measuring" had always been Justin's and Douglas's prerogative; that they, being such giants, even taller than Eugene himself, had fussed and worried and even scolded that Duane was not growing up as tall as they, who were well over six foot three and despised anyone shorter than themselves. *"He's yours to measure, I won't have a hand in it ever."* Duane remembered precisely his father's words to his brothers when the measuring ritual had begun four or five years before.

The more, however, those two, Justin and Douglas, had measured him, the less he seemed to grow. "You aren't going to grow up to be a runt on us now, are you?" Douglas had cried, exasperated after they had looked at the cross penciled above where he had stood for his measuring, and they had seen he was still only five foot ten and three-quarters tall.

Justin had been even more put out, and had stared at the tape as if it had put one over on him. "Maybe it's better, though," he had mumbled after a pause. "If Benj is going to be an ice skater he don't need all our height."

"But *they* always did this, Dad," Duane finally replied as his father picked up the tape measure.

At a look of sudden sneering command from Eugene, Duane began taking off his tennis shoes, and then resignedly went over and pressed himself against the wall.

Eugene extended the tape measure.

"Don't you remember, Dad, that they always were in charge of this?" Duane flinched from the peril of his own remark.

"I declare," Eugene cried, and his voice was the cheeriest his son could remember hearing for some time, "I believe you've grown nearly half an inch!" The pencil marks from his last measuring had been left by his brothers' hands on the white wall. For accuracy's sake, Eugene now measured him again. He nodded, corroborating his first finding.

"You're sure?" Duane stepped away from the wall and came over to inspect the tape measure which Eugene still held at the precise line of measurement.

Mourners Below

"But I won't ever make their ... altitude, will I?" he inquired, absentmindedly taking the tape out of his father's hand. "Will I now, Dad?"

"Why, hell," Eugene replied, snatching the tape back from Duane and putting it in a drawer which the boy had never seen opened before, and from whose inner recesses appeared what looked like old photos of the hero-measurers themselves. "Why, damn it all," Eugene continued, locking the drawer, "boys often grow up until they are twenty-five. Don't you know that?"

"But they," Duane muttered, "were over six feet when they were only sixteen.... You told me once."

"Sit down," Eugene commanded testily. "Look, I'm going to have to go to Maryland with Professor Redpath," Mr. Bledsoe began, after lavishly ignoring as usual the various references to Duane's brothers. "We are working together, the professor and I, on a little brochure re the Battle of Antietam. You remember Professor Redpath, of course." Eugene spoke a little nervously under Duane's silence.

Professor Redpath, who was no more a professor than he was an historian of battles, was, in the still-fresh words of Justin, who had loathed the man, "a broken-down lickspittle of a retired baseball player" who had found in Eugene an easy mark for getting ready spending money, and in whom their father had found a flatterer and a confidant, a hanger-on who liked to draw a picture of a Eugene free of all mortal faults.

Like Justin, Duane despised the man with an inveterate passion.

"Your tutor will be back from his summer vacation in a very short while." Eugene shifted on his chair uneasily. Duane knew his Dad felt guilty about leaving him.

During the summer, which, despite the fact that since their terrible "news" time itself seemed to have frozen, was beginning to draw to a close, Duane had nearly forgotten that he had a "tutor," and that he would soon have to buckle down to plane geometry, advanced algebra, and Latin, if he ever hoped to go to college (which he did not).

"Are you sure you didn't make a mistake in the measurement of my height, Dad?" Duane surprised even himself by returning to this topic.

"Do you want me to do it over?" Eugene spoke in an almost tearful tone. Duane was always amazed at how easily his father's feelings were hurt.

James Purdy
(50)

"I've been thinking," Duane tried to explain, "that maybe you just wanted to encourage me by saying I had grown."

"Why would I deceive you about such a thing?"

And throwing the lead pencil down on the hardwood table, Eugene shouted, "You tell me why!"

The next day Duane went to the depot to see Eugene off for Maryland. He suspected that Professor Redpath was already waiting for Eugene on the train.

"In case you get too lonely," his father told him before boarding, "Mrs. Newsom has agreed to let you sleep at her house. Be sure to leave the porch light burning all night while I'm gone."

Eugene looked at Duane in a kind of wondering way, and then stiffly, almost sleepily, bent down and kissed his son on the mouth.

His doing so made up in a way for his father's awful silence about their loss and was perhaps—who knows?—perhaps a kind of mention of it at last.

The very day after Eugene Bledsoe departed for Maryland to study firsthand the Battle of Antietam, two heavy wooden boxes arrived from the War Department addressed to Duane's father.

Duane helped Mrs. Newsom in with them, and once they had carried them into the living room, they both stood staring at the crates which had come from such a great distance. Of course, both the housekeeper and Duane knew what the boxes must contain, whose property they had once been, but they merely stared at them without speaking. Perhaps Eugene's silence was catching.

"I guess his den is the best place for them," Duane finally remarked after they had begun to get over the strange feeling of apprehension and dread that the unexpected arrival of the boxes had brought them.

A peculiar aroma now came from the cartons, which suggested camphor or perhaps carbolic acid.

"It depends on what is in them, I suppose." Mrs. Newsom spoke apprehensively. "They've obviously come from such a terrible distance. . . . Perhaps we should let them rest in the woodshed until Mr. Bledsoe has had a chance to look through their contents."

"Oh, they should never be put in the woodshed!" Duane could not conceal his shock and disapproval of such an idea.

Mrs. Newsom then gave him one of her searching glances.

They both knew he would try to open the boxes. It was one of Duane's many regrettable habits; that is, he went through his father's "things." This prying open of drawers and closets and even sealed packages which did not belong to him was, however, of recent date. It had actually begun one day when Duane had tiptoed into his father's den and, while rummaging about looking for an English translation of Caesar's *Commentaries,* which he thought he had once spied in his father's desk drawer, he all at once came upon an unopened packet of letters addressed to him and written by his mother. At first he could not believe his own eyes. Or he tried to tell himself that he had read the letters already and had handed them back to his father for safekeeping, for shortly after his mother had left them she had written Duane a letter which Eugene handed to him directly from the postman, and when the boy had finished reading it, Eugene had said, "Anything in it I need to know?" and Duane had handed him the letter and his father had kept it. For some minutes, therefore, after his discovery Duane pretended that this packet of many letters had already been opened, read by him, and handed back to his father for protective custody.

Duane might have demanded an immediate explanation from his father of this high-handed intercepting of his correspondence except for two reasons: first, the enormity of such an action numbed his mind; and second, only a day or so after his discovery of the "theft," his brothers' deaths had been announced, and so the letters and the deaths had all fallen under a shroud of heavy silence and mute oblivion.

Mrs. Newsom protested sharply when she heard Duane opening the cartons from where she still stood perplexed in the living room. She stepped to the threshold of the den.

"Duane, think carefully what you are doing!"

He reminded her of the "stolen" letters from his mother, a secret he had blurted out to her over the dishpan.

"But two wrongs, Duane, don't make . . ."

He sniggered his defiance.

She could not help watching him open the battered boxes, which were now beginning to come apart. They gave off a reeking odor of something which afflicted the nostrils—was it dried sea water? manure? or merely some powerful chemical or disinfectant?

"Oh, Duane," she admonished him as the boy savagely ripped open the lids with a small crowbar from the toolshed.

James Purdy
(52)

Inside the crates lay exposed their hats, trousers, belts, grim un-mended bathrobes, and finally, in the bottom, strange exotic trinkets, which Duane fingered absentmindedly.

"That is Douglas's"—the boy would point out one article of apparel: a hat, a handkerchief, a good-luck charm, etc.—"and this belongs to Justin," and he would hold up a shirt or a necktie or a sweater.

"How do you know whose it is?" Mrs. Newsom spoke thickly.

At this question something broke in Duane, whether caused by his daring at having entered the den and broken open packages not ad-dressed to him, or by the memory of the purloining of his mother's let-ters, or by his father's inhuman and to him fiendish silence over the boys' deaths, or over his failure as a "scholar" and his meaningless bril-liance as an ice and figure skater, or all these things added together. Whatever the cause, a kind of series of groans came from him like the bursting of the accumulation of a festering sore.

"You see, Duane"—Mrs. Newsom tried to put her arm on his shoul-der, but he threw it off—"it doesn't do to look into these things unbid-den and all by oneself."

He turned away from her and walked to the corner of the room, like a reprimanded child, where he suddenly gave over to a quieter if more unassuageable surrender to his grief.

Unable to sleep that night, Duane took up the packet of "stolen" letters from his mother and by candlelight (another of the habits Eu-gene had warned him against—well, then, why did his father have can-dles in the first place!—the excuse always being the risk of power failure during electrical storms), he opened a letter over a year old and read only the first few lines:

> *I think of you so often, indeed I am* always *thinking of you,*
> *and can never resign myself to the thought that we are so far*
> *away from one another. I pray constantly that the barriers*
> *which divide us will before too long be broken...*

Duane knew that at that moment both Douglas and Justin were standing near him and that they were of the same vital consistency as the flames from the candles which had moved twisting and gyrating through the air like silent tongues from their red cups before the face of Jesus in Mrs. Newsom's church.

"I'm not afraid anymore," Duane said, keeping his eyes closed and addressing his brothers. "If I am crazy, I am crazy. I am not afraid."

He looked beyond the candles straight to where the two boys had stood watching him. They were no longer there.

"I wonder what you want?" He spoke to the empty air where they had faced him.

He opened another of the letters. There would be enough of *them* all right so that if he read only one an evening by candlelight, they would at least last him until the first killing frost.

"Perhaps Douglas and Justin measure me with some heavenly measuring tape," Duane said, beginning to fall swiftly into slumber at last, "if they care about measuring in heaven."

The stealing of his mother's letters at his father's hands had at first numbed his mind because of the treachery, the sneaking dishonesty. He recalled his mother's denunciations of Eugene prior to their divorce. Often, in imaginary interviews with his father, he thought of how he would make him face up to this crime of theft.

His anger and resentment against Eugene caused him to think of the two dead boys' bedroom, which Eugene had kept locked ever since they had gone to war. He had heard his Dad instruct Mrs. Newsom and the cleaning lady, the electrician, and the other maintenance men that they were never to go into that room under any circumstance.

"This of course applies to you, as well," Eugene had added, looking brazenly at his youngest son.

As Eugene had stolen from him, he would now disobey his command in retaliation.

One of the things Duane was good at, as a matter of fact, was jimmying locks and loosening bolts.

After Mrs. Newsom had gone home for the night, Duane sat brooding in the living room until the thought of the locked upstairs sanctuary rushed upon him strongly with a desire perhaps prompted by his having opened the War Department boxes addressed to his father. The impulse to open that locked door, as had been his desire to open the cartons, was almost as strong at that moment as a sexual urge. He was in fact suddenly frightened of his own wish to break into their room. The fancy even came to him, especially now that the deepest shadows of night were descending, that upon going into the room he would find Douglas and Justin sitting there dead because Eugene, unbeknownst to

James Purdy

everyone, had brought their bodies back from the front and had had them preserved forever for his own solace. Or perhaps, instead of the dead, he would find Eugene himself waiting for him to walk into the trap.

The fear of what he would find in the room gave him pause.

The deepest part of night had gained possession of the earth, and a cloud-ridden gloom covered the entire sky, blotting out every trace of any stars or the moon. Even the crickets and tree frogs were nearly inaudible. This chilling stillness postponed a little longer his gaining resolution enough to go up the back stairs with their narrow, traitorous, broken steps, and stand before his brothers' door. Even in life they had not liked him to invade the sanctity of their room. They preferred to talk to him in the spacious backyard, or even in his own room, which was actually slightly larger than theirs, with higher ceilings.

Duane had brought along a skeleton key which he had worried out of the possession of a locksmith, who had said on finally surrendering it to him, "If I didn't know you came from such a good family, Benjy, I'd never let this out of my hands."

The door, which he had aimlessly and abruptly smote, the keyhole, which he had touched gingerly, were now ready for his assault, he thought bitterly. He put the skeleton key into the aperture, and its sound was to him loud as a trumpet in the deep stillness of the house. With a few tries of the key, the lock snapped open. He hesitated, however, at least a minute, perhaps two, before daring to push open the door. A soft moan escaped him as his feet moved over the threshold, for the darkness was so complete here, like that of the old oak grove near Yoxtheimer's stone quarry. He had not forgotten his flashlight, but he hesitated to turn it on. Yet he knew he could not go on waiting in this dense blackness, no matter who or what he was to find expecting him!

He snapped on the heavy waterproof flashlight, and its beams caught the shapes of basketballs, a football, a hockey stick, varsity banners, boxing gloves, a skip rope, dumbbells, and Indian clubs. His hand then found the light switch and flooded the room with illumination. There were no corpses or ghosts or giants waiting. His father was not hiding in the clothes closet. The room was vibrant with emptiness.

But on the east wall, by the fireplace, near an outstretched flag, were two large and recently enlarged photos of Justin and Douglas in their Marine dress uniforms. The photos had also been rather inexpertly tinted or colored and were framed with a kind of vulgar convex glass which magnified their impeccable grooming and frowning, chapped male good looks.

His knees buckled as they had the day in the Roman church, and he found himself half bending before the portraits of the two men who would not leave him in death, whom he often thought he had despised, perhaps never loved, who, he was fearful, had never completely cared for him. Yet here they were as in life so near him, so commanding of his least action and thought: he would never be free of them or the man who was the father of all three of them.

"What is it you want?" Duane cried out, slowly rising from where he had fallen to his knees before the portraits. "I know you're here!" He turned around, gazing into every corner of the room. "But what do you want of me? Justin, Douglas!" He went over to the high wild-cherry commode and put his head down on its marble top. As he did so, a solid brass handle of one of the drawers came loose and clattered to the floor. He hardly noted its fall. Eugene would notice it later.

Slowly Duane realized that this was the room where Eugene came to unburden his loss and his grief. It was his Roman church, as witness the recently burned candles which lay strewn on tables and chiffoniers everywhere. And *he* had condemned idolaters and old women who kissed rosaries!

The skeleton key which had been so serviceable in opening the door was of no use in closing it. After an endless number of attempts to lock it, Duane merely shut the door and came bumbling down the stairs.

His anger against his father had, if anything, only increased, but it was more under control, more tightly fastened, and more poisonous. At the same time, an overweening, nearly delirious notion that his brothers were with him everywhere, that they guided his every step, that they measured him constantly and sat by his bedside as he slumbered became the sum and substance of his consciousness.

PART II

"I would never go if I were you, Duane!"

Mrs. Newsom had seldom been so emphatic, so hidebound, so firm
and unsmiling as now, facing the youngest Bledsoe boy. Her false teeth
whistled, almost sang under her strong feelings.

Duane said nothing for a few moments, still holding the thick envelope and formal invitation in his hands. Indeed, he had never received
any invitation that he could remember from anybody. It came from Estelle Dumont, a name not unfamiliar to him or his family, a very young
widow who lived some miles from them in the country. She had been
married twice, and both her husbands had died. Both had been very
wealthy men and had left her, so it was said, large fortunes, which, together with her own not inconsiderable wealth, made her something of

a marvel in the community, if not throughout the neighboring states.

"Why ever not?" He finally broke his silence, but still avoided looking in her direction, and fingered the thick paper of the invitation in almost a famished way.

"I think she's caused enough trouble in your family, if you ask me." Mrs. Newsom, he saw, was every bit as much a killjoy and tyrant as Eugene.

"You mean because Douglas and Justin used to go to see her?" He sneered at her piety .

"See her! If that was all." Mrs. Newsom was positively ferocious, he thought.

He handed her the invitation with a kind of rude flourish.

"What was 'all,' then?" Duane demanded, but she was deep in reading the invitation.

"I said, what was *all*, Mrs. Newsom?" He touched her hand which was holding the envelope from Mrs. Dumont.

"I've said too much as it is," she replied, handing him back the invitation, but fumbling, in her agitation, so that the envelope and its contents fell to the floor. They both waited as if unsure who should pick it up. Duane finally leant down and grasped it.

"Since you've said as much as you have, you should finish your thought, shouldn't you?" He spoke in a scoffing, harsh manner she could never remember his having used to her before.

"I told you I misspoke, Duane, and I'm sorry."

"Do you mean Justin was her . . . sweetheart?"

"Oh, Duane!" She now took on his indifferent, sophisticated tone and walked out of the room.

He went on studying the thick paper of the invitation as if perhaps somewhere in its wording he might find out what Mrs. Newsom had meant.

He soon followed the old housekeeper into the kitchen.

"But a fancy-dress ball, Mrs. N.," he began, using this shortened form of her name which, in spite of herself, she had always liked. "I've never been to one."

She saw that her running down of Estelle Dumont had been the wrong tack so far as discouraging his wish to go to the party, and like his curiosity concerning Roman Catholic ritual, his desire to see a woman who had also "seen" Justin and Douglas, not to mention his curiosity to visit Mrs. Dumont's mansion, was too impetuous to be vetoed, especially by an old housekeeper.

"You'll have to ask your father, then," she grumbled, and began preparing a veal roast for the oven. "I will say no more. I've said too much already. But you can't just run off like a harum-scarum to such a woman's house, without your Dad knowing, and then let me be raked over the coals for knowing you were going to see such a person."

"Whatever 'such a person' means," he shot back at her, "she can't be too terrible if both Justin and Douglas saw her, can she?"

The almost contemptuous, certainly pitying look which Mrs. Newsom now bestowed on Duane flustered him severely.

"I mean . . . if they were all . . . friends."

" 'Friends' is not quite the word for it, I don't believe." She immediately regretted having said this, for she flared up with, "As I say, Duane, you must tell Mr. Bledsoe before you go. I am going to wash my hands of the whole thing."

"Yes, after you've aroused my suspicions and wonder with your sly remarks!" he shouted. "Why don't you come out with the entire story, if you've gone this far?"

"I don't know the whole story. I only know that Mrs. Dumont"— here she paused, and in angry short movements dusted the veal roast with flour and garlic powder—"Mrs. Dumont's reputation is not of the best."

"Well, then, what about my brothers' reputations?"

"They were, after all, young men," she whispered.

"Going to her forty-room house can't be any worse than bending the knee in your church, can it?" Duane exclaimed. "After all!"

He was immediately sorry. He saw he had wounded her feelings, and yet he was glad, too, that he had got back at her. He hated to be crossed. Having gone this far, he repeated some unkind remarks he claimed Eugene had made about her cooking, and the fact she had not properly mended the large Irish linen tablecloth.

"No one can stop me from accepting, I guess!" he cried in the face of her hurt silence and tossed the invitation on the table. And he stormed out of the room.

Smarting from his impudence and his caustic speech to her, Mrs. Newsom, in a shocking betrayal of her own principles, found herself letting slip Duane's secret to his father shortly after the latter returned from Maryland.

Eugene had returned looking as though he had been out in the sun a good deal, and he brought back with him an enormous sheaf of papers, containing maps and notes, and some old daguerreotypes of Civil War soldiers for which he said he was indebted to Professor Redpath.

Mrs. Newsom began with the invitation, handing it to him like a piece of damning evidence, without comment or preparation.

"Estelle Dumont, is it?" Eugene pressed and ruffled the thick paper as if there was something yet more hidden in its folds. "But how would a boy his age have anything suitable to wear to such a thing?" He acted suddenly astonished that anybody could even think of Duane as a possible guest to such an affair.

"I think the ball is beside the point," Mrs. Newsom began, carried away by she knew not what tide of folly, "when one takes into account your son's present . . . mental condition."

She could have bitten her own tongue out once the words were said.

"I don't follow you, Mrs. Newsom," Mr. Bledsoe said in that shocked, stern, deathly cold voice which after all her years of service still made her feel faint with trepidation.

"Mrs. Newsom!" He roused her from what he took to be a fit of absentmindedness.

"He feels he sees his brothers." She now finished her revelation in a voice softer than had she spoken with her mouth covered by the thick paper of the invitation itself.

"He thinks he sees . . . ?" Mr. Bledsoe was thunderstruck. She merely nodded.

"You mean . . . he has confided such a thing to you?" Mr. Bledsoe assumed again his old if now rusty stance of cross-examining a recalcitrant and hostile witness, except that it was clear from the tone of his voice that he believed this particular witness all too easily.

She stifled a sob, then her tears flowed uninterruptedly. Eugene turned away. He loathed weeping.

"What does he see?" he inquired with deadly aloofness.

"I would never have betrayed a confidence such as this, Mr. Bledsoe"—she indicated it might be better if no more were said—"but I am so troubled by his . . . state."

"I said *what does* he see?" Eugene ignored her scruples. "Well?" he thundered when there was no more sound from her, not even sniveling.

"You said he *sees* them, didn't you! Weren't those your words, Mrs. Newsom?"

"They were," she replied. His severity and coldness had stunned her into calm. "He sees their ghosts," she said finally.

Had she spoken the most offensive obscenity and then in the bargain crushed his mouth with her rosary he could hardly have been more revolted. He turned away, however, less to hide his loathing than his consternation.

"His mother, you may remember"—he spoke after a fearful struggle with himself in which he was victorious at least in refraining from blaming the housekeeper for his son's madness—"his mother," he went on, turning to her with a look of rage now turned against the absent Aileen, "had an unbridled imagination. But even she, so far as I know, never went so far as to see . . . *that!*"

He folded his arms and stared at her as if to give her a short breathing space before pronouncing her guilty.

"If you would not tell Duane I have broken his confidence . . ."

"You can have no fear of that," Eugene snapped.

He might have said, she thought, that in any case she could spare all fear that he would ever speak to Duane about any matter touching on feeling.

"I won't mention we have talked," he added, pacing up and down the room. "But I would recommend, Mrs. Newsom, that in the future you do not allow him to expatiate on such a . . . subject at all! Do you hear?"

She nodded.

"There is Dr. Cressy, sir," she volunteered abruptly.

"There is, indeed!" Eugene assented, turning to face her. It was almost the only suggestion of any magnitude she had ever made which seemed acceptable to him.

"Dr. Cressy," he repeated. "You think he might have a notion or two about this?"

She bowed her head in assent.

"As to this invitation . . ." Eugene was lordly now again, and in full possession of himself. He stared at the rather ridiculously luxurious invitation to the fancy-dress ball. He tapped the piece of engraved stationery against his open palm. "Why not let him go? It might distract him from . . . from whatever he may have inherited from his mother."

Mourners Below

Mrs. Newsom looked unconvinced at his assigning the origin of Duane's distraction to his mother, but she could not conceal her astonishment and disapproval that he had given in to what seemed to her more dangerous than ghosts—Estelle Dumont herself.

Dr. Cressy's house was situated about ten miles from the Bledsoes through green undulating hills, interspersed with abundant cornfields, a lone live oak rising unexpectedly here and there, and innumerable scarecrows, more numerous than the trees, owing to the fact that a great cyclone of a few years earlier had destroyed much of the forest which had abounded here. Almost the only tree left standing near the doctor's residence was an ancient and immense thorn which overshadowed the entire west end of the edifice.

Dr. Cressy had retired from practice some years past, but he still saw an occasional patient such as Mrs. Newsom who procured from him an herb tea which she claimed was the only remedy against her occasional kidney distress and insomnia. Time out of mind, she had begged the doctor to tell her what the herb in question might be, but he had steadfastly refused, and finally one day when they had nearly had a violent argument over the precise identity of the mysterious potion, he had reluctantly agreed to leave behind, in the event of his death, a note addressed to her describing the name of the drug so that she would not be left without this cure-all and heartsease.

Mrs. Newsom, since the matter of the herb had been settled, went right to the real point of her visit, which was Duane, and told the doctor "where the shoe pinched" there.

Somewhat to her surprise, the doctor laughed uproariously. "Oh, those young brutes of brothers," he cried, taking off his glasses and wiping his eyes. "Imagine them coming back from the Great Beyond, Mrs. Newsom! Why, that would trouble anybody, let alone a boy barely out of his childhood!"

Mrs. Newsom sat with a somewhat morose look. She was puzzled by the doctor's levity, or lack of reverence, or cynicism and callousness, or perhaps by a combination of all these things.

She finally broke in on his amusement and mirth. "But can't you give the poor lad something?"

Becoming rather sober, the old man stared at her a moment. "Your trouble, my dear Annette, is that you think some sort of pill or elixir can cure or calm anything—even, I suppose, stretching as far as to prevent a boy from seeing his young brutes of brothers appearing out of the grave! Medicine, Mrs. Newsom, does have its limits! It's not, after all, Nature."

Dr. Cressy went off again into peals of laughter. "I've never had contact in all my years of practice with young men who gave off such a profusion and odor of sweat as Justin and Douglas," he recalled. "Mind you, I don't say they stank! Not at all. But they were sweaters. Always exercising, or running, or climbing, or jumping, or turning cartwheels. Their dirty clothes must have been stacked to the ceiling!"

"But Doctor," Mrs. Newsom raised her voice in disapproval, "how can you speak so of the departed?"

Ignoring this interruption, he went on, "Their sweat was not, as I say, unpleasant to the sense of smell, at least not to mine. And I am, compared to most of my patients, a bit on the fastidious side, after all. No, their sweat was pleasant, as indeed is a horse's, come to think of it. . . . A horse's urine is another matter, as we can all testify." He stared at Mrs. Newsom hard as if for corroboration of this last opinion.

Mrs. Newsom sighed.

People said that Dr. Cressy was senile, but she knew better, of course. Her memory of him went back forty-odd years to when he had been a young medic just out of Harvard, and had set up practice in his native village. Though of a good family, he had talked coarsely even then to his patients and friends. Just stepping into Dr. Cressy's waiting room was a kind of education into life, she supposed, and she recalled the day, not too long ago, when she had haphazardly picked up one of the tomes with which the walls of his waiting room were burdened, and read such terrible things in it about the human body that she had had to ask the doctor for some drops of peppermint in hot water to calm her stomach.

"Here you are, again," he had scolded, "writing out your own prescription for me, Mrs. Newsom! Peppermint in hot water, indeed!"

He had cared for his mother, who was an invalid, until only recently (she had died at ninety, bedridden), and he kept a staff of what he called his "valets," young men who had been in trouble with the law, and who stayed on with him as chauffeurs and handymen anywhere from a year to five years, then vanished.

Growing thoughtful now, the doctor spoke in a lower tone. "At one time, Mrs. Newsom, in my early days of practice, I disbelieved in

Mourners Below

(65)

ghosts, but now when my life is measured in days or hours, I am not certain of anything. I even think there may be fairies, as this book on superstition in Scotland makes out." He touched a heavy volume sitting on a chair near him. "Your religion, I believe, forbids you to believe in such things. But if there are ghosts, one can hardly persuade Duane there are none, especially if, as you claim, he has seen them. But"—and here again he began to give out his rather loud, even coarse laugh—"I can't imagine any less spiritual candidates coming back from the other side than those two young thugs and lummoxes."

Mrs. Newsom was considerably taken aback, even outraged, by the use of such epithets to describe Justin and Douglas. At the same time she wondered at a certain feeling of relief she suddenly experienced at hearing the doctor's outburst, for his irreverent words, indeed blasphemy, somehow made her worry over Duane and her sorrow over his brothers' deaths all at once lessen, even snap, at least for a few moments. And though nobody but an eccentric like the doctor would have thought of applying the words "lummox" and "thug" to such fine young men, there had been, she had to admit, something of all that in them. She began to remember their hard, horny, callused hands, with the broken, discolored nails, and the cracked, chapped knuckles, and she recalled too their fearsome sweating and how she had gagged of a morning when she had drawn back the sheets and seen how they had stained the bedclothes with their "masculine vitality," as she put it. At the same time, hearing the doctor's uproarious irreverence, she felt it was impossible that such obstreperous and full-blooded boys could be dead. She had the feeling that one day they would return in actual flesh and blood and probably upset the entire management of the house and dismiss her as their first order of business.

"But why shouldn't I see him, Mrs. Newsom?" Dr. Cressy interrupted her reverie by returning to her supplication that Duane should come to him. "I doubt though," he went on, "that I can get him to talk. The boy is as deep as a well. He should no more be an ice skater than he should walk the mountains of the moon, and whoever put that idea into his head anyhow and promised him the Olympics!"

"None of *us* certainly," Mrs. Newsom defended herself and, at the same time, Mr. Bledsoe.

Dr. Cressy stared at her, marveling at her loyalty to the clan of the Bledsoes, and at the dogged way she always spoke up for them.

"I miss the second Mrs. Bledsoe," the doctor confessed. "Aileen—

Duane's mother. She was a vivacious woman. Always lifted my spirits when I saw her."

Mrs. Newsom recalled for the physician that it was Aileen who had recommended Dr. Cressy's kidney and bladder potions, pills, or teas to her in the first place.

Disregarding this harping on the herbal remedy, Dr. Cressy wondered, "Does Duane ever hear from his mother?"

Mrs. Newsom did not know whether she should share the episode of the purloined letters with the doctor or not, but since Duane was going to consult with him in any case "about this, that, and the other," she let slip the whole story of Eugene's "secreting" of Aileen's letters to her son.

"The downright cussedness of human beings." The doctor chuckled but looked more serious as he took in the story. He continued, "Their hellishness, their deliberate torpedoing of their lives in taking the wrong tack! Wonderful, isn't it, the misdirected energy? Yes, wonderful," he answered his own question.

"Well, when can young Duane come by?" he wondered, getting up and ending the session.

They agreed tentatively on a day and an hour.

Mrs. Newsom insisted the doctor take her money, and they had the same argument over "payment" as they always did, the old man saying, "Not a penny when you need it for your grandchildren's education," and she replying, "Then I'll have to stop my visits, Dr. Cressy. I will not be beholden to you for medical assistance, and that is final," etc., etc.

After his patient had left, the mask of good humor and stoic acceptance of the foibles of human nature fell from the old man's face.

"You could have knocked me over with a feather!" Mrs. Newsom's description of her discovering that Duane had seen ghosts came back to him. He picked up a heavy volume and leafed through it idly, but her words kept echoing in his ears. Finally, closing the book with a sharp detonation, the doctor felt, if not knocked over by a feather, considerably eager to see a patient who was not afflicted with the bodily discomforts of old age and coming death but one who was gloriously young and an ice skater (however ill-advisedly) to boot, and who was in the unusual circumstance of being visited by his two dead brothers.

The day selected for Duane's visit to Dr. Cressy was preceded by a mild frost, so his father decided that it was not advisable for him to go all that distance on his bike but that instead he should take the bus. He also insisted that Duane wear his winter sweater and muffler, against Duane's vociferous protest.

Eugene had agreed to Duane's seeing Dr. Cressy with mixed feelings. Dr. Cressy had been Aileen's favorite doctor, and Eugene felt that the old physician was therefore prejudiced against him personally. But to whom else could he entrust a boy who "saw things"? It was better to send him to an old man who had one foot in the grave and who was not part of the immediate community in which the Bledsoes had to live and appear publicly. And a doctor closer to home with new methods and smart theories might even want Duane sent off to a hospital—who knows?

In addition to the burden of a muffler and sweater, Duane was also handed a large picnic basket containing his lunch, in case the doctor kept him too long and he should become, as he usually did, ravenous.

Duane had hardly crossed the threshold of the doctor's waiting room and cried out a loud "Good morning!" when an emergency arose, which, though at first unnerving, later served both doctor and patient to reach an understanding. A young man who had been hired to cut down some dead trees had badly cut his forearm with an ax and was brought in by two of his fellow workmen, bleeding profusely. Without being asked, Duane assisted the doctor in reviving the woodsman and quickly kept handing to the doctor, as they were required, the various surgical dressings, gauze, and even instruments, and gave other assistance quite like someone who was at ease in an emergency room.

For some time after the woodsman had been sewn up, bandaged, and dismissed with the usual bottle of medication, Dr. Cressy sat gazing at Duane with silent if openmouthed astonishment and admiration.

He came out of his musings when he caught sight of the fact that Duane's expensive jacket and tie and shirt were all extravagantly splashed with blood.

"If you will follow me on in here, Duane . . ." Dr. Cressy spoke deferentially, and ushered him into a brightly illuminated room equipped with several huge shining porcelain sinks. Duane removed his jacket, tie, and shirt, and the doctor proceeded to wash them free of the red stains.

"Blood is very easy to remove from garments when it is fresh, but when dried"—and he looked back at the young man from his task of washing—"well, that's another matter altogether."

James Purdy

(68)

He studied Duane closely as the boy put his clothes back on. Then, breaking into a grin, Dr. Cressy said, "You're sound as a nut, and don't let anybody tell you different!"

The doctor directed him into a spacious kitchen, ample enough for entertaining a family reunion. Without asking Duane what he wanted, he poured him a king-size cup of black coffee.

"I marvel at your sangfroid, Duane. I suppose, though, mayhem and carnage are far from unfamiliar to you, for your two brothers were always coming home battered and smashed from all their countless athletic feats. Am I right?"

Duane shifted uncomfortably when the conversation began to take this particular drift. He realized, of course, that somebody had been here before him and "talked." Nonetheless, he nodded politely at the doctor's query.

Dr. Cressy's visitor, if a bit surprised that the old man expressed no sorrow at the passing of his two brothers, nor even made an acknowledgment of their heroic end, was, on the other hand, relieved that condolence was not in order here either, painful as that would have been in front of the old physician, who, the boy decided then and there, must be of the same stripe as his father; that is, once men were dead, they were to remain unmentioned and unspoken of.

His host was now busy cutting a piece of an enormous homemade jelly roll sprinkled with a deep coating of powdered sugar, and he edged a helping over to Duane on a plate large enough to have held a turkey leg with trimmings. It took the boy only a few moments to gulp down the slice, and the doctor, without needing to be asked, gave him a second helping.

"Just to be on the safe side," the doctor began, but then the attention of both of them was diverted briefly by the sight of several woodsmen walking past the old man's property on their way to cut down more dead trees. "While I have you here," he went on, "we'll have a quick exam of your vital functions."

The physician brought out a curious instrument with a light in the end of it, and gazed briefly into Duane's eyes. He held the boy's wrists rather painfully, bade him roll up his sleeves and glanced at the veins in the crook of his arm. Then, leaning forward and growing red in the face, he listened to his heartbeat with a stethoscope.

"Help yourself to more jelly roll, why don't you?" the doctor said, coming up to a standing posture and leaning against the bright pink

Mourners Below

(69)

and white wallpaper decorated with bluebirds. Duane noted that the old physician stood against the wall in the same posture he himself had assumed when he was being measured.

"Today's dieticians . . ." the doctor began, and then sat down and quickly ate a piece of jelly roll. "These gentlemen are dead set against things like what we are now eating and drinking and, of course, enjoying. Actually, these authorities on diet are themselves valetudinarians, prisoners of the natural, if not Nature. What they do not understand is the pleasure so-called worthless foods—viz., pastries, jellies, and jams—confer on the human soul. If a thing is a great pleasure, Duane, the body has a way of making its ingestion healthful. That is my theory. I am on the road to eighty, and have never eaten the proper foods or drink. But I have enjoyed nearly everything, even oftentimes the unpalatable and unpleasant, all my life. I believe you enjoy life, too, don't you?" He now turned his full scrutiny on the boy .

"I haven't made much of myself, I'm afraid," Duane confided in a whisper. He was on his fourth piece of jelly roll.

"Is it absolutely required in your case that you do?"

"I beg your pardon?" Duane waited to be prompted.

"I mean, you're still a minor and not in dire need."

Duane repeated unintelligibly after the doctor the words "minor" and "dire," and then gave his questioner a look of appeal not to expect him to throw any light on his own problem or condition.

"I'll be perfectly open and aboveboard." The old man now began what appeared to be the actual "consultation" they were to have. "Mrs. Newsom has been blabbing about you and your Dad, and stirred up by her, I suppose, your mother has also been on the phone concerning you. . . . I was very fond of your mother, you know. I'm not surprised, however, that she ran off with another man. Eugene, your father, is a cold fish. Looks like a prince or aristocrat, his nose always in the air, and a far-off look in those robin's-egg-blue eyes of his. Strides about like he is walking over the backs of the rest of us mortals. . . . Your chief trouble with your brothers and your father, Duane"—the doctor now raised his voice as if to give both diagnosis and prognosis—"is you're too short!"

On hearing this pronouncement Duane let out a kind of snort which stopped the old man for a moment.

"Nonetheless"—the physician now resumed his consultation—"if you look about you, which at your age you are probably incapable of, but if you did, you'd see men everywhere who are four to five inches shorter even than you. That is, the average U.S. male citizen is still a bit on the squat side, and what with all the off-scourings and riffraff of the world arriving here hourly, the average height will go down even lower. Take that young woodsman who was in here, all brawn and sinew, putting us to shame, why, compared to your height, he is no more than a dwarf!"

Duane looked down at his jacket to see if the stains on his coat were going away after the doctor's thorough washing of them, and detected no remaining trace of red.

"These modern fabrics at least dry quickly." The doctor followed his eye. "Your father always dressed you better than his other sons, no question of that. Was that deliberate or was it because your brothers were such roughnecks? I wonder ... Justin, for example, must have come here at least twice with broken bones, though you may not remember, and I think Douglas had as many as three slight brain concussions from soccer, tumbling, and that time he slipped from the climbing rope in the gym."

Duane waited now with bated breath for a dressing-down for his having been fool enough to have testified to seeing his brothers return from "over there," but the doctor had lapsed into comfortable philosophic silence, and gave him no indication the subject would be broached.

Suddenly Dr. Cressy leaped up and went into still another adjoining room, where Duane supposed people were operated on. He was gone for quite a while, during which period the boy began to shed scalding tears, which in a trice wet his entire face from the eyes down. It was not really grief, he knew, but a combination of rage, confusion, and humiliation, or even perhaps a result of the immoderate deliciousness of the homemade jelly roll.

The doctor returned with two small bottles filled with capsules. He glanced at Duane's wet cheeks briefly.

"I want you to take these first thing in the morning and at bedtime. The dosage is on the bottle. . . . Now, what is the meaning of this?" The doctor touched Duane's right cheek stained with tears.

The old man sat down and waited. Duane now felt rather comfortable with him again, and after a moment, spurred on perhaps by the blithe song of a meadowlark, he began, "I don't know why they come to *me,* because they were never too nice to me . . . in life."

"They were *nice* to nobody," the doctor countered in a tone which almost suggested that Duane had insulted him. "Yet who had time to teach them to be anything but what they were—brutes!"

Duane's jaw dropped, and then he seemed to be repeating the last graphic word pronounced by the doctor.

"But they did talk about you all the time, Duane. When I was setting Justin's collarbone, he in fact spoke about what a whiz you were. . . . He could take pain more remarkably than any patient I have ever encountered. Most people scream, faint, even muss their pants when having their collarbone set. Not Justin. He just grinned!"

"You're not pulling my leg, are you, Doctor?"

"About what?"

"I mean, I don't see how Justin would talk about me at all, let alone call me—"

"A whiz?" The doctor spoke airily.

"He never paid any real attention to me."

"Are you sure both of them . . . appear to you, Duane?" The doctor spoke in a confidential, almost inaudible whisper. "Or isn't it only Justin?"

"Both," Duane managed to get out as firmly as he could.

And now that his secret was out, and his weakness held up to the scrutiny of day, he was able to cry openly in the old man's presence. The doctor didn't seem to mind.

"I never recall Douglas speaking very often of you," Dr. Cressy went on with what appeared to be his theory that only one of the boys appeared.

"However, I have been reading up on the subject," the old man continued, "in the wake of Mrs. Newsom spilling the beans. . . . One can't really trust her too far, so I didn't know, when she tattled, whether you had actually seen anything or not. But it's nothing to be alarmed about. Remember, Duane, that whatever you may think or feel from now on to the end of your life—and you will have a long life, I see that in your countenance—well, all that you think or feel, some other man or boy has thought and felt before you, and long after you are dead and gone, some other boy will feel and see what you have felt and seen. Nothing that happens is outlandish or out of the ordinary. The people who think so are fools, but of course fools rule the world. If you enjoy seeing

James Purdy

(72)

them come back, though, those coarse, sweating bruisers, don't *interdict* them, do you see?"

Duane appeared to be having trouble with some of the doctor's vocabulary, not to mention his ideas, but he got the general drift, and nodded a great many times in grateful agreement.

"As a matter of fact, I used to *think* I saw my uncle, who died in World War I and who helped to raise me. And I feel sure I hear my mother in the dead of night occasionally pouring herself a cup of tea."

Duane went on weeping, but it was a refreshing kind of grief, and a little like being caught in a summer thundershower.

"I am going to wrap up the rest of this jelly roll and you can tuck it away there with what I suppose is the lunch Mrs. Newsom packed for you."

Dr. Cressy led him to the front porch, where he struck him manfully across the back.

But as the boy was going down the long brick walk toward the bus stop, the old man called after him a final thought and word of caution: "By the way, one last matter. If you do go to that terrible Dumont woman's party," he shouted so that the woodsmen now resting in a nearby copse heard him, "drink a tablespoon of olive oil prior to your arrival there. It will help you with the strong drinks she will foist upon you. But my advice is don't drink anything in her company stronger than maybe a little hard cider. You have a very highly developed case of the imagination, otherwise there isn't a thing wrong with you, and you'll live to be ninety, especially if you give up ice skating, which is a perilous sport in the extreme."

Duane did not fully realize it at the time, but the combined contradictoriness, captiousness, and seeming changeability of Dr. Cressy, Mrs. Newsom, his father, and his mother finally gave him the strength to give very little heed to any of their instructions, opinions, advice, or indeed authority. Since he was sure he had no talent of any kind (unless one counted skating), and since he would never amount even to the hill of beans his mother claimed Eugene never quite came up to, it really mattered very little if he saw the dead or not, and it didn't matter at all why they returned to him. Yet in this very particular he had caught the doctor contradicting himself, for on the one hand he had said the brothers cared for nobody, that they were animals, and on the other hand he had let out of the bag the fact that Justin, even when having a broken collarbone set, which must have hurt hideously, had talked of nothing but his youngest brother.

Arrived home, Duane went immediately to his father's study (off the den, and which, unlike the latter, he was permitted to enter) and consulted the unabridged *Webster's* in the hopes of finding a few of the words the doctor had thrown out that afternoon.

Eugene came into the study and stared.

"First time I ever saw you sticking your nose in that dictionary, Duane. Maybe I can help you find the word you are searching for."

Duane blushed.

"As a matter of fact," the boy said, fearful of what the word now might mean, "I don't imagine anyone not in medicine would know it."

"Well," Eugene said, "what is the word in question, can you tell me?"

" 'Bruiser,' " Duane said hoarsely.

"I haven't as a matter of fact heard that term used for a good while. Not since I was a boy. Who was it used in reference to, I wonder?"

Mrs. Newsom called from the other room just then that Eugene was wanted on the telephone.

Duane leafed quickly then to the word "valetudinarian" after first having some initial difficulty in finding it at all, owing to his ignorance of how it might be spelled.

Since Eugene expected a report from the doctor, very little discussion between father and son ensued after Duane's return from the consultation. Mrs. Newsom inquired cautiously as Duane circled and soared around the dishpan that evening, but he confined his description of his visit largely to the woodsman's half-butchered upper arm, the jelly roll, which Mrs. Newsom had sampled and admitted was better than any she had ever made (of course Dr. Cressy was very rich, she pointed out, and could afford to put more eggs and butter in his sweets), and finally the marvel of Dr. Cressy's countless rooms, medical equipment, gauze, and bandages. Finally, the original purpose of his visit was lost in all these surrounding details, and one would have thought, to hear Duane tell it, that he had merely gone to visit the showplace of a kindly, leisured grandfather.

"Like father, like son!" Mrs. Newsom sighed and spoke to herself, unable to get any word of sense as to the result of his visit. "Deep wells of silence," she sighed again.

Finally, however, Duane showed her the medicine Dr. Cressy had given him. That relieved her somewhat and assured her that Duane's case had been considered, however perfunctorily.

But one thing, though unspoken, came to be generally understood by all under Eugene's roof from the time of Duane's visit to the physician: the youngest of the Bledsoe boys had seen something, it had been recognized and confirmed by professional diagnosis, medicine itself had been prescribed, and, to all intents and purposes, his vision or whatever it was called could not be too important or serious. In a brief exchange of talk Eugene had had with Duane on the latter's now more frequent visits to the unabridged dictionary, the realization had come to be established that young boys, especially when their education had not "taken," had seen such things before and not been confined to lunatic asylums. It was all perhaps—who knows?—a part of growing into manhood, which in Duane's case, along with his tardy increase in height, was very slow.

"I am curious, though," Eugene said to Duane after he had returned from accompanying Mrs. Newsom to her home that evening. "To whom and in what circumstances did Dr. Cressy employ the word 'bruiser'?"

In order to avoid telling Eugene the truth, Duane decided to be as oblique and unhelpful as his father always was with him. He therefore began describing the woodsmen, or tree surgeons, briefly, but then, getting caught up in his subject, he gave a lengthy description of their gear, their climbing apparatus, and their extremely short stature.

"But why would Dr. Cressy consider these perfectly admirable fellows bruisers?" His father raised his voice.

Duane busied himself looking at the lapel of his jacket, which still bore a spot or two now of dried blood, the fresh deposit of what had been missed by the doctor's ablutions, and would now, according to the old man's medical lore, in its present desiccated condition, resist cleaning.

"Dr. Cressy has no use for valetudinarians and nutritionists." Duane finally broke his silence, and then immediately turned back his attention to what his Dad presumed to be his homework, a series of books held on his lap, the topmost of which was Scudder's *Second Year Latin*.

Shaking his head as he often had done with a hostile or intractable witness in the courtroom, Eugene shrugged his shoulders and gave up at least for now the hope of identifying who in the doctor's opinion came under the classification of bruiser, and leaving the room, slammed the door behind him.

What Duane, however, was poring over was not his Latin lesson, but a somewhat battered and stained comic book beneath his Latin textbook, which he had found that day in the woodshed, where it had fallen out, he presumed, from the boxes that had arrived from overseas and which were now stored in the shed. All over the comic book was drawn picture after picture of a girl and under it in his brother's hand the linked names Justin and Estelle written again and again, a kind of rubber-stamp carried ad infinitum.

On the last page of the comic book was a kind of letter, which had perhaps finally been transferred to stationery and sent. It read:

You once wondered if where we went that first time and where it happened also for the first time was some imaginary kingdom. Well, it has a real location and if you don't see it on no ordinary road map you can revisit if you are as homesick for me as you say: you go two mile past old Turley Pike, turn left, skirt the stone quarry, go direct on to the old dirt road, impassable in bad or rainy weather, then on past Burnshaw farm, turn left again, proceed past apple orchard, and it's the first big house with the cupola on top where we were. Don't ever go back though without me, I should not have give you these directions, but if you must go, go alone, for our sake.

Just.

Eugene had returned home in so jubilant a mood over his having found so many new facts concerning the Battle of Antietam and was so busy discussing his finds with Professor Redpath that he barely noticed that the cartons from overseas containing his sons' effects had been opened and rummaged through. Without paying any particular attention to the break-in, he had gone on chatting with the professor as he lugged the boxes off to the woodshed. Returning to the house, he had closeted himself with Redpath, and chuckled and droned on with him about their excavations.

"He must have seen I opened the cartons," Duane confided to Mrs.

Newsom after supper. He dried one or two dishes for her, the large meat platter, and a smaller serving platter of some antiquity to judge by its many little cracks and crevices.

"I dread to think of it," Mrs. Newsom said after sighing several times. "Your father will blame me, of course, no question at all about that."

"I'll shoulder all the blame," Duane said. He kissed her on the cheek. They were both surprised by his action.

Duane tried to imagine how the coming storm would begin. "I haven't even caught up on all my mother's letters to me, from his own break-in. She must have nothing to do but write letters."

"Aileen was one of the most communicative souls," Mrs. Newsom reflected as she poured the pan of soapy water into the sink. "I always remember her sitting at the little spinet desk, holding her green fountain pen, writing, writing, writing. . . . Justin and Douglas were as fond of her, too, as if she had been their own mother." She added this thought after a lengthy pause during which she began polishing a few old solid silver forks.

"Yes, I remember once"—Duane followed her line of thought—"Justin took me aside when, well, I guess he had been drinking a little, and said, 'I wish so beautiful a woman as Aileen had been my mother. You are a lucky . . .' "

Mrs. Newsom gave him a quick glance as much as to say she knew he had cut out something in order to spare her. "The one Justin was fond of was you, Duane." She said this with the formality and hollowness of tone of the final words of an oration.

"Me?" Duane replied in a voice so loud that they heard Mr. Bledsoe open the sliding doors to find out, one supposed, if he was being summoned.

"We must lower our voices," Mrs. Newsom cautioned and took the tea towel out of Duane's hands in case Eugene should come running in.

"How did he describe . . . his feelings?" Duane spoke after a pause in which he appeared to have got lost in a reverie.

Mrs. Newsom became reticent, almost frigid all at once, whether because their voices had roused Mr. Bledsoe to come out from his den, or for some other reason. But Duane persisted, now that she had opened the subject. "You see, Mrs. N., I supposed Justin . . . sort of resented me."

Mrs. Newsom put the last of the silverware away in a box sumptuously lined with purple velvet. "I just can't believe two such young men won't be back." She spoke as if to herself.

Then as she turned toward him and saw the look of extreme begging on Duane's face, Mrs. Newsom, who was almost as loath to say anything grandiloquent as Eugene himself, said, "Justin thought the sun rose and set on you, and you know it!"

"But," Duane almost blubbered, "he always told me I was a ... booby!"

Mrs. Newsom hurled a look at him that was full of pitying reproof. She strode into the buttery where her light summer coat was draped on a wooden hanger.

"But Douglas never said anything to you about ... what he thought of me, did he?" Duane followed her on into the narrow room and held the coat for her. He blushed like a schoolgirl as he inquired as to Douglas's opinion of him.

Mrs. Newsom gave a long and penetrating gaze at the coat being held for her, brushed some lint off it, and straightened the hem. "I don't know why you make me tell you all the time what you already know," she began severely. Then she must have thought of his "illness," for the lines in her face smoothed out, and he could watch her silently phrasing and rephrasing the words to come.

"You were like a pet to them." She again sounded like a public speaker in the finality with which she spoke, but then he saw, as she turned away from him, that she was not happy with this description of what the two brothers had felt for him.

Duane shook his head and followed her on out the back door. This evening they proceeded down Beach Avenue as a change of route.

"All I know, Duane, is that they were constantly talking about you. After all, Just and Doug remembered the day you were born. And there couldn't have been two happier brothers. They went traipsing all over the neighborhood rounding up the kids to come see their new baby brother."

"But weren't they pretty disappointed in me later on?" he persisted.

Mrs. Newsom swung her heavy purse to her other arm. Her mouth tightened over her rather loose-fitting false teeth. He saw how uncomfortable this conversation was making her, but he could not stop, and she, remembering Dr. Cressy perhaps and certainly Duane's "vision," did not know quite how to proceed or diverge or cease or whatever was required in such a circumstance. And perhaps they both wished to continue the painful subject partly because nothing had been done ever to acknowledge so heavy a loss and so swift a tragedy by means of some final and complete pronouncement on the event itself.

"It didn't matter what you did or indeed what you were, Duane." She raised her voice almost to a shout so that a passing car slowed down and the driver stuck his head out the window, unsure or not whether she had called to him.

"Don't you see"—she shot a look of reproof at the driver, but lowered her voice—"for you must realize, for heaven's sake, there were no two human beings closer to you at all and no one will ever be closer to you again than your two brothers."

He stopped in his tracks as she said this.

"With the exception of your mother and father . . . I'll have to add them of course."

"Is that why, then . . . I've been singled out, Mrs. Newsom?"

She had a notion to say *I don't follow you,* but she knew, and Duane knew she followed him all too well in all contexts, so she merely said, "It might be the case."

She indicated she wanted him to leave her now. In fact, she reminded him of Mr. Newsom's feelings about their relationship. He thought it a bit odd that this boy who was after all turning into a young man tagged along behind her every night like her shadow, or even her bashful suitor.

"I feel a little bit easier, to tell you the truth," Duane said to himself and smiled, watching Mrs. N. disappear into a glade alive with all kinds of ferns, evening primroses, and buttercups galore.

Professor Redpath, a tall, raw-boned man of about fifty with tousled, graying hair, had been drinking more than usual, and Eugene Bledsoe, ever since his return from Maryland, had begun to lose most of his buoyancy and jubilation. His extremely good mood had at first carried him over the shock of seeing overseas packages addressed to him brazenly opened and the contents rifled. And much as he disapproved of Professor Redpath's tendency toward alcohol, it was nonetheless the former baseball player's present state which gave Eugene the nerve to begin a tirade, which had the effect, in its violence and mild hysteria, of sobering up his companion and collaborator in matters of Civil War military tactics.

"I am cursed with a son who is not only incorrigible, but obviously, in his idle state, hell-bent on mischief." At that moment, Mr. Bledsoe saw openmouthed the broken lock on his desk drawer.

Professor Redpath had no special liking for Duane owing to the fact that the boy had always treated him with, if not contempt, pretty steady indifference, and often walked out of the room when the "professor" was speaking of how he had made baseball history and won the friendship of Babe Ruth himself.

But the professor had never seen Eugene angry before, and anger frightened him almost as much as being sober. He shrank into his chair as the lawyer vented his wrath against Duane while pacing up and down, stopping only occasionally to pick up a book and put it down immediately with a loud slam-bang.

"He takes after his mother in all respects." Eugene summarized the boy's shortcomings.

"What has he did this time?"

Whether it was the professor's grammar, or the cool and deliberate way his companion asked this, leading Eugene to feel Redpath thought he exaggerated the culprit's offenses, the father launched into an even more vigorous accusation.

"What has he *done?*" he corrected the younger man. "Let me tell you what he has *done!* He has had the gall to open two cartons of belongings ... addressed to me and me alone from overseas, and has broken the lock on my desk like a common thief."

"May I ask who the packages were from?" Professor Redpath inquired with mild insouciance.

Eugene had never minded the younger man's questioning him concerning their joint Civil War findings, but this question somehow irked him greatly.

"Is it imperative I tell you?" Eugene snapped. "Isn't it enough that the packages were addressed to me and not to him?"

"But in a court of law," Professor Redpath went on in his new-found sobriety, "I believe it would have some pertinence."

"You do, do you?" Eugene was quite lordly. "Well, then, by God, I will tell you." He spoke with an almost menacing unpleasantness. But having promised so much, he stopped like one who has lost his train of thought.

Eugene turned several times and stared at the professor as he was pacing up and down the room. One would have thought indeed the next move was up to the professor.

"They were, if you must know, from Justin and Douglas," Eugene finally said.

The former baseball player half rose, picked up his battered Panama hat, and twisted the little ribbon, which had gotten crooked, about the crown.

"I think I'll go up the street and have a bite to eat, Gene," he said.

"Don't get up and go away mad." Eugene began to feel his friend had taken his anger personally.

"I ain't mad at all," Redpath replied. "But I think I have sense enough to know when a fellow would like to be alone. Thank you for the trip, and for all the meals you bought me, and other favors." He stared now fixedly, if briefly, at the broken lock on the desk drawer.

"Don't mention it, Miles," Eugene answered. "I'm more than obliged to you for going with me."

Eugene kept his back to him during these final speeches, and Professor Redpath in the end was forced to say good-bye to the broad and high wall of his friend's back and find his own way out in a stumbling fashion, for once past Eugene's stern presence and ire, his own usual drunken state took possession of him again.

Eugene Bledsoe's only pleasure, at least the only pleasure which remained to him outside of his dabbling in Civil War military strategy, was immersing himself in listening to baseball on the radio.

After his scene with Professor Redpath, he turned on the set and sat listening to a night game coming from St. Louis. He had left the sliding doors open and lay sprawled in his armchair, abandoning himself to the game as Professor Redpath abandoned himself to whiskey.

Puzzled, even alarmed at such behavior on the part of his Dad, Duane passed and repassed the open door, but was fearful to go in and face his father's wrath.

"A pair of homers, both long clouts into the right-field stands that drove in three runs. Both came off fastballs."

"Come on in, Duane, if you want to listen to the game," his father said. Duane froze at the threshold.

"Pitch shot high over the infield, climbed far into the dark outfield sky and cleared the right-field fence three hundred and seventy-five feet away."

Mourners Below

"Have you nothing to tell me?" His father spoke over the voice of the announcer on the radio.

There was a long wait while another voice advertised for a sparkling, thirst-quenching beer.

"He faced six batters and retired all of them. Not only that but he struck out the final four and officially received credit for saving the game two days after he came out of the bull pen. You couldn't ask for anything more unless he struck out all of them."

"I'm terribly disappointed in you, Duane."

Eugene turned down the radio so that only a blur of a voice from the baseball announcer could be heard.

"It's a great pity that a son of mine ..."

Duane barely heard his father because he was thinking of Mrs. Newsom's estimate of what his brothers had thought of him, and was comparing her estimate with the peculiar opinion Dr. Cressy seemed to have, indeed, of all the Bledsoes.

"That you should have, in addition to opening the overseas packages, broken the lock on my drawer containing very private and confidential documents has also come to my attention," Eugene Bledsoe was continuing. "Are you listening to me, young man?"

Duane could tell that his anger was very weak and that he wanted, actually, to listen to the summary of the St. Louis game, and he curled his lip at the phrase "young man." It dated back some years to when he was, in one of the many phrases Justin had heaped on him, a "mere brat."

As he half-listened to his father and hardly half heard the radio broadcast, suddenly, as if to contradict all of Mrs. Newsom's cheery tidings about how Justin and Douglas had cared so deeply for him, Duane recalled the day Justin had purposely bloodied his nose when they were playing softball because Duane had done something "unsportsmanlike"; and again how Douglas had once tied him to an elm tree and slapped him "to sleep" for having busted his tennis racket; and worst of all, yes, it all came back to him now, perhaps because of all the hoarse ruckus of the baseball game, Justin had, in great anger with him for having accidentally hit him with a baseball, struck him with a bicycle chain on his left cheek where he still bore a noticeable scar.

"Do you have any defense of yourself for these two acts of mischief?"

James Purdy
(82)

He heard his father's voice coming from as far away as the announcer in St. Louis.

Alarmed by his son's persistent silence and the peculiar glassy look in his eyes, Eugene jumped up and came over to where Duane stood. "Are you all right?" he wondered.

He touched the boy on the forehead. Eugene had always been slightly uneasy with Duane, while he had felt totally at home with Douglas and Justin, and when all else failed in his rule over them he had beat them soundly with his razor strop or knobbed belt and there was never any hard feeling afterward, but once when he had struck Duane across the mouth, and another time when he had beaten him with the strop, the look of resentment and smoldering anger in the boy's eyes had been so dreadful that Eugene never dared lay a hand on him again.

"What do you say," Duane began at last, and his father gave him perfect attention, "to your taking my mother's letters away from me ... to your having stolen them?"

"Stolen them?"

"Yes, secreted them away from the light of day!" he cried, echoing the phraseology of the comic book on which Justin had written of his love for Estelle.

"Your mother, Duane, was a very evil woman, I am afraid ... I have a bounden duty to look out for your welfare, after all." Eugene spoke with weak conviction, feeble authority.

"She is the only mother I will ever have," Duane said sleepily.

"But she chose to desert us," Eugene reminded him.

Eugene folded his arms, and Duane stared at him with a kind of nausea as he saw how his Dad's muscles bulged under his expensive shirt.

"I will not, however," Eugene was going on, "*not* continue this examination of your opening the cartons and breaking my lock on my desk drawer because of your condition."

"My condition!" Duane shouted, still staring at his father's brawny arms. Then, crimsoning violently, he whispered, "What is my condition?"

Eugene cleared his throat, and at last let his arms fall to his sides, where they appeared less massive and certainly less menacing.

"Your excitability, Duane, which no doubt comes from your mother's side of the house, and owing to the events of the past few weeks ... I don't want you to worry about anything at all, do you hear?

But in the future"—he looked back into the den as if to survey the damaged desk drawer—"for God Almighty's sake, ask before you break into a closed and locked desk . . . or cartons not addressed to you."

"And shouldn't you, sir, ask before you secrete . . . mail . . . from me . . . to whom it was addressed? Which is a federal offense!"

Eugene laughed in spite of himself and was surprised and pleased that Duane chimed in with him until his son's laugh ended in a kind of strangling cough and hiccup.

"Did you take your tonic today?" Eugene asked, approaching the boy and raising his right arm, from which Duane involuntarily dodged.

"Don't do anything," Duane said between his coughing and hiccuping. "I don't want you . . . to pat me on the back or anything when I choke."

"Duane!" Mr. Bledsoe dropped both his hands to his sides and looked indeed as hurt at that moment as if his youngest son had just razor-stropped him

The remembrance of how Justin had beaten him came so strongly and without warning into Duane's consciousness that he felt wounded and hurt all over again, terribly angry and incensed with his oldest brother, and only the now weakened perfume of violets from his mother's packet of letters brought him up short with the realization that there was no Justin to be angry with or hold responsible or accuse or scold or beg forgiveness of or ever again try to please. Absentmindedly picking up one of his mother's letters, he decided she too might as well be dead, for she was as insubstantial and far away now as his brothers. And Eugene and Mrs. Newsom—what were they but ghosts also, ghosts, it is true, who spoke and ate dinner with him, who, in the one case, drew together the sliding doors to shut him out and, in the other, went home each evening to a snug cottage among the hollyhocks and fragrant sumac, totally oblivious to his suffering?

He had been staring at his mother's letter for what must have been minutes without having taken in any of the sense of what she was writing to him about, when, resigning himself to never finding out if Justin did see the sun rise and set on him or merely thought he was a half-feebleminded snot who could not even play softball with any style, the words from his mother began swimming into his consciousness, though the light in the room was so poor that what Aileen was telling

James Purdy

(84)

him was nearly as hard to decipher as Caesar's plans to surprise the Helvetians in his Latin book:

> *I know I should not burden a young man, almost a boy, like yourself with my sorrows, but, darling, I have no one to turn to since your grandmother had a stroke and cannot communicate with me. Duane, I have made a terrible, perhaps irretrievable, mistake, in marrying again. My present husband has, I find, not only deceived me as to his abiding love for me, but has misrepresented from the beginning his financial situation. Far from having a fortune, he has begun borrowing from my own very reduced financial resources. He is also not kind to your mother. . . .*

The thought of anybody being unkind to Aileen infuriated Duane so much that he barely noticed the next paragraph:

> *I saw your photograph in a local newspaper, with the wonderful account of the prize you won in the figure-skating competition in Chicago. Duane, be very careful when on the ice that you do not take a bad spill. It could be serious. Anyhow, congratulations, dearest. . . .*

The violet aroma clung to his face and incipient beard till all hours of the night as he lay tossing and turning, fearful to go to sleep lest he suddenly, even with eyes closed, become aware that either Justin or Douglas was sitting at the foot of the bed listening to him snore, or sometimes (he blushed at the thought) watching him touch his cock. He now felt that only Justin came back and watched him. Yes, he was beginning to lose Douglas somewhere in all that infinitude of space the departed were said to dwell in.

"Aileen, Justin, Douglas," he muttered, and then he sank into the heavy snows of slumber as the courthouse clock struck four.

Once a week Mrs. Newsom would step into Mr. Bledsoe's study and make a few inquiries as to what he might suggest for the coming week's menu. Eugene Bledsoe enjoyed only meat, potatoes, and pie, but since modern dietary information had been repeatedly brought to his attention by the newspaper and by his clients and business acquaintances, he would frequently agree to take a few bites of lettuce or cabbage, and had occasionally even eaten a whole carrot. Therefore, so long as Mrs. Newsom served great quantities of beef, pork, veal, and chicken, with the inseparable potatoes, followed by pie or cake and strong coffee, he invariably approved of or merely ignored the rest of her menu.

He had already, having quickly okayed her selections of dishes for the week to come, said good morning to her in dismissal when she came a bit closer to his desk, and though he pretended to have fixed his full attention on the Battle of Antietam, he finally turned back to her and indicated by a movement of his lips upward that she might say whatever she might have to add.

"About the Dumont party Duane is invited to . . ." Mrs. Newsom came to the point at once.

"Oh, the masquerade ball, you mean." He tried to speak as neutrally as possible.

She hesitated until he tapped impatiently with his lead pencil on the hardwood of the desk.

"Do you honestly think, Mr. Bledsoe, that is the right sort of thing for him to attend at this time? He's only barely seventeen, after all. And a young seventeen at that," she added, immediately regretting that this last phrase had crossed her lips.

Mr. Bledsoe looked thoughful, or rather vague, which was to her his usual expression. He placed his right index finger over his left eyebrow, a mannerism which always annoyed her.

"Mrs. Dumont"—she pushed through his silence—"does not have the best reputation, if I may say so."

"Her family, however, were the actual founders of this community, you may care to remember, Mrs. Newsom. They are among the earliest settlers indeed of the county."

Somewhat riled, he mentioned then their contributions to the Revolution, the Continental Congress, the Civil War, and the fact that they had given the country quite a few senators and a Presidential hopeful or two.

"I only know," Mrs. Newsom spoke with as much resolution as she had on the day they had had their trouble, "that as a mother myself, I would not allow a boy of mine to go there."

Had anybody else pointed out the moral dangers of a visit to Mrs. Dumont's house, certainly anybody of his own class or profession, Mr. Bledsoe would doubtless have torn up the invitation with his own hands and perhaps even punished Duane for being the recipient of it.

James Purdy

(86)

But he felt constrained to oppose Mrs. Newsom in everything not concerned with the kitchen or household management, and he also took her criticism of the Dumonts as in some oblique and insidious way a slight on his own family antecedents.

"Duane is still not quite himself," she went on, despite his growing coldness and the signs of irritability evidenced by his whipping about the loose papers on his desk, "despite Dr. Cressy's remedies, and for that reason alone—"

"Yes," Eugene's voice boomed, "and for that reason alone, then, it's time he went off to see people who are a little more lighthearted than you and me, Mrs. Newsom. We are, after all, too old to be much cheer to him."

"Certainly I am," she said with a bit too much emphasis as she gazed into his pale blue eyes. He glanced immediately away from her scrutiny.

"Thank you, nonetheless," he addressed the housekeeper while looking at a legal-sized document, "for your concern. . . . Your faithfulness, and your care," he went on still staring at the sheet of paper as if the words he was speaking were inscribed on it, "are valued."

But Mrs. Newsom had already broken in with, "Well, then, what about his costume, sir? For if he is to go, he will need one, of course."

Mr. Bledsoe appeared as dumbfounded by the mention of such a thing as if she had hinted that Duane and she would perhaps soon be attending mass again together.

"It is a masquerade ball, you understand." She spoke with a slight, if deliberate, condescension, which was not lost on him. "If we could have the key to the attic," she went boldly on, "there are, I believe, quite a good many old garments up there which I could, with your permission, alter to fit him."

Eugene's face clouded over. He had a great aversion to anybody's using keys which were in his possession, and he liked nobody to go into the attic.

"I hadn't thought of *costumes,* I guess." He laughed tunelessly at his own shortsightedness. "Perhaps you were right in the first place in thinking he should not go."

His beginning to change his mind, however, helped solidify her belief that Duane should attend, and that she should be the person to find him a costume.

"No, Mr. Bledsoe, you were quite right. Duane should get out more and meet younger people."

Mourners Below

He considered now his own recent judgment and ruling.

"I can't for the life of me imagine, though, why Mrs. Dumont would want Duane to attend." He spoke in a kind of whining-jeering tone, and then, rising, moved quickly over to a little cabinet which he opened with noticeable difficulty. Inside it were hanging, as if from the roof of a cave, stalactites, keys, row after row, of all sizes and shapes.

She marveled that he went immediately to the one he required, and taking it out, he closed the cabinet.

"You may keep this key, in fact." Mr. Bledsoe spoke solemnly, handing it to her. His face had assumed its usual calm, unruffled aspect. "I have a duplicate," he explained when she seemed unwilling to take it. "One here, oh yes, and another in my office up the street."

She accepted the key with something like the reluctance he had displayed on picking up her rosary.

"We'll let you see which costume we pick out," she informed him.

"God knows you'll have enough to choose from." He laughed at the thought of what the attic contained, and he thought that if the Dumonts went back to the beginnings of the county, his family went back nearly as far, and under the rafters of the old house were remnants of uniforms worn as far back as the Civil War, together with military apparel from later conflicts which his father and grandfather had insisted on keeping in heavy, opaque glass cases.

"You asked a moment ago, Mr. Bledsoe . . ." Mrs. Newsom began, and then stopped. Something about her manner and the hushed tone in which she spoke made him look over at her. "You wondered, you say, why Mrs. Dumont should want to see Duane."

He nodded and remained gazing at her.

"It might be, don't you think, that Mrs. Dumont and Justin saw so much of one another."

"Saw one another?" he cried. Catching himself and apologizing for his sudden anger, he said, "Excuse me, but did you say 'saw one another'?"

"I supposed you knew that, Mr. Bledsoe. But you see, when you said you wondered why Duane should be invited, I wasn't sure if you had been . . . aware . . . of the other. . . ."

"Thank you." He spoke thickly.

"I hope you know I would not be guilty of gossip."

"I know it. I wish to God it were gossip. And I wish to hell and high water Duane would not go there now. But if it's to be, it will be," he

James Purdy

(88)

finally said, and he gave her a very strange smile, which, coming from another man, would have been called winning.

Neither Mrs. Newsom nor Duane had been in the attic for some time. In the days of his brothers, he had sometimes played tricks on them by shouting taunts down the heat register, through which one could see into Justin's and Douglas's room, situated directly below the attic. Once Duane had even lowered a long cord through the apertures of the register which slowly descended upon Justin's face as he slumbered. He had wakened with a roar and came rushing up to the attic where he pummeled the perpetrator with mock brutality.

Looking about stealthily, Mrs. Newsom picked out several wonderful long silk dresses in plastic bags and two expensive, superbly wrought dummies for fitting clothes. When tired of feasting her eyes on other fineries, she began to marvel at the twenty-foot ceiling and the ample windows which might have made this part of the house the most comfortable place to live of all its many rooms and floors.

Duane's eyes roved to a collection of fencing foils and masks and his father's Knights Templars outfit with sword, plumed hat, and high boots. Still further away he spied some rifles, Marine Corps dress uniforms, and a gas mask, all secured with double locks in a case. A solitary child's hoop occupied a far corner of the great room.

"But still, where are our costumes, Duane?"

Mrs. Newsom then drew his attention away from the guns and the soldiers' uniforms to a little door which must lead to still another room. They entered. One small upper window admitted only dim sunlight. To Mrs. Newsom's delight, an entire wardrobe of costumes of all kinds was waiting for them.

"Your brothers must have gone to endless numbers of parties!" she cried after a long period of silence in which she took in the display before them. "And, see, they are not so old," she pointed out. There was a rooster costume, a jackass, the inevitable domino of course, another of an ape, a stag, a harlequin, the Pied Piper, Robin Hood, and six or seven other choices.

"Some of these must be from school plays," Mrs. Newsom observed to Duane.

Looking at some of the apparel more closely, Duane said, "My mother sewed all of these, don't you suppose?"

"I wouldn't be at all surprised," was Mrs. Newsom's quick rejoinder.

Mourners Below

(89)

In another corner of the room Mrs. Newsom pointed out apparel of less recent times: knee breeches, trailing gowns, beaver hats, poke bonnets, hoop skirts, and giant umbrellas all rose before them with their spectral lifelikeness.

"I can see by your expression, though, Duane, that none of them quite suit you." Mrs. Newsom now opened one of the cases brusquely, and pulled gently at the sleeve of the domino costume.

"It's just that I feel a bit odd about wearing what they wore," he said in a hoarse voice.

"I see," she said, and went on examining another of the costumes, a kind of George Washington frock coat.

"In any case," he tried to explain his indifference to costumes which he could see she found quite attractive and suitable, "don't you see they were so much bigger than me?"

Mrs. Newsom put away the frock coat and faced him. He had gone very pale. Whenever this occurred, one noticed the scar on his cheek, and Mrs. Newsom turned her eyes quickly away from having stared at it, for gazing at what to others was only a slight disfigurement flustered him even more.

"Maybe I should try the rooster costume," he proposed after a silence.

"Oh, put on the harlequin, why don't you?" She had revealed her dislike of the headdress of the rooster outfit very clearly. "Go ahead," Mrs. Newsom said. "I won't watch you change."

While Duane took off his shirt and trousers, Mrs. Newsom removed the harlequin costume from the mothproof bag and looked it over.

"Such expensive material," she muttered. "And all for one evening's show!"

Duane stepped into the tights and then pulled himself into the upper garment.

There was a beautiful pier glass at the north end of the room, and she ushered him over to it.

"Yes, I'm afraid you were right," Mrs. Newsom opined. "Much too big for you."

Duane blushed furiously.

He went back to the other costumes, which Mrs. Newsom had brought out from their cases, reeking of camphor squares. He fingered the stag costume, the ass, the Pied Piper dispiritedly.

"I can easily alter this costume, Duane, if you like it." She referred to the Pied Piper.

James Purdy

(90)

The thought of wearing anything Justin had worn filled him with a kind of soaring, nameless, violent emotion which suddenly caused his teeth to chatter.

"They were ... giants!" Duane spoke with a sort of feverish rage, though his blood was freezing in his veins.

Mrs. Newsom took the costume out of his hands and pressed his shoulder gently.

"We'll look elsewhere, never mind," she soothed him.

"No, no, Mrs. N. You've gone to all this search and trouble. I'll wear ... Justin's disguise for you," he told her and shrugged his shoulders. "See if I don't!"

That evening, just a few minutes before supper was to be announced, Eugene came into the kitchen, holding his hat behind his back, and sheepishly excused himself from dining with them. An unforeseen business matter had presented itself.

Duane listened to this familiar alibi from where he sat in the front room laboring over his Caesar, almost tearing the pages of the thumbed text which had belonged at one time, like everything else, to Justin.

"Did you find anything to wear for the ... party?" Eugene inquired of Duane just as he was about to go out the front door.

"Oh, several things, sir." Duane scowled as he replied.

That scowl was so pronounced that Eugene sauntered back into the room and waited almost penitently before his son. Duane's anger that Eugene was leaving him alone with Mrs. Newsom made his mouth tremble, and as he was growing pale in his anger, he imagined that Eugene, too, was looking at the scar on his cheek.

"Well, enjoy your supper, Duane," his father said abruptly.

"Enjoy your own, Dad," Duane replied in a muffled voice.

A few minutes later Mrs. Newsom rang the little handbell announcing that supper was served, but Duane, idling, looked over his pony, and read: "Caesar swore that he would neither shave nor cut his hair ever again until he had avenged the death of his heroic soldiers."

At the table, Duane picked at his food, though Mrs. Newsom had gone to extra pains to make him everything he liked best: pork chops, spoonbread, fresh applesauce, and for dessert, pineapple upside-down cake.

"Should I let my hair grow longer, do you think?" Duane inquired out of nowhere.

Mourners Below

"You haven't eaten enough for a bird." Mrs. Newsom ignored his question. She was extremely provoked with both Eugene and Duane after all the effort to which she had gone to prepare supper, what with the one going off with no prior warning, and the other one turning his nose up at every morsel of food.

"Think of the many who are going without, tonight," the house-keeper said, going into the kitchen and putting down her own empty plate with a bang. "While here good food goes to waste."

When she returned to the dining room, though, the sight of Duane's face made her stop scolding. He was as pale as the Irish linen tablecloth.

He barely had time to put his napkin back in its ring when his head fell over on the table.

She rushed to him and pushed his head between his knees. She was furious that his father had left him when he was not himself.

After a while, he motioned with his hand that he was all right, and suddenly rising, he left the room and went to sit in his study chair, idly turning the pages of his Caesar again.

Mrs. Newsom waited by the high step which led from the dining room to the front room, watching him in anguish.

His eyes roved over the test questions which his tutor would be quizzing him on in a few days:

Why did Caesar write this particular letter in Greek?

Why did his javelin have a thong attached to it?

"Yes, Mrs. Newsom." He turned to her. "Why did he have a thong on his javelin?"

"Here, here, Duane." She indicated he must follow her upstairs.

She helped him into bed, then took his temperature. It was slightly over 100.

Lying in bed with the daylight still strong about him, Duane could hear the sparrows and the robins giving out their liquid evensong. Having lost his supper, he was too weak to feel particularly restless. When his father looked in on him a couple of hours later, Duane denied there was anything the matter with him.

But as the evening shadows began to take possession of his room, the smell, even taste, of the attic came back to him, accompanied by the recollection of so many weapons of war, the wonder at so many unending

James Purdy

conflicts, his father's Knights Templars sword, the child's hoop in the corner, all these forgotten relics residing silently under the same roof with him gave, in addition to the bitterness it had left on his lips, a dryness to his nostrils which threatened to suffocate him. And everywhere, as in the dancing motes of the westering sun, coming from under the blinds, was the presence of Justin.

"Thank God Douglas, at least, don't come anymore." These words escaped from him when his father looked in on him for the last time before retiring himself.

Eugene made no rejoinder to this remark and left him.

Duane heard the courthouse clock strike midnight. He had come wide awake. He knew he was in for it. His hands moved agitatedly over the frogs of his pajama top.

At about two o'clock, still wide awake, he heard the familiar whistle. He seized the edge of the sheet in his mouth and, before he knew it, he had torn it badly. He thought he heard the whistle again. Yes, three notes.

It was the kind of whistle borrowed from a bobwhite or some other familiar bird, and it had always been Justin's cue for him to come out, no matter what the hour or what he was doing, and in times past, often in the very dead of night, Justin had summoned him to go traipsing off for a late hike or a ride in his roadster. These had indeed been the only times Justin ever recognized him fully, these mysterious nocturnal country walks together during which the older boy would tell him about the girls he was sleeping with, would describe the feeling of merging with another human being, and extol the first intense painful joy of the seed being freed from his penis. "You will soon know that, too," Just had said gravely, putting his hand on his hair.

Duane rose now, knocking over the antique chamber pot near the edge of the bed. His yellow piss started in tiny streams over the bare floor. He went to his clothes closet, brought out a mop, and patiently dried the inundation.

Then he heard the whistle again, more peremptory. He sank his chin painfully against his chest and made a sound so peculiar it scared him even more than the whistle had.

He whimpered a little as, when a small boy, he had once cut the flat of his hand with a buzz saw and had stared incredulous at the copious flow of red coming unbidden from his own flesh.

He went to the window, raised the blind, and looked down. He sucked in his breath as he saw him: Justin in his basketball outfit, beck-oning to him. He could see his lips open, thought he heard the words, "Get down here. On the double!"

"Right away," Duane replied. He did not take time to throw on his bathrobe, a present, as it happened, from Justin on his fifteenth birth-day.

Rushing down the back steps so as not to waken his father, he slipped and suddenly plunged through the protective railing, falling as he held on to the broken banisters to the floor below. The crash and the blow to his head seemed to calm him, make him less feverish.

Presently his father was standing over him, silently questioning him with his eyes, but with no trace of anger or scolding.

"Justin insisted I come down," Duane managed to tell Eugene before losing consciousness.

Dr. Cressy was sitting by the bed when Duane woke up. The boy de-cided that he had been taking his pulse but had stopped when the pa-tient regained consciousness. "He's a lucky boy." Duane heard the doctor speaking to his father. "Nothing broken, hardly a bruise on him, except for a slightly split lip, and now he has very little fever. Yes, Mr. Bledsoe, youth has everything!"

"It was the poor staircase got all the bad news, Doctor," Eugene re-plied, laughing.

Duane raised up in bed and looked from the doctor to his father. "What day is it today?" the ice skater wondered, and Eugene and Doc-tor Cressy burst into uproarious laughter, which Duane finally joined in somewhat dispiritedly and with very little volume.

"You'll be as good as new in no time, Duane," Dr. Cressy added after the merriment had died down. "And fit as a fiddle for the masquerade party—see if I'm not right!"

Nothing was ever quite the same after Duane's fall through the railing of the staircase. An even thicker veil or partition came between him and Mrs. Newsom and Eugene. They were too polite to him, almost as if he were their elder or occupied some distant seat of authority which they did not understand but were subservient to. Also his encounter with Justin, openly avowed in his delirium, drove Mr. Bledsoe into still fur-ther silence and detachment. It would have been easier for Eugene now to have stood stark naked in front of Duane while he shaved than to refer ever again to "them."

Mrs. Newsom would now stay on after supper and "sew on" his costume. As if seeking an excuse to prolong her stay after the evening meal, she decided to make three costumes for him and let him choose whichever he might finally prefer at the very last minute.

The one she was working on tonight with such fearful concentration and perseverance was the domino.

"Are none of your classmates attending this . . . shindig?" Mrs. Newsom almost snapped at him; then modifying her irritable note, "For instance, what ever became of Keith Warner, Val Noble, and Ken Beattie?"

"They've all gone off to college by now," Duane replied, and cast a vengeful look at his Caesar. "Anyhow, Mrs. N., they wouldn't have been caught dead at Lady Dumont's," he finished waspishly.

"Why do you call her Lady Dumont?" Mrs. Newsom said sharply, putting down her needle and looking critically at the upper part of the costume she was altering. "I mean," Mrs. Newsom resumed, harping on this one string, "where did you pick up such an expression?"

Duane flushed a bit.

"From everybody," he spoke evasively. Then staring at her in a rather brazen manner he said in a whisper, "From *them* of course."

She picked up the costume again with great energy. "Well, there'll be plenty to eat, and nice music, judging by the reports I get of her to-dos."

"It's true I won't know anybody there," Duane went back to her remark about where all his classmates had gone.

All at once he felt how very much he had been left behind, as he had the time when he and Just and Douglas had gone to Shepherd's Island and Duane had tarried so long in the concession booth that they had taken the ferry boat without missing him. He had had to wait in a cold driving rain for two hours until they had returned for him in a towering rage, Justin cuffing him several times for his idiotic undependability.

He looked down at his legs and feet. Yes, he would go skating again any time now. At least the rink was open, and Dr. Cressy had told him he might as well.

He hated Caesar so much that he found himself staring at the big green textbook many times during the day as if it were a festering sore on his body which he could not help touching and reinfecting.

Mr. Bledsoe's relationship with Professor Redpath did not go unnoticed in the town. For a man who prided himself so much on decorum and respectability, who himself never touched liquor, it was thought odd that he harbored under his roof a man who was little less than a drunkard. As a young man, Miles Redpath had made a brief and spectacular name for himself in the major leagues, and then, after a distinguished stint of service in the war, he had returned to his hometown and had coached baseball and basketball in the local high school, where his drinking caught up with him and he lost his job. How he lived now, nobody knew; he was married, and a father. Nonetheless, though in many ways ignorant, he had amassed a considerable amount of information concerning the Civil War, about which he had read omnivorously since a boy, and this store of knowledge had been the original meeting ground of two such disparate personalities as Duane's father and the former major-league baseball player.

But although the ostensible reason for Redpath's coming to see Eugene was for the baseball player to help the lawyer with his Civil War research—for which Eugene paid him rather handsomely—the real purpose of their almost daily conferences was to allow Eugene to talk to somebody, and to a somebody to whom, owing perhaps to his very habit of drinking excessively, one could say nearly anything. (The title "professor" had originally been applied jocularly to him in his short-lived career as a baseball player by reason of his extreme youth, and for some reason the nickname had stuck with him.)

In the beginning, Miles Redpath had refused what Eugene called "emoluments." "I don't deserve any pay for what I do," he had protested.

"You are the father of four children, I believe," Eugene had replied. "All girls, I think you told me," he added with a hesitation and tone of voice which implied that the very fact that all his offspring were female was reason enough for him to be given assistance, if not outright sympathy and condolence.

"You, also, Miles, served your country," Eugene went on, ignoring the fact that Redpath suddenly took a brief swallow from a bottle kept handy in his jacket pocket.

James Purdy

(96)

Perhaps embarrassed at Miles's taking a quick one (which he had repeatedly forbidden him to do), the older man went on, "The greatest regret in my life, Miles, is that I never saw . . . action. The war ended shortly after I was called up, you see. Do you understand my feeling of disappointment?" He gave Redpath a searching look.

Muttering a preamble of largely indistinct sounds, Professor Redpath said that he did not believe that anybody would have minded missing what he had been through in the war. His own experiences had been too god-awful, and what he had seen so far away had made all else before and after his being a soldier appear to him to have little or no significance.

"But how you have been helped by your career as a soldier!" Eugene cried. But when his eye fell on Miles and his state, he became flustered and cleared his throat, partly as a result of an expression that came stealing over the younger man's face which was very close to sneering hostility.

"I see." Eugene closed the topic by picking up a recently purchased antebellum map of Virginia which he had been able to locate through an antiquarian.

Together they now went over some observations of terrain and strategy with rude perfunctoriness.

"You see," Bledsoe returned to the earlier subject, "I feel I have missed something almost as fundamental as, say, marriage. Perhaps more fundamental. After all, anybody can get married."

"And how about your two boys lying over there somewhere unburied and untended to?" Miles brazenly pulled out the flask and took a long swallow and almost brandished the whiskey in Eugene's face.

Eugene Bledsoe sank back in his chair, and as he did so, the huge and badly worn map fell to the floor. Miles Redpath made a brief motion to retrieve it, and then, realizing he had said the unsayable in his friend's presence, merely took another surreptitious swallow from his flask.

It is even possible that Eugene did not hear the remark. His absent-mindedness had always been profound, even as a young man, and had of course been growing more pronounced. He had always had a habit of not hearing things he did not want to hear, so that when a few years afterward he became partially deaf, no one was particularly aware of his loss of this faculty.

Nonetheless Miles Redpath was about to ask Eugene to accept his apology for this remark when Bledsoe went on, "My other missed opportunity, as you know, is my leaving my law firm in New York and coming on back here owing to family pressures."

Miles Redpath was about to ask, "What law firm in New York?" but he was still concerned about the expression on Eugene's face when he had mentioned his "unburied and untended to" boys.

"I apologize," Miles said abruptly and extended his hand. "I mean, I am sorry," Miles went on when Mr. Bledsoe took no more notice of his hand or his abrupt contrition than he had of the original insult.

"Shake on it, will you?" Redpath rose and drew Eugene's unwilling and cold hand into his.

"I wish you'd give up that rotten habit," Eugene said after an embarrassed pause, but in so low a voice that perhaps Redpath did not hear it, any more than Eugene had heard the baseball player's remark about his sons.

"I don't see what you think you have missed," Miles began again, cutting short Eugene's explanation about his Wall Street years, which obviously did not interest the veteran. "I mean my body is riddled with ammunition shot of all kinds. I can show you if you wish some of the choicer wounds I got decorated for."

Eugene shook his head rather vigorously.

"I'm a colander of shot of all kinds, if you want to know the truth. The medics used to say I was a damned sieve of bullet holes. But it don't make me proud or satisfied or fulfilled or more of a man, or anything else, like I gather you think it ought to. I mean, if it had done for me as much as you seem to think war and service do for a man, I don't think I would be sitting here today with you over old maps and taking your hard-earned money for doing nothing."

"Now, Miles, that's the booze talking, and you know it."

"No, it ain't either, Gene, it's me talkin', and you know God damn well it's me and not a bottle saying this to you."

"Shall we go on with the map reading, Miles?" Eugene's voice trebled and shot up nearly an octave.

"That's what I'm here for."

"Are you in a condition to go over the maps with me?" Eugene wondered.

"I'd like to see you drunk just once, Gene. I'd like to see what comes out of that steel fortress you got built around yourself. Do you know what I'm saying?"

James Purdy

(98)

For answer Eugene tapped with a Blackwing pencil, sharpened to a murderous point, on the Battle of Antietam.

"Do you see this red line here, Miles?" Eugene was saying. "I drew that, of course. . . ."

But Eugene's attention was drawn to a noise so peculiar that at first he was not certain what it was, and did not indeed think it came from a human being.

It was Professor Redpath weeping uncontrollably and pushing away the tears with his angry fists.

"I can't get to you, that's all," Miles said. "Or through to you, or nothing. You're all talk around everything, that's you. Can't make a dent in you nohow!"

He stared wildly at Eugene.

"Do you want to go home?" Bledsoe inquired with appalled and dumbfounded bewilderment.

"No, God damn it," Miles replied. "I want to read the maps and earn my pay. What did you say you meant by this goddamn red line then?"

Mr. Bledsoe stared at him a long time before replying to his question.

PART III

As fall approached "in earnest," in Mrs. Newsom's phrase, and the schools were opening their doors and taking the brats off the streets again, thank God! Duane's tutor, Duke La Roche, returned from his summer vacation in Colorado, where he had been roughing it, hiking and mountain climbing.

Eugene Bledsoe closeted himself for some time with La Roche in his den before allowing him to see his pupil, and during the last fifteen minutes of their conference, Mrs. Newsom was also summoned.

Meanwhile Duane strolled about in the backyard, picking up a stray croquet ball here and finding a lost jackstraw a little farther on and a ruined cigarette lighter lying half buried under the lilac bush. He knew, of course, that they were talking about him inside. And he also knew he would never forgive his father for having brought Mrs. Newsom into the conspiracy.

"So what did you tell Duke?" Duane advanced on Mrs. Newsom with poorly controlled fury once he heard her come back into the kitchen.

"I told him nothing," Mrs. Newsom responded. She did not, however, look him in the face as she answered.

"I don't believe you," Duane cried.

"Duane! We have only your welfare at heart, and you know it. Duke had to be told that you have been upset."

"And saw ghosts! Did you tell him that too? Did you tell him I was crazy and shortly to be confined to a lunatic asylum?"

The look of commiseration and sympathy on her old face enraged him still further.

"What asylum am I to be locked up in? Did you confer over that, too?"

"My precious boy!" Mrs. Newsom went up to him, her arms opening out to hold him, but he rushed out of the room, leaped on his bike, and went sailing off in the direction of Yoxtheimer's forest preserve.

Therefore, when the lessons began, Duane was more intractable and obstreperous than ever before in the company of his tutor. For instance, he would sometimes put his leg over Duke's thigh, as if the tutor were a piece of furniture. Duke had been a Phi Beta Kappa at some prestigious Eastern college, and had won several prizes for his studies of mathematics and languages, in addition to which he had been awarded a gold medal for being a champion swimmer. Duke had an antiseptic look to him, and his face shone as if it had been scrubbed with Bon Ami. His nails were nonexistent either because he chewed them to the quick or because he purposely cut them that short. From his ample chest, slightly overdeveloped from Swedish gymnastics, there came a strong chemical odor which, although probably a deodorant, reminded one of chloroform. His eyes, behind thick, tortoiseshell glasses, were almost as blue as Eugene's, and his hair was so blond that it sometimes appeared white.

Throwing Duane's leg off his thigh, he inquired, "Did you do anything with the chapter on medians, squares, and square roots?" Duke moved his chair to a considerable distance from the boy.

"I did as many of the exercises as I could alone." Duane **now** spoke in a more cooperative tone.

James Purdy
(104)

"Good," Duke said blithely. "You know how to find the average of a set of numbers now, don't you? You remember last May we had some trouble there."

"We?" Duane mumbled.

"You see, you add them. Then divide by the number of addends."

Duane worked a few problems for the tutor then on a large sheet of ruled yellow paper.

Even more than Duane's own lack of interest in what he was doing, he could feel the tutor's boredom by the very way he sat and looked on at Duane's work, but under this boredom he could also feel Duke's growing curiosity as to what Mr. Bledsoe must have told him in the den. Several times in their working on the problems in advanced arithmetic Duane was aware that Duke was on the verge of saying something to him.

"A little break now?" the tutor finally suggested.

Duane smiled.

"Do you mind if I smoke?" Duke wondered.

"Smoke away." The boy opened both his hands in a gesture of mock beneficence.

"How is your beautiful mother?" Duke lowered his voice, moving his chair now closer to Duane.

Duane's features softened a little. After all, Duke had been one of the young men who had always come to see his mother as much as he had danced attendance on Justin and Douglas. That had been a wonderful time, after all, those old days. Both Duke and Duane exchanged looks which expressed nostalgia and regret and made the lesson on arithmetic and the assignment on Caesar about to come even more unwelcome and onerous.

Duane mumbled something about his mother.

"Does she communicate with you?" Duke wondered. (Mr. Bledsoe had asked Duke never to mention Duane's mother in any way, shape, or form, but Eugene had given him so many injunctions, prohibitions, and caveats that he ended by losing track of them all.)

"Aileen writes me a lot, yes," Duane informed him, blinking his eyes. His mother had secretly encouraged all the young men to call her by her first name, and gradually Duane had likewise assumed this privilege.

Suddenly, Duane was telling Duke about the stolen letters, and he watched his tutor's eyes widen and sparkle.

Mourners Below

"Would you happen to have one of her letters handy?" Duke inquired.

The boy's eagerness to run upstairs and get one immediately caused the tutor to have second thoughts about the wisdom of such a request, but Duane was already halfway to the top of the stairs before he could suggest they postpone seeing the letter.

Waiting for his pupil, Duke puffed greedily on his cigarette, and rustled the algebra and Latin exercises against his pants legs.

Duane appeared with a whole sheaf of letters tied with a scarlet ribbon.

"But so many, Duane!" Duke gasped. He grinned happily.

"He stole every one of these from me," Duane whispered, handing them to the tutor.

"You're positive?" Duke was reluctant to say or hear anything critical of one who was, after all, his employer.

"What a thing to do, eh?" Duane said, eagerly studying his teacher. The tutor's fingers touched the envelopes, and traced Duane's name written there as if it were braille.

"He stole them." Duane repeated the charge.

"But he gave them to you finally?" Duke spoke as if he felt he should say something in favor of Mr. Bledsoe.

"Not really," the boy explained. "I stole them back."

Duke gazed at his pupil in a kind of dreamy fashion, and then they simultaneously looked away from one another in embarrassment.

"Your mother is a beautiful woman," Duke reminisced. "I'd have given anything in the world to have had a mother that lovely."

"You sound just like Justin and Douglas," Duane said in a voice as severe as if Eugene Bledsoe were speaking.

Duke kept staring at the letters. He passed his palm over his face and, having touched the letters with such tenderness, put them aside.

"Those were the days, Duke, eh?" Duane spoke as if begging the older man to agree with him.

Duke smiled at the statement coming from so young a face, for Duane appeared even younger now than when he had left him in the spring.

"I suppose Eugene has told you a lot of rot about me." Duane now spoke with a curt and nasty tone when Duke showed no inclination to talk more about the wonderful days when his brothers and Aileen had all been living together with him.

James Purdy
(106)

The tutor touched the boy's shoulder with his hand.

"I guess it's bad enough for a father to have a son who is pretty dense in the head, but to have one who is also given to ... to ..." Duane gave the tutor such a look of desperate appeal that Duke's own throat became dry and his lips moved in slight little spasms, unable to form any words suitable to the crisis:

"There's nothing wrong with your ... brain," Duke finally got out. "Don't you remember those tests I gave you last winter? Well ... you're as bright as the next fellow."

But Duke's full attention had come to rest again on the packet of Aileen's letters, from which a faint perfume still escaped and went drifting through the quiet confines of the room.

"Well, why don't you read one of them to me?" Duane said craftily, letting the subject of his brightness and his trouble drop, and studying Duke's hopelessly distracted attention. As he said this, he let his algebra book drop to the Navajo rug at his feet.

"Read one? Aloud?" Duke spoke with the pretense that he would be committing an impropriety were he to follow the boy's suggestion.

"Why not? We could translate it into Latin then."

"Aileen," Duke said, unable to conceal his affection for Duane's mother. That, too, had been one of the phenomena about her, as Mr. Bledsoe's lawyer had pointed out to his client. She attracted young men to her like Queen Circe.

Duke's mouth parted, he wet his lips rather self-consciously, and read a few lines from one of the letters to himself. Then, after his eyes had roved quickly over the handwritten page, he pronounced: "I'd give a lot to have *anybody* write me such stuff. I wouldn't care how it sounded, if only she wrote it!"

"What stuff, Duke?" Duane said huskily. "Go ahead, read it."

Duke read thickly:

I sometimes feel if I cannot hold you in my arms again and see you near me, my heart will break in two.

Duane started, then blushed. "I think I must have missed that one," he muttered.

Duke's eyes rested on him now in a singular fashion, as if Duane had injured him or taken something away from him improperly. He then went on reading.

Mourners Below

The sentiments Aileen expressed made the blood rush to Duane's cheeks and caused his hands to feel cold, and he was filled with embarrassment close to torture before the man reading the words. But, at the same time, he knew these letters were all that mattered to him, and he would have hired Duke—if he had lots of money—merely to read them to him again and again until the paper and ink had turned to powder.

"What else matters, Duane, huh? If somebody loves you that much."

Unable to read any more, the tutor put the packet of letters together and painstakingly tied them neatly with the little ribbon.

"Except I don't have her," Duane said. "The letters are all I've got."

Duke frowned. "Is there anything else you want to tell me? After all, we've been apart a long time, and our lessons can perhaps wait a bit if you wish to say something."

"About what?" Duane mumbled.

"About anything at all, Duane."

"You know I am dense and stupid. Don't lie to me!" the boy cried, shading his eyes with his palm.

"I know nothing of the kind," the tutor answered back in an almost brutal voice.

Almost as if a bugle had sounded, they abruptly opened their separate copies of Caesar's *Commentaries*.

As Duane leafed through the text to where they were to begin translating, his invitation to Mrs. Dumont's masquerade ball fell out and landed on the smartly shined shoes of Duke La Roche.

"What have we here?" The tutor could not contain his curiosity.

"Go ahead, open it, too, if you like." Duane smirked a little at the other's unabashed nosiness, very much resembling his Dad's. "Well," he went on at a look of injured pride from the teacher, "if you enjoyed Aileen's letters so much, why shouldn't you see Lady Dumont's note to me? Go ahead, Duke." Duane tried to soften the expression of hurt and wounded pride which had crossed the face of the tutor.

"Aileen and Estelle Dumont are . . . worlds apart," Duke muttered.

"Are they now?" Duane did not know why he spoke in this cutting way to his teacher.

"You certainly know they are not . . . the same kind of people," Duke stammered, and flushed.

"Do you know this Dumont person?" Duane found himself talking with the lofty indifference of Mrs. Newsom.

"Not really." Duke showed the greatest confusion and embarrassment. "I waited outside her house once when Justin went inside to convey a message to her of some kind." He spoke almost inaudibly.

Duane could not believe how flustered Duke had suddenly become. For the first time in their relationship he saw the tutor completely lose countenance.

In his agitated state, Duke opened the invitation, and stared at its thick embossed summons with more concentration than he had ever given to irregular Latin verbs.

"Are you going, Duane?" came the almost ferocious query.

"They've already got me a costume," Duane spoke gently, indifferent because he was uneasy over the change in the tutor's manner. "Mrs. Newsom, and I . . ." He stopped, studying the peculiar rapt concentration Duke still showed as he stared at the invitation. "We went to the attic and looked over some old getups."

"I see," Duke said absentmindedly. Then, coming to, so to speak, he looked up from the invitation to inquire, "And what costume are you wearing?"

Relieved that nothing was being done, even if only for a moment, about Caesar, Duane described the possibilities and selections: the harlequin, the domino, the postillion, and so on.

"I don't think any of those will do, do you, Duane?" The tutor had resumed his schoolroom tone of firmness, and laid the communication from Mrs. Dumont aside.

"You make me tired," Duane snapped.

"Why?"

"Not only is nothing I do ever right," the boy began, "but even when I am invited somewhere, I get treated as if other people's plans for me were my fault."

"Oh, I don't mean to criticize you in any way, shape, or form," Duke replied hotly. "I was, I confess, a bit taken aback that anybody of your age and . . . experience, should be asked to go to a party at . . . Lady Dumont's."

"Oh, so it's Lady Dumont with you, too, is it?" Duane realized he was picking a fight, and not only in order to postpone the Latin lesson; his anger came from whence he scarcely knew and carried him along.

"I'm only speaking from second hand," Duke snapped at his pupil. "In any case, we all know, don't we, who first called her that." He tossed the invitation back to Duane.

"Do we?" The boy sniffed, taking the thick envelope and holding it

Mourners Below

(109)

awkwardly, as if he knew neither what it was nor what he should do with it.

"I sometimes think that all I know about life," the tutor went on in an absentminded way like one suddenly left alone in a room, "is what I learned from him. From Justin, of course." He expatiated on this, aware that Duane was intently watching him. "Of course it was *his* word for her!" he lashed out at the boy. "But as I say, everything I know about those things is secondhand, or better yet, everything I know, except from books, is from him."

Duane sucked in his breath and shook his head.

To the boy's amazement, the tutor all at once snatched the invitation back from him and crumpled it slightly in his hand until his fingers went white. "She lives high and handsome, you know. Like some potentate, with all the money she got from two husbands, who obligingly died on her, not to count all the money she inherited from her mother. Yes," he went on in mild fury, "you'll see how she lives at first hand, no matter what he may have told you in detail."

"That was nothing," Duane said, crestfallen.

"So?" Duke smiled bitterly, and handed him back the invitation again, now badly creased and almost torn. After a wait of fearful tension, he almost shouted, "Shall we do a little sight translation from your Latin now to see if you pursued your studies this past vacation? Take line six, page 396, will you please?"

Duane, in his general nervousness and confusion over Duke's unprecedented behavior, had some difficulty finding the place. But finally locating it after a lengthy fumbling during which Duke snorted his irritation and impatience, Duane bent over the book, the invitation falling from his other hand as he did so, his pupils growing large and black, his tongue protruding from his lips and working its way up as if to reach his nostrils, and recited:

Caesar sat down among the munitions brought from the camp. The leaders of the rebellion were brought thither. Vercingetorix surrendered, and his arms were thrown down.

Duke La Roche nodded, and mumbled some praise, which, however, was mixed with distrust, perhaps even disappointment, that his pupil had done so well.

James Purdy
(110)

"Do you know what happened to Vercingetorix?" La Roche inquired after a moment.

The noon factory whistle blew at that moment, causing the furniture and the springs in the easy chair to vibrate.

"Do you recall, Duane?"

"He was horsewhipped to death by the Romans." Duane stared at his tutor as he spoke with a kind of effrontery which took the older man aback.

"Where did you pick that up?" the tutor wondered. Then, abruptly stooping down, he tied his shoelace which had come undone.

"About the masquerade party," Duke began without waiting to hear Duane's reply, his face pink from having bent over, and a line of wet on his rather thin and nearly always tightly compressed lips. "Come to think of it, I have some costumes which might suit you better than the ones you fetched out of your attic."

"You would expect I was going to kneel before the Pope the way you all fuss about what I am going to wear!" Duane cried. Then seeing he had hurt his teacher's feelings with such an outburst, he quickly added, "I guess you think I would look like a fool in a domino or postillion getup, don't you?"

"I want you to do the next entire chapter in your Caesar." The teacher, as Eugene often did, merely ignored what Duane had just said. "Did you write that down in your assignment book? And I want you to do all the exercises on prime numbers and factorizations for your math homework. Clear?"

"Well, what about the costumes you mentioned?" Duane began again, after having written down his assignments. "The ones you think are more suitable."

"Oh, those?" Duke replied carelessly, perhaps affecting that he had forgotten ever mentioning such a thing. "Why"—he paused, rising from his chair of instruction rather pompously—"you can drop over any evening, and we'll fit you out.... I want you to look nice, Duane," he added, and he buttoned his jacket and tightened his cravat.

"Just before you go," Duane began, and touched the tutor's sleeve as he did so, "there is something I have meant to tell you all summer long."

"Can't it wait until you drop by to see the costumes?" Duke asked, and took out his pocket watch which he noted was slower than the noon whistle.

"I want to say it now while I've got the nerve." Duane looked balefully before him.

"Go ahead," Duke agreed.

"He queered it with my ice-skating instructor and the chance for the Olympics," the boy said. "Eugene, that is. I've pieced it all together, the way my instructor acted, after I won that competition in Chicago, the way the instructor is seldom at the rink now when I skate. From a number of things. Eugene went to him. Told him I wasn't up to skating. Wasn't up to anything. Don't you see?"

Duke gazed at his pupil with wondering, an almost terrified eloquence. "It will have to wait, Duane, even if it's true. We'll talk later, do you hear?"

He put his heavy hand on the pupil's shoulder. Duane shrugged the hand off with fury. "Let it wait all right! After all, he pays you, I don't. Yes, let it wait till hell's cold enough to skate across and back, why not!"

And without saying another word, Duane rushed out of the room and into the backyard through which he fled onward past the catalpa trees and the white oaks.

Returning a few minutes later, like someone engaged in running practice, Duane stood on one of the side porches of the house and watched the tutor passing down the avenue lined with hundred-year-old elm trees.

A remark which he had overheard Duke make to his father last spring in the den suddenly came back to him and smarted in recollection. "Your son is a dreamer, Mr. Bledsoe. His mind is in the clouds. He has the attention span of a small child. I'm sorry to say that."

Duane imagined that Eugene's face must have darkened like a thundercloud on hearing this report, for though he constantly said even worse things about his only surviving son, he did not wish anybody else to make the slightest criticism of him. "Eugene hates the truth," Duane said aloud, thinking of this trait of his father's with something like pride and satisfaction. "I hate it, too! And why shouldn't I watch the clouds?" He went on with his furious muttering.

Mrs. Newsom came out on the side porch. "Are you alone, Duane?" She was not alarmed or troubled that she had caught him talking to himself. She often spoke to herself over her needlepoint or when watering the geraniums. She accepted eccentricity as natural, and that was one reason Duane loved her.

"I was going to ask Professor La Roche to lunch." She spoke cheerfully.

"Well, he's gone," Duane informed her. "Besides, he's no professor."

"He teaches, though, don't he?" She spoke a bit snappishly in reply.

"I suppose, but I wonder what he teaches," Duane said, and went on staring after Duke, still visible along the line of elms.

Around nine o'clock that night Duane began putting on his pajamas in his bedroom, after having soaked his feet in Epsom salts for a while. His skating instructor had recommended this, and he went on doing it nearly every night despite the fact that he no longer expected to become a star ice skater, and certainly did not anticipate ever being in the Olympics.

He sat in Aileen's old rocker and stared at the bed which Mrs. Newsom had turned down. It was always the last thing she did before she left the house, turn down the covers of the bed. "When they quit turning down the covers of the bed at night," Eugene had once said to one of his financial advisers, "life, as we know it, will be over."

The recollection of Duke La Roche's having called him a dreamer still rankled in his breast. Then his anger suddenly changed from the tumultuous beating of his heart and the pounding in his temples to a tingling feeling at the base of his spine. Icicle-like sensations went up and down his back, and his mouth was by turns very dry and overflowing with saliva.

Justin stood outside the window glass in the vertical rainbow reflections from the big streetlamp. He had his full-dress Marine uniform on. He looked at Duane crestfallen and sorrow-laden and reproachful as he had once done when he caught the boy pissing on the front tire of his new racing car and had struck him with his fist, shouting, "You God damn little cur!"

As if weary of the very terror of it, Duane stood up and stared at what he knew could not be real. All at once a gush of water descended from the eaves outside the green shutter half closed against the window. It began raining hard. Without looking to see if he was still there, Duane got dressed slowly. He turned the bedclothes up, undoing Mrs. Newsom's work.

Mourners Below

He hurried down the back stairs, which had been repaired since his fall. Rushing out the door, he did not know where he was actually going, but he knew that he must go somewhere, anywhere, that he could not remain under his father's roof that night.

He sped past street signs: East Main, Cross, Locust, Defiance, Greenoak, Blessington Meadow, Cornhill. And then the signs stopped and he was in open country. He crossed a field, nearly fell into a ditch, and heard dogs barking in the direction of a small stream. He tripped and fell over the remains of an abandoned tractor. The rain had stopped for the most part, and there was only a blind moon. He felt cold. He walked on to where a row of poplar trees loomed forlorn with the wet. From beyond them hove into sight a brick house. It was as though somebody had guided him, he had come to it so directly. The house, of course, was Duke's, and his car and bicycle were parked directly outside the back window of the brightly lit kitchen.

Duane was about to knock when, looking through the glass door, he saw Duke and a young woman whom he did not recognize. Her pale skin was in marked contrast to her rich, very dark braided hair. In profile, her breasts were outlined hard and firm and somehow defenseless. Duke wore only a thin dressing gown, and about his heavily sinewed legs bright red garters were adjusted tightly, parting the thick hair that grew in whorls over his limbs.

They seemed to be in the midst of an argument or altercation. Duke was drinking thirstily from a big mug filled with beer, to judge by the streak of frothy liquid it left behind on his upper lip. The woman was crying, and Duane could not distinguish her occasional words.

Without an indication that he was about to do so, Duke La Roche abruptly advanced and grasped the woman by the shoulders. His dressing gown slipped open and he was stark ballock-naked save for the red garters. Duane stared incredulously at his enormous and violently agitated cock. His companion touched his penis, or rather pushed him and his cock away as if it were the source of her tears. He seized her mouth in his, and they fell in tight embrace on a cot in a kitchen that was as ample as both the parlor and the living room of Eugene Bledsoe's house.

Feeling a terrible thirst, and later wondering what on earth had possessed him to do such a thing at such a moment, Duane, with only a momentary wait, quietly lifted the door latch, walked directly to the refrigerator, opened it, took out the cut-glass decanter containing water, and drank noisily from the neck of the vessel. Wiping off his mouth, he stared brazenly at the couple churning about on the daybed.

It was not clear to him whether they were even aware of his presence, absorbed as they were in their vigorous exertions. He watched them dispiritedly. The woman began to moan and protest, but Duke continued to work himself even more brutally into her body, at the same time giving out his own cries like someone in great pain and suffering. In fact his tutor's cries of anguish became so pronounced that the pupil could not help remembering once when he had seen a car hit a dray horse, drawing from the beast sounds of such hideous volume and agony as he had never believed existed in nature.

At the height of Duke's exertions and vociferations, the tutor turned his head and neck slightly toward the visitor, and then, as if seeing him for the first time, gave out further moans and grunts interspersed with foul words and curses, some of which were unknown to the boy, though his brothers had had the reputation of being the most foul-mouthed youths in town. Indeed, for a second Duane looked about for a pencil to write down what Duke was saying, so used was he to obeying his tutor.

Shaking himself at last like a mastiff which has plunged unknowingly into a lake, Duke came to himself, the woman rose, covering her lower body with her hands, and hurried off upstairs. Duke put on his glasses and came over and sat down at the table alongside which Duane had seated himself. Duane pushed the decanter of water in the tutor's direction, and Duke gingerly took it with a look of murder and drank noisily.

Nothing was said until Duke had put on his trousers and shirt and pulled on his high shoes, which gave out squeaks almost like those of a mouse, so that Duane laughed at the sound.

"Come on along, then," Duke spoke in sultry, vicious tones, standing by the glass door. "Let's go."

Duane followed his tutor, and they walked down the pike road. Directly ahead were the lights of a hamburger and coffee place. Duke opened the screen door and ushered Duane inside.

They sat in a booth large enough for six people. The waitress called out a greeting to the teacher and threw down two immense menus splattered with barbecue sauce and badly soiled by countless unclean hands.

"Do they let you drink coffee at your age?" Duke wondered.

"Oh, yes," the pupil replied cheerfully. He felt very good suddenly, and very comfortable. He had not felt so at one with himself since— well, he supposed since before they had gone off to war.

Duke pushed the sugar cubes, the cream, and a napkin toward his charge with a maniacal fierceness and sizzling energy. Duane put four lumps in his coffee and enough cream to make the top of the cup sop over.

"I forgot to give you something today when we were having my lesson," Duane said, looking at Duke with the cool collectedness of somebody who had run into him by accident in the diner.

He fished up from his pocket a gold amulet on a chain and handed it to the tutor.

Duke's fingers opened and closed on the object—obviously precious.

"Where did you come by this?" the tutor inquired, fetching a long breath.

"I found it . . . in one of their boxes," Duane mumbled.

"One of their boxes," the tutor sassed him, and laid the amulet down on the cheap oilcloth. He folded his arms across his chest.

"And you want to part with it for someone like me, is that it?" The tutor raised his voice now so that everybody in the diner turned around expecting to see an altercation.

The waitress approached their booth and smiled a peculiar smile, then went off into the kitchen.

With unexpected vehemence, Duke picked up the amulet and put it around his neck. "All right!" the tutor shouted. The giver of the gift sighed heavily and leaned back in the booth.

"You know something," Duke began, trying to put into words his tumult and outrage. "Do you know . . . ?" He stopped and beat the fist of his hand into the tabletop. "You beat the Dutch!" he cried. He rose as he said this, and his voice again filled the diner; then, suddenly, wilting, without energy, he slipped back into his seat and covered his face in his arms. Duane continued drinking his coffee and cream and eyed him nervously.

At the sound of the signal which La Roche gave when the lessons were at an end—something between a clearing of the throat and a deep sigh—Duane rose from the booth and followed his tutor to the cashier, saw him pay, then heard the inquiry, "Got an extra quarter, Duane?" But Duane had only three pennies, which Duke did not deign to accept.

James Purdy
(116)

They began walking in a direction the pupil was not familiar with. They crossed empty lots, came into little meadows, went down a declivity and into a huge, unencumbered terrain where tall sunflowers rose in abundance, top-heavy and bowing like personages in a child's story book, and then through a field where Queen Anne's lace, pasture thistle, and a purple nodding flower whose name he did not know grew. He picked one of the latter.

"Put that down, for Pete's sake!" Duke quarreled with him even about this.

Confused at this arbitrary hatefulness, Duane involuntarily handed Duke the flower, which the tutor was perhaps too surprised to refuse; then, having taken it, he crumpled it in his fist and discarded it on the ground.

There was no question in Duane's mind that he was to accompany Duke wherever they were off to, and then without warning there they were back at the teacher's house, but this time they approached it from the main entrance. Duke took a big ring of keys from his pants pocket, unlocked the front door, pulled back a little inner door, and said glumly, "You go first."

They sat down in chairs somewhat far apart in the sitting room, and waited as if a meeting were scheduled to begin any moment.

"Why I put up with it, I'll never know." Duke finally broke the silence. "The rudeness, the uncalled for . . ." Here he waved his arms all at once and stared around the room as he did when addressing a class. "The gall! The brazen, cold-blooded impudence!"

"Where is that woman?" Duane interrupted his tirade.

"What?" Duke replied murderously, rolling his eyes.

"I mean, where did she go?"

"Probably to the river to drown herself. Wouldn't you?"'

Duke bounded up from his chair and began pacing around the room with an energy Eugene Bledsoe could never have hoped to emulate, while giving out a great flow of filthy words and curses which made Duane smirk despite himself.

"Go ahead, laugh, why don't you, if it tickles you. See if I care. Go ahead!"

Actually Duane had made the strange little expression around his lips because Duke's cursing and bad language had made him feel more at home here, for it was like the old days when Justin or Douglas would give him hell and damn him up one side and down the other. All he lacked now was for Duke to give him a bloody nose and things would be back to where they were before, so he lay back in his chair as carefree as someone having his back scratched.

"It beats me hollow!" Duke finally finished his cursing and damning of him and leaned against the mantelpiece.

Duane dug the toe of his loafers into the thick carpet.

"Don't spoil that imported rug, you shitass," the tutor began again. "Let up, can't you?"

Then, as the pupil looked over at his instructor, he saw that the anger of the words did not quite match the expression on Duke's face. Indeed, he was looking at the boy with a kind of eloquent compassion. "I suppose while you're here we should take a peek at some of those costumes I promised you, shouldn't we?"

"Whatever you say, *Mr. La Roche.*"

"Whatever I say!" Duke's anger rose again. "Don't you have any preference, don't you want to go as somebody? Answer me!"

Duane dug his toe into the carpet again. The tutor came over to his chair. "Don't you want to go to see Lady Dumont when you know she was his all-in-all? Don't you want to look at the one he worshiped?"

Duane's Adam's apple rose and fell convulsively. "I always was going, Duke," the boy managed to get out. "Except I didn't know I would be going in one of your costumes."

"Fuck my costumes! You haven't even seen my costumes yet. So what are you talking about?"

"Look," the boy began vehemently, rolling his eyes frenetically, "I didn't mean to spy on you, do you hear?" He almost leaped at the tutor as he spoke. "I'm not like that. I'm not ... brazen. I'm not. I was coming tonight just to see you about the costumes, as a matter of fact. Just trying to get my courage up eventually to see ... Estelle, you might say."

"Well, for crying out loud," the tutor said nastily, standing over the chair like a dentist who cannot proceed with a difficult patient.

"I was so surprised to see you doing what you were doing," Duane went on with his explanation, "that ... I didn't know what I was about. I guess I came inside so you could explain it to me."

"Explain it to you! God Almighty! Do you think I have an answer for everything under the sun for you, including showing you how to fuck?"

"Well, if you don't, I mean don't have an answer for everything for me, I don't know anybody else who does," Duane said with perfect equanimity.

"Well, thanks for the compliment." The tutor took out his pure Irish linen handkerchief and mopped his mouth, his cheeks, and his forehead, looked at the moisture on the cloth, and put it back in his breast pocket.

"I won't tell anybody what I saw tonight, anyhow," Duane added.

"Again, I'm much obliged to you."

"It was pretty much of a shock to me, though. I hope you appreciate that."

"To *you?*" Duke said, smiling nastily. "A shock to you!" He went up to the chair again. "Well, what do you think it was to us? What do you think we felt having you doing a Peeping Tom, huh? Explain, why don't you, what *we* felt! In fifty words or less!"

"But you're used to it, Duke. I could see that. I'm not." Duane was nearly truculent.

"Used to being looked at like fish in a bowl. Oh, thank you, thank you!"

He moved away from the chair now and started walking around in circles and, to Duane's intense irritation, began jingling coins in his pocket just like Eugene at his worst.

"Well, why don't you strap me and get it over with?" Duane shouted.

"I wouldn't touch you with a ten-foot pole and you know it! I'm not a Bledsoe!"

"I see," Duane said in a muffled voice.

"What you have done can have no punishment, correction, or so forth. What you have done is so awful it has no name."

"Oh, I bet you could find one." Duane now half stood up and pushed his shirt down into his jeans.

"As I said a while back, since you're here, we may as well go look at the costumes."

"Is she out of the house?" the pupil asked with a kind of lordly, and certainly proprietary, manner.

"Don't worry, we won't run into her where I hang my old clothes," the tutor reassured him.

Duke La Roche was busy looking through some garments put away in huge bags in what he called his clothes closet, which was actually an area large enough to sleep four or five overnight guests.

"After all, Duke," Duane called into the dark recesses of the closet, "I've come into your kitchen before, uninvited and unannounced. In fact, you told me last spring before you pulled up stakes, *'The latch is always off the door where you're concerned.'* "

Duke rushed, almost leaped out of the closet, and gave his pupil a look of hopeless exasperation. He broke open two of the garment bags from which emanated the not unpleasant aroma of camphor and cedar chips combined.

"Yes, you got an eyeful tonight, no question about that," Duke muttered, staring at the costumes he had taken out of the bags.

"Everything I do is wrong!" Duane fulminated. He had never raised his voice so loud.

"Will you pipe down, and step into one of these outfits instead?" Duke threw two of the garment bags directly at Duane, who caught them but nearly lost his balance.

Duane kept staring at the tutor. He could not get rid of the picture of his teacher stark naked lying atop the young woman and making sounds like some farm animal.

"It's not my fault," Duane went on incoherently, "if I catch hell everywhere I turn. Grown-ups are the unreasonable ones, if you ask me. I go to the wrong church, for example, and my Dad beats me with the razor strop," he said, believing at that moment his father had actually punished him.

"Good for your Dad," Duke replied. "I'm glad he can use his hands for some kind of useful physical labor."

"What do you mean by that remark?" Duane spoke with truculence. The sight of so many garment bags, all on great hangers visible from where he stood, however, had made him forget about defending Eugene.

"Your Dad isn't exactly the community's idea of a man of affairs," Duke remarked with a toss of his head.

"You wouldn't dare say that in front of Justin, would you?" Duane blurted out and then remembered the moment he spoke that there was no Justin. The shock of hearing his own peculiar statement made him abandon abruptly his position near the closet and walk over to the big window where he looked down at the streetlamp around which immense white moths were circling.

"So your Dad thrashes you," Duke inquired, standing in the threshold of the closet, and unaware of Duane's new turmoil.

James Purdy

When there was no answer from the boy, Duke walked over to the window. "Look here, Benjy!" He tried to attract his attention, but Duane kept gazing out the window. "Duane, look at the oufit I've got here for you."

The boy finally turned around and saw a peculiar-looking costume, all pale green and leafy, with a half mask and smart forest-green tights.

Duane's features softened and he touched the cloth.

"What's it supposed to be, Duke?" There were tears in his eyes.

"Pan."

When Duane did not respond, the tutor went on, "You know, the ancient god of sheep and fields and so forth."

"I like the feel of the material, anyhow," Duane said, holding the costume in his fingers, "whatever it represents."

"Then I have this Arizona cowboy outfit." Duke opened out what looked like brand-new and expensive buckaroo-type gear, with silk scarf, chaps, and boots.

Duane touched the chaps and was almost about to put on the broad hat when the tutor opined, "I think you're Pan."

"Where is that woman?" Duane inquired without warning.

"Who cares?" Duke put on the cowboy hat for a brief moment, as he gathered up some of the other costumes and placed them back in their bags.

Duke's indifference to her plight made Duane relax his mouth into a grin.

"Go on, Benjy, put on the Pan costume," Duke urged. "Go ahead. I won't watch you while you undress. You don't care about gawking at me mother-naked giving it to someone, do you? But you're Miss Modesty when you have to take your own clothes off, eh?"

Duane stripped off everything, including his jockey shorts. He stood thus all bare, expectant, even penitent in front of his tutor, as if the latter were a doctor at an induction center.

"Why didn't you keep your shorts on?" Duke complained. "Oh well, step into these tights, why don't you. . . . I hope your ass is clean."

"I resent that remark," Duane said, though there was no real anger or protest in his voice. "Besides"— he flashed a look of indignation at his teacher—"sensible people don't do that in their kitchen, anyhow, and you know it!" Duane's anger overflowed again. A kind of rising tide of rage against everybody was coming out of him, and weirdly enough, at that moment, he felt a kind of fury directed against Justin more than at anybody else, an indignation against him for having died, for not having stood by him. Big thick tears fell, staining the god costume.

"Here, for cripe's sake, let me help you." Duke spoke in a quiet but almost frightened voice.

"That's good," he said, looking appraisingly at his pupil. "There's a big full-length mirror off this room in the hall to the right. Go on."

Duane started to go in the opposite direction, and Duke yelled: "I said *right!* Christ, you'd do beautiful in the army."

"You shut your big mouth," Duane yelled from the hall. Then turning clear round, he cried to the tutor: "And my Dad don't sit on his ass any more than you do!"

"All right, Duane, go study yourself in the mirror."

But when he got to the mirror, instead of looking at himself in his costume, he began to bawl and even to scream a little. Great snorts of grief, rage, and indignation came over him, causing him to double up.

"Duane," the tutor began, coming halfway toward him, "don't take it so hard. Do you hear me?"

The weeping continued—tears, mucus, saliva falling over the fresh costume and Duke's outstretched hand.

Duke put his hand on the boy's shoulder, and his own breathing became rough and arhythmic. "Is it all because you miss your brothers?" the tutor whispered.

"They hated me, too, I'm positive," the boy groaned. "They knew I was a boob. They know it now looking down on us here. I wish I was dead, too, but they wouldn't probably let me even go where they are, so why die and not be with them there, too?"

The realization that his pupil was suffering such misery and confusion banished the last of the tutor's anger and disgust. Almost involuntarily, he pulled the boy toward him and held him against his chest. The wet from Duane's eyes and nose soaked through La Roche's thin shirt and moistened his skin.

"You look good in your Pan costume. You know it."

Breaking away from his tutor, the pupil ran back to the window and looked out wildly at the streetlamp.

"I don't know why you think I hold it against you," Duane began to say in an almost croaking tone, "just because I seen you doing what you done tonight. I don't think the less of you at all." He wheeled about and faced his tutor. "I was sort of proud of you." Fearful that he had

James Purdy

(122)

again said something inappropriate or even insulting, the boy turned away and looked out the window.

Standing in the center of the room, his arms dropped lifelessly at his side, La Roche felt too numbed by this last observation by his pupil to make any rejoinder. The whole evening's activity came over him all at once with overwhelming force. He felt very tired and sat down.

"I can see," Duke said after an interminable silence, "that I am going to be stuck with you. I can kind of see all at once what they had on their hands. Well, all right, God damn it, then! If they could stand it, I guess I can, too. And after all," he said, looking down at his hands which he had bruised slightly on one of the bent hangers, "what do I have to occupy my time with anyway? I'm getting nowhere in this backwater. Might as well be saddled with you"—he raised his head to look over at Duane—"as anybody else. And, by God, you're going to that party if I have to beat your ass all the way there."

Turning fully around, Duane gave Duke an almost beatific smile.

"You're my catechumen, I guess." Duke spoke between his teeth. He was glad to observe that Duane appeared not to have heard him say this; and of course even had he heard it, he would not have understood it, or remembered it, although the word had once been referred to in one of their history texts.

For the next day or so, Duane picked at his food at the table, and whole platefuls of grub had to be thrown out by an outraged Mrs. Newsom, while this waste was surveyed by a glowering but silent Eugene Bledsoe.

"Make him take some more of that beef, blood, and iron tonic in the cupboard," Eugene advised the housekeeper.

Holding the tablespoon full of the tonic to his mouth, Mrs. Newsom scolded, "If you're not going to eat, Duane, and your Dad is going off up the street every evening to dine where he pleases, I have a half a mind to quit—this time for good. I won't cook for empty mouths and sit down by myself to a table of empty chairs, and that's that."

Having swallowed the tonic, he gagged and hurried over to the sink to spew it out.

Mrs. Newsom, implacable, held a second tablespoonful ready. He took it, one might say, almost by his teeth, thinking as he did so how loathsome and ridiculous Duke had looked as he lay atop the woman, and he no more than got this second spoonful down when he began to laugh uproariously.

"Now what's so funny?" the housekeeper wondered, and picked up the bottle to stare at its label, for fear, perhaps, that she had given him the wrong medicine. She felt relieved in a way that he could laugh, but she supposed it, too, was a bad sign.

"I wish I could tell you, Mrs. N." Duane sat down on a little three-legged stool while she went at her work of stacking the supper dishes for sudsing and scalding.

"There's very little I don't know, Duane, or at least haven't heard of. It's one of the things menfolk like to pretend among themselves, that women know nothing about what they feel they're so expert on." She gave out a dry little laugh.

"I wish, oh how I wish I could tell you!"

"Suit yourself." Mrs. Newsom went on stacking the last of the big plates in a pile for their first scrubbing. The Bledsoes followed a kind of ritual, which, had Duane known it, was common in the army. Dishes were subjected to a number of cleanings and scourings and final plunges in varying immersions of boiling water so that an entire atmosphere of clouds, steam, and smoke from bottles, kettles, and vats swept over the entire kitchen and adjoining pantry.

"If I tell you, Mrs. N., you won't go blabbing to Eugene or anybody else?"

"You know me better than that," she responded with not much conviction. "But if you are about to give away somebody's confidence, I don't want to hear it."

Duane thought carefully if such a thing was at stake.

"Is that the case?" she wanted to know.

"Mrs. Newsom," Duane began, and he walked to the open door beyond which the rose of Sharon bush was in full bloom, moving in the evening air. "I have done a terrible thing."

She kept sudsing the same serving dish again and again, for she knew now he was going to both give away a confidence and probably tempt her own weakness to pass this confidence on.

"By the way," he began abruptly, "do you have any catechumens in your church?"

"You leave my church out of this," she cried with extreme irritation.

James Purdy

"For goodness sake! I don't want to go into all that again with you and your father."

"I can't tell you, Mrs. N. It's too graphic."

"Then quit teasing," she warned him. "Either tell it or forget it. I'm not that interested, to tell the truth. But I did see you going home past my house very late last night, Duane. It must have been after midnight. So I hope you were not anywhere you shouldn't have been."

"I went to my tutor's house," Duane confided.

"Good."

"But it wasn't, Mrs. N. Not if you hear what I saw there. No, siree."

Duane blushed now, not because of what he had seen, but because he felt he was about to betray his friend. He didn't want to, but he had to tell somebody, somehow. Of course, one could not tell Eugene such a thing, one could not tell him anything except maybe that it was raining or that it had just struck twelve noon or that the President had been shot.

"I used to know Duke La Roche's mother," Mrs. Newsom reflected. "She was very ambitious for her boys, and I think Duke has turned out in a way that would have pleased her. He's very young to be a professor, too."

"I suppose . . ." Duane reflected on his tutor's youth. "Anyhow, he gave me some costumes for the ball."

"I couldn't help seeing them in the hallway." She spoke coolly. "I guess my selection didn't quite fill the bill, eh?"

"I just haven't made up my mind yet which to wear. I guess I have to go though."

"According to your father you should." She was even more icy now.

"Mrs. Newsom," he began with a rush. "As I say, I did a terrible thing."

She poured a second spoonful of soap flakes into the dishpan until the whole vessel was bursting with great violet and red bubbles.

"I admit I showed up at his place unexpected, uninvited." He stood directly by the dishpan, and picked up a little tea towel from the wall hanger and began drying a meat platter.

"After all," he continued like a once reluctant witness who is now testifying with the slight hysteria of full candor, "I've gone to his house uninvited before. In fact, he once said he liked these 'unpremeditated' visits, as he called them."

"I'd hardly use that word myself." Mrs. Newsom was very dry.

"So being at loose ends," he went on, toweling another platter, "and walking around Yoxtheimer's, and beyond, I just found myself, as I say, near Duke's place. It was a decent hour still. The lights were all blazing in the kitchen, and the door was not locked as it has often been. I looked through the curtains, and he was all bare, Mrs. N., as bare as a newborn babe."

"Duane, for pity's sake, are you making this up now?"

"Duke was stark naked, and on top of a woman!"

He spread his arms as he said this, as if beseeching her to impart to him what action they should now take.

"But the worst part is still to come," he went on. "Much worse. You see, Mrs. N., I walked right on in and took a seat, like it was choir practice or something, or a meeting of one of his college classes."

Mrs. Newsom scalded the dishes again from a boiling kettle and wrung out the biggest of her dishcloths.

"I just sat there," he informed her, and gently touched her sleeve, "sat there and looked at them, you see, while they let out their infernal choking and hollering sounds, and—"

"Duane! Stop. Stop right where you are. I don't want any details, and I think you should close this chapter of what happened right here. And please do not help me dry the dishes. You know that is forbidden as well."

"But, Mrs. Newsom. You don't understand. I didn't mean to! Don't you follow me? That's why I'm telling it to you. I wouldn't have done such a thing on purpose, don't you see? Never. I'm not that kind. I don't know why I stayed on, when I should have fled."

"To say the least! To say the least!"

He sat down on a chair and held the tea towel over his knee.

She finished putting away the last of the dishes, poured out the dirty dishwater down the drain, hung up her apron, and put out all the tea towels and dishcloths to dry by the snowball bush.

Standing in the middle of the kitchen, she asked, "Do you want to walk me home, Duane?"

"I give up," the boy said and shook his head. "You're just like him—my Dad. When I try to explain something to you, all you care about is scalding the dishes and stacking the china plates in the right place. I thought you'd at least be interested in me admitting I made a bad mistake."

James Purdy

(126)

"Come along, Duane, and don't be silly. The air will do you good."

As they walked along in silence, Duane broke off little branches from the privet hedge they were passing, and whistled off-key a popular tune of a few seasons past.

Mrs. Newsom would from time to time remark on somebody's hedge which needed trimming, or the poor way some other homeowner was keeping up his property.

After a struggle with herself, she finally got out, "It's very disappointing, Duane, to discover a chink in somebody's armor. I know from experience. We look up to somebody, and then find out he has feet of clay. Perhaps you looked up to him too much for your own good. That is one of your ... weaknesses, if I may say so."

"Maybe I look up to him now more than before," he snapped and stooped down to pick a clump of wild asters.

"I see." She tried to speak as indifferently as possible.

"What I tried to tell you, Mrs. N., but couldn't, because you wouldn't let me," he began, and they both stopped short. She gazed at his mouth, which was somewhat stained by the beef and iron tonic. "You see, I didn't mean to do what I did last night, go in and stare at them, but he will never believe me and I know he will hold it against me till the Last Judgment. Do I make myself clear to you now? That's why I wanted to share it with you, not to tell you how disgusting a man and woman look naked together."

Mrs. Newsom started walking on again, and he followed a pace or two behind.

"I think Mr. La Roche is too much of a man to hold a thing like that against you forever. See if I'm not right." She stopped and gave him one of her winning smiles.

They parted at the former site of the old Crozier vegetable farm, and Duane watched her with a half-assuaged expression in his eyes as she sauntered on into the gathering gloom of night.

Instead of going directly home, Duane took a detour off toward the stone quarry and passed through a field similar to the one near Duke's in which a vast array of joe-pye weed and Scotch thistle, run to seed, was swaying in the mild night breeze. He began running, and then after a while, short of breath, he stopped at the limits of our small town, where his family had lived for generations. Somewhat to his surprise, the high granite walls of St. Michael's Church rose into view. A strong urge to see the altar of votive lights where he had lit a candle for Justin and Douglas, and where he was forbidden to enter, conquered him.

But he entered the church this time from a different door, and stood confounded and confused as to where the candle to his brothers might have been.

As he hesitated near a marble crucifix, an old man who was sweeping the aisles with a huge broom cried: "Take your hat off, you young heathen! Have you no sense of where you are?"

Duane pulled off a little stocking cap which he wore only because Justin had worn a similar one, and turned to an altar with many candles burning, lit one, put some coins in the slot, and not sure which knee to bend, fell awkwardly on both his knees for a minute or so, and then fled from the church, running all the way home and slamming the door behind him as he entered. Eugene emerged from his den and said, "Is the devil chasing you? You came in like a whirlwind."

"This not sleeping at night!" Duane muttered through the protection of the linen bedclothes. The clock struck two, then, after what seemed an eternity, three. Duane leaped out of bed, dressed, and slunk down the back stairs, leaving the latch up on the kitchen door. He ambled out over the endless backyard with its summerhouse, wicker porch furniture stacked and tied ready to be put away for the winter, a half-assembled croquet set, and the remains of a target for archery. He began running frenetically in the direction—whether he knew it or not—of Duke La Roche's house.

His face was still hot with shame at having intruded on Duke's privacy and pleasure, and also at having subsequently betrayed him by confiding what he had seen and done to Mrs. Newsom. She was probably telling her husband about it even now in bed, as they lay sleepless with horror over what he had done. No, he knew better; Mrs. Newsom was too prudish and hypocritical and modest to tell Ab such a thing. It would make her look off-color.

Sure enough, Duke's kitchen was ablaze with light—he must not care about his electric bill. Duane walked noisily up the steps and knocked. There was no answer. He called his tutor's name, but only silence. He opened the door and tiptoed in. He blushed all over again, as he did every time he thought of his having gone in to gape at Duke making love and then sitting himself down as one would at a basketball game one had arrived late for. How could he have had so much gall! He

James Purdy
(128)

realized he didn't know himself at all. He might do anything, in fact! Would do anything!

He began walking up the wide front staircase, holding onto the banister and calling Duke by name. He knew he should go back downstairs and go on home, but the dread of not sleeping, the terror that one of his brothers might be sitting on the foot of the bed waiting for him, drove him on up the staircase.

He thought he heard a noise in one of the little rooms at the back of the stairs. He stood there a moment, called Duke's name again, then, advancing to the closed door, he opened it as softly as he could. Duke was sitting in a chair before a long table, fully clothed, his head cradled in his arms. Probably he had shot himself to death! Duane was about to go over to investigate his condition when, looking around him, he saw the entire room was papered with photographs of a young woman with long whitish blond hair, immense eyes with lashes as long as if they were false, a mouth full and plump as red raspberries on the vine, and a dimple equally appetizing just in the middle of her chin.

Studying this elaborate display of one face reproduced so many times on the walls, Duane was unaware that Duke had raised up and was gazing at him malevolently.

"Well . . ." Duke began.

"I came to . . . ask your forgiveness," Duane stammered.

Duke's face was wrinkled and red from having slept in the crook of his thick, heavy arms. His expression, one of distrust, weariness, and outrage, somewhat resembled that of a fox the boy had once come upon unawares in the woods.

"Who is she, Duke?" Duane moved his head in the direction of the photographs covering the wall.

"What in hell time is it?" the teacher cried, and fished in his desk drawer for his wristwatch, but could not find it. "Where in Christ have you been, coming in like this?" he went on. Then after a pause, during which he plowed his fingers through his hair, he muttered, "Somebody's got to take you in hand."

"Is she your fiancée?" Duane went back to the girl on the wall.

"I wish to Christ Almighty she was," Duke cried. He opened another little drawer in his desk and took out a package of Players cigarettes, pulled one out, and in a trice had lighted it and was inhaling.

"I thought you were going to give up smoking," Duane observed.

Mourners Below

(129)

"I did," Duke replied. "That is, I'd quit until just today. I've been so rattled, I've begun again."

"Over her?" Duane wondered.

"Over you!" Duke screamed at him. "Oh, of course, not over you," Duke amended his words shamefacedly, but Duane felt he had spoken the truth in the first place.

"You mean to tell me," Duke said bitterly, "you don't know who she is?"

Duane shook his head. He was suddenly afraid of something.

"No one else has ever been in this room till now." The tutor spoke again in a more acerbic tone than the boy could ever remember having heard from him before.

"So I've spoiled it for you, too," Duane observed.

"Well, isn't that why you tiptoed in?" he barked at him, again looking like the fox in the wood. He offered Duane a cigarette, which was refused.

"Why not?" Duke derided his refusal.

"I don't like the little pieces of tobacco that stick to my teeth," the boy explained almost coquettishly. "But it's not as bad as the chewing tobacco . . . they used to make me . . ."

"I see."

Duane came and sat directly beside the tutor but avoided looking at him.

"What's her name, Duke?"

Duke stared at him for a full minute, until finally Duane turned away.

"You mean to tell me you don't know Estelle Dumont when you see her?" the tutor said, giving him a searching look. "Your brother's girl friend, the one who's invited you to her party. You don't know her face?"

Duane lowered his head, then after a moment bit his lip and shook his head—but said nothing.

"How long have you been . . . drawn to her?" Duane asked hoarsely.

The tutor blew smoke rings as expertly as the giant face did on the billboard in New York, but his eyes rolled with hateful displeasure and irritation which only drove Duane on.

"Do you want to marry her?"

"She wouldn't wipe her feet on me." Duke almost spat these words out.

James Purdy
(130)

"Do you want me to speak to her about you . . . when I go there?" Duane said in a kind of idiotic confidentiality.

Duke merely blew out more rings of blue smoke.

"Duke," the boy began again, "I have come to apologize, to make up for what I've done to you. Furthermore . . ." He was starting to tell Duke about his indiscretion with Mrs. Newsom, but glancing surreptitiously at the tutor's face, he was so alarmed by what he saw there that he became mum.

But as Duane could not bear the silence either, he abruptly said, "Why can't I intercede with her for you? After all, if she knew . . . Justin . . . why shouldn't you marry her if you want to? Huh?" He spoke, and spread his hands as if to shower the teacher with his magnanimous plan.

Duke rose wearily, like a man who has suffered a toothache for several nights and can find neither painkiller nor dentist, went over to the window, and laid his head in the crook of his arm again.

"I'll do anything to make up for my misdeeds." Duane had followed him over to the window.

"You can't help being the way you are," Duke observed in a muffled voice.

"What do you mean by that?" Duane spoke testily.

Duke turned almost dreamily to him now, but didn't expatiate on what he had just said.

"I *said,* what do you mean by your statement, Duke?" Duane touched the tutor on the cuff of his sleeve.

"I don't know what I mean by it," Duke flared up. "Does that satisfy you?"

"Your mind was poisoned by them before I started to take lessons with you. That's what it all boils down to."

"I don't know who you mean by 'them,' " Duke sniffed, hiding his eyes again in his arm.

"The only *them* I have or ever will have. The dead ones and the one still living!"

"And, of course, I don't have a mind of my own, do I?" Duke inquired with nasty sarcasm.

"And what do you mean by *that?*"

"You think I couldn't form my own judgment of you unaided by the living or the dead?"

"But you've come up with the same opinion they had of me."

Mourners Below

"I don't even know their opinion!"

"But you ran with them all the time—Justin and Douglas." And he pronounced these two names as if they were the sound of his simultaneous salvation and damnation. "And you're in love with the girl they were in love with. So it all fits together."

The tutor shook his head. He acted drunk when he was actually as sober as if he were standing under a cold shower.

"Well, Justin loved her, according to what you just let drop. Didn't he?" Duane thundered at him.

"Don't you shout at me!" Duke growled. "Now tell me what you want to know," he said in a sleepy voice.

"You said," Duane began, "just a while ago," lowering his voice to the whispering of a conspirator, "he loved her."

Duke nodded.

"You mean he ... slept with her?" His voice was nearly inaudible, his eyes on the carpet, his hands crossed.

"I think that's all they did toward the end," Duke also whispered. "They slept and slept and slept in one another's arms. They would be sleeping there now for all I know if he hadn't put on a uniform."

To Duke's consternation, his pupil had quietly put his head on his shoulder as if he had decided to take a nap there.

Freeing himself from this embrace, the tutor cried, "Why do you cross-examine me like this?" He went over to his desk and plumped down in front of it. "At this god-awful hour to boot! Wanting me to tell you who your brother slept with, when the poor bastard is lying buried over there in that hellhole!"

"He's not lying anywhere," Duane said in a clarion voice.

"He's not?" Duke's eyes kindled fearfully. Then, almost sweetly, "Well, where then?"

"They're not buried." Duane looked directly at Duke's lips, avoiding his eyes. "There was nothing to bury but maybe a dog tag and some scraps of clothes. They couldn't bury what they couldn't find, and there was nothing left to find." Looking into the tutor's eyes now, he went on, "That's why they're out. I've read about it in books. The unburied are out. But I don't know why they call on me. They never cared for me in life. Not like they cared, according to you, for her." He waved his hand at the photographs. "They should pay their visits to her."

Duke La Roche had lit two cigarettes almost simultaneously and he would puff now on one, then another as he sat hearing all this.

"So you love this woman too, La Roche?" Duane spoke with folded arms and hollow voice.

"Yes, judge, I do. Your honor, I'm guilty," he scoffed.

"Because Justin loved her, you do? Is that it?"

Duke shook his head and was about to say, *"You are one hell of a sick boy, aren't you?"* but he guessed the expression on his face must have conveyed what he thought to the pupil.

"I've loved Estelle Dumont for years," Duke testified.

"Shall I tell her that at the party?" Duane inquired patiently.

"It was me introduced them." Duke's attention was far away. "Put them in touch, pushed them into one another's arms. That's why she put up with me at all. She knew I would bring him to her. She was too high and mighty to go out to meet the men she wanted. They had to be brought. I was, in his case, a bringer."

The boy volunteered his complete cooperation. "I'll tell her anything you want me to tell her. Leastways I want to make up for the pain I've caused you."

"Where did you pick up that expression?" Duke came out of his fog.

"What expression?"

" 'Leastways.' "

"Oh, I didn't know it was . . . an expression." Duane colored and looked away.

"I suppose you heard it from your cook," Duke sneered.

Duane lowered his head. It seemed to him that Duke had not heard his offer at all, or if he had, he held it in contempt.

"Well, who did you hear it from, then? Why don't you tell me?"

"Why are you making so much of . . . an expression?"

"Don't I teach you? Then I can make as much of it as I want. Where—"

"As a matter of fact"—Duane looked at him worriedly—"I think it was in the pool parlor."

"You're a liar," Duke told him. "Tell me you're a liar. There's only one person around here says 'leastways' and that's *her*. So how did you pick it up then without you must have gone to her?" Duke lapsed into his own country grammar.

"I did go there once, but to tell you the truth I had almost forgot it. I mean"—Duane thought back on that day—"it seemed like I dreamt it and am dreaming it now. But you're wrong about 'leastways,' Duke. I'm surprised at you. That was Justin's word. She must have picked it up from him. That's the only way."

"You leave me out of it when you go to her party, do you hear?" Duke was winding his Swiss watch, though it didn't need winding. "I'll tell her myself in the event she ever summons me again, which, judging by her not inviting me to her party, won't happen. So leave me out, do you hear, if you know what's good for you."

It was three o'clock in the morning when Duane left his tutor. The countryside was covered with a soft, gliding mist which rose against his mouth and eyes as he walked.

Yes, in actuality, Duane knew all about Estelle and Justin, but he had purposely forgotten it, purposely forgotten he had ever gone to her that day, and on purpose told Eugene and Mrs. N. he did not know her.

Back in his room he stared accusingly at the bureau which stood solemnly before him now like a sentinel in need of relief. It was locked in that drawer, what he wanted. And as he unlocked the middle drawer he realized he was his Dad's son, as crazy and crotchety as him, as nuts and as underhanded. For who had taught him, after all, but Eugene, to hide everything in the first place, to hide his secrets, hide himself, hide his memories and feelings and deny anything that ever gave him pause or meant anything deep? He nearly tore the drawer out of the bureau and uncovered a sizable lacquer box decorated with herons and trees and lagoons and a full moon. He opened the box and took out from it an undershirt still stained with blood, and with the initials in thick blue embroidery:

J. C. B.

He moved his fingers over the initials, then slowly brought the cloth to his face and let it rest a moment against his cheek.

"You said 'leastways' all the time, Justin." He spoke to the cloth, or to the ghost, or to time. "I ain't ashamed to say 'leastways' if you did. No woman would know how to say it like you did, anyhow, even if she learned it from you in your arms."

He sat down in Aileen's rocking chair. It was between very late and very early, and from the room down the hall he could hear Eugene snoring. He snored like a horse.

Holding the undershirt, he remembered the afternoon as clearly as if it had just now come to a close. It was only a few days before Justin had been inducted into the Marines, and the older boy had been sharpening all his different knives. It was one of Justin's pastimes which scared Duane, his fondness for keeping all his knives sharpened—his hunting knives, his pen knives, the knife he kept his pencils sharp with—and sometimes in these moods he would step into the kitchen and sharpen all the butcher knives there.

Justin had looked up from his work and given that funny look to Duane.

"If I tell you a secret, will you know how to keep it?"

"You know I will," Duane replied. They both looked at one another as though time was running out for one of them or for both of them.

"I bet," Justin retorted, but without his familiar cocksureness, "you'll blab it the first time my back is turned. I know you."

"Cross my heart," Duane replied, at which Justin's lips curled a bit.

"Can't trust you, Benj," Justin complained. Then in a smothered voice, "Let's go out to the summerhouse."

The summerhouse was the stillest and strangest place one could go to, except for, perhaps, Yoxtheimer's woods. The reason it was so beautiful, if so unsettling, was that Aileen had almost lived in it when she was having her trouble with Eugene. She had left her touch on everything there—the lavish curtains, hand-carved furniture, and costly, thick rugs.

"Fetch those over there." Justin had pointed to a box lying atop a broken wind-up phonograph.

"You mean these?" Duane faltered, picking up a box of thumbtacks.

"I pointed there, didn't I?" was the retort.

Duane followed him dutifully into an adjoining room but, for the first time in his life, was badly frightened in the company of his brother.

Justin slammed and locked all the doors to the little house—side, front, rear—and bolted the basement passageway, then turned almost savagely to Duane.

"I've got to have her, or I'll die," he said.

"Yes."

"What do you say 'yes' for?" Justin inquired. He took a chew of tobacco and offered the plug to Duane, who took a bite also. "Do you know what I go through because I can't be with her?" Justin went on.

He walked up and down the tiny back room of the summerhouse. Then he pulled down the two blinds.

"Don't hurt me," Duane begged.

"Hurt *you?*" Justin turned to him in bewilderment. "I ought to for that remark!"

Just then the thumbtacks fell out of the box from Duane's shaking fingers.

"Pick them up," Justin said without stopping his pacing.

"I know it will work, Duane." Justin stopped his walking and gazed down at the boy gathering up the last of the tacks.

"When I do this to myself, Duane, she will have to acknowledge me, do you hear? I say, do you hear?"

Off came his shirt and off the many-times mended undershirt. Justin always insisted on mending his own clothes; he handled a needle, as Mrs. Newsom had once remarked, in a way which would have put many a housewife to shame.

Then, as meticulously—with his mouth slightly puckered—as it always was when he threaded a needle or bit off a piece of thread, Justin picked up a small hammer and pounded one thumbtack after another into his chest and arms. With each tack inserted, Duane cried out as in some kind of refrain, "Stop! Don't! Don't! Stop!" to which objurgations Justin only smiled and nodded. Some forty tacks protruded from his chest and arms.

"Now take them out of me," he commanded Duane when he had finished, and pressed his back against the fancy wallpaper.

At first Duane did not obey him. Instead he went to an old porcelain chamber pot and vomited.

"Wipe your mouth on this," Justin said coolly, handing him a handkerchief from his back pocket. "Go on," he said patiently as the boy hesitated.

Then, as Justin had once taken a great splinter out of Duane's thumb, the younger boy, his lips still awry from his nausea, now patiently took out, one by one, all the thumbtacks from his brother's chest and arms. It was Justin, however, who wiped his own chest and arms of the blood with his mended undershirt. He walked over to a sink to wring out a bit of the running red, and then, wheeling about suddenly, he said almost into Duane's teeth, "You take this shirt now to Stelle, do you hear? Show it to her, and tell her what I done. . . . Hey, are you listening to me? What are you so pale for? Aren't you my brother? Then don't look so cruddy pale."

Duane turned his face away and nodded many times.

In his memory now, looking at the shirt, he stood almost the next instant in front of Estelle. The undershirt was wrapped in tissue paper, and the tissue paper was in a box which had once contained expensive kid gloves. She unwrapped the "gift" slowly. He admired her from the moment her hand touched the garment, still wet with blood, one thumbtack still attached to the cloth.

He didn't have to explain what it was or meant.

Cautiously, she handed him back the box with the stained garment.

"You keep this for both of us," she muttered, and then she inquired, "Care for a smoke?" handing him one as she asked. He took it but did not light it, holding on with his other hand to the gift box.

"Tell him I'll see him tonight." She smiled. He knew she was pleased with him, for her eyes looked appraisingly, approvingly even, before she went on to say, "But only because he sent you to ask, tell him."

"I can keep the . . . rag?" he asked, pointing to the box.

For a second he was sorry he had said "rag," but he saw then that she liked it. It was also the word Justin would have used, along with "least-ways." He had for a long time kept scribbled over his Caesar vocabulary a list of words which Justin had used, as if Justin had invented and for-ever appropriated to himself all these words. And the worst things he had called Duane, like snot-face and puke-shit, were, as he now touched the stained undergarment in recollection, sweeter than praise from an-other man.

The next day Duane could do nothing but doze over his Latin lesson, his finger over the section concerning the defeat of the Nervii; then, coming awake, his eyes focused on a strange paragraph which he was somehow able to translate from the Latin at sight, and with consider-able comprehension. It had to do with the Gauls' contempt for the Romans because the latter were of such short physique. "I must remem-ber to tell Eugene that Caesar was considered a runt by his enemies," Duane muttered aloud.

Even as he said these words, whether it was the events of the night before or his having had no breakfast (he had got up too late for it, and Mrs. N. was gone), he felt somebody standing over him. The sweat came out on his forehead. He could feel the beads of perspiration rest-ing on the two or three furrows there.

"For God's sake, leave me alone. I'm not up to . . ."

It was Douglas who stood before him, but of the consistency, and even color, of lemon pie. It was a final farewell, Duane understood. He would not stand before him again, or communicate with him in any way until that far-off day in space, perhaps, when all is understood. The wall was closing on Douglas forever.

A pang of remorse came over Duane, for he knew that Douglas was aware that Justin and he were closer, and yet at that moment, Duane's regret for Douglas's death was almost keener than his sorrow that he would never see Justin again in this life. Perhaps that was because Justin was somehow so much more in communion with him than this other brother.

He closed his Caesar with a bang and there was nothing facing him now but the view through the window of the rose of Sharon bush in gorgeous bloom.

Now that fall had begun to show its presence in earnest, the nearby baseball field was crowded with blackbirds creating the infernal din they always do prior to flying south; the trees had begun to turn, especially the maples and oaks; and none of his former classmates were anywhere in sight, all having elected to go ahead to college or to gainful employment, or in some cases, to enlist in the armed forces.

Duane sauntered down Main Street and noted that four out of the five billiard parlors in our town were closed "until further notice." The one that was open, not to mention the four closed ones, had a hard-and-fast rule that no one under the age of eighteen was allowed to enter the premises.

But by reason of the fact his brothers had been such favorites with the owner, who was simply called Colby (no one seemed to know if this was his first or last name), he took the liberty of entering his parlor this morning.

Although Colby's pool parlor was referred to at least by the police as the Stars and Stripes, Colby himself insisted his place had no name—certainly it had none over the door, and it had no telephone number listed in the directory. Its front window had never been washed, the electric ceiling fan had never worked, and there was a huge American flag, which, along with a gigantic eagle, dominated the room. Beer only was served, together with a plate lunch of stale bread and cold cuts.

Colby came into the front of the parlor when he heard footsteps and scowled heavily at Duane, but he finally shook the boy's hand with an iron grasp and his lips ruffled a faint smile.

James Purdy
(138)

"Shoot a few if you like while nobody's here." Colby jerked his head in the direction of the big green table, and the cues along the wall.

"Thought you would be off to school," the pool-parlor owner went on suspiciously. "Ain't you graduated like everybody else?"

Without waiting for an answer, he began sweeping the floor with a heavy broom, revealing a faded blue and red tattoo above his elbow with the name "Louella" and a heart transfixed with an arrow.

"Was sorry to learn of your bad news." Colby stopped sweeping as he said this and, perhaps noticing Duane staring at his tattoo, pulled down his sleeve over it, but as soon as he moved his arm the tattoo was visible again.

At first Duane thought the pool-hall operator was referring to his having failed his senior year, but then the actual meaning of the remark came home.

"Oh, yes," Duane responded. He took up one of the cues from the wall.

Colby looked at him for a while, then went into the adjoining room where the bar was and came back with a glass containing an orange-colored liquid.

Duane took the glass stealthily and stared at the spots surrounding the rim.

"Go ahead, it ain't alcohol."

Duane sipped it, and then, liking its sharp, zesty taste, quaffed all of it.

Colby took the glass from him and set it down on the edge of the billiard table.

For some reason Duane was remembering how he had overheard Eugene talking to himself the other evening, as, pacing and jangling coins in his pocket, of course, he had muttered between his teeth, "If I guaranteed the damned mortgage on the Garfey property, I could, I suppose, invest in that land deal over at Bentwick's. By God, I've got to get my hands on some ready cash."

"See here, Benjy," Colby was saying as he flashed a lighted match under the boy's eyes, and then laughed. "You're a thousand miles away, and you know it. But look here," he went on, blowing out the match and putting its remains in his shirt pocket, "my dad, my two uncles, and three cousins never come back from World War I. So I've been where you are and then some."

Mourners Below

(139)

Duane turned to the billiard table, his hand pressed the cue, and he shot a ball.

"You still don't hold it right," Colby advised. He held the cue for him and adjusted his hand over it.

Duane shot a few more with the cue, using his thumb and fingers as Colby had instructed, while the owner went on back into the room beyond the bar, which must have been where he slept. He could hear Colby rummaging around in some drawers. When he returned, he looked chalky in the face and held something behind his back. Duane put down the cue.

"I was always wondering when you might drop in again, Benjy," he began. "You used to pay us a visit quite often in the days of your two ... pals."

They both looked at one another when Colby said "pals."

"It always pissed off Just that regulations would not allow you to play here too," Colby added after a long wait.

Gradually he brought his two hands forward. They held an envelope. Duane put down the cue, then picking it up, quickly, he replaced it in the rack on the wall.

"I have wondered what to do about this for some time—over a year now." Colby spoke as if he were talking to the envelope he held. "Thought any day you would drop by and I could explain it. Don't like to approach your Dad, you know."

Duane nodded. He had gone deathly pale.

"Then we was closed for violations, you may remember. Shut us up for over a year. But I kept it safe just the same." He tapped the envelope against his fist.

Going up to the wall again, Duane took down the cue and began shooting balls furiously.

"You got some real power for a little guy."

Duane flushed furiously and shot again. All the billiard balls on the table flew about as if under some invisible centrifugal force.

"So if you would relieve me of this letter, I'd thank you for it," Colby said in a booming voice. "I ain't read it."

Duane put down the cue and kept his back to the billiard-parlor owner.

Then he wheeled about and faced Colby. Colby looked uneasily from Duane back to the letter he was still holding in both hands.

James Purdy

"Do you know what the Gauls called Caesar?" he inquired, livid. "A runt. . . . Yet he conquered the world."

Without warning, Duane seized the letter from Colby's hands and looked at it.

"Do you want that I should read it to you?" Colby spoke in a smothered voice.

"God in heaven, no," the boy groaned.

Colby sat down on a stool and took his handkerchief out of his pocket and wiped his forehead.

"It fell out of Just's pocket the last night he was here." Colby kept his gaze on the letter itself. "You know it's his handwriting from the envelope. Them bold capital letters and no crosses on his T's."

Duane nodded.

"As I think I said, I ain't never looked or glanced inside, or read the message. It's still sealed as it was when he dropped it."

Duane nodded again, and stared down at the sawdust on the floor.

"If you won't take it, Duane, shall I hand it over to your Dad then . . . ? *Duane!* Look here! I can't keep this letter; it ain't right now."

He went up close to the boy and put his hands on his shoulder.

"Don't you treat me like this, Benjy. I am your friend."

"Treat you like what?" Duane roused himself.

"Like I was guilty of something toward you."

"Oh, I show that, do I? . . . Well, go ahead, read the letter to me," he ordered him. "Why not? Go ahead, if it amuses you, read it." Duane stirred under Colby's unflinching gaze. "I ain't Eugene. I can admit he's dead, for your information. Go ahead. See if I care he's dead. The police can't arrest you and close your place again for readin' a dead man's letter to his dumb runt of a brother, can they? I won't tell them anyhow."

"You mind how you talk now, Benjy. That ain't proper speech, coming from Just's brother, do you hear? I've always tried to be good to you, and you know it."

Duane caught at Colby's hand, held it tight, then dropped it and looked away.

Colby held the letter at some distance from his eyes like someone soon in need of reading glasses, and then with a quick movement of his forefinger opened the envelope. He took out the paper, unfolded it, brought the letter itself closer to his blinking eyes, his tongue moistened his lips, and he had already said "Dear" in a hoarse grouchy voice when two men carrying a hot-water boiler came into the parlor.

"Tell us where to put it, Colby, on account of we can't hold on to it while you read your mail."

Colby gave Duane a look of torment and pressed letter and envelope into the boy's hands. He motioned for the two men with the boiler to follow him.

For some time, Duane stood holding the letter and envelope, as Colby had at first, some distance from his own unimpaired vision, then, like a thief on the run, sprang out of the pool parlor and raced all the way home.

"What is that paper you're crumpling in your hand?"

Eugene's voice reached him as if from a city block away.

Duane gazed in a kind of reverie at his father.

"You look as if you had run a marathon," Eugene remarked, approaching the boy and looking him over with the same distrustful, aggravated glance with which he cleaned his rifle or took apart the grandfather clock to rid it of dust.

"Your face is streaked with dirt, and you're dripping with perspiration. One would think you were training for . . ."

Duane put the "crumpling" paper in his hip pocket.

"I asked you a question, Duane."

"You've ordered me never to bring up the matter," the boy replied. As he said this, only the whites of his eyes were visible, and his long eyelashes fluttered in a manner which would have struck Eugene as comic had he himself not been so out of humor with his son.

"Here you rush into the house, looking as if you had been working at Knight's Brickyard, reading a suspicious-looking paper, which you now hide from me, and explain it all away to my disadvantage: that I have forbidden you to speak of something or other. As if I were some tyrannical old potentate!"

"Well, you are a very peculiar man. Everybody says so! Everybody can't be wrong!"

"And who is everybody, Benjy? Do you refer to our housekeeper?"

"God, no. She is as close-lipped as you. One can neither tell her anything nor get anything out of her. I guess you muzzled her for keeps when you had the row with her over the Roman religion!"

James Purdy
(142)

"I had no row with Mrs. Newsom!" Eugene defended himself uneasily.

Tightening his blue and gold cravat, and pulling down his sleeves so that his cuff links shone, he inquired, "Was it Mr. La Roche, then, who spoke of me as a tyrant?"

"There's another for you!" Duane cried, his eyes in a noon blaze of indignation. "I wouldn't trust him as far as . . . I can spit!"

Eugene shook his head. "These past few months," he began, "I declare, you are no more the boy you were once than . . ." He paused, for along with his habit of pacing and jingling coins in his pants pockets, Eugene's failure to complete a comparison was well-known to his son, as indeed it was to his fellow lawyers.

". . . Than a rooster is like a buzzard?" Duane finished the sentence for him.

Eugene laughed in spite of himself. "And if I didn't know you better," the father went on, his hands resting briefly on the suspenders under his jacket, "I would think you had something concealed in that envelope you were ashamed of. Tell me at least, will you, where you got it?"

Bringing out the letter from his pocket now and studying its single page as if trying to find in the lines an answer to his father's question, Duane replied, "The *crumpled* paper was handed me by Colby, the proprietor of the Stars and Stripes billiard parlor."

Eugene whistled shrilly.

"Proprietor, my foot," he scoffed, having narrowly missed using another expression which he would not have wanted Duane to hear come from his lips, certainly not now when there was hint of an explosion. "Billiard parlors have no proprietors—those fly-by-night shacks."

"Well . . . some fellows very close to you once thought different."

"Is that so?" Eugene's voice grew syrupy with malice. "Do you mind telling me who thought so well of a billiard-hall operator?" He raised his voice as Duane's countenance grew more and more wrathful and his manner more uncooperative.

"You shan't steal this letter from me as you did the others!" the boy finally vociferated. "It was bad enough you took Aileen's from me. But this is my own letter, and I've hardly had time to glance at it, let alone pore over it."

"I didn't know you were the recipient of such a large correspondence."

Mourners Below

Duane advanced toward his father, holding the letter and envelope before him with his two hands, and as he came forward, Eugene winced slightly.

The boy brandished the letter almost in his father's face.

"I'm forbidden by you to mention his name, so take it and see for yourself. Look to your heart's content, why don't you!"

He pressed Justin's letter into his father's hand

"I don't know how Colby would have in his possession something which evidently I am not supposed to read," Eugene cried, astonished, but his tone, for him, was almost conciliatory, if not downright benign. He stared at the envelope.

"Am I to read it, young man, in your presence?"

"You can suit yourself, sir," Duane replied with stinging impudence.

"And will you deign to keep me company while I do so?"

"If you command it, sir."

"Very well." Eugene gave a half smile. "Consider yourself commanded then."

Duane shielded his eyes with his palm. The terror of what the letter might say overwhelmed him. He felt almost sorry for Eugene, for he knew more than anyone else how ill-prepared his old man was for anything "real," certainly for anything which could not be solved by adding up a column of figures or figuring out a percentage.

The sound of the stationery stirring in his father's hands sounded to him in his agitated state almost as vibrant as the blare of a trumpet.

"My dearest Stelle," Eugene's voice boomed,

> *You can't be ignorant that you were the first to teach me all I know about love and are the same teacher who has now shut the door on such bliss forever.*
>
> *Am I to have to stand outside your door forever waiting for you to change or at least thaw in your coldness to me?*
>
> *I hope someday someone will tamper with your feelings as you have with mine, and subject you to the coldness and finally the exile you have visited on me. I have no shame or pride left. My only wish is to be with you as we were that first long night, forever, but since that is not possible, I am glad I am going to put on Uncle Sam's clothes and go as far away as they can ship me.*

Eugene got through the letter pretty well, speaking in his cold, resonant baritone, pronouncing each phrase as if the import was clear, if

James Purdy

(144)

meaningless, to him, as if the sound and the enunciation were all that were important; but when he came to the signature, he failed to pronounce the name written there, he faltered, he turned his back on his auditor, and Duane thundered out for him, "Signed, Justin."

Had a gunshot rung out at that moment rather than Duane's voice, the effect could hardly have been more pronounced. Eugene bent over double; the paper dropped from his hand. He went, in this stooping position, on into his den, and pulling the sliding doors closed with great effort, he locked himself in.

Duane went over to the spot on the carpet where the letter had fallen and picked it up gingerly as if it were covered with something wet and sticky. He held the page fluttering now from the breeze coming through the open window.

"So let it upset him. Why should he be spared when nobody else is?" the boy said, and slightly bending his knees, holding the fluttering paper like a communicant, he now read the words in a whisper, as if checking to see that his father had got every syllable of it out, and had not, as he had with the signature, omitted a single word.

Shutting himself up in his den, there suddenly came back to Eugene, as leaves will without warning rise from the ground and buffet and sting a hiker when a sudden storm strikes the countryside, the recollection of Aileen's taunts. But more stinging than the leaves that blow against one in a storm, more like bitter hail and wind, her jibes, her constant complaint against him, her exact words echoed again:

"You are afraid of the human body, of its birth, its maturation, and certainly its death. Yes, death is unsavory to you, Eugene Bledsoe, but then so was birth! If I live to be a hundred, I will never forgive you for how you looked at your newborn son as the doctor showed him to you. You shrank from him as I have seen you shrink from looking at the dead in their coffins. You were not meant to deal with the human. . . ."

Eugene bowed his head under this powerful remembrance of Aileen at this moment in his life. Her presence and words were more real to him than had she stood breathing upon the back of his neck, or letting her tears scald his carefully manicured, albeit massive, hands. And all at once, he recalled having heard Duane recently say to his tutor, "Well, my Dad dresses much better than any of us boys ever did. He is the dresser in the family."

The whole room was dancing with carnage and birth and howls of newborn infants and men in their caskets, all the orchestration of this infernal whelp, Duane, and here again Aileen's voice came back to him as he remembered one of the last things she had ever addressed to him, in his lawyer's office: "He has been a thorn in my side since his birth while you lived in the probate court and in litigation. Now let him be one in yours!"

Should he write to Aileen? Should he tell her she had been right? Should he admit in short he had been and was still a fool? The very thought of capitulation terrified him not so much as something which might occur, but as an end to the very idea of the Eugene Bledsoe whom he and the world recognized. For if he admitted to Aileen that he had been wrong, that he could not control Duane, or face the death of his two sons, was there anything pertaining to his life which would not fall? Having admitted, that is, to Aileen (in the imaginary letter, or interview, he was now engaged in) that she was right and that all he had done was pure error, where would his fall end but in total capitulation and impotence? He would sit in his chair in his den and drivel and mouth idiocies. He would finally have to be helped to the toilet and not remember what month or day it was.

No, Aileen had been wrong, for she had believed only in the body and in pleasure. So she had been able to accept all the "facts of nature," which was her phrase, for she talked constantly about "life" in a steady stream from sunup to sundown, and even mumbled to herself while she slept. She had hated his silence, any silence, his thought, his brains, and rather than have a smart man for a husband, she would have preferred a coarse day laborer who would have been able to repair the roof, fix the faucets, climb ladders to the attic, clean out the eaves, and drag home planks from the lumberyard. She loathed his sedentary contemplation. In only one area was she in awe of him: he could shoot a gun better than any other man she had ever met, and in this arena he had forbidden her to impinge on him. His glory as a marksman only reached her from hearsay and whispered asides from his colleagues, and a glimpse of his martial excellence was only once accorded her, very briefly, when she saw a citation given him by the local military reserve.

"They are dead, and there is nothing I can do about it," Eugene finally muttered to himself after the ordeal of Justin's letter. "But I will see Aileen, God damn it, whether the provisions of the divorce forbid me to set eyes on her again or not."

He rolled back the sliding doors, and the sound frightened both

Duane and himself. Duane was sitting as immobile as his father usually sat, the crumpled letter still clutched in his hand.

"Where are you going?" Duane rose from his chair as he said this, for his father looked so beside himself, so desperate, that Duane forgot how angry he was with him.

"I am going to see your mother about you!" Eugene thundered. "I am going to tell her how grief-stricken and utterly at loose ends you are. How ungovernable and underhanded! She must assume her responsibility! How can a mere man know what to do!"

"But you told me the court forbade you to meet," Duane whispered. He had never seen his father so wild. His blue eyes had turned black in hue; his mouth, usually as expressionless as a brass padlock, opened convulsively, letting his white teeth reveal themselves in their immaculate splendor almost for the first time in his son's memory; and his tongue, likewise seldom visible, moved out of his mouth like some threatening weapon.

"I cannot save you!" he cried. "Do you understand?"

"Who ever thought you could?" Duane shouted back at him.

"What? What did you say?" He lunged toward his son with his hand raised, but the ringing of the front door bell aborted any further movement on his part.

Professor Redpath came hurtling into the room and without warning threw a baseball directly at Duane, who caught it with both hands.

"You're drunk again!" Eugene's fury turned on the former ball player. "Would you either tie your necktie or take it off," he went on, turning his full attention now on Redpath. "Well, come on in, why don't you?" He motioned his visitor to accompany him into the next room.

Aileen was considerably surprised to see Professor Redpath coming up the driveway to her home rather early one morning. She had not yet removed all the night cream from her face, and she was occupied with preparing herself a cup of hot lemon juice for a sore throat.

Professor Redpath's appearance could, of course, mean only one thing. Eugene wished to speak with her. The court had forbidden them to see one another except in the presence of a third party, and for some time now Professor Redpath had accepted as one of his many duties the role of the third party in interviews between Aileen and Eugene.

"Miles, what is it?" Aileen was at once frantic, fearing more bad news.

Professor Redpath sauntered into the living room and, going over very close to Aileen, whispered to her his usual inquiry, would she give him a drink and not tell Eugene.

"I asked you a question," she raised her voice. "Are you bringing me more bad news?"

"The only bad news I'm bringing," he replied, "is that Eugene is waiting outside in the car and wonders if you will see him."

Aileen daubed some of the night cream off her face with a tissue. "You'll find some liquor in the little cabinet over there, and a tray of ice cubes in the refrigerator." He made a beeline for the kitchen.

"What is it about, Miles?" Aileen followed him to the refrigerator.

He did not speak until he had mixed himself a drink and was sipping it. "Let me down this quick before I tell him to come in."

"But what does he want to see me about?" she prompted him.

"Your boy."

Aileen raised her eyes to the ceiling. "Let him come in then, for heaven's sake."

As soon as Eugene and Miles Redpath were seated in the front room, Aileen began to cry. She was unable to explain why she lost her control whenever she saw Eugene.

"There's very little I can say or do, Gene," Aileen began after she had wept for a while and the two men looked awkwardly out the front windows. "The court saw fit to give you custody of him. . . . Consequently my hands are tied, I'm afraid."

"Well, Aileen, you certainly put up no fight to keep custody of him, if I remember correctly."

"I had no money to go on with endless lawsuits, and you know it!"

Eugene stared at her. He was astounded that she had grown no older, that indeed she looked considerably more youthful than when she had been his wife. Her yellow hair was untouched by gray, and her throat in its strawberries-and-cream freshness would have complimented a girl of twenty.

"My other sons never plagued me so!" he rebuked her.

Aileen exchanged a glance with Miles Redpath and then said softly, "Gene always loves putting me on the witness stand." She laughed. "I wonder who now bears the brunt of his countless rages and disappointments?" She kept looking at Redpath as she spoke.

James Purdy

(148)

Eugene Bledsoe snorted for reply.

As he sat near the window, with its unflattering light streaming in from the street, she saw that his face had grown considerably more weathered and worn than when they had been married, and his hands had lost some of their rather soft appearance, and despite some hint of home manicuring, the nails were cut or chewed almost to the quick. His hair was rapidly going white. His eyes and his mouth, on the other hand, looked juvenile to her, and, yes, she thought, inconstant.

"I don't think Duane ever loved me," Aileen said with bitter abruptness.

"Did he ever love anybody?" Eugene wondered, straightening the rather savage crease of his new trousers.

"He idolized one person, no question of that," she struck out at him. "You know," she said in a deep, accusing voice, "who I mean."

But somehow, in the presence of this beautiful—if in his eyes disgraceful—woman, he could more easily bear to hear the reference to Justin than in his own house, among his own possessions.

"Well, lay the blame there—why not?—for his carrying on," Eugene said wearily, looked at Professor Redpath for a second, and then, as if disgusted at the baseball player's condition, let his gaze fall to the highly polished surface of his own high black shoes.

"How does he carry on, Gene?" Aileen spoke in a cold and precise manner which actually echoed her former husband's tone.

Eugene silently enumerated, then summarized aloud: "Nurses his grief and doesn't sleep. Falls down the staircase and stays out all night. Tears his bedclothes in two and won't eat. And hounds poor Mrs. Newsom nearly out of her mind!"

"Mrs. Newsom is a very strong lady," Aileen pointed out.

"You wouldn't take him from me, Aileen?" He extended both his hands toward her with an eloquence which even suggested that she might wish to take him back likewise.

"Take him?" Aileen spoke with real heat. "Hear *him!* After you saw to it that I should never have him, and played your cards so well that the judge allows me to visit him only five days a year! You who always preached about the evils of my inconsistency, my changing my mind and general dizziness! I couldn't take him if I wanted to! You and the judge have seen to that!" She now turned her full gaze on Miles Redpath, as if handing over the entire matter to his jurisdiction.

"I can't contradict you," Eugene said in a hollow voice. He shook his head. His concurrence, his spineless acquiescence made her falter and dried up her volubility for a moment.

"If you don't think the courts will hear of it, Eugene, or have the sheriff take me into custody, I could, however, drop over for a talk with Duane ... if you believe it would do him any good, that is."

"I'm sure the courts won't be sending a process server under those conditions," he retorted in a hoarse voice.

He gave Miles Redpath a swift look as he said this, then, raising his eyes nowhere in particular, went on, "He's being tutored at great expense by Professor La Roche." Then he threw in, perhaps in desperation to show he was doing something for the truant in question, "He's going also to a masquerade ball." This abrupt non sequitur brought Duane's mother to galvanic attention.

"Where on earth, and by whom, is a ball being held?" Aileen's eyes had opened wide, and her tone of icy suspicion brought back to him Mrs. Newsom's own lofty infallibility and disapproval with regard to the matter now being broached.

"It seems to be a special invitation, Aileen," Eugene began in an apologetic tone, "from a Mrs. Dumont."

"Mrs. Dumont, is it now?" Aileen gushed and then adjusted the hem of her dress while shaking her head both in amazed horror and pitying contempt.

After waiting in vain for further elucidation from Eugene she went on, "And you mean to sit there and tell me the boy will be allowed to attend!" she cried. "Have you quite lost touch with everything that goes on?" She rose to whisper, "God help us all!"

Rising then, and giving Miles Redpath a lordly nod to get up also, Eugene spoke to Aileen: "He will attend."

Aileen folded her arms solemnly and bowed her head, perhaps indicating an attitude of defeat or perhaps only one of prayer.

"Mrs. Dumont, Mrs. Dumont," Aileen muttered again and again, and going over to a little marble-topped table, took out an extremely long cigarette from a slim Italian glass box and lit it swiftly and malevolently, blowing smoke rings with the facility of a cabaret entertainer.

Eugene had always loathed the practice of smoking by women. Indeed, he had never permitted Aileen to do so in his presence while they had been man and wife.

Turning about to face him, she said, with great whorls of smoke coming out of her nostrils, "If you don't put your foot down now,

Gene, you are in for real trouble which will make all the boy's present carryings-on mere child's play. But after all, he is in *your* custody. The court forbids me actually to say a word. That is, I am deprived of my son while you have carte blanche to send the child to a dissolute, depraved, albeit irresistible, creature like Mrs. Dumont!"

"Dissolute, my eye!" Eugene turned again to Miles Redpath, seeking support from the ex–ball player, but the latter only looked down sheepishly at his somewhat unsteady hands. "The thing I can never get over," Eugene went on, "is how women hate one another." He turned away and snorted to show that the cigarette smoke irritated his respiratory tract.

"Oh, that's prefect rubbish, Gene, and you know it." Aileen laughed. "I have many women friends, which you yourself can attest to. Do you expect me to approve of *all* women"—she went directly up to him, almost invisible to her now by reason of the cloud of heavy tobacco smoke—"even, say, when they are as degraded as she is? Though rich as Croesus, of course, which is no doubt the reason you take her part and apologize for her so eloquently!"

"I take her part? I don't recall ever meeting the woman!"

"*Hardly!*" Aileen sneered, and turned away from him in sly triumph.

"I do know," he said weakly, "that Mrs. Dumont comes of a long line of distinguished forebears."

"One could say the same of many famous criminals."

"Whatever you and I may think, Aileen," Eugene began, and then took his hat in both hands to indicate that he was bringing his visit to a close, "I don't see how Duane can back out now. The invitation has been accepted, I believe, and he will go unless you can think up a better excuse than your vague insinuations about his hostess."

"Vague!" Aileen slapped her cigarette case down on the mantelpiece. "You never fail to amaze me with your utter contempt for facts."

He made a sudden movement with his lips. His eyes had a very strange glint in them at that moment, and then he merely turned away from her and put his hand on the knob of the door.

Professor Redpath sprang after his friend with the alacrity of a bodyguard who fears his charge faces danger, and the two men then made their departure after a few cursory good-byes and a nearly inaudible thank you from the former baseball player.

"Tell Duane I will be paying him a visit very shortly," Aileen called after the departing pair. "I will telephone him from the hotel before-

Mourners Below

hand," she went on, "unless, of course, the court meanwhile issues a staying order against our reunion!"

She waited on the porch until they were out of earshot.

"Did the sky ever look down on a bigger pair of fools than those two!" she said before going back into the house.

When Eugene returned from his visit to Aileen, he was already in a state of eruption, but his anger had not yet found a satisfactory target in the environs of his den. Duane was absent, and Mrs. Newsom was busy baking bread and cutting pie dough. Eugene paced from his den to the front parlor, finally going over to the great grandfather's chair in which Duane usually sat while poring over his Caesar. His eye fell on a pile of books. At first he paid them no particular attention; perhaps he even felt mollified by the fact that his son was getting less indolent and "illiterate." A glance at a single title, however, brought him to uneasy attention: *The Home Life of Borneo Headhunters*. He picked up the musty volume, its spine broken but its print and paper still almost mint fresh. He turned a page or two, then closed the book quickly, an expression of disgust on his mouth. A second volume lay near the one he had just opened: *Dispersal of the Dead Among the Andamanese*. This volume, also very old, gave out a kind of powdery flux over his hands, descending onto his new trousers, but before putting it down he read a few pages which were, in his opinion, in even worse taste than the first book he had glanced at. A pamphlet, *Circumcision Among the Dwarf Tribes of the Gaboon,* and the tomes *The Harvest Cock in Picardy* and *Savage Childhood* gave conclusive proof, he felt, that it was what Duane read which had brought him to the brink of insanity.

He summoned Mrs. Newsom, who emerged covered with flour, but with a look of such forbidding self-possession and dignity that Eugene could for a moment think of no way to catalogue his discontent.

"Have you seen this *bilge* he has been perusing?" he said at last.

Mrs. Newsom's eye took in only *The Home Life of Borneo Headhunters.* Bridling, she acknowledged that she had looked through this volume.

"You mean you actually spent your very valuable time in the company of such a book?" Eugene's rage now broke loose, and his usual baritone voice climbed to that of a tenor, almost a countertenor, so that Mrs. Newsom felt for a moment that another person had entered the room and was giving vent to this outburst.

Then his pacing began, his jingling of half-dollar pieces in his pocket, his sniffling, and his clearing of his throat, but Mrs. Newsom, whose self-confidence about—indeed, indifference to—what he might have in store for her had increased steadily, told him she could no longer leave her pastry untended in the kitchen.

"You can rest assured, however"—she shot a glance now at all the ancient volumes arranged in moldering piles—"that the books are not Duane's property. Furthermore, I doubt he has carefully read any of them, Mr. Bledsoe. The books belong to Professor La Roche," she concluded.

"They are enough to distemper a dog!" Mr. Bledsoe thundered when he was left alone in the sitting room.

Sitting down heavily in Duane's chair, he leafed through one after another of the tomes, all of which had the bold proof of ownership, he now saw, in a bookplate with the illustration of a naked nymph dripping from her bath in a forest stream, over which blazoned in bold Gothic letters:

EDWARD DUKE LA ROCHE

PART IV

"The one thing I cannot bear, Richard, is being crossed."

Estelle Dumont spoke these words in the attic of her forty-room house to her dressmaker, Richard Flodman, who since being released from prison two years before on a sentence for attempted murder (he came recommended to her by Father Mellors of St. Michael's Church) had with indefatigable energy and concentration made nearly one hundred gowns of every style, material, and variety, and in the bargain, had listened to almost every sorrow and disappointment his employer had experienced in her twenty-seven years.

Richard's handsome, swarthy face was framed by tight ringlets of hair. His astonishing eyes, light blue, shone out of his dark face like those of a forest beast. Had she thought about such things she might

Mourners Below

have remembered the whispers of his having Portuguese and African blood.

Richard studied the transparent muslin dress Estelle wore, cut too short for his taste, but whose faded blue color enhanced her ash-blond hair and luminous green eyes.

Lately, Richard had been treated to more hours on the subject of her present chagrin than to any other: the fact that her invitation to Duane Bledsoe to attend her masquerade ball had received no acknowledgment or reply.

"They must have got the invitation by now, don't you think?" Estelle would cry again and again, and Richard would nod and grin mischievous encouragement.

"Then why don't I hear?" she erupted. "When they must know the party is in effect some kind of tribute to Justin's and Douglas's sacrifice! It is my way of commemoration, at any rate, Richard—say what you will.... Do you know, by the by, old Eugene Bledsoe refused the mayor's offer to have a public ceremony in honor of his two sons' heroic deaths? Yes, old Eugene gave a categorical *no* to the mayor!"

The remarkable beauty of the new dress being made for her, however, quieted her rage over the unanswered invitation and her remembered sorrow of the two soldiers' deaths. She looked at herself in the ceiling-high mirror.

"You could not have learned to sew this well just in prison, Richard!" She turned about to face him with an almost childlike expression of thanks.

"I think I've told you fifty times where I learned to sew," he intoned sulkily.

Richard had spoken to her several, if not a hundred, times of how his mother, grandmother, and great-grandmother had all been seamstresses of great skill and fame in this community, that they had more work than they could handle, and that he had been given needle and thread when only a little boy of five, and finally, that under their tutelage and encouragement he had when only in the second grade made an entire dress in his secret moments and then presented it to the astonished matriarchs. From then on, he had spent all his idle hours sewing by their side. He had, in fact, made a dress for his great-grandmother's funeral, which his mother and grandmother were not ashamed to let her be buried in.

Thus Richard, in the wake and to the tune of her despair over the unanswered invitation, never tired of repeating the story of how he had learned to sew, which Estelle, falling into his mood, would pretend she had forgotten, all the while repeating as in a chorus, "I knew you could not have learned it all in prison!"

"To be treated to this kind of contempt!" Estelle, having heard yet again the history of his learning to sew, went back to the unanswered invitation. "Who does Eugene Bledsoe think he is, I ask you! And where does that little beggar Duane think he gets off?"

"Why do you need him for your party?" Richard asked gloomily, his words nearly unintelligible owing to all the pins he had in his mouth as, kneeling down before Estelle now, he went on working on the hem of her dress.

"Because this party is my way of remembering his two brothers," she patiently explained. "If Duane doesn't attend, well, the whole thing will be meaningless to me—and to everybody else. Why can't you see that?

"But true, their ignoring the invitation doesn't come as a complete surprise to me either," Estelle went on fulminating. "When Justin was practically living here, at the beginning of our . . . close affair, you see, and we couldn't get enough of one another, why even then he refused to take me to his home and introduce me to his father and his youngest brother. No matter how many times I begged him, he always said, 'Not quite yet. I've got to prepare them, you see.' Even after the day he said he was going to marry me, he stalled about taking me to his house. At last, one day when we had lain together in one another's arms in this very attic for twenty-four hours without budging, I told him, 'At least let me come to your place when your ogre father is absent. I want to see and touch the rooms where the only man I ever loved was born and has spent most of his days.'

"Black silence on that request, too," Estelle added, after a pause which was followed by a burst of muffled laughter.

"Come now, Justin Bledsoe wasn't the only man you ever loved," Richard Flodman scoffed, now standing back at least six feet from her and inspecting the dress he had just completed.

"But that is exactly what I told him that day," she said, suddenly going pale. "He was the only one! And I think it would be what I would tell him if he came through that door right now." She sat down and looked indifferently at the veins in her wrist.

"Why shouldn't you just go to the Bledsoe house then and ask them if they received the invitation," Richard said in bilious sarcasm, "if you were his betrothed!" And he snickered.

She turned to look him full in the face.

"Go where I wasn't permitted even in my good days!" She smiled craftily, however, after her initial surprise at the idea.

"I could go for you."

"You, Richard! You? My God!"

"We could go together. . . ."

"Come here, Richard." Estelle spoke in silky, almost inaudible tones. "Let me see the fingers of my magic dressmaker. . . . Come on, don't be that way."

He came clumsily over to where she sat.

"Spread them out," she commanded.

He held his hands out to her like a culprit before his arresting officer.

"So strong"—she caressed his fingers and brought them to her lips—"so sensitive and mobile, like long wire grass in the wind. I am quite in awe of your fingers. Tell me, your grandmothers and your mother, weren't they in awe too . . . ?"

"They certainly wondered at me," Richard confided quietly.

Something in his voice made her go cold.

"They were afraid for me though, I guess, afraid for what was in store," he mumbled.

"I will see you have nothing to fear." Estelle spoke almost as softly as he now, and she kissed, almost nibbled his fingers. "If you stay with me! And if you go with me to the cursed Bledsoes, will you? Let's make our appearance together! Your idea is a splendid one."

She abruptly leaped up and began dancing around the room. He fell to the burgundy carpet and watched her with grudging amusement, grinning and kissing his own hands where she had kissed them before.

"All right!" he exclaimed with affected gaiety. "I will go and ask for an explanation from them, either with you or by myself. We will find out, Estelle, about the invitation, one way or another."

"Of course we will." She spoke sleepily. "And the sooner the better, Richard. We'll go together to the Bledsoes, arm in arm, we will, and demand to know the reason why. After all, my family goes back as far as theirs."

"And what about mine?" Richard suddenly raised his voice at her.

"What about yours?" She turned to him, a slight smirk on her lips.

"You with the money and the houses and the landaus," he began,

James Purdy

(160)

flecks of spittle coming out on his deep ruby lips, "I could tell you things, Estelle Dumont, except you never ask. I could tell Bledsoe where my folks come from and how far back. . . . I have a book from my great-grandmother. . . ."

"Look at your hands, Richard," Estelle said in a low voice. "How they're clenched and flailing. . . . For God's sake!"

"You look at them," Richard shouted. "I've looked at them since I was five years old."

Then going directly up to her and pulling her toward him, he said, "My family goes back the furthest of any of yours, and I want you to think of that while I work for you, Estelle. Hear? I'm the oldest of any of you. I go back and back and back—to the forests and the time before a gun was fired."

"Don't hold me so tight, dearest." Estelle wrenched loose from him.

"That's why I'm not afraid to go call on old Bledsoe, Stelle. Do you hear?"

"I'm glad you're such a soldier," she said in chidden tones, "because I'll tell you the truth. He scares the life out of me . . . Eugene Bledsoe," she cried out to the question in his eyes. "I can admit I'm afraid even if some people can't."

"Your damned digs and innuendoes," Richard sneered. "As if I wasn't afraid at every breath I draw! Look here"—he took her face in his hands—"we'll get the answer about your invitation, and then whatever they say at the Bledsoes, we'll have your masquerade ball or shindig or whatever you call it anyhow." He kissed her impudently on the lips.

The next morning the car and chauffeur were already waiting in front of Estelle Dumont's house (the chauffeur lived all by himself in a small cottage directly behind the barn where the masquerade ball was to be held). Richard was dressed in an Oxford dark suit, with a thick wide blue cravat which matched his eyes. When Estelle came down the staircase, she called to him as if she were addressing a postman who was bringing her a special-delivery letter, "Tell Mr. Bledsoe that I regret I cannot come myself this morning." (She had sent him a telegram the night before informing him of her impending arrival.)

"What do you mean, can't come?" The smoldering anger suddenly broke out.

"That I am ill," she said, as if rehearsing the text of another telegram which she was about to send, "but that my trusted messenger, Mr.

Flodman, will convey to him my worries and concern. Whereupon you will broach the subject of the unanswered invitation."

"And what if I disgrace myself and you when I speak to him?" Richard said.

She turned, but then gave him only a sidelong glance. He had become suddenly quite formidable, and it was not just because of the Oxford suit.

"I thought we were already disgraced in any case," she replied.

She sat down on a tiny divan, and brought both her spike heels tightly together.

"I cannot face him, Richard. Go or stay. If you stay though, I must send another telegram."

"I'll *go*," he said, and went racing down the front steps, spoke to the chauffeur as if he were commanding him to shoot someone, was admitted into the car, and the door was closed on him by the driver. A moment later, the car and its occupants had disappeared, leaving behind a cloud of small proportions and blue tinge.

"For God's sake, he *has* gone!" Estelle cried and burst into angry tears.

Eugene Bledsoe recognized Richard Flodman immediately. After all, Richard had grown up in the community, and his having shot a young man in a roller-skating rink had created a good deal of notoriety. As a matter of fact, Mr. Bledsoe had even attended the short trial in which Richard had pleaded guilty to manslaughter and was sentenced to one year in the penitentiary. His year of confinement had made less impression on him, however, Mr. Bledsoe was inclined to bet, than his stint of service with Mrs. Dumont.

For a moment after Richard summoned Eugene to the door by ringing the eloquent bell situated under the green mailbox, both men froze, but it was Richard who first spoke, in an icy, "How do you do, Mr. Bledsoe. I have a message from Mrs. Dumont."

Had he employed a megaphone his voice could not have carried farther. It reached Mrs. Newsom, who was just taking a pan of Parker House rolls out of the oven. The smell of the fresh bread had almost immediately drifted out to the two interlocutors.

"Come in then, Richard." Mr. Bledsoe opened the door.

On passing into the living room, the dressmaker wheeled about suddenly, like a bird which has unaccountably made the mistake of flying into a room that has no exit.

"Take a seat, why don't you?" Mr. Bledsoe indicated Duane's big study chair. "Go on," he urged as the young man hesitated. "Please sit."

"It won't take long," Richard replied, his bravado now beginning to break down, and he backed into Duane's chair.

"I only just now received Mrs. Dumont's telegram that she and you were coming to see me," Eugene went on, and he took a yellow envelope from his breast pocket.

"To tell you the truth," Richard babbled, "Mrs. Dumont is rather afraid to meet with you."

"You don't say." Mr. Bledsoe smiled faintly and crossed his legs.

"I don't think she thought I would come either, but the matter has to be settled."

To Mr. Bledsoe's relief, if not approval, Mrs. Newsom now stepped into the living room. "Would you and your guest," she inquired, "like some refreshment?"

"Richard is alone this morning," Eugene told the housekeeper, "but I am sure he could partake of something, can't you, sir?"

Richard raised his head and nodded.

Mr. Bledsoe closed his eyes heavily for a moment, as if to sniff with more concentration the aroma of the freshly baked rolls, and then abruptly gave the old housekeepeer a nod to bring in the refreshment.

"I have tried to imagine," Eugene went on, "what is so pressing about her wish to see me," and he looked again at the telegram.

"Oh, it's fairly simple," Richard assured him. "But you do remember who I am?" the young man inquired.

"Perfectly." Eugene lowered his head. "Of course I do."

Richard sighed and lay back in his chair.

Mrs. Newsom now entered with a tray of tea, Parker House rolls, homemade peach preserves, and the usual fresh linen napkins.

Richard helped himself almost greedily and soon sank his teeth into the hot bread; the color was restored to his dark cheeks, and he smiled a little.

Mr. Bledsoe also attacked the rolls with unflagging appetite, and the two men chewed rather loudly together while Mrs. Newsom looked on, gratified and almost smug.

"What, may I ask, Richard, are your duties at Mrs. Dumont's?" Eugene said after they had masticated the rolls and jam, and he picked some crumbs off his severely pressed trousers.

"Dressmaker," Richard replied.

"I beg your pardon?" the older man inquired cheerfully.

"I make and mend her dresses. Her wardrobe."

"I see." Mr. Bledsoe spoke gingerly, and gave the impression, although still seated, that he was about to leave the room.

"I had always sewn some at home," Richard went on, nodding to Mrs. Newsom who without being asked had sat down in the far corner of the room—much in fact to Mr. Bledsoe's relief, if not his complete approval.

"I knew your mother and grandmother very well," the housekeeper commented.

Richard bowed his thanks. "So that," the dressmaker went on, "when they wanted to find some sort of work for me in prison, they set me to sewing there also. So sewing is I reckon what I do best."

"Good," Mr. Bledsoe said, but more with an inflection of dismay in his voice than of congratulation.

"Mrs. Dumont is a very high-strung woman, of course," Richard went on, drinking some tea. "Do you by chance have a bit more cream?" He turned to Mrs. Newsom.

"To be sure!" she cried and rushed out to the dining room, where she had left a small pitcher of thick cream, and rushed on back in soon to pour some into his cup.

Having thanked her, Richard continued, "Seldom does a day pass that we do not have an altercation."

Both Mrs. Newsom and Mr. Bledsoe seemed to find this very satisfying, and both laughed heartily.

"But because she is so high-strung, she felt she could not come today."

Mr. Bledsoe's smile, as well as that of Mrs. Newsom's, faded upon hearing this, and they looked grave while managing to encourage their visitor to expatiate.

"So I have brought you her message myself."

Mr. Bledsoe beamed and his lips formed the word "fine."

"He is absolutely to come," Richard said in a voice almost as hearty and loud as a cheerleader's.

"*He* is?" Mr. Bledsoe fumbled and looked toward Mrs. Newsom.

James Purdy

(164)

"Duane! Duane."

Neither Mrs. Newsom nor Eugene, however, gave him any helping hand here.

"The invitation, Mr. Bledsoe. Mrs. Dumont's invitation to your son Duane . . . unanswered these last three weeks!"

"Oh, the invitation, of course!" Mr. Bledsoe said, as Richard scowled heavily, looking from the old housekeeper to the father and then back again. A suspicion crossed his mind that both were in the early stages of deafness, if not senility.

"It was received, was it not?"

Mr. Bledsoe now turned his full gaze toward Mrs. Newsom. Eugene would be grateful to Mrs. Newsom for the rest of his life for her having seated herself without permission in the room. He now, in effect, turned over to her the entire business of Richard Flodman, Estelle Dumont, and Duane Bledsoe.

"Of course." Mrs. Newsom drew her chair closer to Richard.

"And is Duane coming or isn't he?" Richard spoke with a kind of hush in his voice now, for his suspicion that these old persons were far from responsible had not yet been dispelled.

"Estelle—Mrs. Dumont, that is—has been in quite a temper about it. You, as lifelong residents of this community, know that she has rages. Of course you do. The entire ball is to commemorate . . . your two brave boys. That is why Duane's presence is so essential. And why the invitation, being unanswered you see . . . irked her so tremendously."

"We have had no end of trouble thinking up what he is to wear." Mrs. Newsom now came forward with an explanation of the delay. "Until we had quite decided that, you see, we have procrastinated on replying to Mrs. Dumont's invitation."

"But, you see, she must know . . . *today*," he said with a peremptoriness, even a belligerence, which, however, did not seem to upset the old people.

Mr. Bledsoe nodded and cleared his throat. "As a matter of fact," he said, and rose, "I have the invitation somewhere about, and if you will allow me, I will write the acceptance now and hand it back to you."

Rummaging about among some papers he had left lying on a huge deal table, Eugene soon came up with the nearly forgotten, certainly mislaid, invitation, seized it with the firmness and distrust he might have shown to something alive and wriggling, and quickly wrote a few words across its face and signed his name.

"There!" he almost bellowed, and gave the document to Richard Flodman, who placed it immediately in his breast pocket. Then, picking up his cup of tea, Eugene was saying, "I am sure Mrs. Dumont will be more than delighted and relieved to have this matter straightened out at long last," when suddenly the dressmaker's gaze was directed to the front door, which was being swung open with a flourish. He dropped his teacup, which fell and broke into countless pieces as it hit the somewhat threadbare Persian carpet.

"Indeed, Mrs. Dumont *will* be delighted and marvelously relieved, Richard!" A strident contralto voice rushed from the threshold and went echoing throughout the entire downstairs.

Astonished, Eugene and Mrs. Newsom turned their heads to take in the spectacle of Estelle Dumont, now dressed entirely in shimmering white silk, advancing toward them, carrying a huge bouquet of roses in her arms.

"Wherever there is an important or delicate mission to be accomplished, my great-aunt Lou always told me," Mrs. Dumont continued speaking (but now in a slightly lower but perhaps more vibrant voice), "go accomplish that mission in person!" She immediately thrust the bouquet of flowers into Mrs. Newsom's arms. "In any case," the visitor went on, turning now to Mr. Bledsoe as she removed her long white gloves, "I have decided it was not fair to put all the burden on Richard here as a spokesman or intermediary for me, however adept he is. But the truth is, I could not wait a minute longer! My patience, you know, has vanished! I had to have an answer to my invitation at once! I could not wait even a split second longer. So I summoned the livery to fetch me. And here I am!"

Eugene came out of his stupefaction, offered the best chair in the house to the guest, and choked out unintelligibly, "Mrs. Dumont, make yourself comfortable."

"Thank God formal introductions are not in order," she almost cooed, and took Mr. Bledsoe's hand in hers, at which point Eugene's head tilted forward slightly, as if, were he not careful, he might perhaps fall to his knees before her. For although, as Aileen had always claimed, he was always a pushover for a pretty face, he was not at all prepared for the dazzling magnificence of the visitor before him, with her fresh good looks, her jewels, her picture-book gown, and her bouquet of roses. And the sudden appearance of Justin's "sweetheart" brought to him a hundred confused thoughts and remembrances, which, racing through his

James Purdy
(166)

brain, gave him the sensation that somebody had put something in his tea, or that he was about to have a stroke. At any rate, he was blank before her grandeur, and turned a furious beet red.

Dropping Eugene's hand, after giving it a kind of wrench, Estelle cautiously but perhaps menacingly turned her attention toward Richard, and she studied him like a prosecuting attorney about to begin cross-examination.

"I am not here to undercut my messenger," she began. "Richard is an obedient boy." She now drew everybody's attention to the dressmaker. "A trustworthy, an obedient boy. But I often fancy that he has a grudge against me, Mr. Bledsoe. He feels that owing to his wonderful skill as a fashion designer, he has made me grander than my native endowments meant for me to be! You knew he was a dressmaker?" She stared at Mr. Bledsoe's expression of bemused wonder. "No finer in the land, I can assure you," and she frowned at Richard.

"Mr. Bledsoe knows all about me, Estelle." Richard spoke softly but put a warning note in his voice.

"As I said a moment ago," the visitor interrupted him, "I cannot wait a minute longer, messenger or no messenger! I have to have an answer to my invitation at once. And the thought kept coming to me, what if through some slip of the tongue, or other indiscretion, my dressmaker should say something—inadvertently, of course—which might queer the whole thing with Mr. Bledsoe! After all, we have never been formally introduced, and you don't know me from Adam!"

"I can assure you, Mrs. Dumont . . ." Eugene began, greatly flustered, and it was clear to Richard and Mrs. Newsom that Mr. Bledsoe was going out of his way to be affable and conciliatory. "I can positively put your mind to rest that nobody here has said a thing which could prejudice you or your invitation."

Mr. Bledsoe looked Mrs. Dumont full in the face, but was somewhat astonished to observe that instead of paying attention to what he was saying, she was looking eagerly and with undivided attention at the little sideboard on which Mrs. Newsom had deposited a second plate of Parker House rolls.

"May I, my dear?" Estelle asked Mrs. Newsom (who had just finished sweeping up the remains of the broken teacup) and then turning back to Eugene said, "Please continue with what you were saying, but I suddenly feel quite famished." She took one of the still-hot rolls in her mouth and ate the whole thing very rapidly, letting out little exclama-

Mourners Below

tions of delight, licking her fingers, and finally cried, "Perfectly delicious! Uncommonly marvelous!"

"If Mrs. Dumont had stayed home, where she belongs"—Richard's deep baritone voice now broke into his employer's ecstasy over hot bread—"I would have brought her the invitation signed, accepted, sealed, and finalized, with Duane's presence vouched for. But she *would* have to make an entrance, and in fact, I think she has planned the whole thing this way. Of course, I am left looking like a fool, a role I am not unused to playing." As he finished he put both his feet down with a loud *thump*.

Everyone was too thunderstruck to say anything, except Estelle, who went on chewing so loudly that these sounds almost gave the impression that this was how she meant to reply to her dressmaker's statement.

He continued: "She has not only made me look like a fool as a messenger, she has cast doubt on my ability as a tailor by appearing here in a dress which I have not finished, and which is in the worst possible taste for this morning occasion. She is furthermore"—he looked at Estelle balefully—"laden with jewels which do not suit her gown. She is, in short, a fright. I apologize for her to you all."

"Do you see what I have to put up with, Mr. Bledsoe?" Mrs. Dumont appealed to Duane's father after a lengthy pause during which she gulped down the last of the Parker House rolls. "And the rest of my servants are just as impudent and impertinent as Richard here."

"I am not one of Mrs. Dumont's servants!" Richard fairly shouted.

"You are not?" Estelle spoke in a nearly inaudible, scornful voice.

"I am not only not one of her servants, but if the truth were told, I am more like her actual husband. Even in the eyes of the law. But whatever my legal position may be," he went on in the heavy silence which had taken possession of the room, "my occupation is that of a true artist in cloth, and nobody but a vulgar upstart would associate me with the role of servant, servingman, or paid messenger!"

"Now, now, Richard, is that any way to talk to a pretty woman?" Mr. Bledsoe's bass now rose as the final words of the dressmaker died away. But to everyone's astonishment—especially to Mrs. Newsom's—Duane's father gave every indication of enjoying the altercation in progress, with its roster of accusations and general opprobrium. At least his voice at that moment was most jovial and good-humored.

"And here is the document you could not wait another second to have a reply to," Richard began immediately Mr. Bledsoe stopped speaking. He had taken out the invitation to the masquerade ball from his breast pocket. "Here is your heart's desire." He flourished the thick paper before all their eyes like a magician about to perform a feat of sleight of hand. "You spoiled, rude, insensitive, very vulgar dame, you! You frump, in fact!"

And Richard tore the invitation to bits and pieces and threw them in the general direction of Estelle Dumont.

Both Mr. Bledsoe and Mrs. Newsom made sounds of shocked amazement, but Mr. Bledsoe's countenance was still wreathed in an expression of merriment.

"Oh, I am used to such scenes," Estelle apologized to Eugene and the housekeeper. As a matter of fact, Richard's employer spoke with a certain kind of tolerant amusement at this point. "Yes," she sighed, "I am used to being abused by husbands, lovers, and permanent or present houseguests." Before she had quite finished saying this, Estelle bent down and with perfect equanimity began picking up the shreds of the torn invitation.

"Here, let me help you, my dear." Eugene comforted her and stooped down and also began gathering up shreds and bits.

"Please do not bother, Mr. Bledsoe. Let me reap the fruit of my own folly. Besides, it always gives Richard such pleasure to see me on my hands and knees. Furthermore, if you can endure his rudeness under your own roof, who am I to complain about it, after all?"

As they were gathering up the torn pieces of paper, Estelle and Eugene's heads nearly bumped together, and for a moment each exchanged with the other a long meaningful look, which was not wasted on either Mrs. Newsom or Richard Flodman. It was crystal clear to them then, if it had not been before, that Mrs. Dumont had won Eugene over to her side.

Everyone now rose as if a gong had sounded announcing the end of a session of some kind.

And everyone looked toward Estelle, who occupied at that moment the center of this small circle. Looking down at the scraps of paper, she inquired of no one in particular, "Is my invitation, then, to your son accepted, may I inquire?"

"I don't see how you can doubt it, after our very pleasant, if all-too-brief, meeting, my dear." Mr. Bledsoe spoke in strong, booming, almost indignant tones, and he flashed a quick look at Richard Flodman.

Mourners Below

"Duane will most certainly attend. You can lay all doubts to rest on that score."

"Then despite our little moment of drama"—Estelle looked down at the scraps of paper—"my intervention has after all been a success!" Then she laughed so shrilly that everybody, even Richard, looked taken aback.

"But I cannot take leave of you, dear Eugene—may I be allowed to call you by your Christian name?—I cannot walk out of this house leaving you to think badly of this young man here," and she moved her head in the direction of Richard. "We must be understanding and patient with him not only by reason of his great talent, for no one sews as he does, dear Eugene, but also because he has been corrupted to no small degree by enforced imprisonment with common convicts. I wonder if we would behave any better had we been so treated." She now went over to embrace Mrs. Newsom, who did not appear greatly honored by this expression of affection.

Then she swiftly took Richard's hand in hers, kissed it effusively, and indicated she was ready to depart.

A moment later, as if overcome perhaps by her own strong feelings, and, as a last gesture, Estelle ventured to kiss Eugene almost fiercely on the mouth.

"I will always be grateful for this," she cried, holding in her free hand the torn pieces of invitation. "It makes my commemoration jamboree a reality and a certain triumph, generous understanding man that you are!"

The chauffeur was already opening the street door for her and Richard, as Estelle waved one farewell after another to Eugene and Mrs. Newsom, so that one would have thought she was taking leave now and forever of her own kith and kin.

Richard, accepting her arm like a man who has just been released from a hospital after a serious illness, was reduced to utter silence and near immobility, but in another moment she had hurried away with the dressmaker to their seats in the limousine, and then almost as instantaneously they were whisked out of sight of the Bledsoe house.

"Mortified! Mortified! Mortified!" Estelle kept repeating the word all the way back to her mansion. "Only my own self-possession, poise, and the training given me by my maternal grandmother allowed me to retain my dignity in front of that ogre! What other woman could have walked out of there with her head up, I ask you! Being disgraced in front of Bledsoe by you, Richard! God, God, I will never forgive you for it if I live to be a thousand!"

"A thousand, piffle!" the dressmaker scoffed. "You will *never* die."

"After all I've done for you," she went on sniveling. "Taken you in off the streets, made a home for you, given you of my attention and encouragement in lavish amount and in lavish surroundings.... And to have you mouth those insults in front of Eugene Bledsoe! Telling him you were my husband! Tearing my invitation to bits!"

"That is truer than your telling him I was your servant!" the dressmaker fulminated, choking with real rage. "I am nobody's servant, and won't never be! Do you hear me, you gilded bitch?" He abruptly seized her hand and painfully brought it to his chest.

"Richard, you are breaking my arm.... For Christ's sake, let go of me!"

"Your arm! Nobody could break any part of you! You're made of cast iron—or who knows?—steel and diamonds. You certainly had enough of the latter on to light up the sky."

"Calling me a frump, though, I think, was the hardest thing I had to bear." She spoke as if she were alone in her bedroom. She began weeping more vociferously, while the dressmaker let out a short loud snort, followed by a coarse and prolonged series of guffaws.

"Look at it this way, love," Richard began, "they're sending the last of the family to what you called back there your jamboree, so you accomplished what you set out to accomplish. Which I could have done just as well alone, but you must have melodrama, your day in court. And old Bledsoe is as big a ham as you are. He should have been an actor! All that posing of his, strutting around like some little English squire, when he's a nobody from back to the Indians! Oh, you're two of a kind! Maybe, come to think of it, you should marry the old man instead of seducing little Duane. Or why not do both? Go ahead and marry the youngest, wear him to ribbons, and then work back to the Dad. You will, probably—mark my words! Yes, sleep with the old man, and go make your way through the entire family."

The limousine came to a sudden halt.

Richard sprang out and helped Estelle, still weeping, out of the car. He then curtly, rather grandly, dismissed the chauffeur. Blinded from her tears, she accepted Richard's arm up the long flight of front steps to the parlor. Seated, their angry glances at one another indicated that their quarrel would continue.

"*You* mortified! *You* disgraced!" Richard began after clearing his husky voice with a few violent coughs. "You couldn't be content, could you, with letting me be your ambassador? No, you had to bolt in like Juno or the Virgin descending on a cloud, make me out as your lickspittle of a servant, incapable of being trusted out of your sight, remind Bledsoe I am a lady's tailor and a criminal to boot, and that you are a noble, magnanimous philanthropist to put up with the likes of me. I should have torn that unfinished gown off you right in front of them, that's what I should have done. Making me look small and nasty and a jailbird while you glowed, the queen of munificence, the benefactress of all who encounter you. And Bledsoe fell for it! That stuffed-shirt no-account little lawyer with his manicured nails is smitten with you!"

"He's taller than you, Richard, if you are going to use the epithet *little!* He's taller than Justin was, for that matter," she added, biting her lip, as if shocked by the thought.

"Then, as I suggested a moment ago, sleep with the Dad, since you've been running through the family!"

To his considerable astonishment, she now burst into what looked like genuine tears and sobs.

"I've planned this party for weeks." She tried to gain control of herself. "And it's all been held up by that beast's refusal to answer my invitation. I was telling the truth in their tacky old parlor! I had to know if there was to be a party in poor Justin's honor or not. The suspense was driving me crazy! You know this as well as I. I came on your heels only because I couldn't wait any longer. Not to make you contemptible and small, I swear it! Oh, Richard, this party means so much to me. Don't ask me why . . . I don't know myself!" she whimpered, sobbing inconsolably.

"So," she attempted to continue, gulping down her sobs, "if I insulted you and made you look mean and abject before Duane's father, I didn't do it on purpose." She looked about desperately for something to dry her eyes on.

"Here, use mine." He extended his large blue workingman's handkerchief.

James Purdy
(172)

At the sight of it, the volume of her weeping increased, but she seized the cloth from him and blew her nose loudly.

"I was brought up, I would have you know," she went on, "by terrible old women who respected nothing but money, and who taught me only company manners. But I didn't go there, Richard, to make you look small! I merely had to know, I had to be sure!"

Richard sat down on a straight-backed chair near her and put his head in his hands. "You always have to undercut me," the dressmaker said in a sepulchral voice. "You never let me receive the credit. I am not even your dressmaker." He removed his hands from his face. "I am your nigger."

"You told them you were my husband," she spoke drily, and her weeping had ceased. "How do you think that made me look? Wonder is he didn't cancel Duane's acceptance of the invitation right then and there. And you talk about humiliation!"

"Ain't I as good-looking as any of the Bledsoes," he shouted. "Stelle, look at me! And don't my family go back just as far?"

"I don't question any of that." Estelle was almost pathetic. "But you risked the invitation again by telling him—and that pious old Catholic woman to boot—that you are sleeping with me!"

"Are you ashamed of my love?" Richard demanded. "Go on, tell me, are you?"

"I didn't say that," Estelle replied, a quaver in her voice. "But to put it so bluntly, so malapropos. Oh, Richard, Richard!"

All at once he knelt down where she was seated and methodically took off her shoes, then fastidiously removed her sheer hose. He kissed her feet in a kind of dizzy rapture.

"Oh, Richard, no, no . . . Not after what we have been through!"

He lifted her skirts and kissed her legs and thighs with famished concentration.

"If I ain't your husband, who is?" he mumbled, pressing his lips and face against her flesh.

"Yes, I suppose," she said wearily. "And after all, we've caught the golden fly!" she almost crowed. "Little Duane is in our net, whether I made a vulgar entrance or not."

Pushing him away from her brusquely, Estelle cried, "But do I look like a frump, Richard? Now be truthful!"

"Yes, yes," he sighed, kissing her legs again, "you looked tawdry and

Mourners Below

(173)

gorgeous, dreadful and luscious, hideously fetching, radiant and god-awful."

"To think you are my husband!" she whimpered under his caresses.

Without warning, he uncovered her petticoat and pulled violently on it.

"Where did you get this undergarment?" he yelled. "This is not anything I ever made or approved for you. Do you hear me?"

She stared down at him with trepidation.

"Oh, what does it matter where it came from, dearest?" She spoke with real fear.

"I *said*"—he faced her with bared teeth—"where did this petticoat come from?"

When she could give no reply, he took the garment in his two hands, holding it as if it were a lever he was about to pull, and said, "When you appointed me here, you told me I was to dress you from the skin out, that you would wear nothing I had not picked out or sewn for you. And here I find this strange thing under your skirts!"

"Richard, I do believe you have taken leave of your senses. Will you let go of me!" Looking down uneasily at his powerful hands, she muttered, "That petticoat belonged to my grandmother."

"Then take it off!" He removed his hands from the article.

"I will not!" she almost spat at him.

"I said remove it, and I mean it."

When she merely stood motionless, he bawled, "I don't like that damned look of defiance on your face!" And he tore the petticoat into two pieces without further ado.

"You should have been a prizefighter, Richard, rather than a lady's tailor. Do you hear me?" she cried, worried at the look of him, for he held the two pieces of satin steadily before him, dazed and driveling.

In another second, he had rushed out of the room still holding her grandmother's torn petticoat in his hands.

"I wonder if there was ever a woman who was so put upon!" she addressed the walls and the high, frowning ceiling. "Men! Goddamn men! All I get done is endure their bravadoes and assaults! No rest for even a minute! Lifelong battle! Oh, my Christ, where will it all end?"

She sat down on a little hand-carved stool and cried her eyes out.

———

James Purdy

(174)

"I wasn't prepared, I must confess, for such an attractive young woman, Mrs. Newsom," Eugene finally commenced, after their visitors had departed. "Nobody had forewarned me she would be so fetching! She is a real ... picture book, if you ask me."

Eugene had noticed the chill that had been coming over Mrs. Newsom ever since Estelle Dumont had set foot in the house. And this chilliness was even more pronounced now that he had begun his encomiums of the young widow. The housekeeper busied herself in redding up the table from the remains of the repast, and then, without a word, she hurried to carry the dishes and soiled linen out to the kitchen.

Without perhaps being quite aware of his need for her approval, Eugene followed her on out to her own undisputed realm, and began, "Mrs. Dumont means well, I'm sure, and she has gone to this great bother of planning what she calls her jamboree." He chuckled on the word.

Under her growing, almost crabbed, silence he got out, "You don't think a mistake is being made, do you?"

"I think you should proceed just as you see fit, Mr. Bledsoe." Mrs. Newsom finally raised her eyes to his. "You must be the judge." She plunged her hands into the hot suds of the dishpan.

"I see," he said. His ebullience suddenly vanished, and he assumed his more customary manner of grouchy superciliousness and vague boredom. "You are in other words not overenthusiastic about Duane's going there."

Mrs. Newsom fetched a deep sigh.

"I thought the whole visit was little less than scandalous, sir, since you ask me." All at once certain recollections flooded her own mind. She could picture again, a year or so ago, Justin and Estelle going by her house arm in arm, gazing with almost ridiculous rapture into one another's eyes. "In fact," she continued, "I'm rather surprised you don't seem to think so, too."

"Go on, Mrs. Newsom," he said gravely.

Mrs. Newsom shook her head wearily and proceeded with sudsing the plates and cups and saucers in the huge dishpan. "Well, for one thing," she commenced, "having to hear from young Richard Flodman that he is to all intents and purposes ... her husband! A boy like that! And his unceremonious tearing up of the invitation to the ball! And

Mrs. Dumont's egging the poor chap on, tantalizing and teasing him in front of all of us, just as if the two of them were alone together in her boudoir!"

Eugene gaped open-mouthed at the vehemence of his housekeeper's sentiments.

"I felt almost sorry for Richard Flodman," she rushed on. "Having to live with such a woman and eat her bread. Whatever his faults and misdeeds may be, he is more than punished by having to work for such a Jezebel. In fact, Mr. Bledsoe, I had the feeling I was attending a vaudeville show."

"I can see your point, of course"—Mr. Bledsoe was meekness itself now—"but I'm afraid I found it all rather amusing and diverting." Her outraged moral sentiments, however, dashed his spirits.

"I'm glad your mother was not here to have to witness such goings-on!" Mrs. Newsom, now with the upper hand, spoke with a loftiness, even grandeur, that rendered Eugene still more unsure of himself.

"Oh, come now, Mrs. Newsom." He began to come out of his retreat before her fury. "Mother's views belonged to quite another day and time, after all."

"Yes, I am afraid you are right."

"I don't see how we can possibly back out now," he went on in the softest voice she had ever heard him employ with anybody. "It wouldn't look at all . . . courteous . . . or neighborly . . . to cancel at this time, and keep the boy at home."

Mrs. Newsom's lips moved in an expression of contemptuous indifference.

"I agree with you, of course"—he appealed to her with his eyes—"that Richard's behavior left a great deal to be desired!"

"Richard's behavior!" Mrs. Newsom practically shouted.

"Yes, and, of course, Mrs. Dumont's, too. But he is, after all, no matter what he said, a mere servant, and will doubtless be put in his place when they get home. I am thinking of Duane's welfare too, you must be aware of that. But, Mrs. Newsom, I feel it will do the boy good to get out of this house and see something of the world, of people," he went on, faltering, in a chastened voice, "see a different side to life." He almost giggled now under her immovable disapprobation, her sudden invincible and implacable righteousness.

"I cannot imagine sending a young man in to a worse environment," Mrs. Newsom gave her final summary of her views and feelings. She

James Purdy

(176)

dried the last of the dishes as she made her pronouncement, then wrung out the tea towel and hung it from a great shiny nail near the sink.

He stood silent for a moment, looking at the timeworn boards of the floor.

"I respect your forthrightness and concern, Mrs. Newsom," he said at last. "Thank you. I am glad you feel you can speak with the frankness you have expressed here today. I mean that. But it's all out of our hands now—at least that is my feeling in the matter."

With a kind of wan smile, he bade her good evening, and walked toward his own secluded part of the house.

He stood over his desk littered with papers, pencils, a barometer, and several calendars. He looked out at the setting sun. All his euphoria of the afternoon had deserted him, but there was a faint whiff of violet perfume, which could have emanated only from Mrs. Dumont, still pervading the house. Yes, he thought, the air was still sweet with her presence, and his eye was drawn to a shaft of sunbeams coming through the half-drawn blind. Gradually the motes of sunbeams, as he stared on at them, grew dimmer and dimmer, and finally he had the impression that he was looking at nothing but long dark shadows. He recalled out of the blue the letter Justin had written to this same Estelle Dumont, a letter "rescued" from the recesses of the Stars and Stripes billiard hall, and all at once his enthusiasm for the party to be given in honor of, it would seem, all his sons, living and dead, appeared as questionable and ill-advised as the salvaging of dead Justin's letter from Colby's grimy archives.

A kind of not unfamiliar dread came to haunt him again. He felt now, as he always had, that Duane was somehow the bearer of ill-fortune to him, and to his house, and to the boy himself. To his own shame and even horror he now wondered why a boy like Duane had been spared when his two nobler and more manly sons had not.

He again questioned Mrs. Dumont's motives in inviting Duane. A spoiled, intractable, not over-bright, still largely beardless boy whose mother had schooled him in every variety of self-indulgence and idleness. Why should such a boy be chosen as the guest of honor for a gala? And with the lame excuse that it was an affair commemorative of his two dead hero brothers!

Picking up his straw hat, he started off he knew not where, and then feeling a bit revived by the bracing autumn air, he quickly decided he would pay a call on the tutor. After all, he cost him enough! And he received so little in the way of reassurance or encouragement on the part of Mr. Edward Duke La Roche as to his pupil's progress.

Once arrived at his destination, Eugene found that nobody either answered the front doorbell of the tutor's house or replied later to his hammering at the side door. Hearing voices coming from somewhere inside, however, Eugene took the liberty of walking on in, cleared his throat a score of times, and then proceeded down the dark, wainscoted hall with a heavy tread.

Presently, he was standing before a thick walnut door, behind which he heard something like the following:

"Now if you divide a parallelogram lengthwise into several small parallelograms, and take the diagonal both of this whole and its parts, then the diagonal of the whole might more easily be counted the same as (that is, both parallel and equal to) the long side than could the diagonal of any one of the small parellelograms as compared with the corresponding long sides. . . ."

All at once Mr. La Roche's voice (which had been pronouncing the above) came to a halt, a vibrant kind of silence followed, and then the tutor cried out in something like alarm, "Who is out there? Hello, hello!"

"It's Duane's father, Mr. La Roche," Eugene's voice boomed in majestic and slightly crabbed pitch.

An even deeper silence followed. Then the door was flung open and Mr. La Roche appeared on the threshold. His brow was deeply wrinkled, the flesh surrounding the upper lids appeared as if someone had held his fist to them, and his lips looked slightly, even fiercely, inflamed.

"Good evening, sir." Mr. La Roche unbent a little. "Just finishing a remedial lesson." He spoke almost guiltily, certainly apologetically. "He's just leaving in any case," the tutor explained and turned his gaze toward a bronzed young man with a snub nose and tight black curls who was discovered seated on a campstool at a large conference-type table. On being pointed out by his teacher, he sprang up in relief and, with a hurried good-night addressed both to Eugene and La Roche, and an added "Excuse me," rushed out from the room carrying a battered copy of *Remedial Geometry* pressed tightly against his chest.

"I often think I would as soon dig ditches, Mr. Bledsoe," the tutor expostulated after both men had seated themselves in chairs situated, it appeared, as far from one another as possible. "Look at me," La Roche went on, "I am sweating like a dray horse after trying to teach that last cuss." The instructor raised his arms to reveal the area under his arms where enormous circles of perspiration had soaked through his shirt.

"I don't, however, mean to compare the bonehead who was being coached here this evening with your son Duane," La Roche hastily volunteered on seeing how black and beetling Mr. Bledsoe's countenance had become.

"Oh, why not, Mr. La Roche," the older man snapped. "Duane seems to have a stovepipe for a head, I sometimes think."

"Not at all," the tutor defended the boy. "He's natively bright. Brighter, I sometimes think, than me, if the truth were known."

Mr. Bledsoe's eyes shone briefly, then appeared to go out like an expiring log.

"I have had a very unusual visit this afternoon," Eugene began in his orotund and slightly pompous forensic manner, and Duke La Roche recalled a time in the not too distant past when he had attended a trial at which Bledsoe had been the prosecuting attorney and had held the attention of the entire court by dint of his gloomy, doleful, and booming elocution.

La Roche shifted in his seat and begged permission to smoke, while wondering if some wrongdoing of his own in some disremembered epoch was now about to come to light. He bent over his lighted cigarette as cautiously as if it might go out, never to be kindled again.

"Richard Flodman has been to our house," Eugene began, "and was joined later by Mrs. Estelle Dumont."

As he pronounced this second name Duke La Roche stood up with such precipitous alacrity that Bledsoe immediately went silent.

Muttering some inaudible excuse, La Roche sat down again.

"As I say," Eugene resumed, with a hint of uneasy suspicion now in the way he looked at the tutor, "their visit came out of the blue. . . . Well, not entirely, perhaps," he backtracked. "They came to me about the shindig, you know. And especially about the invitation we hadn't answered."

"Oh, Estelle's party." La Roche blew out his customary enormous smoke rings as he nodded and pretended nonchalance.

"Naturally, I supposed you knew about the party," Eugene muttered with that faraway look in his eyes which had always discomfited the tutor. "I supposed also that you know her ... the heiress." Duane's father spoke almost in accusatory tones.

"Not formally," Duke confessed, turning his eyes uneasily away from his questioner. "I used to see them together, though, in the old days," the tutor remarked under his breath as if he were talking to himself. "Estelle and Justin, you know." He studied the father with close scrutiny. "They ... went together, you know."

The father did not say anything for a while, but the sucking in and expulsion of his breath in violent and irregular vehemence were quite audible.

Eugene found his voice after a struggle. "I don't know why the past cannot be laid to rest and forgotten. ... Let me tell you something that has been on my mind the last few hours, if you will let me. A letter was brought to me not too long ago by my youngest boy. A letter which had been in safekeeping with a certain Mr. Colby, operator of a pool parlor. You may recall the place, or even know him by sight." Eugene stopped, perhaps hoping to receive some sign from the tutor that he knew what he was talking about, but Duke merely puffed more vigorously on his cigarette. "The last place on earth I would want a boy of mine to go, and the last place I would have expected a private piece of correspondence to be stashed away in. Duane, in his usual addlepated way, contrived so that I would read the letter ... aloud! I fell into the trap and obliged him."

Duke La Roche was studying his visitor with open-mouthed attention.

"As I say, I was fool enough to read the letter aloud. And I was dense enough not to put two and two together at the time. I failed to connect the 'Stelle' of the letter with the fashion plate and knockout, Mrs. Dumont, who came to our house. I am aware, of course, that both my older boys were ... harum-scarums."

Duke's jaw dropped open even wider on taking in the final word of Eugene's speech, and Duane's father felt like asking him to close his mouth.

"It's too late now to do anything about it," Eugene went on, "forbidding Duane to go. But somehow I can't stomach the idea of his following the same path trodden by his two older brothers."

Duke La Roche did not, of course, realize that Eugene had violated his own code never to mention his dead sons, certainly not to refer to their wild past, and how could the tutor know how far the father had gone in betraying his own notion of what was proper or correct? Duke only knew that he had before him a very overwrought, even very ill, man.

"Can I get you a cup of hot tea?" the tutor inquired at last, in a fumble as to what to do at this juncture.

"I detest tea," Eugene groaned. "After all, we are Americans."

Duke smiled painfully.

"See here." Mr. Bledsoe spoke now in almost frantic desperation. "I will take your word for it. That's why I've come. If you are of the opinion that Duane should not go, I will not let him set foot inside her house. Just say the word, Duke. I will follow your advice implicitly. I don't want to make any more mistakes."

Duke studied Eugene's face as cautiously as a photographer who has only one last shot in his camera.

"Mr. Bledsoe, listen. I can't give you any decent or honest advice where she is concerned, or even where Duane is concerned."

"I beg your pardon," Eugene barked.

"I can't tell you, I say, to let him go or not. I can't tell you anything, because I am your wrong witness. I am in love with her. That's right. I am in love with Estelle Dumont." He moved his lips again in painful grimace at the older man's look of dumbfounded surprise. "Have been in love, what is more, for years. Head over heels. Deliriously, crazily enraptured with her. And I don't even know her. She don't even know I exist. I've never been properly introduced to her. It was all a gift of Justin's. When I saw how much he loved her, well, the feeling must have been contagious, or infectious, or maybe both. I caught it from him, you could say. And I've kept it without ever losing it for a moment . . . the contagion, you know. So how can I tell you what to do? I'd perjure myself if I were to tell you. What will be will be."

A short but seemingly interminable silence followed.

"This certainly does not make my decision any easier, Duke," Mr. Bledsoe muttered.

He took his watch from his vest pocket, held it in his hand without looking at it, and then put it back.

"Yes, this comes as quite a revelation to me, Duke," Eugene continued in a choked undertone. "No question on that score."

He turned and put his hand tentatively on the tutor's shoulder. "And if I knew how to help you with your own problem, I swear I would . . . but . . ."

Mourners Below

"I shouldn't have brought up my own case, sir. I apologize."

"I don't see that at all. I'm glad you have spoken, even though it makes everything still more of a muddle."

"That's what I mean, Mr. Bledsoe. I shouldn't have made it any harder for you."

The older man stood there a moment longer in the heavy silence of this old and vast empty house. "I don't suppose there is anything I can do now but let the scamp attend." Eugene turned an eloquent look of petition to the wallpaper of the room.

"Before you go, sir," Duke spoke up huskily, "I want to ease my own conscience a little more if you will let me. I take it you will." He paused, dry-lipped, his eyes wild and roving over the same wallpaper. "You spoke of a letter which was found at the Stars and Stripes billiard parlor, I believe?"

Mr. Bledsoe gave an exasperated movement of his left hand as if to cut off further testimony.

"That letter, and many others like it—I wrote them all for Justin! Do you follow me? I wrote them at his suggestion, or I should say, rather, his command. For he did command me. He said he couldn't think up the right words to write her, though he had all the sentiments, of course."

Eugene gave the tutor a sidelong look of grim disapprobation.

"I'm afraid also . . . I enjoyed it, writing what I felt as well. I'm afraid I did."

"Shall we let it all rest right there?" Eugene said. He took both the tutor's hands in his and pressed them hard. "For everybody's sake."

Duke nodded, and in a moment felt his hands freed from the older man's grasp. He watched the retreating figure of the lawyer until he was out of earshot, and then Duke heard his own voice saying, "You are too late to stop him from going, don't you see, Mr. Bledsoe? For if it isn't this party where it will happen, it will be another rendezvous somewhere else. They will meet and fulfill the hero's commands. Why do you come to me about what is inevitable?"

PART V

The day of the masquerade ball was flooded with sunshine despite the occasional appearance of an angry blanket of clouds and a hint of frost in the air.

From the way both Mrs. Newsom and his father looked at him during breakfast, Duane had the feeling he was going away on a journey. The housekeeper even allowed him to have a second cup of coffee, and instead of eggs and bacon, she had prepared beefsteak and homemade biscuits.

"You've finally decided what to wear, I take it," Eugene said after gobbling down three helpings of steak and potatoes. His thirty-second degree Masonic order pin sparkled in the sunshine streaming in from the opened shutters.

"I elected the cowboy outfit," Duane mumbled in reply between masticating his portion of steak.

"Nothing wrong with that choice, is there, Mrs. Newsom?" Eugene queried.

The housekeeper smiled, wiping her hands on her apron, and looked wistfully at Duane.

"Why don't you sit down and have something with us?" Eugene beseeched her. "After all, it's sort of a special occasion, to say the least."

Removing her apron, and tucking in a loose hairpin which had fallen about her ear, Mrs. Newsom seated herself. Her heavily veined but rather small, shapely hand with the thick gold wedding band was laid across the ancient but still serviceable linen tablecloth as if to bless the day.

Later, Duane insisted on mowing the grass despite his father's expressly forbidding him to do so on the grounds that he would tire himself for the "blowout." He was, in fact, still trimming the places the lawnmower had not reached with sheep shears when Mrs. Newsom rushed out late in the afternoon to the backyard and cried, "The limousine is here!"

He had not bathed or combed his hair or put on his costume!

However, he was a fast dresser when he chose to be (over the past month he had taken to heart Justin's and Douglas's warnings that he learn to dress more swiftly in case he was drafted, when he would be expected to clothe himself in a flash), and in only a few minutes he had rushed out in his cowboy outfit, having donned at the last moment the mask from the rejected domino getup. Then, slowing his pace, he walked out giddily to where the chauffeur was waiting for him in poker-faced indifference. It was a different driver from the one who had conveyed Richard Flodman to the Bledsoe house on his first and only visit, and he ordered Duane not to touch the handle of the door. He then, after a lengthy wait, came over and opened it for the guest, and while Duane blew kisses to Mrs. Newsom, who watched from the porch, the car majestically pushed off into a lowering west, where the sun had begun to set in angry mauve clouds.

Eugene came up the walk just minutes later, and when he was told Duane had already departed, sighed, whether with relief or foreboding or mere deflated exhaustion, his housekeeper could not determine.

"We'll not know for perhaps a year or more maybe, Mrs. Newsom," Eugene confided to her, "if we've done the right thing in letting him go or not," and he opened the evening newspaper by banging it against his imported high Scottish shoes.

"Just stand like that—the way you are. Don't move, if you please!" Estelle Dumont said these words as the chauffeur marshaled Duane into the large, poorly illuminated parlor where she sat in a high-backed settee which only she was ever known to occupy. She wore a loose-fitting beige dressing gown and a long string of amber beads.

"That's good." She smiled as he stood obediently silent before her.

"He never told me exactly who you were, you see, though he talked about you incessantly. He never, that is, mentioned you were his brother. I never knew until a few weeks ago you even existed! I thought 'Duane' was his tombstone buddy. That's the way he was." She spoke almost inaudibly.

Looking somewhat greedily at her now, Duane saw that she looked much older in this light than she had appeared in the innumerable blowups on the wall of Duke La Roche's room, or even from the brief visit he had paid her as messenger so long ago.

"I felt since he had lied to me about your being his brother," she was going on, "and since your father has forbidden, I take it, that any mention be made of either Justin's or Douglas's death, we would celebrate both your appearance and their passing by a commemoration such as we are having tonight."

He smiled almost imperceptibly, but even this slight movement appeared to anger her, and she shook her head.

"It is a good thing in more ways than one that I had you come early," Estelle went on after a brief pause. "Your costume, for one thing, will never do. Not for a shebang"—she pronounced this word almost with venom—"such as we are having tonight. I am somewhat appalled, to tell the truth, that your father would allow you to come in such a garb."

She rose after saying this and stood facing him with a formality and hostility of an adversary in a duel.

"The costume I have on," Duane said in a booming voice, "didn't come from my Dad but from my tutor."

"And who is he?" she asked with ill humor.

"Why, Duke, of course," he replied.

"To be sure." She laughed drily and then coughed. "Another of the men he kept in the dark. He was good at keeping people apart. Once he

Mourners Below

had corralled someone," and Duane supposed she referred to herself, "one never left the circle where he had placed one. But I hardly need tell you that!" she spoke in a fairly threatening tone.

"So you've come from your tutor." She indulged again in her grand contemptuous manner.

He bowed his head.

She stared at him for a full minute this time.

"And what on earth does he impart to you?" she said finally, after wetting her lips repeatedly. "I mean what is the subject he instructs you in?"

"They vary," Duane almost whispered, and his head raised ever so slightly.

"Music?" she said.

"No, I don't think he knows that."

"Do you?"

"Only the harmonica"—he brightened a bit—"and I used to be allowed to play Justin's saxophone before he got tired of it."

"Did he play well?" she wondered, and almost turned her back on him.

"Of course."

She moved almost fully to face him again, but kept her eyes on the window which looked toward a great meadow.

"Well, he must teach you something, since you call him tutor," she went back to her inquiry.

"Latin, geometry, algebra, some calculus," he enumerated the disciplines.

"He must be expensive if he teaches all that," she almost wailed.

She studied him again lengthily.

"And what is all this study preparing you for, may I ask?" she went on in her implacable way.

"I don't know. For nothing, very likely."

She laughed uproariously at this, but he did not join in. "That is like the Duane he described to me." She went on laughing. "Yes, you are beginning to come alive to me as he gave you out to be. I wonder if you would be as real as you are, though, without those long descriptions he made of you. Probably not. I am seeing you, of course, partially through his eyes."

"Can't we forget him?" he said wistfully.

"Yes, that's what you Bledsoes are good at, isn't it?"

James Purdy

(188)

"Oh, I don't mean that, and it's my Dad after all who is good at forgetting ... I've remembered him pretty thoroughly, if you ask me."

"I believe you." She flashed rather a blinding glance at him.

"To go back to your costume, though," she spoke now in an almost schoolmarm way, "we don't have all night to think one up for you. But if we can't find something better than what you have on, you may as well go home."

They both suddenly looked taken aback at the thought of such a contingency.

Estelle now went to a partition in the wall and pressed a button, and, after a slight pause, one heard the sound of chimes echoing throughout the entire house, a house which, whether one gazed at it from outside or observed it as one walked through its many rooms, appeared to extend endlessly over pasture land and meadows.

Richard Flodman entered. Whether by reason of his mouth being so full of pins, or owing to his generally intractable nature, he was not able to reply at all intelligibly to the fire of questions Mrs. Dumont put to him.

As she scolded and ranted to the dressmaker about Duane's lack of a suitable costume, one detected some sort of accent in her speech, which could perhaps be laid to her having been educated abroad.

After having exhausted her disappointment and anger on Richard, Estelle asked nobody in particular if the two knew one another. After a prolonged silence, chilly introductions were made on the part of their hostess.

Richard Flodman blinked his eyes at Duane by way of acknowledgment of the introduction, and Duane colored violently.

"We may as well go to the fitting room at once," she chided, looking as she spoke at where the sun had sunk behind the small hills at the edge of her property. "I hope you've left some space in your workroom, Richard, for us to get through without breaking an arm or leg."

Indolently trailing after Estelle and the dressmaker, Duane reflected that it might be just as well that his reception was such a cold one, and that he had received his cross-examination and scolding so early on in the evening, for the whole party was obviously to be such a trying and unnerving affair that it was better it had been unpleasant from the start.

"Now take off what you have on." Richard spoke to him in an exasperated manner as soon as they had entered his sewing room, which was full of dummies and mannequins. From the ceiling, depended from wires, were countless dresses and skirts, blouses and gowns of every color and description.

Duane's cowboy costume had been easier to get into than out of, and seeing the boy's difficulty in undressing, Richard rather gingerly began helping him out of it with the result that he tore the shirt badly.

"Oh, I can fix that in no time if you will leave it here for a day or so," the dressmaker said.

Estelle appeared to be paying no attention to the two of them as she walked about the room appraising the different women's dresses in different stages of completion.

Richard had removed all of the boy's clothing now except his shorts and socks, which Duane indicated by a glance he should keep on.

"But we have better and cleaner ones," Richard observed. Then sniffing rather obviously, the dressmaker said loud enough for Estelle to hear, "Somebody could stand with a bath!"

Going over to a chiffonier, he brought out some pearl-buttoned shorts, and a handsome pair of jet-black socks which had a gold arrow ornately running down them.

"The chauffeur came before I had had time to bathe," Duane, stark naked now, began to explain to Richard, who was sorting through a pile of underwear. Presently Duane became aware that in addition to Richard's being unable to speak properly owing to the pins, he was also hard of hearing, as a result, he learned later, of a punctured eardrum the dressmaker had suffered while in prison.

Estelle took in Duane's nakedness with about as much outward show of interest as if she had been staring at a brick wall. She paid considerably more attention to the underwear Richard had produced for their guest: a hand-stitched pure silk undershirt, with shorts to match, the latter of a pastel blue. Richard nodded to Estelle to take a good look at the boy's armpits, streaming with perspiration and soon wetting the immaculate never-before-worn underwear.

"Now what have you got for him that he can show a little more to advantage in?" Richard's employer wondered, eyeing the dressmaker narrowly.

"I thought we had agreed on the tuxedo," Richard announced coldly.

"What tuxedo?" Estelle answered in the most disagreeable voice Duane could ever remember hearing from anybody.

"We certainly discussed the tux some evenings ago." Richard

jumped right into the argument with the vigor and confidence of one who is used to such frays. "You indicated then that you thought it was a good idea."

"Indicated *then*," she lashed out at him. "How did I indicate it then, will you tell me? You must know I loathe tuxedos if you know anything. And on him!" she cried, looking now accusingly at Duane.

"Well, then, what is your pleasure if a tux won't do?" Richard said airily and began straightening out the folds of a dress he was working on. Duane wondered if all the dresses in the room in different stages of completion were Estelle's or if this was perhaps actually a dress factory.

"As if my pleasure were all that was at stake!" she went at him again. "I wonder what I pay you for if you can't come up with a number of options. And here all you can offer is a tux. I won't have it!"

As if to irk her even more, Richard hurried off to a corner of the room and came back holding what looked like a bandbox-new tuxedo.

"Just look at this, if you don't say it's beautiful. Examine the material! Look at the classic cut!"

"Well, wear it yourself if it's so wonderful!" She refused to look at or touch it. "I offer it to you as a gift. Wear it tonight."

"You know perfectly well that I will not attend the party, so don't rub it in," Richard told her, putting the tuxedo back on a gold hanger. "If you think I'd make a fool of myself attending a party at which I'm not welcome . . ."

"How could you be unwelcome if I invited you?" she shrieked.

"Because everybody there would look down his nose at me, and you know it!"

"So what, if I were pleased!" she shot at him. "I am truly shocked by your disobedience and bad manners, Richard. Are you behaving so badly because you wish to impress someone, by chance?"

"I will not discuss such matters now," he said, struggling with his wish to say even more, "precisely because strangers are present."

"Duane is hardly a stranger." She attempted to control her own temper. "Very well, what alternatives do you have to the tux?"

"None," he told her.

"What do you mean, none? Are you my dressmaker or not?"

"I am your dressmaker, ma'am," he said, shooting a look of great contempt and haughtiness at Estelle and then eyeing Duane narrowly.

"Did you hear me the other evening speak of the Sicilian shepherd getup?" she wondered.

Mourners Below

"I did," he said, nodding several times.

"And where have you put it?"

He put down the dress he had begun working on—and which might have been the one she was to wear tonight—walked over to a small wardrobe which seemed to have been recently constructed, and brought out a shimmering pale garment resembling a nightshirt, decorated along its edges with golden forget-me-nots. He handed it to her coldly.

She held it up admiringly.

"I see nothing at all wrong with this for him," she went on in angry contemplation. "What is your objection, may I ask?"

"Duane is an American boy, and if you opened your eyes you would see he is." Richard now gave signs that he was completely losing his temper. "The costume you are holding up to us is a nightgown—expensive enough, God knows, to hang in the costume section of the Louvre, but still a nightgown, and quite inappropriate for tonight's party."

"A nightgown, my eye!" she lashed back at him. "Have you seen the gold crown that goes with it?"

"I'm afraid I have," Richard replied, no longer looking at either of them.

"Richard, I wonder at you, I truly do!" Estelle commenced now in a more reasonable if still threatening tone of voice. "You are a superb dressmaker, milliner, tailor—an artist, really. At the same time you can come up with ideas that would shame a clerk at Woolworth's."

She walked up and down the room as she said this. Richard had sat down and was busily sewing on the gown.

"I will stick by my opinion that the shepherd costume is right for him," she said desperately, and went directly up to the dressmaker. "I want to see him in it and I want your opinion."

"My opinion has been given, ma'am. It is the tux or nothing."

"I see," Estelle said, shrugging her shoulders.

Then, in a turnaround which surprised the dressmaker, Duane, and probably herself, she said, "Very well, let it be the tux. I bow to your decision. . . . But you must create a special mask for him, of course—not that tacky domino mask."

Richard began to remonstrate, but Estelle held up her hand:

"Not a word more," she cried. "The tux, but the mask . . . I will not be further contradicted under my own roof. God, I never saw such a puffed-up bully and tyrant," she cried. "Why I put up with it, I'll never know. You are the only man I think I ever met who can beat me. I hate you for it, and I will always hate you for it. Very well, fetch out the damned tux, and put him in it, and quit stitching on that dress, do you hear me? Put that damned dress away, will you!"

Richard dropped the dress so that it fell to the floor, and his hands folded themselves over his lap. The gold thimble which he held on his right index finger glistened.

He rose and perhaps deliberately stepped on the dress at his feet and walked out of the room.

"It's become so uncommonly hot in addition to everything else going wrong," Estelle remarked to nobody in particular. "What an infernal climate. Snowbound from October to June, and after that, baked and broiled and roasted: I arranged what Richard calls my *fête champêtre* this late hoping we would have some fine autumn weather. Instead it's sticky and damp with not a breath of air stirring. And how I hate to be bested!" Then, holding the Sicilian shepherd "nightgown" roughly in her two hands, without warning she ripped the garment in two.

"Now see if I am not right!" Richard's voice brought her up with a start.

But as he stood before her with the tux, his entire attention became absorbed in the spectacle of Estelle holding the two pieces of the torn nightgown in her hands.

"How dare you destroy a costume I have worked on!" he cried, livid with anger, and holding the tux now in one hand, he seized the two pieces of the nightgown in the other. "What do you mean by such an act," he shouted as if to the rafters, "you coarse, ignorant, vulgar harridan!"

"Now, now, my dear, temper, temper!" Estelle retorted, and instead of roaring back at him as might have been expected, she almost cooed out these words. She acted delighted and relieved that Richard was so angry.

"You have no right to humiliate me in front of others, and I am resigning."

He threw both the tux and the nightgown to the floor, and began to retreat toward one of the many doors all marked in great red letters EXIT, as one would expect in an opera house.

"Stop right where you are. If you go down one step of the staircase I will call the police. You may call me what you like and drive me to acts of destruction which your ridiculous rages prompt me to (although I

Mourners Below

will take the torn costume out of your salary later), but you can no more leave my employ than fly. You know it, I know it, and the authorities know it. Come back and set to work, or go out of here in handcuffs."

"You filthy—" Richard began, turning back. Then, sitting down in a Yorkshire chair which he had purchased only the day before yesterday at great cost, he burst into tears.

"Now, Richard, control yourself. It's no time for histrionics. You know I am your best friend." She kissed him coldly on his eyebrows. "Bygones be bygones now, and so on, and set to work. The bands will be arriving at almost any moment. Go on, pick up the tux, and I'll put the nightgown away in your rag drawer."

As this altercation was in progress, Duane had moved as far away from the principals as possible, but Estelle, looking around for him, said in a soft voice, "Richard will have you fitted in no time," and she smiled in a way which resembled Aileen when putting on her lipstick.

Estelle was examining the tux suspiciously as she spoke.

"I wouldn't handle it any more than I had to, if I were you," Richard warned her, drying his eyes on a piece of sheer cotton.

"Yes, it is quite superlative," Estelle admitted with a toss of her head. "Well, let him step into it, for heaven's sake."

Had Duane joined the army and heard reveille he could not have jumped into his clothes faster than he put on the tuxedo.

"I have to admit it," Estelle said. "It's right for him in every way. No question about it."

Both she and Richard now stood some few feet away from the boy and looked at him severely but approvingly.

"One must always be surrounded by perfectionists, no question about that either," Estelle said with a bitter glance nowhere in particular. "I am going to make another suggestion with regard to Duane's costume, and I suppose I will have my head chopped off when I do," Estelle began after a pause with clasped hands as if she were a singer about to favor her audience with an encore. "May I speak?" She looked over toward Richard.

"You may speak, but I will keep my own counsel."

"Good," Estelle replied, bending her head ever so slightly. "I would like to propose that he have a mask *painted* on him."

Richard moved his lips angrily.

"I will leave all the details to you, Richard," she said, batting her eyes, and looking somewhat uneasy. "I hope you won't overrule me on this, also."

"Very well," he said in his sultry way, "I'll yield on this one point or I'll probably never hear the end of it. But it's wrong, and in execrable taste. It's cute-silly!" he raised his voice. "All right, I'll agree, if you will only let me finish what I am doing." And he angrily shook out the dress he was working on across his lap.

"Come, Duane, my dear." Estelle stretched out one hand. "Let us go and inspect the pavilion where the dance is to be held, and leave Richard to his labors. Come, my fashion plate."

As they walked toward the great barn where the dance was to be held, Estelle confided, "Those dark eyebrows of Richard's that form one continuous line scare the life out of me sometimes, I can tell you."

She took Duane's hand as she spoke. The boy studied her out of the corner of his eye. It was hard to believe, he felt, that anybody could ever have frightened her.

As they reached the aperture of the barn itself, they stopped and watched a swarm of men finishing the last work on the two platforms on which the orchestras were to take their place. From the high roof of the barn many streamers, pennants, and flags were in evidence. The walls of the barn were hung with all kinds of wonderful cloth which moved back and forth like great wings propelled by giant electric fans. Duane felt he was a thousand miles from home.

"I still cannot get over his never having peeped he had a younger brother." She dropped his hand now and turned about to face him directly. "Doesn't it strike you as barefaced deceit? But I hardly know what to call it. . . . You have no explanation for such double-dealing?" She harked back to the subject when he said nothing in reply.

"Maybe he didn't think I was important enough to mention," Duane stuttered.

"But I've already told you he spoke of nobody but you. You were the subject I was treated to hour after hour!" Her anger seemed to have returned, or at least her exasperation.

Just then Richard hurried up to them and handed Estelle a folded piece of notepaper. Without either of them saying a word, she accepted it, and he hurried off back to his workroom. She read the paper by holding it a long way off from her eyes.

"He is the most ungrateful, meanest, and most insolent man who ever drew breath!" she began. They entered the barn, but Estelle's whole attention was occupied with the note. "He came to me right out of the reformatory, where they had taught him to sew. . . . I am held responsible for his good behavior, you see. But nothing I do for him is enough or right. Were I to cut off my two breasts and hand them to him on a platter, he would feel I had shortchanged him."

Duane was in hopes that Estelle would return to the subject of Justin's unceasing praise of him, but it was evident that Richard now occupied her entire attention.

"You may read this, if you like." She handed Duane Richard's note.

At first, Duane started to read the note upside down, for Richard's handwriting was almost illegible. Estelle turned the paper right side up, and he read out loud, rather to her discomfiture:

You know I am the greatest couturier living, and a genius with cloth of any kind, while you are a coarse, insensitive, common pretender to social graces, and even with all your dishonestly acquired fortune, without my dressing you properly, you would be ignored everywhere for the commonplace tasteless frump you always were.

Richard, Couturier Nonpareil

"That word 'frump' again," Estelle sighed. "Well, aren't you outraged by it?" she inquired indignantly when Duane handed the note back to her without comment.

"I think you would be beautiful in anything at all," he told her. "Even in that shepherd nightgown you picked out for me."

"I see," Estelle said, looking at him sideways. She put the note in her bosom as if it were very valuable or extremely dangerous.

"To go back to your brother, though," she said, as they walked quickly through the barn and received nods and bows and salutations from the many workmen engaged there, "I've made up my mind to get even with him for not having told me you existed."

"Can we get even with the dead, if you don't mind me asking," Duane spoke huskily.

She turned to look at him.

"An inexcusable action is an inexcusable action," she said rather softly. "Of course, only a month before he went away the last time," she went on huffily, "he had promised to introduce us, but even then he never breathed a word that you were his brother. Can you make head or tail of it?"

Duane thought he began to understand Eugene a little better, for now he did not want to hear about Justin, certainly not with regard to his shortcomings, deception, or outright bad conduct, and from a person he knew as little as Estelle, and in a barn where a big dance was going to take place.

"Just the same," she said a little more sweetly, "we will all try to have a good time tonight, since the gala is in honor of all you Bledsoe boys, and, of course, that goes for Douglas, too, though I was never so close to him. We will try to celebrate just as splendidly as we can." She stopped to survey the barn, which had suddenly grown, it seemed, even larger, more replendent. With the colored searchlights being turned on for the first time to catch the many moving banners, pennants, and flags, the whole place was a phantasmagoria.

Still amazed at the vastness of the barn, Duane finally inquired, "Were horses kept here at one time, Mrs. Dumont?"

"Mrs. Dumont cannot say," she replied, between sneering and giggling. "But I suspect they were, along with sheep, cows, and doubtless goats."

"I hope it was horses, ma'am."

"You're so like Justin, and yet so different!" Estelle abruptly cried, and took his hand and pressed it briefly. "When we speak of him, Duane, you look as if you begrudged me having known him, I do declare you do!"

"Do I?" he wondered, reddening slightly. "I suppose, though, if I knew how close you were to him, I might feel different."

"You mean you would be sure you begrudged me his affection."

He opened his mouth for a long while, then shut it.

"How close were you?" the boy finally said.

"As close as I could be," she replied, looking, he thought, crestfallen.

"But how close were you *both,* I mean?" he went on, slightly stuttering and turning now a brick-red under his sunburn.

"I am a bit surprised you don't know," she spoke now almost with a whine, "since he assured me you were his confidant."

"His what?" Duane almost snapped at her.

"That was the impression that he gave me, that he told you everything."

"And while you were both as close as you could be, you say he talked about me?" As he got these words out, he let out a great breath of air as if he had said all he could ever say with regard to the two of them.

"He knew, you see, that I didn't think he was as close to me as I was to him."

Just then they heard Richard hallooing them.

"You will permit him to paint the mask on," she said nervously and in great agitation. "It's so perfect a finishing touch to just a plain tux, however fine it may be. It won't be too hard to remove, either, afterwards," she added.

The word "afterwards" seemed to impress both of them.

"Richard can certainly see that there's no trace of it remaining. I suppose, too, you wouldn't want your father to observe it on you, or have it come off on the bed linens. I learned how you live at home, you see, from him. Run on ahead of me now back to the millinery room!" she joked, "and more bad temper and abuse. Just the same, I can't cashier Richard. There's more than a grain of truth in that hateful note he wrote me. And, after all, he is a criminal. One can't expect him to be like other men. Go on ahead, dear," she motioned to Duane with both hands stretched out. "I'll follow."

He ran.

Richard immediately handed Estelle the finished gown of flaming red satin, bedizened with sequins, as she entered the millinery room and, grasping the garment almost desperately, without a word more the hostess departed, leaving the two men alone together.

Richard was already mixing the paint for Duane's mask.

"This is not my idea, of course," the dressmaker began. "But what can one do? She did yield on the matter of the tux. Have you any particular choice as to the color of your mask?"

Duane shook his head.

"If I were you," Richard whispered, coming up close to the boy and studying his face, "I would run as fast as my legs could carry me from here."

"But it's in my honor," Duane muttered.

"The only thing ever in anybody's honor here is her," Richard said. "I feel more a prisoner now," he went on, "than when I was behind bars. I also miss the direct punishment I received there, instead of the uncertain, vague, and crippling kindness I get here twenty-four hours a day. Why don't you get out now while you can?"

"She didn't even know who I was till a few days ago," Duane imparted this information to the dressmaker.

"Oh, her ridiculous crushes and fancies!" Richard scoffed. . . . "Well," the dressmaker advised after a silence, "you had best remove your jacket and shirt, if we're to put on this mask and not spatter your tux. She falls in love with someone new every fortnight," Richard went on bitterly, thinning the paint now, and inspecting it bellicosely.

Duane gave a start when the first makeup was being applied, and Richard advised him, "Just relax, why don't you?"

"Were you here in the days when . . . ?" Duane began, his voice unsteady from the bracing and unpleasant shock his skin got from the application of the paint.

"When what?" Richard wondered coolly.

"When he came?"

Richard stepped back a few paces to inspect the application of the lacquer.

"The big tall fellow with the sunny smile?" the dressmaker inquired.

Duane had never thought of Justin as someone with a smile, sunny or otherwise, but he nodded.

"Yes, I remember him," Richard said in a kind of grudging, grieved tone.

"You see, we were both surprised." Duane spoke as if in a tone of argument.

"Who is *we*, Duane?" Richard worked now very quickly and with fierce concentration, painting the boy's lips and chin with a different color from his palette.

"Mrs. Dumont and I . . ." Duane began again thickly.

"She wants you to call her 'Estelle,' for heaven's sake. She asked me, as a matter of fact, to speak to you about it. It won't do to call her 'Mrs.' in any case. . . . Well, go on with your story."

"She and I . . ." Duane continued hopelessly, and he put his hand to his face.

"Watch out," Richard cried. "You must not touch the makeup!"

"I say, Richard, were they *sweethearts?*" Duane all at once blurted out and, as he did so, he grasped the dressmaker's hand.

"There's a mirror right over here you can look at yourself in." Richard raised his voice, while giving Duane a look counseling silence, for Estelle had just come into the room.

"The mouth is much too full," she cried, and cast a critical appraisal at the seated boy. "And the color on the lips themselves is too much on the vermilion side, don't you agree?"

Duane rose deliberately and walked toward the full-length mirror. He gave a kind of soft moan when he gazed at himself in the glass, which caused both Estelle and Richard to laugh.

"You'll get used to it!" Estelle could not control her laughter. "Go ahead," she urged him, becoming a little more serious. "Go on looking until you like yourself.... Go on! It will come, Duane, it will come! See, you're getting to like yourself now, aren't you?"

Duane turned away from the mirror and gazed helplessly from Estelle to Richard and back to Estelle again.

"I rather like the way you described Justin's and my relationship," Estelle said in a cold matter-of-fact voice. "The words you chose ... Didn't you like how he described it, Richard?"

"Oh, very much indeed," the dressmaker answered coolly.

"I never thought of him as a sweet—" Duane began to say, but then suddenly, whether it was the mention of his brother in such loud obstreperous volume after the silence and evasion practiced concerning him at Eugene's, or the nauseating odor of the makeup, or the dread of the evening ahead, Duane suddenly keeled over and fell close to Estelle's high-heeled shoes.

It was therefore necessary to pour a considerable amount of cold water on his face to bring him around, thereby spoiling a good deal of the makeup Richard had applied. In addition, some of the ammonia used to revive him ruined the delicate touches here and there which the dressmaker had been at such pains to apply to his cheeks and throat.

When he came to, he found himself in a small room with elaborate and brightly colored wallpaper on which were depicted great wading birds standing at the water's edge and flying through the golden clouds of the sky. He had been propped up on a daybed, and behind his head were soft cushiony eiderdown pillows.

"There! About time!" Estelle's voice boomed from a dark recess of the room. "You had us truly wondering," she began.

"Where's Duke?" he cried.

"Duke?" she spoke with angry impatience.

"Ain't I in his house?"

"His house, my foot!" she cried, and then she was by his side with such speed he had the impression she had flown through the air to reach him.

"Don't you know me?" she said with bitter ill-temper. Then after a pause during which she acted like a person trying to read a printed page in total darkness she cried, "Who is this person you are calling on when you should be giving me your sole and undivided attention? I ask you!"

He rose up, for she appeared near tears.

"But you certainly must know Duke!" he challenged her.

"I know nobody at all, it would appear, or the ones I did know have deserted me!"

She had risen and now walked about the room, and her shadow falling across the daybed on which he lay stretched was extremely long in this light.

"Who on earth would have the gall to go by the name of Duke, I ask you?" She stopped and faced him. "Well, who is he?" she fairly screamed at him.

"I thought I told you he was my tutor, but before that," and here he stopped a moment, "he ran with Justin, of course."

"Of course!" she flung at him. "Naturally the one would follow the other."

At that moment, to his surprise, he saw someone give her a glass of something, though it was so dark in that part of the room he could not see who the person handing it to her was. She drank from it thirstily.

"But Duke La Roche is actually his name," Duane said, watching her. "It's on his birth certificate that way: Edward Duke La Roche."

"I won't ask you how it comes about that you had the opportunity to inspect your tutor's birth certificate." He heard her drink again.

"His room is papered with photos of you."

"How papered?" she asked, advancing toward him and holding her glass as if she were going to throw its entire contents in his face. "Or what did you say?"

"That's right, over all the walls of his den is nothing but photo after photo of you. That's what Duke is like."

She looked down at the brim of her glass frosted with salt, which Duane mistook for sugar.

Turning away, she managed to say, "It's an appalling name for anybody ever to go through life with. One would expect him to be a nigger jockey."

Estelle shook her head repeatedly as she sipped from the liquid.

"What did he say when he showed you all the photos of me?" she wondered. "For I gather he showed you."

Duane straightened up in bed.

"No, I walked in and seen them unbidden."

She looked appalled or at least bested.

"Don't you get out of bed," she scolded, seeing he was putting his feet down on the floor. "Do you hear me?"

He stood up nonetheless, shakily, and said, " 'She's got nowhere to go but here,' Duke told me, pointing to the photos."

"He said that?" She was very quiet. "What do you think he meant by it?" She seemed to put the question to herself.

"He's desperately in love with you," Duane muttered.

"Those photos must come down." She spoke now in her normal voice. She walked about the room. "I'll see to that!"

"But how will you do that . . . take them down?"

"I'll go and tear them off the wall."

"Maybe that's what he wants you to do." Duane offered this to her. "That would be how you would go to him."

"And he really said I had nowhere to go but there?"

"To the best of my recollection those were his words."

"The nerve, the arrogance! How dare he look at me all the time in his private room!"

She paced and stomped about the room holding her glass in hand as if it were a flashlight, spilling some of it from time to time.

"We should go at once to his place and tear every one of my photos from off the wall!" she cried. "But I suppose you are too sick," she complained bitterly. "And then, of course, there is the party ahead of us, but we could cancel it or let everybody wait until we come back from his place. I must have those photos down! Well," she said, looking at him appraisingly, "we will go tomorrow and take them off. You should have told me this long ago," she went on. The matter of the photos had almost completely swept her off her feet.

"And so he says I have no choice but to go to him!" She waited in silence, then, "You're not sick often, are you?" she inquired as she finished her drink, and set the huge glass which had contained it on a chiffonier.

"Oh, off and on, I guess," he mumbled the response to her query.

She sat down on the edge of his bed and bent over quickly and kissed him. The softness of her lips made his heart slow, then quicken. She kissed him deliberately again.

"You are so like the other one it sickens me, too," she whispered. "I don't suppose you dance either. Even he was a terrible dancer, but it didn't matter, you know—just to be next to him was more than good enough. Just to know he existed, it would have been all to the good had he thrown me down and walked over me instead of keeping step.... Do you know what scent he used, Duane, by the way?"

In his state, he did not get the word, and as she waited she kissed him again.

"What *what?*" he inquired, returning her kiss.

"His after-shave, what was it called?"

"Oh," Duane responded, thinking carefully.

"It smelled like nasturtiums, I always thought, mixed with something else. Well?" she prompted him with incipient, blustering impatience.

"I'm trying to think, Mrs. Dumont."

"Oh, there we go again!" She leaped up and walked about the small room. Returning to him after a bit, she said, persevering worriedly, "Would your Dad know, do you suppose?"

"Why Duke feels this way about you?"

"Duke be damned! The nasturtium after-shave I asked you about! I have to have it. Does your Dad use the same kind, by chance?"

"I think he uses just plain rubbing alcohol ... Estelle. I don't shave much yet, you know." He made a motion to touch his cheek and then stopped, letting his hand fall.

She sat down on the bed again. "Yes, you're so like him, but you're so different all the same. In this light you look like he did in the high-school annual." She kissed him industriously and he raised up. She saw how excited he was, and she smiled briefly. She permitted her hand to rest lightly for a second on his thigh and was pleased to see how much more flushed that made him.

"I want us to go and take all those photos off his wall," she whispered, toying with the hair about his ears and kissing him on the eyelids. "It would take no time at all."

"But that would be robbery, Estelle," he protested. "They're his photos."

"*His?*" she flared. "He got them from Justin, and you know it. Justin told me someone had taken them from his room."

The name "Justin," pronounced so vigorously, authoritatively, as if he were still alive, perhaps waiting in the next room, quieted Duane's furious erection a bit, then it flared up more violent than before as he felt her breath on his face.

"What on earth is it now?" Estelle's voice boomed out, reaching to someone in the hall outside the room where he lay. She wrenched his hand painfully as she got up and strode out with great long but noiseless steps to the corridor and whispered something to someone standing there.

"Duane, dearest?" she called to him from the threshold. "I'll be back directly. I must see to the musicians just now." She blew him a kiss.

The person to whom she had been speaking remained shrouded in the doorway. Presently, however, someone came on into the room and stood over the bed. It was Richard.

"Now's your chance to skiddoo," he said through his strong, dank, liquor breath.

"Why would I do that?" Duane replied after a pause.

"It's too much for you." Richard sat down on the bed just where she had been seated. "There'll be nothing left of you," he whispered.

"I'll stay," Duane answered, staring at the dressmaker in the very pupils of his eyes.

"If you go now, she'll leave you alone forever," Richard went on. "If you stay, you'll stay forever." He rose and waited there at the edge of the bed.

"I understand you," the boy muttered.

"Except you don't," the dressmaker breathed heavily. "You just don't."

"It would be like going back on him, if I went now." Duane looked up into the face of his visitor.

"*Him?*" Richard said coldly.

Duane nodded.

"So you mean you just do what you're told?"

"In the case of this party, it's in his honor."

James Purdy

(204)

"Then you're just staying to honor him, and not for her."

"I came invited, I am expected to remain, and I'll stay on my own until the party is over," Duane said in rapid fire.

Richard walked away from the bed a bit. "You're a fool to stay when you still have your own life free of her," he said. Then he walked over to the threshold from which he had come and waited there in the darkness. Wheeling around abruptly, he shot back at the boy, "Don't come to me then when it's over. Understand? Don't ask me then to ever help you, for I won't."

"We'll have to dance presently. We'll have to do something," Estelle was saying as she sat by Duane's bedside. "Your color is much better," she went on when he did not reply to her adjuration. She took his hand in hers. "No question about that. . . . How different you look from the summer day when he sent you to me. Do you remember it?"

"Like it was an hour ago. I mean, it seems recenter than when I arrived here with your chauffeur."

"Richard tries to make me admit I never loved your brother," Estelle said, her hand freed from his and moving over his forehead and smoothing his hair. "He says I never loved anybody. But how does anybody know what another person feels about anything? To the best of my knowledge, I loved him," she said like a witness in court. "Justin." Her head fell down gently toward her breast.

"People are arriving from miles around," she remarked after a long silence. "You know the little hills that face the west? Usually they're black as deepest midnight. Well, tonight you can see cars coming down them. I've literally gone out in the highways and byways to invite people. We'll have five hundred here tonight. Yes, the hills are all blazing with auto headlights coming to Mrs. Dumont's shindig." She began to weep.

Suddenly, she engulfed his mouth in hers, plunging her hand through his curls and then somehow placing her tongue in his nostrils, then again licking his outer lips, his chin, and even biting his throat; she kissed him on down to his breast.

"We must stop," she said after a while when the response from him was even more impassioned than her own kisses. He put his hand on her breasts and pressed.

"When am I to steal the photos?" he inquired.

Mourners Below

"So Duke was Justin's nigger." She spoke vacantly. "I lied to you a while back, Duane. Of course, I knew about Duke. I have even met him somewhere. Probably in the ice-cream parlor." As she mentioned the parlor she looked at him quizzically, perhaps accusingly.

"I'll steal them if you say the word."

"Yes, steal them," she said, breathing heavily. Her hand touched his penis and held it through the pajama bottoms he wore, held it in a curious way, as a surgeon might do before applying a local anesthetic; yet held it, he felt, for keeps.

"Your brother told me once when he was very drunk that he felt he had shit Duke, and that is how Duke came into being. He had made him out of his . . ."

Duane pulled away from her as she said this, and his distaste for what she had said reached her immediately. She kissed him as if to expunge what she had told him.

"Adorable," she said. "Not as adorable as you were the day he sent you as his messenger, but adorable, adorable." She kissed him hungrily. She covered his throat with kisses and made long succulent sounds like a blind person eating an orange which has been only partly cut for eating. She put her tongue on his Adam's apple, and he gave out cries he had never heard come from himself before.

"You're all I can hope for," she said after a while, her words coming spaced out between short heavy breaths.

"What you don't know is I was Justin's real nigger. Not Duke."

"Oh, no you weren't. Never! Never."

"But—"

"There's a difference between blows directed by love and those directed by the wish to order and command. Besides, he could never command you. You commanded him."

"I?" He spoke as breathlessly as she now. "I—"

"Shut up," she said. She kissed him all over his face, allowing his face to swim with spittle.

"Steal the photos from the nigger, if you like," she said during one of her pauses for breath. "Or let the nigger keep them, for he'll be here one day or another, and I'll require them of him at that time."

"He ain't coming tonight?"

"Who knows how many will slip into that barn and out."

"But you didn't send him an invite?"

James Purdy

She either hadn't heard him or she was too liquored up to answer, for she merely looked out the window, watching the lights of the cars come down the black hills.

"You're all I can hope for," she said, helping him put on his tux. "God," she exclaimed when he was fully into the suit. Traces of the painted mask were still visible despite the passing of the hours and her many kisses.

In the dark she had changed into another person, someone he had perhaps dreamed of but could not believe was Mrs. Dumont. It was almost, too, as if Justin had turned into a woman and gave him this tenderness, this strong affection. He dissolved into soft ecstatic weeping, which caused her to baste him with more wet kisses.

"We must go outside and hear the bands at least, dear Duane." After a pause she said, "Justin's brother, just think. . . ."

The barn was full of dancers, and at the opposite end of the building—now alive with moving lights of all kinds which illuminated the streamers and pennants hanging from the roof as if they were innumerable tongues of flame—were the three bands, one playing, the other two on call and waiting for the first band to cease so each could sound out in sequence. The vibrancy of the illumination and the ear-splitting noise of the bands caused Duane to feel even more intoxicated and unreal, so that he seemed to melt into Estelle's body. It was as if he were inside her sumptuous sequined evening gown, nestling against her breasts and her flat, hard belly and sleek, soft thighs. Whether it was the cacophony of the music or his closeness to her, he did not want—ever—to stop dancing. Finally he wore her out, and, panting, she begged for the respite of a drink.

"Of what?" he said belligerently.

"Said just like him! Yes, yes"—she shook her head—"said like the one and only!"

It was now she who needed nursing, she confided to Duane, but instead of fainting and lying driveling and drooling, she said the night air would be good for both of them.

"We're both dead drunk." She spoke to him as soberly as Mrs. Newsom might have, and then abruptly, "There's nothing wrong with you for seeing the departed."

As they stood outside the huge entrance to the barn, lit by magic jack-o'-lanterns alive with purple and scarlet searchlights which explored the ancient barn's roof and craggy rafters, a knot of men stood staring at both of them.

It was later, Duane knew, that the sight of this knot of men carried him higher into ecstasy than perhaps his most perverted embraces of Justin's sweetheart.

Perhaps the knot of men felt the same as they saw Estelle and Duane standing there together. Each of the men, one after the other, put out his cigarette as one does when some person or procession quite out of the ordinary crosses one's field of vision.

"For a moment we thought you were—" The tallest of the young men came out from the knot.

"Yes, we could have sworn it was—"

Estelle's pearls bounced and danced forward and around as she shook their hands, then kissed each one of the young men, and pushed Duane into their midst so that they all formed a circle.

The men were Curly Rogers, Bud Phalon, Will Redfern, Ted Defoe, all classmates of Justin and wearing their Marine uniforms.

From inside the barn came the sharp cadenzas of four pianos playing in concert.

The circle of the buddies and Estelle and Duane knit closer, against the sharp wind that was coming from the hills beyond and the November sky, and the odor, from some far-off farmstead, of burning leaves.

"So you're carrying on the family tradition," Curly Rogers said and put a cigarette between Duane's lips.

"That's enough," Bud Phalon said, taking the thing out of Duane's mouth and taking a drag on it himself. He offered it to Estelle, who declined.

"Why didn't you invite the whole goddamned nation, Stelle?" Ted Defoe grinned at her. "Do you know this is the biggest party this part of the country has ever saw?"

Estelle was about to say something when a young man dressed like a store dummy in tight, poorly fitting, but perhaps brand-new plus-fours came forward and said softly, "Duane! Oh, Duane."

But Duane was staring at the four buddies.

"Don't smoke any more of that, do you hear?" Estelle watched him. She had got over her malaise but she did not understand why he stared at the knot of men so feverishly.

James Purdy
(208)

"You're all alive, aren't you?" Duane said with the inflection of a small boy awakening from a nap.

All the buddies roared with laughter. Yes, the laughter, he was assured, came from real lungs, bellies, and moving rib cages.

"Duane don't want to say hello," came the crabbed voice of the young man in the plus-fours.

"Oh, for Christ's sake," Duane said, and he went over and threw his arms around Duke La Roche in the ill-fitting long knickers.

"We both have on some getups," the tutor cried, staring with frightened eyes at Estelle, who looked straight through him up to the hills and the purple-black sky.

"Well, this is him, Estelle, the guy who papers his room with your smile." Duane spoke, however, to everybody.

An argument had now broken out among the young men who had just a moment before been like a group posing for a fraternity photo. Fisticuffs followed, and soon one of the men was lying on the grass, his mouth cut, bleeding profusely.

Estelle pulled Duane away from the fray and Duane pulled Duke. They entered the barn, with Duane, however, looking back, throwing out his one free arm imploringly, for now it seemed to him that he had merely dreamed this circle of Just's buddies, had imagined the whole thing, but he could not imagine the sound of knuckles striking against flesh and bone. They were all in a fracas now.

"Let them get it out of their systems," Estelle said with icy command. She was herself again.

Without their quite being aware of it, Duane, Duke, and she were all dancing together, and every so often kissing one another, but at the last Estelle kissed Duke a long simmering wet kiss, and then perhaps feeling something was not quite right with this, she commanded Duke to kiss Duane.

He demurred, and she pulled him toward the boy.

"When you hear me say something," she said in a voice which carried above the pianos going at lightning speed, "you do just that."

Duke kissed Duane, and Duane turned away. He went over to a long bench and sat down, and Duke and Estelle went on dancing together, their mouths very close, almost kissing again, and Estelle's rope of pearls flying dizzily here and there, like something actually alive and trying to fly upward.

A young black man with a tray of drinks came over to Duane and said, "Wash your mouth out with a potion, why don't you?"

The Negro held a glass to Duane's lips and said, "You could stand with another, go on! Takes two to fly anyhow, and we have a hundred more trays circulating."

"Have you ever kissed a dead man?" Duane asked him.

Just then they heard the police sirens. After a while, the black man with the tray returned and said, "They just arrested some of the guests. Ain't you glad you stuck in the barn?"

Immediately Duane rushed out of the building and hurried over to where two squad cars stood parked with their revolving red lights rising and falling against the black outlines of the barn and making the November sky look even more somber.

Going directly up to the vehicles, ignoring the state troopers who shouted for him to depart and stood scowling at him, Duane peeped into the cars.

"Curly Rogers, Bud Phalon, Will Redfern, Ted Defoe." He called out the names in a loud toneless voice. He noticed they all had bloody noses, as if Richard Flodman had painted them with stage blood just for the occasion.

The young men all lifted their heads dispiritedly. It was Ted Defoe who limply raised a hand at last. It was handcuffed to Will Redfern's.

"Let me ask you something." Duane went to the window of the car, but the trooper took hold of him and held him back. Duane struggled to be free and talk to Ted, who now looked at him wonderingly.

"As Marines, guys who saw action," Duane cried, "tell me something!"

"You better go back to your party, sonny, or we are goin' to pack you in along with your smart-ass friends here. Now I mean it!" the state trooper bellowed when Duane didn't budge.

"Just one question. To that fellow there," Duane pointed to Ted Defoe.

The trooper let go of Duane's arm and the boy pressed his face to the window of the police car.

"Put me straight on one thing," Duane implored. "Is he really dead and buried? Go on now and tell me. Swear to me you know."

"Duane," Ted looked at him piteously, helplessly. "You've had way too much down the hatch."

James Purdy
(210)

"No, no! Drink don't have nothing to do with it. Just tell me if we've been informed correct, Ted. Did you see him, for instance, laid out? Did you see his body?"

Then, after a pause in which only the motor of the police car was heard, "I mean, Ted, how do I know you ain't a ghost, too?"

Ted looked away and shook his head, and as he did so more tiny trickles of blood came out from his nose. He refused to look at Duane again.

"I won't warn you again now, bud, to go back to the party with friends your own age or I'm going to have to let you keep company with these heroes here."

Duane must have missed something then, like falling asleep for a few moments in a movie, for when he started to say something else to Ted all he could see was the taillights of the retreating squad cars and a cloud of smoke from the exhausts.

"I wonder if they will shoot them," Duane said, then ran on back into the barn.

By the time Duane returned to the ballroom, if he had been capable of noticing details by now, he would have seen that the crowd had thinned out considerably. In fact the only two noticeable dancers were Duke and *her*.

But what was wrong with Duke's legs?

He went over to the couple and stared. Estelle looked relieved, almost overjoyed to see Duane.

"He's asleep on his feet," Estelle pointed out.

The two of them put their arms around Duke and led him away to the back of the house. It would have been easier to have carried off the barn door.

"Put him in the Jonquil Room," she said when they had reached the kitchen of the house. "Right off here," she pointed.

In the Jonquil Room they laid Duke out on a massive king-sized bed covered with handmade quilts. Duane took off his shoes and made a great to-do about the stench of his feet. He pulled off his trousers too, on which Duke had been sick.

Duane stood gazing at his tutor, who was making hideous sounds through his nose, from which strings of mucus dripped.

"Well?" Estelle said peevishly.

"Well what?" Duane turned to her. He was aware that he must be slightly cross-eyed as he looked at her.

"Aren't you going to take off all his clothes and put him to bed? Why, I mean, half-measures?"

"Oh, all right," Duane cried, and with a rapidity he was sure any army sergeant would have been envious of, he stripped Duke down till he was mother-naked.

"Do you want this good-luck charm took off his neck?" Duane turned to Estelle. She was looking with half-opened eyes at the tutor.

"Why not?" she said shakily. Duane handed her the amulet, which she accepted, but she kept her gaze fixed on Duke.

"Throw the blanket over him," she said and took hold of Duane's hand.

How many times, how many actual times, Duane was later to remember when, a year or so afterwards, he had more or less "grown up," did he make that poor woman rise from her bed to dance again so that he could get the cramps out of his thighs and legs, and then, having held her to him in the ballroom now dwindling of dancers, would take her back to bed and, in her words, give her a Turkish steam bath all over again. ("I have never in my life heard of anybody who could produce the amount of perspiration you can; for the love of God, you must have drunk all the wells in the county dry. You could deflower a woman with what pours out of your armpits!")

For Duane found that once the dam was broken, the conduit in disrepair, and the sluice, the flood running high, he might be lying on her till doomsday.

She had suggested while they were still in the barn that he partake of the same drink she was sipping, and which they procured from a small bar that did not serve the other guests. But he insisted on tasting the liquor from her own mouth before she swallowed it, and which she somberly permitted him to do—that same pale yellow, sweetish-sour concoction with the salt around the rim of the glass which he both detested and could not, however, resist when it came from her own mouth. (That was the moment when he had felt the sweat falling in icy droplets from his armpits.)

Then a dizzy recollection came back to him of a day in mid-August when he and Justin had wrestled together on the grass and he had nearly whipped his older brother, when, without warning, heavy thick drops from Just's chest had come down first upon his own mouth and

James Purdy
(212)

then fairly blinded his eyes. At the rushing remembrance of that afternoon, he turned in a frantic wish for stability to his new friend and
kissed her vehemently, tasting again the peculiar drink he had been
sharing with her. A thin thread of saliva hung in the air from their two
slightly disengaged mouths.

"You have a phenomenal recovery rate, my precious!" she cried in reference to his having keeled over a while back. "While look at me!" She
pointed to her wilted gown. He had already taken her hand and led her
back into the milling mass of dancers. He held her so tightly she kicked
him, though she did not want him to stop holding her.

"Just look at me, Estelle," he whispered to her with his lips against
the hair around her ears. "Don't let's ever again see the passed-over. Do
you hear? I'm me, you understand, or I'm him, but I'm all that's here
before you. I'm all you've got!"

"You're certainly an armful, too." She looked at him carefully. She
was sober, and he was drunk from the liquor he had tasted from her
mouth.

"Did you hear what I said, Estelle?"

"I thought I did."

"You mustn't see anybody but me tonight. Especially when we go
inside presently."

"We're going inside?" She was grinning, and she no longer looked at
all like she had a few hours earlier. Indeed, every time he looked at her
she had a different glance, even a different face. Of course, the flaming
streamers and lights, the smell of so many bodies, too, changed all one
felt and looked at, and he supposed he must himself look momentarily
like a vast array of different men, different faces, different dancers.

"Hold me just as tight as you want to, go ahead," she said, and she
accentuated her own height as he held her like a half-drowned swimmer.

"Go ahead, throttle me," she whispered.

"Where did you round up such a crowd?" he wondered, and he put
his mouth against her cheek.

Right in the midst of this number, she took his hand and led him
through the surly, often enraged dancers back to the house.

They entered a room new to him. She slipped off her evening gown.

He stood before her swaying, his lower lip hanging, his hair suddenly
as tousled as if he had been wrestling again on the grassy knoll with
Justin.

"Here, let me," she said, and helped him off with his tux. "God, it weighs a ton."

When he was all bare but his socks, she thought for a minute of that other unending night now so out of reach and time.

He had started to reach for a thick Turkish bath towel to dry off some of the sweat, but then he considered it like the salt around the brim of the sweet-sour drink: Why would one spoil all that? He had sweated in the first place for her, so why dry out the gift with a towel?

Then there they were together closely pressed, her own body wet from his, her own expensive perfume dissipating and rising invisibly away from her, never to be sniffed again, her mouth swimming with his embraces, her face swimming with so much wet from his mouth that for a moment she thought he had kept back part of his drink and emptied it on her. She gasped and choked like someone taking a first swimming lesson. He never stopped to ask if she was all right, as her other recent lovers had. He never spoke. He was more audacious and more brutal than any before him.

"Tell me I'm not him," he cried, working into her body with all his hard, untried force.

"Not like the devil?" she coughed out.

"Tell me I do it like myself, like Duane, that I'm not the other one."

"Jesus, you're better." She had all but swallowed his mouth, but the words must have got through, or were communicated clearly enough by her body.

"It's Duane that is taking you," he said. "Duane, Duane, Duane. He's dead. This is Duane."

The rush that now came from him swept her past herself, took her over some boundary she had only half envisioned before. She lay back as if he had broken her neck, and now only the whites of her eyes were visible. But as he was already at her again, she raised her head weakly and said, "Don't worry, you're nobody but you!"

She might as well have warned a speeding engine.

But at the height of her surge of feeling she was suddenly enraged by the thought that between Justin and Duane there had been some bond which she could not touch, fathom, encroach upon. It both spoiled her pleasure and made it more intense, doused it out and made it flame again.

"What did you have?" she cried in her peculiar strident voice immediately after her greatest crest of sensation.

James Purdy

(214)

He was staring at her ears. They were pierced like Mrs. Newsom's. He pulled his wet organ out of her, but it was throbbing and hard as if it had not yet entered her.

"What did *who* have?" he said, panting.

"What did you and Justin have between you?" she wondered.

His head, his mouth fell over one of her small hard breasts. He touched the nipple to his mouth, and she lay back for a few moments, but then came up again like a diver who has gone below the usual safe depth.

"I say, what was your eventual plan, do you think? I mean, two men that close must have been planning something. You had some grand scheme, didn't you?"

He stared at her in amazement. She was, he saw, desperate to know.

"He never told me," Duane replied, his head between her two breasts.

"But he knew?" she coached him.

"Don't, don't," he cried plaintively.

"Was it adventure?" she proceeded. "Going to the ends of the earth together?"

"I think it was all over when he went away," he confided.

"His worship of you?" she prompted him, winding his wet hair around her finger. "It couldn't be over."

"Estelle." He raised his head, but the darkness hid her eyes from him, even though outside he could see jack-o'-lanterns glowing from the dancing pavilion. "Just told me—of course he was drunk—he come into my room wearing his nightshirt. He hated nightshirts; he liked only to sleep raw but he wore it to please old Eugene. He said, 'I can't reach any higher crests than I have, Benjy, so it won't matter what happens to either of us from now on, will it? On account of how many reach the crest we have, huh?' "

He did not tell Estelle that Justin had kissed him then. It was the only time he had ever kissed Duane that way, as he might have a woman, but it was a fiercer kiss than any man would dare give a woman. It was a death kiss.

"But did you feel you had reached the crest he was talking about?"

He did not reply for a fearfully long time. Then he said, "I only reached everything through him, or past him."

———

Mourners Below

It was the sunlight stirring from under the green blinds that made him come awake.

He found himself at the foot of the bed, his mouth pressed against Estelle's tiny, sweet-smelling, soft feet. He looked up at her body and its mother-of-pearl hue, the blue veins standing out so delicately on her small, perfect breasts. He stirred again with longing, but then whether owing to the taste in his mouth or the pitiless searching rays from the sun, he lost heart. He painstakingly dressed, putting on, instead of the cowboy suit in which he had arrived, the dazzling if slightly crumpled and soiled tux. Except he could not find his shoes. He walked through room after room looking for them.

In the kitchen under an empty milk can rested a large note. He picked it up and read:

When you read this I will have put as many miles between you and me as the fastest mode of transportation is able to achieve & where you will never be able to break my heart again. Don't look for me and don't be damned fool enough to send the police. Remember all I have got on you before you do a thing like that. Goodbye forever this time. You've got enough dresses to wear until you're ready for your coffin anyhow.

Richard

He looked in the room where they had deposited Duke. Empty also. Not a soul anywhere.

A few gray cats were picking up pieces of spilled food and lapping up melted ice cream near the flagstones by the barn.

He sauntered out somewhat aimlessly to the back road where two men were driving a bay horse and flicking a whip almost too short to reach its haunches.

"Whoa," the more tanned of the two said, and took off his broad-brimmed straw hat.

"What are you doin' on my road?" he said, fanning the flies away with his hat, and then reached for a bottle and drank from it. "What happened to your feet?" he went on, scowling and threatening with his icy-blue eyes and snarling mouth.

"Ask him if he's been stealin' chickens, Tych," the younger boy taunted, and helped himself to a swallow from the older man's bottle.

James Purdy

"Yeah, are you the little fox that's been robbin' the hen roosts around here?"

"I been to a dance," Duane said in a hoarse, thick voice.

"Dance, my ass," the older boy snorted. "Ain't been a dance around here since they shot McKinley. I reckon, Keith, he is one of the gang been robbin' us of our livestock, what with no shoes and all."

"He's guilty as shit fire, tha's clear," the younger man opined.

"Wait a minute, now," Tych, the driver, said, scratching his chin with his tobacco-stained forefinger and thumb. "Look at his puss, would you now? Just look at his goddamned puss, will you? Now look, you blind little crud, why didn't you see it first, why do I always have to be the one to see things, huh? Well, I am a see-er and if he ain't a dead ringer for *him*. Look at that cocky little banty rooster, would you? He's a dead ringer for him, spit and image, 'cept his hair is fair, and he don't have no beard, at least none you could put a razor to. We'll fix that. We'll fix it for no other reason than he looks like him!"

"Looks like who?" Duane shouted, terrified.

"Looks like the one we've been spoilin' to get even with since we tangled with him four years ago!"

"Oh, why don't you tell him he beat up on you, how he knocked you into the middle of next week, why don't you?" Keith taunted the driver.

"All right for you, Keith." Tych flicked the whip in his left hand in the direction of Keith. "We'll take care of you when we get to the house, if you ain't careful."

"I'm always careful, Tych, you know that."

"You button your lip, then, or maybe I'll bust it shut."

"You get up here, and we'll look you over," the driver now commanded Duane.

"Do as you're told, you little piss-fart." Another flick of the whip and Duane climbed up beside the driver.

They started to drive on then, in a slow teeter-tottering pace, like a boat that might capsize at any moment.

"So whose bed did you leave your shoes under?" the driver wondered after a long silence during which they had proceeded down the road, which grew steadily narrower and narrower.

"I went to a masquerade ball," Duane confided in a hopeful way.

"Masquerade ball, my mother! We don't have our balls a-masqueraded . . . do we, Keith?"

Mourners Below

(217)

"Damned well we don't, Tych," Keith replied.

"What do you take me for?" He spat full in Duane's face, and his spit was largely tobacco juice.

"Look here," Duane said, "you can't talk to me like that." He wiped the tobacco juice off his face.

"Like what?" the driver said. "Ain't you in my wagon? Ain't you here on forbearance?"

Duane spat in the driver's face and jumped down.

"Get him!" the driver commanded Keith, who jumped down and grabbed Duane's arms. In their struggle, they fell to the side of the ditch.

The driver jumped down also and helped pinion Duane.

"I want them fancy clothes he has on," the driver told Keith.

While Keith held him, Tych pulled off with some difficulty Duane's tux, under which they saw the expensive shirt and underwear given him by Estelle.

"This here banty rooster must come from quality, what do you know." He studied the boy's underpants. "We'll take all he's got on then, Tych, by Christ we will."

Hardly had they spoken than they had accomplished their intent, and Duane was stripped of everything but his socks.

"Shall we leave him barefoot, too?" Tych wondered, eyeing his socks and the prostrate boy as if with insufferable disgust.

"You know that black paint we have in the back of the wagon?" Keith raised the topic.

"Oh, the kind too thick and clotty to be any use, yeah, I recollect that paint."

"I think this little piss-fart's hair is too silky and fair for a boy's and we'll do him a good turn by dyeing it black with our no-good, clotty paint."

"You got good ideas today, Keith," Tych said. "Damned good ideas, if I do waste a compliment on you by sayin' so. Well, what you waitin' for? Go get the paint while I hold the bugger down."

It was Duane's loud cries which caused them to gag him then with a burlap bag that Keith also brought down at the same time as he fetched the can of paint.

Gagged, and then partially tied, Tych quickly poured the entire contents of the can of paint on Duane's head. Gasping for breath, kicking violently, he had soon turned, thrashing, over on his belly.

James Purdy

"We can't leave the little pig like that all inconsolable, now can we," Tych said, "without somethin' to comfort him with. Go get it, go on."

"Aw, Tych, no," Keith disagreed.

"Do like you're told." He slapped Keith across the face. "Git!"

Keith jumped up laggardly in the wagon and brought back a small, rounded piece of wood which resembled the end of a broom handle.

"Stick it up him," Tych commanded.

"I won't. We done enough, God damn it." In response, Tych struck Keith with vicious precision across the mouth.

"Then I'll do it, you chicken-heart of a cocksucker," he spat at Keith.

Jumping down on Duane, sitting on his outstretched legs and thighs, which jerked violently, he masterfully, methodically, relentlessly stuck the broken-off broom handle up the prostrate boy's backside.

That was how the state police found Duane a few hours later.

PART VI

"I want to ask for your pardon," Professor Redpath said, standing at the door, his fall felt hat in his hand, his necktie stringently tied against his rather prominent Adam's apple, his knuckles showing white as his right hand grasped the lapel of his cotton jacket tightly. "I did not speak, I'm afraid, as a gentleman."

"Step in, Miles, come on, don't stand out there like a salesman trying to palm off something on an unwilling customer," Eugene Bledsoe responded. The wrinkles around his eyes betokened his extreme joy and relief.

When they were both seated in his den, Eugene interrupted a further volley of apologies, heartfelt regrets, abject sorrow with, "Miles, it's all been stashed away, forgotten, never to be mentioned again. So ..."

"The thing I admire about you, Mr. Bledsoe, is that you can turn off unpleasant thoughts so easily. You have, if I may say so, an iron will. You can shut off, I do believe, the past and never consult it again when it is not in your interests to do so."

Eugene Bledsoe cocked his head slightly to the side, so that his cheeks, grown thinner in the past weeks, almost touched his stiff collar. "You mean that as a compliment, of course." He finally accepted Professor Redpath's encomium. "I'm ... much obliged for your saying so," he concluded after a prolonged pause.

"I would give anything to be able to do so myself," the baseball player continued, blushing, and fidgeting in his breast pocket for something.

"I'm afraid, however," Eugene Bledsoe commenced again, "that I am not quite so perfect at expunging unwelcome thoughts as you may think. I am in fact, Miles, a much-aggrieved and tormented man."

Professor Redpath interrupted this confession of inadequacy on the part of his idol by chirping out, "I came here to ask your pardon, and ask it I will. ... For my quite inexcusable and rash contradicting you in our arguments"—here he consulted the long piece of foolscap he had extricated from his breast pocket—"having in effect denied you the right to prefer John Brown to President Lincoln, for having acerbically questioned your opinion and right to hold it that Abraham Lincoln was an 'opportunist' rather than an 'intellect' and that your admiration for John Brown is so high you put him in the class with Socrates, Jesus, and ..."

As the professor fumbled with his notes, Eugene cleared his throat in magisterial and ominous gruffness, but the younger man, having begun, could not bring himself to stop, and said, "... and your recent very unorthodox and, if I may say so, unprecedented evaluation not only of the Battle of Fredericksburg but of the accomplishments of Generals Burnside and McClellan."

Eugene colored, nodded, touched his collar, and closed his eyes several times. Professor Redpath saw that he was exercised, and attempted to say something else, but only a few sounds, barely describable as words, came from him.

"I wonder if you could have heard me properly." Eugene glanced at the foolscap. "Of course," he continued, "when one is in the midst of a heated discussion, as we were, and touching of course on the Civil War, which you as a Southerner and, I believe, a Catholic ..."

"I have told you, sir, again and again, that I am a Northerner, although my maternal grandfather was born in Virginia."

"There you are!" Bledsoe grinned, as if the argument had been conceded. "Don't tell me blood doesn't tell."

"And as to being a Catholic, what do you mean? I am Episcopalian!"

"If you will excuse my saying so, Miles, only a Southerner could have argued the way you did."

"If *I* may say so, your calling President Lincoln an opportunist, and your rather wild enthusiasm for General Burnside ..."

"If I called Abraham Lincoln the epithet you claim I did"—Eugene glanced at the long, legal-size paper again—"I meant it as a compliment."

"I see." Professor Redpath nodded and jotted down something on the fiercely scrutinized paper. "I'm glad to know that, Eugene. It relieves my mind a good deal."

"I am not an authority on the Battle of Antietam or General Burnside. You know that, for God's sakes. The disaster of Bull Run we agree on I think ... as we do on the outrageous cashiering of General McClellan. ..."

Redpath stirred uneasily, then folded the paper, preparing to put it back in his coat pocket, and sighed rather too audibly, for Eugene fixed him again with his glance.

"I am a bit more taken aback, however, that you should believe me capable of expunging all unpleasant or tender thoughts from my consciousness. I am not quite that sort of iron man."

Professor Redpath saw that Eugene did not know whether he had accused him of being a hero or perhaps a cold-hearted egoist.

"I regard you as the finest person it has been my pleasure to know. Your example has cheered and inspired me. Any misunderstanding, rancor, or ill-will between us, sir, would ... would ... it won't do!" Redpath cried, half rising and pushing the paper into his breast pocket. "I also wanted to tender to you," he continued in his most sepulchral voice, "I wanted to express ..."

Eugene moved to the edge of his chair, like a defendant about to be ensnared in some dangerous question by the prosecutor.

"I have heard the terrible news about ... Duane."

Mr. Bledsoe at first said nothing. It was the last topic on earth he had wanted raised, unless it was the deaths of Justin and Douglas, but Professor Redpath's voice had been loud, had in fact reached the street. Anyone passing would have heard it.

"That such a young man should have been so brutally . . ." Professor Redpath wanted to stop, but like a man in a car with faulty brakes going down a great hill, he could only go on with, "Have they caught the . . . ruffians?"

Bledsoe sighed, perhaps with relief that he had used another quaint Civil War term or perhaps because the worst had been asked and he could surrender to the inevitable—that the shameful topic at least was out in the open.

"No," he said thunderously. "They haven't."

"If you could give me a description of them . . . By God, sir, if I could lay hands on them, I . . ."

Mr. Bledsoe seemed to have dissolved under the continued and unhampered mention of the forbidden. He looked both deaf and dead. As no other topic seemed fit to pursue, and because he was already so rattled by his difficult meeting with Bledsoe, Professor Redpath could only go gabbling onwards, touching a hornet's nest here, stepping on a snake there, falling in a ditch at another step.

"He's not permanently . . . damaged, then?" Miles Redpath blurted out in an even louder voice.

"Who? Duane? Outside of sore limbs and racked hips . . ." Eugene began with a sudden, almost idiotic volubility. "God damn it," he suddenly informed the neighborhood with his own volume, "those boys of mine are made of iron, though they mope and loaf and are idlers and are always into something if not unsavory, questionable. But, by God, they have the health of a county-fair ring-nosed bull, if I do say so myself. What I fear"—he came down to a very resounding whisper—"is that he may have slain his assailants. It's possible they may be lying in some ditch somewhere."

Mr. Redpath fell back in his chair, his head pressed against the soft cushion decorated with wild morning glories.

"Except had he done so, they would have found the bodies by now. But he ain't harmed, just sulky and odd, and his hair, you know, is the color of a lump of coal. He's ashamed to be seen, and he looks exactly, damn it . . . looks like . . ."

Mr. Redpath gazed at his idol with both pitying consolation and

James Purdy
(226)

abetting encouragement, for the name was coming, like a piece of something swallowed inadvertently which must be coughed up now or the consequences would be more than serious.

The sound of the ticking clock was almost deafening, as both voices had ceased; then, if not the name, the referent came out in a long-drawn thin scratch of sound like a fingernail on a pane of glass.

"... unaccountably like ... my oldest, you know."

Professor Redpath walked over to Eugene, took his friend's hand, put his other hand on his shoulder, and then hurried out, stumbling over a footstool and closing the door so loudly that all the windows shook.

Eugene hardly knew he had left, his head folded into his outstretched heavy farmer's hands.

"I've heard only bits and pieces," Duke La Roche apologized to his pupil for having asked. "After all, your Dad is more closemouthed than a bank vault at midnight."

La Roche stopped, but Duane only smiled and said nothing in reply.

They were in the east parlor, seldom used before Duane's "accident" and now opened up and aired out. It had been chosen in the first place because of the sun streaming in all day, and was deemed less depressing than the rest of the house.

"We've done nothing today, Duane, with geometry, and little more with your Latin." Duke rose and went to the window. He jingled coins in his pants pocket like Eugene.

Turning about violently, he faced his pupil. "You didn't, did you? Say you didn't!"

Duane knew exactly what the tutor meant, but he could not answer him, for a number of reasons, and also because he marveled at, if not admired, this display of such strong feelings—love, he guessed it was—for Estelle Dumont.

"It's so long past," Duane stuttered out.

"A month or so is long past! What a bright little procrastinator you are. It's your best gift along with wriggling out of everything. If you took a gun and shot twenty men to death, you'd convince the jury that someone threw the gun at you, and, as you caught it, it fired."

"As my teacher, follow your own rules. Always ask a concrete question to receive a concrete answer."

"I'm afraid to ask—or get an answer, you know that."

Mourners Below

(227)

"Then, here I go. . . . I made love to her all night, not once and then good night, but once and then again and then again and then again. Between the whiles, we danced, then again, again, again."

Duke La Roche fell into the chair like a teepee collapsing, and despite his bulk, he gave the impression he was sitting entirely on the floor.

"Couldn't you tell her I care for her, too?" he almost whimpered.

"I already have," Duane informed him.

"Already . . . told her how I feel, you mean?"

Duane nodded emphatically. "Also about the photos you have put all over your study wall."

"Oh, you didn't!"

"Yes, she took that all in, you can depend on it."

"But what did she think!"

"What could she think if you have a whole room papered with nothing but photos of her? She knows you . . . care."

"And you did it, you say, again and again?"

A long silence ensued.

"She would allow me, then, you think, to . . . look her up?"

Duane stared at Duke and repressed a smile, for "look her up" sounded so like Eugene.

"I wonder what she thinks," Duane finally said. "I've never been back or dropped her a line or called or . . ."

"She knows you were . . . attacked."

"How do you know she does?"

"Your father told me she had telephoned."

"And he never told me!"

"Duane! Duane!" Duke was on his feet again, was standing over his pupil, was shaking him like the times when the pupil could not get some simple problem in math through his head. Wild with exasperation, the tutor was yanking him by the lapels of his jacket. "Don't you love her, don't you long for . . . more? Aren't you crazy with longing?"

"Yes, but . . ."

"But, what then, why aren't you there now with her? Why haven't you married her?"

"Married! . . . Can I marry?" He spoke as idiotically as when they had failed with geometry together.

"If you are already her lover, why can't you be her husband?"

"I?" Duane placed his index finger on his chest. "It . . . it . . . it was like ..." and he stood up and went to the window. Then, turning around, he said, "It was just like Justin had come to her again, but let me act, you see, for him."

"I don't see. I don't." Pulling Duane roughly by the arm, the tutor said, "Weren't you deliriously happy in any case, to have had such an experience? Don't you see I would cut off my right arm to lie down with her?"

"I see," Duane said.

"But you don't."

"But Justin ..."

"Hang that rotten Marine. Hang him!"

"Watch out, Duke. Watch out." A kind of foam had formed on Duane Bledsoe's lips.

"You can marry her if you like, Duane, if you ask me." He picked up his hat.

"I didn't ask you."

Duke turned back. His anger gave way now to his need, and he implored, "Since you don't want her as badly as I, or perhaps as Justin, can't you go to her and tell her of my desperation?"

"Your desperation! You expect me to ..."

"You won't help me?"

"Of course, but ..."

"But what!"

"I don't know how to help anybody, can't you see that?"

"But if you were instructed ... by your teacher now ... Told what to do or say ..."

Blinding tears stood in Duane's eyes. Without warning he threw himself into Duke's arms, knocking his new hat to the ground. Duke could only hold him and smooth his hair. They clung together like that while Duane sobbed.

"If she knew how much I cared," Duke explained, extricating himself at last from the boy's embrace. "If you pleaded my case, you see."

"You'll have to rehearse me, Duke," Duane whispered.

"You don't want to marry her?"

"Marry Justin's ... girl ... wife." Duane beseeched him for assistance.

"Does she love you?"

"She's like," Duane began white-lipped, "going through a forest in flames. Yes, I felt I was jumping through burning hoops, or going into a whole sea of black molasses, I felt I was riding the ocean, and also dying in the fire of the charred forest. But she's his . . . Justin's . . . second helpings."

"But she . . ."

"She loves me best, she said. Yes, she said that. But that only made it worse. Made it the worst of . . . loves. He had been there before me in everything else. He stood behind me. He told me how to love her, in fact, and improve on his . . . performance."

Duke again held him close. He did not understand what was at issue quite, but he knew it was grave.

"Then you wouldn't mind if I followed after you, too?" he finally inquired.

"It might be a relief to her after me," Duane told him.

"Whatever that might mean, Duane."

They were both reluctant to pursue that idea further.

"As soon as I'm all together," Duane told his tutor, "we will, that is I will, go to see her, and I will . . ." He looked up into Duke's face, then getting his cue from his lips, finished, "plead your case for you."

Duke took both the boy's hands in his and held them with a powerful grasp, then hurried out down the stairs.

"Well, see who is coming up the driveway," Estelle cried from the front porch on which she was unaccountably sitting.

Duane took in first of all her dress, a raw silk, shimmering green, which, if he had known anything about dresses, he would have realized cost enough to feed a family of four for a year.

"You talk in a different way," he said as she rattled on about latecomers, truants, and prisoner invalids.

"The last time I met you," he went on, "you spoke like a foreigner. Now you talk like one of us."

"I am one of us," she said. "And I will be more like one presently. Why didn't you take a year to return, or two, why didn't you stay away as long as some others I've known?"

Duane sat down gingerly. She pretended not to notice that he had something wrong with his lower body.

"I wasn't in such good condition, and besides, they watched me like a hawk."

He cautiously took her hand, which had two sparkling rings on it, and which he pressed to his mouth awkwardly. She relaxed her face a little.

"I've never been allowed the use of excuses," she told him. "People expect me to be a liar, so I always tell the truth. And they think I'm telling whoppers. I might as well tell them. I'm never believed. Your Dad treated me like a gypsy. I've never met such a facade on a human being. Where is the man underneath it all? How can you stand to have a father like that? Why don't you run off? Letting him keep you as a prisoner!"

"Why didn't you come to me? You knew they . . . nearly murdered me. I didn't know a thing for two weeks. I . . ."

"Somehow I can't be angry with you. When I should be foaming at the mouth! Here I haven't seen you for going on what seems months, I have called at your home, been treated like a door-to-door salesman by your insufferable stuck-up father, who would barely let me step inside, have been told only that *you were not yourself.* I only learned that you had been assaulted from a piece in an out-of-town newspaper under the headline 'RURAL CRIME.' And as if that weren't enough, you have the gall to send me this idiotic letter pleading your tutor's suit: *'Duke is in love with you. Can't you have pity on him, Stelle, can't you see your way to do something for him?'* What drivel!" She tore the letter in two and cast it on the porch floor.

"Now let me give you some real news: I am pregnant, I tell you, *pregnant.*"

"*Pregnant?*"

"Yes, my dear little boy, you are going to be a father."

"How do I know you are pregnant by me?" he got out.

"The oldest dodge in history: 'If you let me, you must have let others.' No, Duane, you are the one."

"This will come as a terrible blow to several people," Duane said. He rose stiffly. Since he had been "assaulted," as the newspapers put it, he did not move about as jauntily as when he had been an Olympic aspirant.

"But that is of only mild interest to you, I take it!"

"Duke will be beside himself." He turned his eyes to her in an imploring expression which drove her to even greater lengths of impotent anger. She could only scream, then cry softly and daub her eyes with her handkerchief.

"I won't dare tell him!" young Bledsoe whispered.

Mourners Below

She wept now without restraint, but even Duane saw it was the tears and sniffling of pure anger.

"Don't think . . ." she began again when her composure had partially returned, "Don't think for a minute . . ." She advanced very close to him, and he could see almost no resemblance to the "bewitching" young girl he had danced with last fall; she was as monumental and beyond him as his grandmother had been when she threatened to bomb the bank if it should foreclose on her property. "You doubtless think, since you are a Bledsoe—that is, impervious to reality—that I intend to make you marry me."

"It never crossed my mind," he spoke up.

"What?" She could not quite believe he would say this, though how many times must the scales fall from her eyes? "Locked away in that house of yours with your idler ne'er-do-well of a father, waited on hand and foot—"

"Look who's talking," he roared at her. "Ain't you an idler yourself? You're known as an heiress. Look how you live, talk about me, you bitch, and my Dad, and sass me for having had brothers I looked up to. Look at how you live. We never lived so, and you know it."

"I earned this. If you only knew what I had to put up with, with my two husbands, you would want me to live in even greater splendor than this backwoods palace. We'll not talk about me, we'll talk about you and your ambitions to know nothing, but, like your father, to live on mere moonshine and hero-worship. You were all the same—Justin, Douglas, Eugene, even poor Aileen, all in love with somebody who never existed."

"Then why did you pull me into it all, why did you make me stand in Justin's stead? Wasn't it him you worshiped, too? But now you've pulled me in. I'll tell you what. I'll marry you if you will be good to Duke La Roche."

"You wouldn't wait till I came to what I brought you here for today, would you? Do you know why you're here? How could you? You don't know what you're about from sunup to sundown. You're here because you are the father of my child, but you are never to be my husband. Your father knows that!"

"You dared tell him!" And after passing his hand over his face three or four times, his tongue flicking in and out of his mouth as if it might pick up his next cue, he said, "Then I'll tell him there's doubt."

"Doubt as to what, will you tell me?"

James Purdy

(232)

"Doubt we ever so much as sat in the same room alone for more than ten seconds, let alone slept together."

"I can't imagine anybody sleeping with any of you, so I'd have to agree. Sleep with a wild mountain cat would be more like it. I'll tell you what." She went over close to him, her breath moving against his face, so that he felt his eyelashes flicker. "I'll see Duke. I'll see him."

He lifted his hand.

"Yes, and you can tell him I'll give him more photos to paper his whole house with. I'll see him!"

"And you'll tell him *everything* to boot?"

"Everything I can remember, yes, everything, I'll tell him."

"About us, about Justin, about all of you. And don't forget Douglas!"

"You . . . ?" She turned her back on him, and, as she bent over, sobs and even groans came from her. "And while it was pouring down rain, it would have to pour harder, and I lost maybe the one person I had come to need the most. Richard, of course." She sighed deeply when she saw he did not know who she meant. "Richard! Richard! He went out like a light, or a thief, or a last leaf or whatever. He left me one of his notes, but not one of his good ones. He didn't even bother to insult me when he left, or say where he was going. A dumb note was all! I knew then I'd lost him forever. He told your father on that great day of our meeting that he was my husband. And though he never actually touched me, and I never knew any more than a tepid kiss from him, in a way he told the truth to your Dad. He was my husband. He cared for me, and I think he loved me. Certainly he knew how to dress me. I believe that was the only time I was ever happy, when he was making dresses for me. I don't think he loved women, but he loved me. I believe he loved me the most of all. And I lost him through you.

"Not one word in months from you," she managed to add.

What Estelle Dumont had always dreamed of was that she had lost all of her fortune (which was already dwindling away owing to her improvidence and poor management) and that she would be married to a common working-man who would come home at five o'clock, begrimed and sweaty with blackened nails and greasy fingers. She would help him remove his overalls and blue shirt, would take his shoes off and put his feet in a large basin full of hot sudsy water and Epsom salts. They would sit together at table lighted only by a kerosene lamp, and after a frugal repast prepared by herself, they would slip into bed together, and she would nestle against his sinewy body content never to leave his embrace.

It was her principal dream and wish, and she knew that if she lived until she was ninety, she would never give it up.

Often she had her chauffeur drive her through the working-class neighborhood of our town shortly after the factory whistles had blown their last, and she would stop in front of some little white-framed house and watch the breadwinner in his front parlor waiting for supper. The wife in kid curlers would come out and say something to her main support and hand him a cold and frothy glass.

Although Justin's death had been, she was sure, a greater blow to her than it could have to the Bledsoes and the possessive, all-knowing Mrs. Newsom, it had ended, she knew, any hopes she would ever have for marriage. She and Justin had been capable of making each other acutely miserable, acutely desirous of one another, and incapable of spending one hour together without a fight. That was what made marriage with him an impossibility; no one human, even with the strength of a lion, could have survived such incessant torture as they had ready and waiting for one another.

Yet Justin's death had ended any hope for her. For a few brief weeks she had thought that Duane might be a kind of counterfeit of what Justin had been for her. Duane was if anything better looking and, she now knew, a better lover. But it was the fact that Justin, with all his overbrimming masculinity, had never satisfied her bodily need; it was the fact that she felt deprived after leaving his body that made her wish for him immediately again. Duane satisfied her completely, overwhelmingly, but as soon as it was over and she looked at his peaches-and-cream throat and face, his beardless chin, she remembered Justin's description of him as somebody who would always keep the imprint of the pot ring on his ass and the mother's milk on his lips.

That left only Duke. No workingman would have her, even if he were dead drunk constantly and continually. A college professor was the last thing she desired, but the fact that he had papered an entire room with the reproduction of her face caused her to throw caution to the winds.

"The reason I look so untarnished by time is that life has passed me by almost entirely except for my unfulfilled longings," she finally addressed her own image in the pier glass.

Seating herself abruptly, she looked down at the carpet. Her face was composed, there were no more tears, but a kind of tearing sound came from her breast. Then it stopped also.

James Purdy

"I believe you." Duane spoke at last. His eyes were directed nowhere, were barely focused.

"What?" she ordered him. "Believe what?"

"Believe I am the father."

Her laugh chilled him into a kind of motionless rapt attention, as if it explained all he had ever been or hoped to be.

"Why on earth," Duane cried, "did you take all of her pictures down? What on earth, what on earth!"

As was his "ingrained custom," in Duke's words, he had come into his study stealthily, without warning or knocking or making any noise.

"Did you burn the photos?"

Duke's big veined hands moved spasmodically on the table next to his slide rule, his compass, and his pencil sharpener.

"I threw them in the trash late one night," Duke explained. "I tossed and turned all night. In the morning, I thought better of it and went down to the trash bin to salvage them. No point in throwing innocent photos away, in any case."

"And did you?" Duane prompted him when he said no more.

Duke looked up at him. His glasses were off, leaving red marks at the sides of his nose, and his eyes were bloodshot, but without his glasses they were a startling gray, almost silver.

"I went down to the garbage pails, and they had been emptied. I got on my motorcycle and drove over to the dump. A Negro with a steel hat on came out and I told him my problem. 'You're about ten minutes too late,' he said, pointing to a black pillar of smoke on his right. 'That's where they'd be now,' he said, 'if anything was left of them.' I walked over to the pillar of smoke and looked at all the things on fire—old settees, dressers, hatboxes, davenports, Japanese screens. Some of the things I wouldn't have minded grabbing from out of the flames, like a beauty of a hard-oak kitchen table, a spinet writing desk, a stuffed buffalo head . . ."

"She'll be relieved to know they're gone up in smoke."

Duke went on enumerating other articles which the rich and the spoiled had thrown out in their trash.

"Otherwise she would have made me come over here, you know, and steal them off of your wall."

"God knows you are the one to break and enter here. I may as well give you this bunch of keys while I'm at it." Duke fished in his desk

Mourners Below

(235)

drawer and threw a ring of keys at Duane, who caught it awkwardly in his left hand.

Duane presently sat down, not listening anymore to his tutor's babbling and enumerating. "You think you feel bad? Why don't you consider what I feel, huh? Always worrying about me breaking and entering your house when I am about to become a father. How do you like that?"

Duke put his glasses back on and looked at Duane. His fierce eyes were of a totally different color behind the lenses, but their ferocity was, if anything, more pronounced.

"Say that again," the tutor prompted.

"I am about to become a father."

"By whom?"

"Whom but her. I've never . . . been with any other woman."

"But you only just met her."

"Three months ago," the boy corrected.

"And she will have it?"

"She will."

"And you'll get married?"

Duane shrugged his shoulders.

"Do they allow boys your age to get married?" the tutor wondered to himself. "I guess the law permits nearly everything today." He laughed abruptly, and then made a sound like sniggering and sobbing together.

"Duke." Duane spoke in a comforting but frightened voice. "I've made all the arrangements with her. She shall sleep with you."

"What?" he bellowed. "What are you doing to me now?"

"Doing to you now? For God's sake, why can't you lower your voice? You hurt my eardrums." And he put his hands to his ears.

"A father to the child of the one woman I care anything about," Duke went on. "I should strangle you to death. *Fix it up with her now!* What's left after you've finished with her? What would I have left, huh?"

Then there she stood!

Duke had not heard her enter the room. In his astonishment he was unable to rise from his chair. He had been up all night grading his students' papers, and his brain was fogged from excessive drinking of coffee and aspirin and Irish whiskey.

James Purdy

(236)

"Estelle!" he got out. *"Estelle."* He emitted a little moan.

Her appearance suggested that all the photos he had thrown out had come back to him in one all-encompassing, life-sized transfiguration.

"Yes, it's Estelle." The picture spoke and then came to sit beside him. She took hold of his hand. He stared at his hand in hers and gently shook his head.

"I think we have a friend in common, Duke," she went on, and pressed his hand harder.

He took off his reading glasses with his free hand and pressed the bridge of his nose.

"Give them here, Duke," Estelle said, and letting go his hand, she picked up his glasses and put them on a nearby table.

He had lit a cigarette meanwhile, and after a wait, she took it from him, inhaled deeply, and extinguished it.

"Even if it was that little jack-in-the-box who introduced us, I don't think we should waste any time giving thanks or looking backwards."

"No," he responded.

"No?" She was harsh, imperious.

"I mean, true, there's never enough time," he agreed.

Without warning, she kissed him full on the lips.

"Oh, God," he responded, near to weeping.

"Duke, Duke, you must know why I've come," she spoke between sweetness and harshness. "You can't be totally ignorant. We're . . . so . . ."

This time he took her hand.

"But I'm not here this morning—if it is morning"—she looked at the heavily curtained window—"to hear you tell me what Duane means, or meant, to you. I came here for you alone, Duke. I don't mean to leave without . . ."

He grinned feebly, and a few tears began to spatter his flushed cheeks. "Without . . . ?"

"Duke, you are to marry me." Estelle raised her voice.

He looked into her eyes with an intensity which made her own go shut for a moment, then she said in a leveling voice, "You are to be my husband!"

He reached quickly for his glasses, put them on, and peered at her in a manner which recalled the way he had sometimes looked at Duane.

"If I said you were my last chance, I don't suppose you would be flattered," she was going on. "But I can't wait, Duke, and I won't be refused, won't hear the words 'no' or 'never' again. And since the death of the Bledsoe brothers, I have felt time is not only running out, but that we are on the last thread of it. So I'm here to ask you to be my husband, and I am not leaving this house until I've heard you swear you will."

She waited, but he could not reply except in strange sounds deep inside his throat, which resembled those of a drowning man.

She rose.

"For Christ's sake, don't leave!" he got out. "Now that you've scared me more than an army of ghosts and told me the only thing I ever wanted to hear in my life, don't shake the dust off your feet and leave me alone to go crazy and cut my throat with my straight razor!"

She waited.

"Oh Estelle, all you have to do is say what you want, anything, and it's done." He hurried to her and began kissing her hands, which she had raised to his face. "Anything. Just command, and it's done. Oh, Estelle, if you only knew . . ."

"I know or I wouldn't have come." Her fingers moved to the top button of his lavender shirt.

"I'm entirely . . . reserved for you," he mumbled as he felt his shirt being unbuttoned still further.

"Of course, you must give up Duane," she said, "once we are married."

He knitted his brows, then raised his eyes to her and smiled. He took her to him and kissed her solemnly, then passionately.

"You have been more than a faithful housekeeper and certainly more than any hired girl we ever employed in the days of my mother. I can think of no praise high enough for your sterling character."

Mrs. Newsom listened to Eugene Bledsoe's encomium of her years of service with a masklike expression. Her worn hands touched a dead leaf on the potted fern next to her seat in his den. He did not look at her but kept his face turned toward the front window, outside of which a thick wet snow was falling.

"One never believes winter will come, Mrs. Newsom, and then one day we look out and see nothing but white drifts. It's the same with

James Purdy
(238)

growing old. One believes one will always be, say, twenty-five, and suddenly people are offering one chairs, and are looking about to see where one has left one's cane."

She knew it was coming, of course, his terrible news, and she cleared her throat noisily to let him know she was prepared for it.

"Estelle Dumont is pregnant," he announced at last.

He now looked over to her corner, but she did not return his gaze.

"She would have us believe," he went on, "that Duane is the father, and he has not bothered to deny it. He has admitted in fact to prolonged intimacy with her the night of that ill-fated masquerade ball, on the subject of which, Mrs. Newsom, you were absolutely right. Absolutely. In fact, I have learned since the ... event"—here he stopped and looked about him searchingly—"since the day when all things seemed to stop." It was the only time he had come anywhere near to speaking to her of the catastrophe of his sons' twin deaths. "I have learned that I am wrong on a great good deal. I should stick to my law books, and not be an authority on human nature, which the good Lord knows is beyond me."

"Oh, Mr. Bledsoe!"

It is doubtful he heard her exclamation.

"I am prepared to accept, therefore, that he is the father. He will not, however, marry."

"Praise be," she managed to get out.

"This note from the lady has just come." He handed her a piece of elegant blue letter paper. "Kindly read it, why don't you, aloud. I can hardly bear to touch it. It is scented in the bargain!"

Mrs. Newsom took off her regular glasses and put on her reading pair. Her lips moved convulsively before she found her voice. She read the date and the salutation in a whisper, and then in a booming contralto began the epistle proper:

> *If I did not make myself clear when I called to inquire after Duane's well-being, I wish to apprise you of the fact that the child when it is born is to be given to you for upbringing and education. I will defray whatever costs this may entail, totally and indeed beyond the outlay. I cannot be a mother to a Bledsoe. You would interfere with me at every stage of the game, not only because you are a tyrant in your own right, but because the poison of your*

resentment against both Duane and me would fall upon the blameless heart and mind of my child. Your great sin outside of the fact that you hate women is your inability to accept the most elementary facts of human nature. You seem to have been born immaculate and you have shed even the slight shell of humanity you must have been born with. I, on the other hand, am a total intimate of Mother Nature. You are what is wrong not only with humanity but with history. When history is rewritten in the future, it will be because you have ceased to exist. You are incapable of love, of tears, and even of death. I do not think you will ever die. You will disappear, probably, and no one will mourn you, though your passing will be felt with the same kind of relief one experiences when an immense boil bursts on one's neck. I will send my lawyer to you just as soon as the child is born.

Estelle Dumont

Mrs. Newsom read the letter loudly and without any expression. Mr. Bledsoe did not know whether he was relieved or annoyed that she made no comment. He was, of course, sure that nobody could quite comment on such a consummate piece of impertinence and rudeness. It could hardly have been worse had she accused him of killing his sons, which is about what the letter amounted to.

Mrs. Newsom handed the expensive stationery back to him, laid aside her reading glasses, pressed the two corners of her eyes, and then put her regular spectacles back on.

"One would think she had plotted it all from the start." Mrs. Newsom spoke in a huffy outraged voice. "The masquerade ball must have been planned long ahead. She was Justin's mistress, you must know."

Eugene Bledsoe had been smiling bitterly and unpleasantly just before he heard this last statement, for he often smiled like this when he was extremely ireful. The smile vanished like instant lightning, and his face assumed a black and almost insane expression.

"Where did you dig this up from, may I ask?"

"There was hardly a night my husband and I did not see them walking hand in hand past our house," Mrs. Newsom began.

"*Him?*" Eugene thundered, for it was as near as he could get to pronouncing the name of the hero.

"Justin. Yes. Justin," Mrs. Newsom went on with great authority, for it was clear he could never assail her again. She not only belonged to the house of Bledsoe, she was assured of a place in its inmost sanctuary. "Who else!" she cried in a tone reminiscent of himself and of his mother before him. "Why, they were inseparable! There was a time, mostly at night, when wherever we went for a drive in our auto we met them walking along the country roads, clutching wildflowers they had picked and looking into one another's eyes as if they saw all the heavenly galaxies in one another's glance."

"And did this whore enjoy my other boy also?"

"Do you refer to Douglas?" She spoke with the phlegm of a high jurist.

He bent his face over and held it in his outstretched hands.

"I wouldn't put it past her." Mrs. Newsom spoke in an indifferent whisper.

"So she caught all three of them in her net."

"She has done one good thing all the same." Mrs. Newsom indicated by a glance at the grandfather clock that her time, if not her patience, was running out.

"Don't give her that benefit, don't give her any!" he expostulated.

"She has given up the child, I mean, Mr. Bledsoe." She spoke in a muffled voice. "She knows that with her way of life she could not abide a baby under the same roof with her. For, Mr. Bledsoe, you do not know the half—"

"That was all Duane needed, wasn't it, to have his promise and his youthful freshness dampened by such a creature, such an initiation into the meaning of . . . life?"

"Oh, he will get over it." She rose.

"I'm surprised at you," he mumbled. "Duane is not the kind to get over anything, and you know it. He has never mended . . . from his grief. Nor will he ever," he added with bitter finality.

"I understand, sir," Mrs. Newsom replied, subdued now and more like her old self.

"He at least had their love before he was sullied by hers," Mr. Bledsoe finished, and with a terrible look gave her both thanks and permission to leave the room.

"Well, well, Doctor." Eugene overcame his usual reluctance at seeing old Cressy. "I heard your car coming up the drive. I'd know that motor of yours if I was a thousand miles from home." He was holding both the storm door and the inside oak door open for him.

Still he always had bitter memories when he looked at Dr. Cressy's face. He had been Aileen's favorite doctor, but then he had also attended his mother during the last years of her life.

"Sit here, why don't you?" Eugene pulled out the cushiony, sprawling easy chair that must have been reupholstered, remodeled, refashioned, and refurbished twenty-five times.

Eugene stared at the doctor's lips. *By God, he chews. I was unaware a man of his fastidiousness did. Wet snuff, I'm damned,* he said to himself.

Dr. Cressy held on to a heavy gnarled walking stick which had a kind of glass eye gleaming on its top.

"She won't go to the hospital," Dr. Cressy commenced.

Eugene felt the urge to say "Who?" but he knew the doctor knew he was perfectly aware who *she* was.

"She's the damndest, most impractical woman ever drew breath," Eugene ventured cautiously. He didn't want to curse her too roundly just yet. "What does she have in mind, to drop the baby like an Indian squaw somewhere?"

Dr. Cressy grunted in an approximation of a laugh.

"I'll tell you something, Doctor." Eugene hesitated, looked away. He almost never looked anybody in the eye, never had, never would. "I'm beyond my depth and have been ever since . . ."

The doctor was not too unlike Eugene in his manner of looking at people: he looked in their direction, but his gaze rarely connected with theirs; he just went on looking at or through his interlocutor, while Eugene always looked about, beyond, and all around them.

"I've had your story from two faithful witnesses, Eugene," Dr. Cressy said, and the younger man wilted, almost gave the impression he was kneeling before the doctor for a blessing. "The fact is, as we grow older, we're generally beyond our depth."

"You know then, I judge, who the father is."

Dr. Cressy said nothing for some time.

"I suppose there's nothing to do but take it at its face value," Eugene went on in the wake of his silence. "My boy don't deny he has . . . been with her."

"I wanted you to hear my side of the story." Dr. Cressy now began the purveying of information he had come to give. "I retired four years ago, and there are those who aver I should have quit ten years before

James Purdy

(242)

that. I've reminded Estelle Dumont of this. There are twenty better men nearer to you than me, I told her."

"Oh I doubt that, Doctor, I do."

"She wouldn't listen, of course. 'You'll deliver the baby or I will call in that Indian woman from Catoctin Creek. And I'll say you recommended her to boot!' "

Dr. Cressy wiped his lips with a fresh cambric pocket handkerchief. Eugene stared at its immoderate elegance and laundered perfection.

"Is this her way of killing herself and taking the baby with her?" Eugene wondered.

"I don't think so," the physician replied. "I think she's the kind wants to live forever."

Eugene nodded.

"But that don't apply to the baby."

Eugene pushed his chair back and swore. "You'll have to expand on that statement, Doctor," he said at last, when his visitor made no further elucidation.

"As soon as the baby is born, and she's strong enough, she's going to leave. Furthermore"—he waited a while for his first statement to sink in—"she's going to marry Professor La Roche."

"You don't mean Duke?" Eugene adopted his old courtroom method and manner of clarifying for the jury an unusually implausible statement just voiced by a witness.

"Duke La Roche," the doctor obliged Eugene.

"And does Duke La Roche know this?" Bledsoe's voice boomed as it had so often during a trial.

"I'm only telling you what she told me. And I'm only telling you this because I don't see any way out for me but to do as she bids, that is, be her obstetrician and deliver to you your son's child."

The utterance of this last phrase had so wrenching an effect on Mr. Bledsoe that Dr. Cressy not only looked at him directly but rose in a professional manner and advanced toward him.

"I'm all right, Doctor, there's no need to . . ." But Dr. Cressy had already taken hold of his wrist and was feeling his pulse.

Whether it was Dr. Cressy's somewhat famous manner with the ill, or the silence which had followed on the heels of his upsetting remark, or the mere fact that someone was touching him and paying some personal attention to him, but Eugene soon came out of the suggestion of apoplexy which had so alarmed the old physician.

"I think for once Mrs. Dumont and I may be in agreement," Eugene said when the doctor had dropped his hand but still continued to stand by him.

"On what grounds, may I ask?" Dr. Cressy said in the very low voice he often used in the sickroom.

"On what grounds, damn it all, but you being her doctor, obstetrician. You're not that old, for God's sake, Dr. Cressy!"

"I wish I could agree with you," the physician said, seating himself again. "I'll come with a young interne just in case, and she need know nothing about him. Medical authorities today don't like delivery at home anymore. They regard it as barbarous and dangerous, unsanitary and in very bad taste. Of course, all my early deliveries were never held anyplace else. So I won't notice any of the perils and outrages they make such a fuss about. And that Indian woman she threatened me with, Eugene, she'd be in a lot safer hands with such a midwife than with some of these recent medical graduates. But I've acceded to her wishes."

"So she's to . . . whelp and deliver her offspring to my door?" Eugene spoke in the savage tone of voice usually reserved for his soliloquies.

"You don't need to feel that is the end of the world either, Eugene," Dr. Cressy said, still eyeing Bledsoe rather directly. "Mothers die every day and their infants are turned over to others, live and grow up, and prosper."

"I never heard of such an infernal mess, or such a disgrace! Duane taken practically out of his bed, dressed up in a ridiculous suit like a carnival performer, led astray by this slut, beaten up by two men who I wouldn't put it past her she hired for the purpose, then called the father of a child who could be any man's offspring, the marriage refused, her engagement announced to one of her other victims, and then the bastard, we are informed, is to be deposited at my doorstep as if I ran a foundling asylum. By God, it stinks to heaven! This strumpet should be arrested and sentenced to hard labor!"

"She's going to draw up some papers so that all will be aboveboard and legally sound," Dr. Cressy said.

"Is that so?" Eugene was musing deep. "I suppose if it is my son's child, there will, in time, be telltale signs and obvious indications."

"One would hope so." The doctor spoke through his handkerchief, which he had again brought out, this time with somewhat ostentatious deliberateness.

James Purdy

(244)

"You medical men are always so damned cautious, if I may say so. You're deep."

"I'm not sure of much, Eugene, and if I live any longer, I may come to the point of not being sure of anything at all. There should be signs, as you say, if it's Duane's child or not, but Mother Nature can be capable of many a deception."

"Well, if Mother Nature has anything in common with the breed of women on earth today, by God, you can say that again," Eugene told him.

"I think you should come for a general checkup one day, Eugene," Dr. Cressy advised him abruptly.

"There's not a damned thing wrong with me except I've probably lived too long, Doctor."

"That statement doesn't hold water, Eugene, either as common sense or scientific fact, and you must know it. You've a lot to accomplish yet, and you'll soon be needed as never before."

This time Eugene looked the doctor square in the eye as he bade him good morning.

"Ask him, why don't you, if it is absolutely essential that I see him." Eugene Bledsoe spoke mournfully and humbly to Mrs. Newsom, who had announced that Duke La Roche was waiting in the vestibule.

"I've already explained to him that you are behind in your work as a result of the constant stream of callers." Mrs. Newsom almost exactly quoted Eugene's complaint which he had made to her about "excessive company."

"He won't take no for an answer," she sighed. "He's awful stubborn, anyhow."

"Show him in," Eugene said. As she went out, he swore and kicked a little footstool clear across the room. "I know how God must feel," he raged quietly, and walked over and set the stool back in its proper place. "I realize I know nothing whatsoever about people except this: they are all of them without exception crazy as poisoned bloodhounds and all on the wrong scent."

"Come in, come on in, Duke." Mr. Bledsoe spoke with his back to his visitor, and attempting to calm his own emotions, which were, more than at any time since Aileen had deserted him for another man, at the breaking point.

When he finally wheeled about, since he almost preferred to show his eyes red with the effort to control his tears of rage rather than give the tutor the sight of his back any longer, he was shocked to see that Duke's own two eyes had been very thoroughly blackened.

"What on earth!" Eugene began, then stopped himself and instead went over and shook hands with him. At first, Duke's handshake was limp, but as he saw that Eugene, too, was under great stress like himself, he finally held the older man's hand with pressure and tenacity.

"Sit down, why don't you, Duke. I don't need to tell you that for several months now I have been through hell and high water with that boy. I see no end in sight, as a matter of fact. Whatever you do, Duke, think twice before you become a parent. It's one occupation where you get nothing but hell and brickbats from morning to night. If you do anything good for your offspring, nobody notices it, and if you fail to do something minuscule you should have done, or do something people think you shouldn't have done, a thousand thunderbolts fall from the sky on you. Take my word for it."

"I hardly know how to proceed after that speech, sir." Duke spoke affably and almost with affection for his pupil's father.

"Just forget I said anything at all on the subject," Eugene advised. "An old fool's advice is not worth the saliva required to express it. I am feeling my age, by God, Duke, and you can engrave that on my tombstone."

Duke had the wind taken out of his sails by Eugene's abject and tragic demeanor and by his obvious "licked" posture. He hardly knew where to begin.

"Duane has disgraced all of us, first by going crazy, and now by knocking up this Dumont dame." Eugene spoke in a fashion which he himself realized had little of his delicacy and decorum.

Duke drew in his breath loudly and shook his head.

"Perhaps I should return at a later time when you are feeling more composed, sir," he ventured.

"When will I ever be composed again, Duke? God damn it! Don't mind what I say at all. I'm glad to see a fresh face." But even as he said this, he looked back questioningly at Duke's two black eyes. From his somewhat specious but perhaps, after all, genuine patrician and genteel altitude, black eyes, like being tattooed or frequenting pool parlors or making love to women in parked cars in the cemetery, were things that divided gentlemen from riffraff. It was certainly not to be mentioned. Therefore, seeing Duke with his eyes blackened was an added trial and indignity.

"I have come, Mr. Bledsoe, to tender my resignation to you, not willingly but for the best interests of all concerned."

"Resignation? What resignation?" For the life of him, Eugene did not associate such a term with Duke's being wretched Duane's tutor and "guide."

"Why, as your son's tutor, of course," he said.

"Oh, that," Eugene said, somewhat taken aback. "Of course! Of course!" He now considered this contingency.

"Has he made no progress at all?" Eugene thundered, for now that he knew what Duke referred to, he felt again a bit insulted and offended that he was about to hear more proofs and examples of Duane's not having come up to snuff.

Duke was straightening his tie and swallowing the great amount of saliva which had been accumulating in his mouth, always a sign for him that he was under unendurable pressure.

"Was he, I say, a total failure, then?"

"Not by a long shot," Duke countered with no real conviction or certainty in his voice. "Let me put it like this, which is the way I explained it to Duane many times. For instance, take Julius Caesar ..."

Eugene now turned his full gaze upon the tutor, for if there was one topic or personage he had grown dog-weary of hearing about from his last remaining son it was Caesar, and if it was one book that the boy had burdened himself to death with—and his father to boot—it was Caesar's tedious and hackneyed account of his own butchery of the hapless Gauls.

"Julius Caesar," Duke went on in the face of this growing thundercloud of hostility, "was able to dictate four letters while he was simultaneously writing a fifth letter with his own hand. That was the kind of mind and attention Caesar had."

Eugene snorted, turned his back again, and paced halfheartedly up and down.

"As I told Duane again and again, nobody expected that kind of attention or brilliance on his part."

"And how many letters can you dictate, Duke, while, say, writing by hand another letter to one of your girl friends?" Eugene demanded to know. "Well, answer me, man!"

Mourners Below

(247)

"Mr. Bledsoe, I believe you misunderstand what I am trying to prove."

"There you have it, Duke, you've certainly hit the nail on the head—or do you hit fifteen nails on the head simultaneously while preparing your history lectures?"

"All I am trying to convey to you—and what I tried to convey to Duane—is that he is a perfectly normal young man and is proceeding quite evenly along the way he is meant to proceed."

"You know as well as I that Duane has no ability whatsoever with books or learning of any sort, and that so far as I know he has no calling for anything under the sun except to involve himself and others in one confounded mess and imbroglio after another. In that, sir, he is a genius and would certainly put Caesar to shame, for whereas, according to your own words, Caesar could do five things simultaneously while conquering the world, Duane Bledsoe can raise the dead, turn a decent family into pandemonium, impregnate a woman damn near old enough to be his mother, and turn the whole community where he was born into a madhouse. Let Caesar top that, even if he was a genius at massacre and letter writing."

"Very well," Duke said, quietly. He was close to tears. "What I wanted you to know is I feel very close to Duane, and I will never regret the time spent with him. He is a wonderful young man in every respect."

"I see," Eugene said coldly. "Thank you," he added in an even colder tone. Then, turning about, his face pale and haggard, "And is that all you wish to confer about today?"

"Not quite, Mr. Bledsoe. There is another matter which I hesitate to broach. I wish, sir, you could realize what an imposing and even awe-inspiring man you are to others who may not know you. You tower over us all, sir!"

"What is your bad news? I'm ready for more. I thrive on bad news, terrible telegrams, and doctors' reports. Go ahead, blacken my eyes, too."

"These were quite innocently acquired, I'm afraid." Duke touched his castigated eyelids. "I fell downstairs. On account—I suppose—I have been so overwrought . . . I had not been drinking, but I was beside myself with grief and confusion, and—yes—love."

"Love?" Eugene cried with outrage and loathing. "What do you mean?"

James Purdy
(248)

"I am going to marry Estelle Dumont, Mr. Bledsoe."

"You don't say!" Eugene approached the chair Duke was sitting in and grasped both its arms as if he might be thinking of throwing him backwards or perhaps, such was the strength in his own arms, picking up both occupant and chair outright and throwing them out the front door.

"Yes, sir, we are to be married. She . . . has proposed." He did not feel the indecorum, even grotesqueness, of such a statement, albeit it was the truth.

"We will be married . . . once she has given birth to her child."

"*Her* child!" Eugene sneered, releasing his hold on the chair arms. "She's the mere receptacle—or bag, to put it bluntly—of what has occurred. The child, sir, is ours!"

"I have not come to contest that fact. But Mr. Bledsoe, I loved Estelle for years before Duane ever . . . came to her. Or Justin! Or anybody. I have loved her from the time we were both mere children."

"This is the most confounded mare's nest I ever saw, and I think the damndest muddled hash in the history of the world. It's enough to drive a decent man to the bughouse or to take to smoking opium. My head is splitting!"

Going on, he shouted, "It reminds me of stock farming!" Eugene had now raised his voice to such a pitch that Mrs. Newsom, who had been tiptoeing about outside the closed doors, opened them and asked timidly if Eugene needed anything.

"Presently, Mrs. Newsom, presently, I will indeed! You may retire, my dear, though for the moment!" he roared on.

"That woman," Eugene lowered his voice, "is a rare gem, a jewel. I don't think I would have kept my sanity without her. Despite her popish ways and her rosaries and candles and the rest, I am on my knees before her at this moment and in time to come. I think if she were not a married woman, I would be marrying her, since marriage seems to be in the wind. But to return to stock farming, artificial insemination, giving the cow the sperm and then turning her out to clover again . . ."

"Mr. Bledsoe, I cannot allow this. I have come here in all humility as your friend and as Duane's . . . And," he said, unsure whether this was the right thing to broach or not, "it was Duane, after all, who was the matchmaker in Estelle's and my case."

"Duane, the matchmaker?" Eugene moved to within an inch of the tutor's mouth and eyes. "Explain that if you will." He made fists of both his hands.

"He wanted us to be together, Mr. Bledsoe. Cupid was never more persuasive. That is one of Duane's many talents, persuasiveness in a strange hard-to-put-your-finger-on-it way. He ushered us into our ... lovemaking."

"I learn each day, don't I, about that boy?" Mr. Bledsoe sat down and looked as if he had turned to rags and straw.

"But I never hear anything direct *from* him, do I? I learned that he saw ghosts, never mind whose ghosts, but I learned that from an unimpeachable source. Now I learn he is a matchmaker for the very woman who, if he had any decency, he would marry himself. My trouble, Duke, is I have lived too long. I can make nothing of the modern world. It does not even have the consistency or logic of an insane asylum. I could deal with inmates of lunatic asylums, have, indeed, dealt with them in my capacity as an attorney. But I cannot deal with my son as a visionary and a Cupid, or with that whore Estelle Dumont and her giving away of my son's bastard."

"But to *him,* and to *you,* we are giving it, Mr. Bledsoe. Don't you understand?"

"What right have you to bestow a gift of a bastard on anybody, even to the rightful father? Answer me that, Duke! For Christ's sake!"

"Don't call her a whore. Please!"

"Tell me the right epithet and I will frame it in diamonds and letters of the finest gold! Tell me what she did, for I have lost the thread of the entire story! Tell me who Estelle is."

"I have done my best, sir." Duke rose. "I will not stay longer. Give my sincerest regrets to your son ... Mr. Bledsoe." He stopped and helplessly raised his right hand upwards. "I love Duane as if he were my own son. That is what I have been trying to tell you. I would teach him forever if I thought there was any hope ..."

"Hope of what, Duke? Hope of what!" The old man turned his back again.

"Please give me your hand, won't you, and try not to think ill of me?"

With his back still to Duke, Eugene extended his hand, and the tutor grasped it fiercely.

"This is the saddest day of my life, sir," the tutor said, and then, rushing out from the house, he hurried on foot down the icy street.

James Purdy
(250)

"I have never seen your father so distracted and beside himself, and that is saying something," Mrs. Newsom confided to Duane after Eugene's interview with Duke La Roche. His pacing and jingling of the small coins in his pants pockets, his muttering between clenched teeth, his rattling his heavy gold watch chain and consulting the hour only a few seconds after he had already looked at the dial on his watch, his talking to himself, all these habits which had annoyed Duane for years in his father were now accentuated to become almost the marks of madness.

The thing which nearly drove him over the brink, as Eugene would have been the first to acknowledge, was the fact (ridiculous though it was to admit or even acknowledge) that he was to become a grandfather; for such a contingency he was entirely unprepared. It was even worse, he felt, than had he been informed by Dr. Cressy that he was going to die someday.

He had, he admitted only to himself, thought that Duane was still a child, and the deaths of his two hero sons, though this calamity had crushed him (in his own unspoken thoughts) to the very earth and had broken him ("I am a destroyed man"), had, if anything, only made him feel younger. When they had died, though the sorrow had paralyzed him, certainly deprived him of speaking of it—for had he begun, he would have run crazy with words; torrents of grief would have caused him never to cease speaking—he had somehow felt to be the same age as his dead heroes. But when Dr. Cressy, like some ebony night bird, had come with his drooping clothes and his tobacco-stained mouth and brought the news that his own baby—his Duane—was to be a father, that he was to be a grandfather, the pinnings that had held him up collapsed. He longed for death. He sometimes stood in front of the mirror for hours at a time, gazing in fierce scrutiny, in merciless judgment on his own physiognomy, seeing that he had not taken in the fact that his thick crest of hair was all gray, not one strand of black left; that the marks of disappointment, enforced bachelorhood, abstinence, unreturned passion, and withheld love had all left their marks on him; and that in a certain light he looked what he was, an old man, but an old man who would live on in bitterness and lovelessness and loneliness and pain.

He might have gone on with his pacing up and down the floor of his den and muttering between clenched teeth until he was carried away in a straitjacket had not Duane, in direct disobedience of the standing rule on his father's part, opened the sliding doors and screamed at him, "Will you give us no rest from that goddamned stalking up and down in your room! Or that confounded muttering and mumbling! Don't you know we are distracted from it all, too, and can't you sit down and be quiet? Can't you rest, God damn it!"

The sight of his own son's eyes rolling around, with nothing but their whites visible, the accumulation of what looked like slime on his lips, the mad flailing of his arms about, made Eugene suddenly calm. When the boy broke into a tempest of wild weeping, Eugene, for almost the first time in his life, took him protectively in his arms and held him, allowing the boy to cry, mucus and saliva falling all over his fine broadcloth shirt. He was as quiet under this outburst as he had been nervous and unresting in the wake of Dr. Cressy's and Duke's terrible tidings and confessions.

"We will live through it, Duane." He had wanted to add "At least you will!" but some restraint, given him perhaps by the dead, held his tongue. "Life is one long succession of disappointments, confusion, and bitterness, Duane, but we have to hold on and not go down. I suppose I have paced a good deal. And muttered. Would you rather have a Dad that paced than one who hit the bottle and ran after fast women?" As he spoke, he pressed Duane's head so tightly against his sinewy arm that the boy was almost strangulated, but he would have let himself smother to death rather than free himself from the pressure.

"I suppose I am a washout in many ways, Duane." He himself released his son now from the embrace and helped him to sit down on the little footstool he had so often savagely kicked and butted about like a football. "But we are the way we are. Whether God wanted us to be so or not is beside the point. I've tried to do a few things right, but by Christ, I didn't know"—he stopped suddenly and looked out at the trees white with frost and snow—"I was so far advanced"—he spoke now in almost a whisper—"down the shady path of my life, ready to be laid on the shelf and not looked up to anymore by anybody. This has caught me like a thief in the blackest night."

"I don't think anybody in his right mind sees you that way," Duane managed to get out.

"If nobody else does, I do. I know I am old, and I suppose one day I may get used to it, as I suppose I used to take it for granted that I was young and thought I would stay that way come hell or high water. Well, hell and water enough to drown this whole edge of town has come, and looking in the mirror"—here he left Duane and stood in front of the pier glass—"has taught me who is looking back at myself. It is a man I do not know or recognize, but I have to admit it is all there is left of me."

"And Duke is to marry her!" Duane's voice brought him back to the present, for whether old age or death comes like lightning or in slow stages, the world we see is going forward with or without us.

"Yes, that is what I have been led to understand," Eugene told him. "How long such a match will last I haven't the faintest notion, but I can tell you one thing, I'm glad it isn't you."

"You are?" Duane cried, and his father didn't know whether this was thanks on his son's part, or a mere hysterical, choric comment on an event which, like everything that had happened to the boy in recent months, was almost beyond his endurance or his ability to fathom.

"We're to have the child, and that will be all to the good. After all, it is ours."

Duane looked at him with awe and disbelief.

"Ours?" he echoed dully.

"Exactly," Mr. Bledsoe replied.

"What will we call him, Dad?" Duane wondered, holding his hands over his eyes.

"Justin, of course," the father answered with unswerving confidence. It was the first time he had said the name since the arrival of the telegram. Forever afterwards, Duane never remembered hearing him say it again.

It didn't occur to the boy to protest or even comment on his father's choice of the name. It was too dreadful a choice to be anything but accurate. And hearing his father pronounce a name that must have been more difficult for him to draw up from his innermost self than when he had to face his image in the mirror and say, "Eugene Bledsoe, you are an old man, and you are even older inside than you are out," filled Duane with pain.

They sat there then together in absolute silence for nearly an hour, until Eugene rose, jingled the coins in his pocket, and said, "I have to go up the street now, Duane, to see a fellow on a business matter."

"It is not any fixed amount added to an impression that makes us notice an increase in the latter, but that the amount depends on how large the impression is in the first place."

Duke La Roche said something more or less to the above effect as Duane Bledsoe darted into his bedroom unexpectedly but in accord with his long-standing habit. Duke had on a new dressing gown and his neck was buried in a huge scarf. Both articles of clothing probably came from Estelle, Duane presumed.

"I wanted to hear it from your own lips," Duane said, falling easily into his tutor's classroom speech.

"I thought I had told your father everything."

"I said firsthand, Duke."

"Right-o," the teacher replied. "Well, then," Duke went on, "when I heard your unmistakable step on the stair carpet, I thought, *I suppose young Bledsoe has come to shame me, deride, beat me up, maybe. Well, let him. All that has been done to me already by stronger hands than his!*"

"Eugene didn't touch you and you know it," Duane interrupted

"I wish he had. And he's still strong enough to. How does he keep his youth, do you suppose?"

"Uninterrupted leisure, Aileen says." Duane smiled.

"No, we spoke as one gentleman to another."

Duane grew aware that Duke was pacing the floor as idiotically as Eugene, except that he did not mutter between his teeth or have any small coins to jingle in his pants pocket.

"You opened the door to this new life that stretches before me." The teacher finally began his lecture proper. "She has agreed to have me after testing me. The very mediocrity of my performance, in her odious words, makes me ideal for marriage. She says she needs a rest after the Bledsoes, which includes, by the way, your father. Oh, no, no, she has not been intimate with him. But she says his corrosive tongue and vaulting, insolent coldness was like being ravished by a cave of stalactites. Her words, Duane, her words. She is obsessed by all of you, and will hate you forever. . . . As you know, the child shall be yours."

"I'll see to that." Duane spoke with perfunctory belligerence.

"She put me through my paces like a stud horse," he went on doggedly. "You have no reason to be jealous of me, none whatsoever. But I was through at the college. I could no longer prance up and down in front of history maps and talk about military leaders whose existence is totally foggy to me, using nomenclature invented by other deadheads

James Purdy

(254)

who never saw a battle or were treated to any more blood than a scratch from a safety pin. I would have shriveled up in any case and gone to seed, never been as alive as your Dad is even. It's better to accept the humiliation and second-rate post of her husband than be a walking phonograph and hear myself repeating the same grade each year with new empty faces, for being a professor is like a pupil sentenced to having to repeat in failure the same courses year after year after year after year."

"I don't suppose it ever occurred to you what will become of me now," Duane interrupted, his lips quivering violently. "You complain about having to repeat the same courses year after year with deadheads. . . . At least you were able to complete them once, even if you do repeat them. I have had to repeat what I haven't learned over and over again. I wish you would tell me to my face that there is something defective in my brain, Duke. Tell me, that is, that I *can't* learn. Then I could make a clean break."

"I told your father, and I will tell you, though I've already told you . . ."

Here he began his pacing again, and Duane sat down and loosened his necktie. "Can't you just stand in one place for even half a minute, Duke?" he implored.

"You are more sensitive to boredom than most young men," Duke proceeded, still walking up and down the room and making all the little paperweights, pencil sharpeners, flashlights, and pincushions vibrate under his heavy tread. "Everything bores you but heroism. That is why I guess you did as well with Caesar as you did, and learned some Latin, while you could barely get through beginning algebra and plane geometry, and sank to rise no more in trigonometry. You should have been a soldier. It's not too late, of course." He looked up brightly.

"Oh, yes it is. I am sure if I became one, no bullet would kill me. They would see to that. They would prevent my heroism."

"Without you to teach, Duane, I don't know what I would have done . . . I mean I was only myself with you."

Duane was too surprised by this latter remark to respond at all.

"She has already told me how many times I am to . . . gratify her daily," Duke went on without waiting for a comment from his pupil. "And that is one thing about me I guess you may have suspected, since you once broke in on my privacy, God knows, but good," he lapsed into the vernacular. "I am, if anything, overendowed in that way, though as she and every other woman I have been with will testify, if

Mourners Below

(255)

untiring, indeed untirable, I am unexciting in almost direct proportion to my indefatigability. I have even been compared with Niagara: steady, overpowering, and monotonously thorough. While you, with your ignorance of women, your untutored force, drove her to the wall, to madness, to unconsciousness, delirium, and illness. But you fathered her child. She is about as fit to be a mother as to preach from the pulpit."

"Who'll pretend I am anything at all now, Duke?" Duane interrupted, and the tutor realized that his pupil, true to form, absorbed only in his grief at losing his lessons, had not taken in the shameful terms of his marriage contract with Estelle. "You are leaving the country, I hear, in the bargain." He raised his eyes on the last phrase.

"Oh yes, we are never coming back here, she says, never."

"You don't have a substitute you can turn me over to?" Duane wondered, toying with one of Duke's many imported pipes.

"I don't know who," Duke said somewhat harshly.

"They would only have to pretend, wouldn't they?" Duane whispered, still fumbling with one of Duke's pipes.

"As you please," the tutor said bitterly.

"But I mean that as a compliment. I mean, Duke, don't I know how well you pretended I was learning something, getting somewhere?"

"I told you you were good at Caesar."

"Rot, Duke, rot. I went into the bathroom the other night when I couldn't sleep and turned over page after page of the *Commentaries*. The only thing I could make head or hair of was a description of an elk in the Gaulish wilderness.

"The only human beings I have ever talked with are you and Mrs. Newsom," Duane went on when there was no rejoinder from his tutor.

"You may as well get used to the fact that I am never coming back," Duke said. "Maybe meanwhile I can think of a substitute. God only knows."

"If you found a substitute, Duke, if he could be persuaded perhaps just to pretend we were getting anywhere, you understand . . . just talking as you and I did, as though we were taking up something . . ."

"Well, you know no college professor could stand to pretend he was teaching you something he wasn't."

"Except you?"

"The reason for that, Duane, is that I loved you," the tutor said

"You did?" Duane responded before he had quite absorbed what Duke had expressed. His toe worked itself fiercely into the emerald carpet.

"I loved you as if you were my own flesh and blood. So I had that incentive and reward. I didn't care if you learned or not, I guess, as long as I stood for something to you. Which I think I did."

Duane was too broken to speak. He rose silently afer a bit, his eyes all watering, took Duke's hand savagely then, and rushed out from the room.

"Come in, I wanted you to come, I wanted you to see me, if not as I am, the way events have brought me to the pass I'm in now. I want you also, if you feel like it, to gloat."

Estelle had sent her car to fetch Duane to her bedside. The interne was strolling around outside somewhere, winter had come and gone, an uncertain icy spring with sleet storms was yielding already to an early hot thunderstorm-ridden summer.

Most of her "foreign" accent had vanished, she used fewer French phrases, and as she lay there he thought that, had he come in unbidden and unprepared, he would not have known who she was.

She took up his unspoken thought: "When I have the strength to do so I walk to the great hall mirror that dominates the west wing, and wonder who is looking back at me, Duane. Who is she? For it must be she; no man ever looked that out of shape unless he had swallowed a calf. Bloated, twenty corsets wouldn't get me into shape, my legs swollen, the veins distended like a woman of eighty, my hand shriveled and veined, one minute I am burning up, the next my heart is encased in ice. Where is the young woman Justin was so fond of, do you know?"

Duane sat down as close as he thought she would want him to, but she said, "Move your chair back a little so your shadow can shut out some of the strong light, if you don't mind."

"I don't know why you think I would gloat over you," he said.

"Don't you find me disgusting to the sight?" she demanded.

"I'm used to seeing people sick," he confessed.

"Sick?" Her hands almost tore the little ornaments embroidered on the quilt which she drew up to, and then threw away from, her full breasts.

"You're waiting, I can see that," Estelle said after they had sat and looked at one another for a few minutes. "Waiting to take him away. That's part of the bargain, isn't it?"

"You put all kinds of ideas in my head. Everybody does," he stormed. "Of course, if you don't want him, I want him."

"I think it's all preordained, if you ask me. It had to be the way it was. I've never told you a thing that has been on my mind a lot, and I may as well tell you now, because later, when I look like myself again, and I am across the ocean again where I belong, and we are married, Duke and I—"

"Yes, I know all about that, he has filled me in."

"Will you let me finish before that damned doting old fool of a doctor comes in here to poke me and look inside my body and show how impersonally a man who does not like women can treat someone about to give birth? Look here, are you listening? Duke had it right about that!"

"What are you saying?" Duane cried out and rose, and she put her finger to her lips, meaning, don't create a fuss now, of all times.

"Before I called for you," she continued when he had sat down again and quiet was restored (the interne had looked in for a moment, then gone off), "you know, last fall—it seems a thousand years ago—when I gave the party—"

"The masquerade, I thought it was called."

"By Eugene probably. . . . Anyhow, before I gave the party, Duane"— she stopped and spat something out into a little box and wiped her lips as if she were removing all her teeth at the same time, but, of course, her teeth were her own and were splendid, and had she been an ugly woman, her teeth alone would have won her lovers by the droves.

Duane bowed his head, prepared for more blame, more censure, more misunderstood and misplaced responsibility, and heard her crying a little, "Why is it so hard to say? I even told the interne. *He* grinned! Duane, look here, why can't I just be myself, do you suppose, with new gowns every day, and though not too much drinking, enough to take the edge off the twenty-four hours? I don't think you have ever realized, you and Eugene, how long a day is. You have so much to fuss with over there in your big, ugly old Halloween house. You manage to fill the hours. I never could fill them. Hours, minutes, even seconds, Duane, are so heavy for me. I feel sometimes that I am impaled on the hands of the clock, going round round round, every second like a year. But, you see, I missed him even before they said he was killed. I mean Justin."

"And how about Douglas? Don't tell me you didn't count him among your victories and acquired addenda," for suddenly sentences and phrases swam into his mind from poaching through Duke's library, and he unexpectedly recalled the day when, looking through a book on physiology, he had been struck dumb by a certain sentence which he went on whispering and muttering until the tutor had said, "What on earth are you poring over?" and Duane had let his finger stay in the spot that said, *"The penis is cylindrical in shape when at rest, but when stiffened has a triangular and prismatic form with rounded angles."*

Duane sat there now before her struck dumb, not at what he had heard or read, but because he sensed what it was she was going to tell him, and, in fact, he had tried to listen so carefully that he had not heard her first words, so that only now was he aware of her angry voice: "You didn't hear it, I've humiliated myself all for nothing."

"Just then," he said, "you looked like yourself again. Fresh and beautiful, Estelle... It will come back."

"You didn't hear," she cried. Dr. Cressy peeked in on them absentmindedly, then immediately withdrew.

"What is he waiting to tell me, I wonder?" Estelle mumbled. "As I said," she went on in a formal kind of lecture-hall voice which she must have borrowed from Duke La Roche, "in the quiet hours after I came back here, I could not sleep at all. I know he was in the room, Duane."

"Don't, please," he implored.

"I knew eventually I would see him. I don't even believe in God; think of that, will you? It wasn't drink or cocaine either, though I had plenty of both of them that fall. I just knew eventually I would see him, and he would tell me something."

Duane walked over to the big window that overlooked a series of hills and little creeks beginning to flow now under the late spring sun.

"Justin came right up to my bed, Duane," she went on. "He had on a kind of bright colored sweater like one I made for him several seasons ago, but it was a sort of crocus color I have never set eyes on. I think I looked at the sweater more than at his face. There was something wrong with it. He said only a few words. He said, 'Go fetch Duane and go through the whole shebang, ceremony, and blowout for me.' "

"He used those words!" Duane sprang away from the window and bent over her.

"Yes, for I wrote them down right away in my memorandum notebook." She pointed to a thick, expensive little volume lying on her night table. Duane stared at it accusingly.

"So I didn't even come to you on my own either," he said. "Everything is a command. So . . ." He looked away and wiped his eyes furiously. "Just the same"—he kept his face turned to her, but she refused to look at him just then—"listen, are you listening now? You all like to accuse me of being the prize woolgatherer. . . . Let me tell you something. I said I was going to take him, the baby, and I am. You took Justin, and Douglas, and Duke. You would take my father away from me if you set your mind to it. Maybe you will come back for him when you're through with Duke, huh? But I am taking your son as he—"

"Yes?" she taunted him.

He plowed his hand through his disheveled hair.

"Take him, I've already agreed to it, so why do you make us quarrel over a fixed understanding? Anyhow, I've told you something I don't even believe in. I've told you what couldn't have happened to me and yet did, against my will: He came, don't you see? Against all I believe or rather don't believe in. I don't believe in graves or heavens or gods, and yet . . ."

"I don't think we'll see him again." Duane spoke with husky, offended syncopation. "After all, what more can he command or do than he's done?"

"I do love Duke, Duane, you must believe that."

He opened his eyes the widest she had ever seen them, and his mouth relaxed a little.

"And after all, you're to have Justin's child."

He stared at her now with complete terror, then rising slowly he walked out of the room, almost knocking the interne down as he left.

Duke La Roche had turned into a more indefatigable pacer than Eugene Bledsoe himself. And he had more rooms in which to pace, since Duke lived alone in his fifteen-room house, for which extravagance the college, especially the faculty, had criticized him repeatedly. Most of the older faculty members were convinced that he lived alone so that he could satisfy his well-known sexual appetites undisturbed and unobserved. At any event, Duke now paced upstairs for a half hour or so, and then, descending the back staircase, visited each of the downstairs rooms with his heavy and rhythmic tread. A caged tiger could hardly have been more thorough. It was the concentration of his pacing which prevented his seeing old Dr. Cressy coming up the brick walk and squinting at the name on the mailbox in the early morning light to see if he had the right residence.

The doorbell did not function too well, and Duke was so preoccupied at the moment by both his own pacing and his talking to himself that he would not have heard it in any case, but he happened to have just reached the front window in his march over his aunt's Persian carpets when he saw the old man beating on the front door. He swore, and spat out displeasure in seeing him. It seemed that all he had done for days was talk and hear talk. His books, his mind, his peace were all being neglected, and he laid the whole thing at the door of the Bledsoe clan.

"Come in, sir," Duke told the physician. "Allow me to take your coat."

The old man declined, but removed his hat and looked about wonderingly.

"Now don't tell me I should be ashamed of myself living here all alone, Doctor," Duke began.

"I'll only tell you what I know." Dr. Cressy followed the young teacher into the parlor and, at his host's invitation, sat down in the mahogany armchair.

"I was going to say," the doctor began, "that you must know I wouldn't have come here were it not an emergency."

Duke's face lengthened, and his feet continued to move over the carpet, even from his sitting position in a low-bottomed cane chair.

"I hardly know where to turn. You see, since Estelle, young as she is, appears to have outlived all her relations and kin. .. She is the last of her line, it appears."

Duke swallowed and nodded worriedly.

"If you are planning, therefore, to marry her, as she mentioned you were, you must not lose any time."

Duke's mouth opened in curious wonder at such a statement, and then shut itself tight in displeasure.

"Let me come to the point at once." The doctor studied the young man's eyes. "I do not think Estelle is going to pull through. I have already summoned a specialist from New York who has been here all morning. . . ."

"But we were only talking the other day"—Duke seemed to appeal to the wall and the front windows—"of our trip to South America and perhaps, after the war, to Europe."

"Well, she probably didn't want to let you know how seriously ill she is. For she is as aware of her condition as I or the specialist. Estelle always knew everything from the time she was a small girl. That's what's wrong with her. She's too advanced for her own good. I think she had exhausted her curiosity about everything by the time she was fifteen. Well, Duke"—the doctor now threw the whole problem at him—"what do you wish to do?"

"What would you do, Doctor, if you were about to marry and your wife-to-be was in this condition? If you had planned a honeymoon, and then . . . then you come and tell me she is going to die? What would you do in my case? And what do you expect me to do or say under these circumstances?"

Duke broke down and sobbed violently.

Unlike Eugene Bledsoe, Dr. Cressy was not disturbed or embarrassed by grown men weeping. He saw it all the time, and Duke's sudden outburst gave him time to consider what he had best say next.

"You're sure she's bad off, very bad off, Doctor?" Duke said after a few minutes during which he wiped his face and blew his nose.

"One is never sure in cases of serious illness, but doctors, especially if they have been practicing as long as I have, do have a certain sense about grave illness. I do not think Estelle will be with us much longer. Barring an improbable miracle."

Duke studied the old man's face as he daubed his own red-rimmed eyes and convulsively twisting mouth.

"That is why," the physician went on, "if you want to be married, you must act at once. Estelle wants to have this ceremony . . . today . . . this afternoon . . . four o'clock . . . at the Dumont mansion. All of which surprises me, for she has never wanted anything the world wants or approves of, least of all marriage. But she has nobody now but you."

"She has the father of her child, doesn't she?" The tutor spoke with extreme bitterness, a wide idiotic grin on his face like that of one of the jack-o'-lanterns at the masquerade ball.

James Purdy

"She would not dream of marrying anybody but you, I can assure you, Duke."

"I see," he said, ever so slightly mollified. "Then I will do so." He raised his right hand perfunctorily. "I will marry her."

"However, before we go back to the house," the doctor said, "I want you to examine a document she has had her lawyer prepare. As it is a very strange document, you will want to read it more than once. But we have very little time, Duke, so please go over it now as quickly as you can."

The physician handed Duke a sheaf of long legal-sized yellow pages which the tutor read with difficulty, hands shaking.

"May I make a suggestion?" The doctor interrupted his reading. "I would like to give you something which will quiet your nerves."

"I don't want anything, Doctor. I can brave this through without it."

"But you must consider that you have never been married before, either," the doctor pointed out. He had already opened his black bag, and brought forth a bottle of a deep red color and a small glass. He poured the glass about one-third full of the red medicine and brought it over to the tutor.

"Now I insist, Duke, that you swallow this."

The tutor's hand trembled so badly the doctor had to hold the glass to his mouth. He drank it off at once, making a terrible sibilant sound with his mouth afterwards.

"But Dr. Cressy!" the teacher cried after a few moments of reading the document, "this paper gives the child, or as it says here, Estelle's son when he is born, to *both* Eugene and Duane Bledsoe! Am I to sign this? Is this, I mean, a proper document?"

"All I can say, Duke, is that if you do not sign it, there is to be no marriage this afternoon."

Duke dropped the document and gave the old man a look of wonder, exasperation, and weary despair.

"I think I will be known in this town as the greatest fool who ever lived if I sign this. And do you know what, Dr. Cressy? For some reason I am going to put my John Hancock on it. And for some reason I am going to marry Estelle, even though she does not love me . . . and may die after the ceremony!"

The doctor took out a pen from his coat pocket and handed it to Duke.

"But you love her, don't you?" the doctor mumbled. "Love, in fact, has taken a very deep root in your heart. Admit it!"

"That doesn't say the half of it," Duke replied, and signed his name to the document.

"I would marry her," the teacher went on, "I guess if she had made me also sign a document to the effect that immediately after our marriage she would be permitted to shoot me and run off with another man she liked better than me. For she doesn't care a straw for me, but, as she said to me the morning when I consented, she couldn't marry anybody else if she hunted the wide world over . . . or the mountains of the moon."

"We don't have much time, Duke. I don't like to be so insistent." The old man looked at the clock in the corner, which, as he studied it, he decided was even older than himself. "You might want to change clothes." And then, looking at Duke's tear-stained face, "Best to freshen yourself up a bit, and shine your shoes. They're spotty. Estelle always liked men to have nicely shined shoes, if I remember correctly."

"But you'll make every effort to save her, won't you, Doctor?" Duke said, rising and going toward Cressy.

The doctor barely nodded. "Now put on a fresh shirt and a nice colorful necktie. I think the draft I gave you is making you feel a little better already, is it not?"

Duke stood silent, thinking, and then, giving the old man a look of earnest appeal, said, "Don't you think she might grow to love me in time?"

Dr. Cressy, whose fame in part rested on the fact that, in addition to being a doctor of infinite conscientiousness and ability, he was also always the standard-bearer of truth, replied, "I don't think so. No, I don't."

"Thank you, Dr. Cressy." Duke smiled, and walked out of the room to put on his wedding suit.

"Where in the name of God do you suppose Duane was during the wedding service!" Mr. Bledsoe blew up as he and Mrs. Newsom reached the parlor after having attended Estelle Dumont's marriage to Duke La Roche.

"Did you ever hear of such a damned outrage? Tell me, Mrs. Newsom, if you ever have, for if there's nothing to equal this, I want it

James Purdy
(264)

written down in all its full particulars. Not to attend the wedding of the mother of his child!" Eugene thundered.

Mrs. Newsom took off her flowered hat with the veil, and, at a severe nod from her employer, sat down in the best chair in the house, the one which had belonged to his mother.

"You must see it this way, if you'll excuse my saying so." She interrupted his tirade for at least a moment, but then had to allow him to speak his mind on some other points first, mainly Duane's incessant lateness, his irresponsibility, his being spoiled, by *others*. (He came perilously close to mentioning the brothers here, and both he and Mrs. Newsom cleared their throats and allowed for a few moments' silence.)

"As I say, I can sort of understand his not attending the ceremony." Mrs. Newsom was surprised at the clearness of her own voice (she was constantly being criticized by both Mr. Bledsoe and her husband for mumbling through her false teeth).

"Would you care to expand on such a statement?" Mr. Bledsoe spoke in his most cutting tone.

Mrs. Newsom was no longer afraid of him, if for that matter she ever had been. Indeed, she was almost smug now about the strength of her position here and her power.

"You'll have to admit he's been through a lot. And he has not been happy losing Duke to her."

"Losing Duke?" Mr. Bledsoe spoke with pitying surliness.

"Since his other . . . losses"—she spoke very cautiously now—"since his loneliness and his illness, there has really only been Duke, you see, to keep him steady company. And, then, Duke La Roche is marrying, after all, a woman who I believe Duane feels he should have married."

"You don't think for a moment, Mrs. Newsom, that a sixteen- or seventeen-year-old boy of the limited training and capacity of my son could marry a worldly, designing, and unappeasable woman like Estelle Dumont! Do you think any court in the land would sanction such a marriage? And even if it did, and they took the plunge"—here Mr. Bledsoe shook his head so vigorously that his fountain pen fell from his breast pocket—"that such a marriage could have lasted out the weekend!"

"I'm sure the poor boy hardly knew what to do," Mrs. Newsom replied.

"Mrs. Newsom, and I do not say this critically, it seems to me you always take his part. You have spoiled him, my dear, as shamefully as

... *they* did! He has, on the whole, been treated as a privileged being from the moment he was born. Wonder is he is not worse than he is. Wonder is he has not brought all of us to disgrace sooner than he has."

The wonder and disgrace entered at that very moment. He was dressed to the teeth, and had Mr. Bledsoe not been so angry, he might have noticed, as Mrs. Newsom did, that Duane had been drinking, indeed was drunk.

"Well, your empty chair certainly proclaimed your absence as loudly as a whole orchestra of trumpets, Duane," Mr. Bledsoe began at once.

"I knew and know," Duane began somewhat incoherently, "that I would never live this one down."

"You have certainly summarized the situation quite well," Mr. Bledsoe snorted.

Pleading her duties in the kitchen, the housekeeper hurried out of the room and closed both the dining-room and the kitchen doors securely behind her.

"The cold lack of feeling you have demonstrated," Mr. Bledsoe continued, "especially to Duke, who has befriended you more than almost anyone within memory ..." Here his father again bumbled and stumbled, and came to a momentary halt. "A marriage which he has undertaken only because of your own lack of self-control and folly. Only to save you. Yes, your tutor has sacrificed himself body and soul for you!"

Duane let out a guffaw which was both so vulgar and so loud that, had not Mr. Bledsoe been so riled, he would have seen exactly what condition his son was in.

"It will be an insult neither of the matrimonial pair will ever recover from, to say the least."

"I tried to get there, Dad." Duane attempted to exercise some control over his dizziness and tried to focus his eyesight on where his father sat. "Nobody could have tried harder, but time just seems to have zipped by for me. And as a mere matter of fact," he went on, adopting one of Mr. Bledsoe's favorite courtroom phrases, "I couldn't bear the thought of Duke marrying a woman who is after all going to be ..."

"Well, why not finish it?" Eugene sneered.

" ... a mother. I didn't think it was a proper kind of wedding, and I couldn't bear it. Do you hear, I couldn't bear it? I would rather have been horsewhipped by ... by ... oh, anybody," he said, avoiding any mention of by whose hands he would rather have been castigated. "As to Duke's being a human sacrifice ...!"

James Purdy
(266)

"Years ago you would have been whipped and tarred and feathered and ridden out of town on a rail," Mr. Bledsoe interrupted. "Be glad you live in a more refined era."

Now, however, Eugene began to study his son's "condition" with a bit more care, though since he was averse to gazing at any member of his family for any length of time, he had to do his looking in very brief takes, and then, as his suspicion grew, he finally gaped at the boy in one long, conscientious, and prolonged stare.

"Duane, may I ask you where you have spent the morning and early afternoon hours?" He looked away immediately he had spoken.

"I went to the pool parlor, wanting to ask Mr. Colby something— who by the way has for his first name Merle. You see, I never knew before what his full name was, so I asked him, and he has told me now . . . Merle." Duane smiled vacuously after repeating the name.

Had he said that he had visited a cannibal, Mr. Bledsoe could not have pretended greater disapproval and disgust, and the fact that he should talk about a man like Colby's having a Christian name at all he found insufferable.

"After all," Duane went on doggedly, "Merle did know . . . everybody in our family."

"And so he proceeded to let you get stinking drunk, did he, and miss *my* wedding?"

Duane shook his head. "He talked so much about them," he went on almost mirthfully, "that I felt somehow *they* would rather have me there with him than at a ceremony that ain't right at all. Don't you see that?"

"I don't know who you mean by *they,* and I don't want to know!" Mr. Bledsoe pretended to rage even more violently, but drunk as Duane was, he noted with relief that his Dad's anger was spent and that the very idea that Duane had been talking to someone about *them,* he found too upsetting to deal with.

"Estelle Dumont," Eugene began now in a different manner and voice, "Estelle La Roche, that is, asked me to describe the ceremony for you, though she will of course give you all the details herself soon, she said to tell you."

"Thank you, Father," Duane cried, in his most drunken voice yet.

Glaring at Duane for one second, Eugene began in an unsettled voice, "She was, as one would expect, beautifully dressed in a wedding gown which I believe had belonged to her grandmother and had, I suppose, been artfully let out. She wore a full corsage"—here the father consulted some notes which he had jotted down while being driven back to his house in Estelle's limousine—"and she was able to stand during the whole ceremony. Reverend Laforgue officiated—he's from quite a ways away, I've forgotten where, since I never heard of him before. There was a distant female cousin or perhaps acquaintance, and that was about all. Oh, yes, some of the servants stood about as the vows were taken. Duane, are you listening to me? Will you, for God's sake, sit up in your chair? Put your feet down on the carpet. The surprise for me and, I think, for Mrs. Newsom was that Duke La Roche really looked impressive. He had a nifty new Palm Beach suit on, cuff links, and his hair was for once properly groomed and didn't stand up all over like he had put his head in some electric socket. But I must say, Duane, that Estelle does not look at all well."

"I couldn't have stood going, Dad," Duane began with such passionate earnestness that his father merely sat silent, staring at his collection of notes. "I can't stand any more of the terrible events that are always happening to me."

"Well, terrible events are the order of the universe, what are you talking about?" his father rejoined, but his manner and his way of speaking showed he was mollified, even perhaps that he understood. "Nobody is spared, Duane. You think even rich people in the end are spared? These things are, I repeat, the order of the universe."

"Well, I'm sorry to be drunk," Duane told him.

"Sorry? I should hope so." Bledsoe tried to think how to finish his thought, but stopped.

"Did they kiss at the end of the ceremony?" Duane wondered.

"Well, of course, for God's sake. You didn't expect them to just shake hands, did you, after being joined in holy matrimony? Even preachers expect the bride and groom to kiss. I declare!" He pretended again to be angry.

"You see I thought taking a drink, and Merle thought so too, would allow me to witness them . . . take their vows. I walked and walked trying to get there on time, believe me. But I ended up in a place where we used to go picnicking, all of us. Remember the old fairgrounds that now is just pastureland? I went there and sat down in a chair by some picnic tables."

"Duane, let me tell you something, and I will never mention it again. Your whole life is before you. When will you stop looking back? Do you understand what I am saying to you? Looking back *has* brought you, it *is* bringing you to the brink of disgrace!"

"Disgrace?" the boy asked. "What disgrace?"

"It's brought you to stopping as if your life was through."

"I feel . . . it is, sir."

"What?"

"No, I don't mean that, of course. Sir, I am drunk." And leaping up, he rushed out of the room and Bledsoe heard him running up the stairs.

"They spoiled him," he muttered aloud. "Gave him constant attention, filled his head with I don't know what. All he thinks about is them. Heroes, heroes! His head is full of the dead and the past, poor sucker. God, what will I do with him? I can't be properly mad at him. They spoiled him from the day he was born and they traipsed all around the neighborhood boasting to the kids about their new baby brother. Filled his head with strange notions from that day hence."

Mr. Bledsoe looked up to see Mrs. Newsom at the door and heard her announce Sunday supper.

"I don't know what an apology is worth in such a case," Duke La Roche was saying. He wore only a new magenta bathrobe; his feet were bare, slightly wet, and covered with some strong-smelling talcum powder. He looked drawn and peaked. He was much angrier than Eugene had been, and he was, of course, talking to Duane.

"I would have thought that of all people you were the one who would not dare be absent!" Duke went on.

"But I've explained three times now, Duke, why I didn't get there. I've never been that drunk before," he added in almost a sob, but this sob, so like that of a child, only infuriated Duke the more.

"And the way you speak of Merle Colby as if you had gone to consult some eminence instead of debauching yourself in a dive with riffraff!"

"My God, you are worse than Eugene! This does come as a surprise to me, this does reach me, Duke."

"Nothing reaches you! You do just exactly as you please, which is nothing! What have you done with your life, what are you doing with it, I ask you? Where are you headed?"

"You talk to me as if I was thirty years old!"

"You will be before you know it, and then where will you be? Will you be able to hold your head up, or will you continue to retreat into dens like Merle Colby's and spend the rest of your life drinking and shooting pool?"

"I've seen Merle Colby no more than a dozen times in my life, and so far as actually talking to him is concerned ... well, the first time he gave me a kind of letter which Justin had left behind the night before he was inducted."

"And so that gives him the right to influence you and detain you from my wedding!" Duke advanced toward Duane until the latter fairly cowered before him.

"Oh, have no fear, Duane," Duke now sneered, "I am not going to strike you. You are not worth it!"

"You can't mean that, Duke, after all our close friendship."

"We have no friendship and you know it. I was merely paid to hear you stumble and bumble about in your lessons. You learned nothing under my stewardship. Absolutely nothing!"

"I beg to differ with you. In fact, I don't know what I would have done, Duke, if you had not come along. I mean, who else would have bothered? I did learn *some* things."

"What, for God's sake?"

"I got a very real feeling of how everything, yes everything, is fight fight fight."

"And where in God's name did you learn that?"

"In Caesar's *Commentaries*. Everything is one man taking something away from another."

"You must be the first reader in history ever to have got that out of Caesar."

"Those little runts of Romans running down the tall handsome Gauls." He looked blank if not rapt. "It's all there anyhow. Burning their towns and stealing their grain." Going further, Duane intoned, "You also taught me the metric system, which ... my son will need, even if I don't last that long."

Duke flashed a look of great surprise at his pupil's eloquence.

"Why can't you forgive me for missing your wedding?" Duane whispered.

"Suffice it to say that I cannot. That's all I can say. That will have to be good enough."

"I will go and apologize to Estelle. Actually I don't think Eugene cared very much that I was absent. He gave up on me long ago in any

James Purdy
(270)

case, as you have. I guess there's only Mrs. Newsom now, and she doesn't hear a thing I say."

"I never met anybody, young or old, who expected as much of other people as you do. And who gives absolutely nothing back in return."

"But, Duke, I would give it if I had it. I don't seem to have anything anybody needs. I mean, after all . . . I am empty-handed."

"Well, your presence at the wedding . . . that was needed. And you played truant. You flunked out!"

"But I've told you a hundred times I didn't do it on purpose."

"Why in the name of reason did you go to a pool parlor one hour before the ceremony was to begin?"

"I can't tell you."

"Why *can't* you, since this may be the last time we ever speak to one another?"

"Oh, Duke." Duane went very white. "I wish you hadn't said that."

"Well, it's said and I mean every word of it."

"Very well, then," Duane began. "I didn't feel strong enough to go to the wedding, and actually . . . " He struggled badly now, like someone enmeshed in a net. Then wriggling partially free, he went on, "I thought if I touched some of the billiard cues and balls . . . he used to touch . . . You know, he sometimes spent whole days there, why it was as if he lived there, and to tell the truth"—here the pupils of his eyes became very enlarged and a pink flush suffused his cheeks—"he no longer comes to me, you see."

"Duane, Duane!"

But Duane was going on. "I thought maybe in that dark old billiard hall he would somehow appear again and give me the strength, but he didn't, and I think Merle sensed I was bad off. Anyhow, after watching me for a long time he said, 'I believe even Doc Cressy would prescribe a drink at this juncture.' But you see it wasn't Colby that made me drunk. I sneaked all the other drinks when he was out of the room. You see, it was then I knew that Justin was never going to appear for me again. That I was all on my own from here on in, and frankly . . ." He stopped and hunched up, then, straightening his shoulders and throwing out his chest, he got out, "From here on in I knew I would never have anybody again."

"Duane," Duke said. His voice had changed, and the hurt and anger had gone out of it. "There's nobody like you, Duane, that's for sure," he finished.

Mourners Below

"So that is, as far as I can tell it, the whole truth. If there was more I'd tell you, no matter how it cut me up inside, because, Duke, you are all I've got, don't you see? If you don't esteem me, if you don't keep me, what's really to become of me? I can do without your lessons on account of you know better than anybody else in creation I don't have no brains or talent, but how can I do without your good esteem? You tell me that."

"Duane, look here." The older man spoke with his back turned to his pupil. "You have it, you know you have it. You know when I speak in anger. But who can resist you, Duane, when you are you? God damn it, you know I love you like a brother or father, I don't know how. Anyhow, Duane"—he turned toward him—"it's all right."

Duane sat down. "Am I crazy, too, Duke, as well as . . . slow-witted? Tell me the truth."

"Duane, you're neither. Neither slow-witted nor crazy, neither of those."

"You're sure?"

"Sure, sure."

"Do other boys . . . see their . . . dead brothers?"

"Other boys don't have brothers like yours, that's your trouble."

"Can you explain that to me?"

"Oh, Duane, Duane, I can't explain anything. I don't know anything. Only I am your friend, I can give you that forever, even if we never meet again."

"So you'll go off like all the others, then." The boy spoke as if he was in an empty room. "But I'll have your faith and friendship." He smiled. "Yes."

"And you accept my apology, Duke?"

"Oh, yes."

"Duke, can I ask a favor of you? Feel my heart as it is beating now.'

"But why? Why, I mean, do you—"

"Just put your hand on it and feel it beating."

"But, Duane . . . "

He walked gingerly over to his pupil and awkwardly put his hand on his chest and held it there.

"Yes, it's racing, Duane," the tutor said, "I guess I see what you mean, but it will slow down in time. But it is a racer." He smiled and turned away.

"I don't think it will never slow down," Duane said. "It isn't that it's racing, Duke. I'm not asking for sympathy either. That heart is busted in two."

"Oh, Duane, for God's sake."

"All right, all right, I'll stop. Thank you anyhow for . . . for all and everything."

Duane walked past the tutor, out into the hall, and began the long hike downstairs.

"Duane!" The tutor called from the top of the banister. "Duane, I am your friend. You know it. . . .

"He left the front door open as usual," the tutor said after a long silence.

There seemed then nothing to do and nobody else to see about his disgrace but Estelle herself, and Duane reluctantly set out on his way there, riding his bike in a long roundabout detour so that he wouldn't get there too soon to face either her wrath or—who knows?—her death. In that event, he supposed, Eugene and Duke and, of course, Mr. and Mrs. Newsom would blame him for killing her, no question about that.

The maid answered the door and gave him an extremely sour look, and replied to his question of whether Estelle could see him that she was not sure she was at home.

He walked on in past her without being asked and sat down in the hall on a recently upholstered antique chair crested with sharp brass ornaments. He saw himself in the mirror which faced the chair, and he was surprised at a pronounced change in his countenance. He could not quite tell what the change was, but he looked a little older and even slightly belligerent, he thought. His mouth was redder and more full, and his eyes had a certain defiant gleam. He straightened his necktie and, seeing a piece of mud on one shoe, he spat upon it and erased it with his finger.

After a wait of about fifteen minutes, the maid ushered him into the living room where Estelle sat on a large green ottoman which she had purchased in Europe or on some of her antique-hunting expeditions in the United States.

He barely recognized her, and she saw his look of bewilderment and frowned.

"I am a bit too weak to see you for very long. Will you have something to drink or nibble on as we talk?" she wondered.

"What is there?" he said rather airily.

She smiled at his rudeness. He noticed that in her hand was a sheet of notepaper which must have been torn out of a ledger.

"Oh, we have the usual beverages and, of course, bread and butter and jam, and I think pie and homemade apricot pudding."

He said he would take the pie, and Estelle called to the maid and asked her to bring what he wanted and some ice water for herself.

"Is that a list of your grievances against me?" He moved his hand toward the piece of paper she was holding.

"I found this in one of La Roche's lecture books," she said thickly, and smiled again. "He gave me permission to tear it out. I imagine you have already heard it. I don't know who wrote it, some great intellect I suppose, of the recent past, or of hoary antiquity."

"Estelle, I am sorry."

"Well, don't be," she said. "After all, I've been married before. Don't be anything you don't want to be."

"Well, according to everybody," Duane went on, "I've succeeded pretty thoroughly in being nobody."

"Who says so, though? That is, who are your judges? Great luminaries themselves?" She took a cigarette from the end table near her, and lit it. She coughed immediately on inhaling and looked at him. Then she took up the piece of paper again and laughed as she read it.

The maid brought him his piece of pie on a little tray with a cup of tea, and served Estelle with a crystal goblet containing the water she had requested.

Duane ate the entire piece of pie in only four or five bites, ignored the thick linen napkin beside his tea, and wiped his hands free of the crumbs on his trousers. Estelle pursed her lips and looked out the window.

"This quotation from the great mind of the recent or hoary past . . . I wonder if Duke was thinking of you when he copied it out. Perhaps not."

"Well, I suppose it is something unflattering, then," he replied, still chewing on the pie.

"Not particularly." She looked at him studiously. "I don't think so, Duane. Anyhow, here goes.

"It is unqualifiedly true that if any thought do fill the mind exclusively, such filling is consent. . . . The thought at any rate,

James Purdy
(274)

carries the man and his will with it. . . . But it is not true that the thought *need* fill the mind exclusively for consent to be there."

There was a toothpick wrapped in a little sanitary envelope on the tray, and even though he did not require a toothpick, he opened the little package and picked his teeth with it.

"What do you make of it?" she inquired and folded the paper and put it down on the end table.

"Estelle, didn't Duke tell you by now how . . . stupid I am? I have no idea what that quotation means, and you must know it."

"At first I thought it was meant for me, because he had left his book of lecture notes behind and this passage had been underlined in blazing red pencil. He denies it. Is it about Duane? I inquired, and he would say nothing. He claims he does not know why he copied it down, or to whom or what it refers. But I can't get it out of my mind. It's like some song the melody of which keeps going around in one's head and on one's tongue, often a melody that one does not even like. I wish I knew what it meant."

"Well, read it again," he said, and put down the toothpick.

"I guess it means I've only got one thing on my mind," he said after hearing her recite it again.

Estelle laughed very heartily and she suddenly looked pretty again.

He got up and came over to her. "You won't die," he said desperately. "Estelle, don't die. My God," he said.

"So you think it is about you," she said, toying with her bracelets. "That sly old thing Duke. Always studying human nature. I think you know more about it than either of us, Duane."

"A lot of good it has done me if I know it," he said. "That pie was very delicious," he added.

Estelle smiled very faintly and put out her cigarette. "You can have some more if you want it," she whispered.

"Why did you read me that . . . quotation, Estelle?" he wondered rather urgently.

"I think it describes you, Duane. Whether he meant it to or not, and whoever wrote it didn't, of course, know you and your story."

"What is my story, Estelle? I didn't know I had one."

"Everybody has a story, Duane."

"Oh, I suppose that's so."

"But yours is special and has touched me. Your mind is full exclusively and by your consent."

"What is it full of?" His voice was choked.

"Worship," she said very faintly. "Worship. That's why the baby will be yours. No one shall have him but you. I doubt I die, despite old Doc Cressy. Your mind is filled with worship by your own consent. You are rare, there is nobody like you, and you must have my son. Duke knows that, and he shall not interfere."

"But what will I do with him?" he said, his voice sounding like that of one who is on a boat that is already a considerable distance from shore.

"That is the least of your worries, Duane. Once you have him, you will know the rest."

He went over to the ottoman and knelt down by her and took her hand.

"Don't die, Estelle. I can't stand any more . . . of that."

"Oh, I doubt I do, but I know I will have the boy, and that I will give him to you."

She put her hands through his hair.

"So you know everything," he said.

"I think I do about you, Duane. I love you, and so I know."

"I want that quotation."

Her hands stopped moving through his hair.

"Estelle, I want the quotation."

"Very well, you can copy it. I'll get you a pen and paper presently."

"You don't know who wrote it?"

"Don't know and don't want to know. Don't want you to know either. It explains you, explains us, and so don't inquire further."

"I see," he said. He looked up at her and then he took her in his arms and kissed her. He was crying.

"So you know everything, Estelle."

"I do now, maybe, about us, that is. I just know about us."

"And he will be mine," he mused.

"Of course."

"And I will know what to do with him, Estelle?"

"Who else would know better than you?"

"But I'll have to have help. I mean I don't know anything about . . . babies."

James Purdy

(276)

"Help will be everywhere."

They held one another's hands. The day faded and night came and still they sat on there together, in silence, with an occasional embrace or sigh or quiet laughter.

On learning of Duane's predicament, Aileen had a mild heart attack. Partially recovered, she conferred interminably with Eugene by telephone. She threw up to him all her previous warnings against the "Dumont creature," and finally she blamed Bledsoe alone for all that had gone wrong.

"You and the court barred me from any real relationship with my boy," she told him. "Now see what your lax and crude upbringing of him has led to. Had he had a mother's protection, advice, experience, and love, this sordid and disgraceful chapter would never have been written. As it is now, the wound that has been inflicted on his manhood may never heal, and even if it does, he will carry the scar to his grave."

Then the letters to Duane began, many special deliveries, followed by telegrams, each communication a tearful bewailing of his "ruin."

Duane did not finish reading all of them, and often, stealing out into the kitchen, he would beg Mrs. Newsom to read them first herself and convey to him the general drift of his mother's communication.

Mrs. Newsom had hesitated. She had been partial to Aileen, who had done her many favors, had even once helped her out of financial difficulties, and the two women enjoyed a deeper level of understanding than Mrs. Newsom had ever had even with old Mrs. Bledsoe or, of course, with Eugene.

And though Mrs. Newsom could understand Aileen's sorrow over Duane's "having gone wrong," it was clear to the boy that the old housekeeper did not approve of the giving of such a free rein to one's emotions, together with the complaints and frightening prophesies of Duane's "never recovering from the pit into which he had fallen." In every epistle, Aileen showered Mrs. Newsom with praise and affection, as if she suspected that the housekeeper would be treated to the perusal of her letters.

" 'More even, though, than the ruin she has brought on your young life, the moral blight that will always linger over your name, my dear Duane,' " Mrs. Newsom read aloud, then hesitated whether to go further, looking up quickly at Duane, who, like his father, however, merely paced up and down the room, " 'the thought that Eugene has agreed to let you become the adopted father of the child has brought me to my sickbed. How you, Duane, who know nothing of life or people (as her having led you astray in the first place demonstrates), how you are to be the tutelar father of an infant—this has caused your mother grief from which she may never recover! Indeed I am so ill from it that I wonder if you will ever see me again in this world. I am also appalled that anyone who calls herself a woman could so easily part with her infant offspring as Estelle Dumont evidently soon will. But the other thing which torments me more than all this, my precious boy, is how on earth are you sure you are the father. Are you positive that she is not lying to you, a woman who has been intimate with so many—indeed almost an army—and who has indeed, dear Duane, made a life of entrapping as many men as possible, whose whole pastime and life—' "

"I think that about does it," Duane said, taking the letter from Mrs. Newsom's hands. He was somewhat disappointed in her, disappointed that she had read as much of the letter as she had. He had thought her of a higher character evidently than she was.

Mrs. Newsom, to his further chagrin, looked somewhat hurt that the letter had been snatched out of her hands as she was reading, and she was cool and uncommunicative to Duane for several days thereafter.

"I didn't mean to tear the letter out of your hand," he said to her once when they met in the hall.

"I understand how your mother feels," Mrs. Newsom said drily. "A father cannot feel the same way because, well, because he is just what he is, a man."

Duane reported this "ado" to Eugene, largely because he did not know where else to go—his relations with Duke were, if anything, too close now for comfort, too painfully intimate.

"One good-looking woman always runs down another, did you ever notice that?" Eugene chuckled over Duane's reporting of Aileen's epistles. "Also, women are very jealous of one another, especially older women of younger, good-looking ones, and I never knew a woman yet who would not stab another in the back when the right occasion arose. They hate their own sex. The minute a man enters the room they become rivals and enemies."

James Purdy
(278)

To Duane's somewhat bitter amusement, Eugene now began to say some things in favor of the "much-abused" (his phrase) Estelle Dumont. He recalled how she had had a drunken mother and a worthless spoiled rich father, neither of whom gave the girl ten minutes of their time in a month of Sundays.

"But I guess Aileen is right about one matter," Duane interrupted his father's chronicle of family history, "I will be one strange father! Won't I?"

There was an interminable hiatus in this conversation, during which Eugene neither paced nor jingled the coins in his pocket.

"I think, if anything, you will be too good a father, God damn it!"

Duane smiled faintly, for he knew that this outburst of anger was really directed at Aileen. But it was Eugene's hatred for her, his feeling that she had spoiled his life, had hurt his self-esteem and manhood that perhaps kept him going. For the watchword of all these latter years had been his cry, "I'll show the bitch yet what I'm worth. I'll make her long to be the wife of a really rich man, which is the only goal the scatter-brained fool understands. By God, she would marry a wart hog if he had prospects!"

"Are you all right?" Merle Colby finally addressed the man who was sitting on the curb with his head down.

Merle was closing his pool parlor down for the night, and had seen what he thought at first was a drunk, but the man was too well dressed for any ordinary toper and looked faintly familiar to boot. "Do you need tending to, sir?" the billiard-hall owner inquired in a softer voice on recognizing the professor of history and humanities. "Let me help you."

"I'm all right," Duke replied antagonistically, and then he looked into Merle's face. The sight of so much pain and humiliation, and a kind of pleading bid for help, made the volunteer of succor stand hesitating there for a moment. Then, without waiting for another signal, he lifted the professor up by hoisting him more or less by his armpits and dragged him into the billiard parlor, where Duke slumped down in a chair.

"By the smell of your breath, sir, you have not been drinking, and that is why I'd like to suggest you have some whiskey. Or do you want me to call the doctor?"

"By no means, Mr. Colby, don't you dare."

Mourners Below

Merle went into the bar and brought back a bottle and a great beveled yellow tumbler.

"This can't harm you none." Merle Colby put the glass full of whiskey to the professor's lips. "Swallow some, see if it don't help."

Duke drank thirstily and wiped his mouth with the back of his hand.

"Thank you, Colby, thank you," he said. He could hardly have looked worse had the owner of the billiard parlor found him in the wilds of Hudson's Bay.

"I guess you're wondering how I got in this state."

Merle Colby was already pouring him another glass of whiskey.

"I don't have no wish to pry into your private affairs, sir. If I can help you, I'm glad to do so, and no more need be said."

"Thank you, Colby, thank you again." He drank some more and wiped his mouth again with the back of his hand. Colby then proffered him a small paper napkin such as might be placed under a lady's cocktail glass and, seeing his guest get it sopping wet, handed him still another.

"I have been put through the ringer, believe you me, Mr. Colby," Duke said, and took off his glasses, stared at them, and put them in a little black case which he put away in the breast pocket of his jacket.

"Your friend, your boon companion, Duane Bledsoe, has about finished me off." Duke tapped the whiskey glass, meaning he required more. Colby, distressed both at the uncomplimentary reference to young Bledsoe and to the professor's consuming thirst, hesitated a moment, then poured him another, less generous shot of liquor.

"At two A.M. this morning there was born to my wife a son," the professor went on. "And at the moment of birth—are you listening, Colby, because someone should hear the unhearable? Are you listening, man?"

"I am, and if you don't mind a word of caution from one who knows what he's talking about, you'll drink less quickly than you're goin' at it now, and you'll also recall, sir, that Duane Bledsoe is a good friend of mine, and his brothers too, before him."

"It started with the brothers." Duke seemed to have heard only the last of the billiard-hall owner's speech. "That's where it began, and that's who, you might say, is behind it all. Justin and Douglas. Yes, who but Justin and Douglas? But especially Justin."

"Remember, Professor La Roche, you now are speaking of the dead and departed."

James Purdy

"I am speaking of the cause," La Roche shouted as if warning him. "Do you, sir"—he spoke as if mimicking Colby's own peculiar deference to him—"do you wish to hear my story, or shall I just drink more generously against your advice and pass out on the sawdust of your floor?"

"You may say what you like, but let me warn you again that the Bledsoe boys are close to my heart. And the two elder being dead, should be spoke about in reverence."

"You entirely misunderstand my drift," Duke La Roche responded with a thick tongue. "Howsoever that may be, I married a woman ten days ago and have seen her give birth to a son tonight. Is that clear?"

"Your words are clear."

"Let me make my meaning clear then, too. It began, with your pardon now, Mr. Colby, with Justin Bledsoe, who loved Mrs. Dumont, and he bequeathed, if you will, his youngest brother to her attention and special favor. Is that all perfectly understandable?"

Merle Colby nodded coldly, and his lips formed a tight little, almost purple, line. He held the whiskey bottle locked in his hand.

"It was a command, you see, from, as you called it a moment ago, 'the departed,' urging Duane to finish what they, or perhaps only he—I mean Justin—had begun. Little did they or I know I would be involved in such an improbable, painful, and convoluted chain of events, the culmination of which happened this morning at two A.M."

"No more just yet, Professor La Roche." Merle Colby took the bottle and walked a few paces away as a result of the professor's having reached out for the whiskey. "Just go ahead with your story, to which I'm paying full attention."

"Under command, then, of the only one he ever looked up to, you follow? *Our* Duane . . . and *his* Justin."

Here the billiard-parlor operator nodded encouragingly, deferentially, but somehow, all the same, superciliously.

"Duane attended her famous masquerade ball, an event which, if all else does, will never fade from the memory of this landscape or from popular memory. On that night or early morning, he went in to her, commanded still, of course, on cue, and they remained in one another's embrace, when they were not dancing at the ball, interwound, locked, entwined, close at it, working as hard I suppose as Venus and Mars may have worked prior to their attempt to escape from the iron mesh another unseen power had laid as snare for them. They sweated and strained and groaned and heaved and labored, for hours. The result of which, Mr. Colby—thank you." The professor now spoke almost to the bottom of the bottle, which was being raised and its contents poured for him again by the pool-hall owner. "That's very good, fine bourbon, excellent—the result of which was that this morning was given to the world . . ."

The professor stared at Colby and Colby stared back with righteous dignity and with the calm contempt of a man who is in his own house and under his own unencumbered roof.

"I say when my wife gave birth to Duane Bledsoe's son, then, and Duane Bledsoe, unasked and uninvited, stormed into the room where she was being delivered, hardly had the umbilical cord been cut and the baby spanked and brought screaming into breath and life—let me tell you, it was the most wonderful, horrible, unforgettable sight any man has seen since maybe the Creation itself or Joshua commanding the sun to stand still—the actual father pushed the old obstetrician aside—do you follow, Colby?—and took that newborn child of his, still dripping with blood and mucus and all the massacred look of afterbirth which had made me deathly sick to see, and holding this bleeding crying mess in his arms, he turned to all of us, including my wife, Estelle, who lay there conscious throughout, and said, 'This is by right mine, and none of you shall ever have him, do you hear? I am his rightful owner. He belongs to me and only to me till the crack of doom.' "

Merle Colby turned away, went to another bottle, still carrying the professor's with him and out of his reach, poured himself a couple of jiggers of rum, mixed that with some lemon juice and Coca-Cola, and then sauntered back to where his guest was still talking interminably.

"And it was after all that that you found me on the curb, and why you found me there, and why I looked—I could see it in your eyes— worse than had I been drunk for a month. Do you think I will ever forget such a thing, or live it down even if nobody in the world outside of the people in that room hear or ever get wind of it? No, I cannot tell why. Do you think psychology will explain it? Rot! I will never be the same any more than Estelle, Duane, or even that hard-bitten old gran-ite-faced obstetrician, Cressy, for what happened in that room in the early morning hours, none of us will ever look on the daylight in quite the same way hereafter. And he will keep that boy. He has been com-manded to keep him, as he was commanded to beget him, don't you see that?"

James Purdy

Merle Colby's head now had fallen nearly flush with the mahogany smoothness of his bar. His hair, thick and untouched by gray, was remarkable in a man his age, at least remarkable for a man whose face was so lined with care and worry and disappointment. He could say nothing. From his mouth a thin string of saliva descended.

"I have made you unhappy, too," the professor said, in a sudden rush of sobriety.

"You have that," Colby replied, his head still almost touching the polish of the mahogany. "Yes, like a good many of my customers, no evening goes by I don't hear something about as cheerful as attending four burial services in one hour. You have brought the evening's work to its usual sobering conclusion."

"I wonder, though, if you had not been here to listen," the professor began again, "I don't think anybody in this town would have paid me the benevolence of even spitting in my eye had I begun on the Bledsoes and their success."

"Success?" Colby wondered, raising his head.

"Yes," La Roche replied. "What other word would you use to describe them, to describe the event, to ... "

Colby watched him, wiped his own mouth with his open palm. "I just would never have considered using the word 'success.'" He seemed to be appealing to the long row of empty bar stools standing around them.

"Well, what word would you have used in its stead?" The professor waited to be enlightened.

"Search me," the billiard-hall owner mumbled after a moment and put the rim of his glass to his exposed teeth but did not drink any more. "I do know," Colby said finally, "every time I ever saw any of them, and even before they was soldiers, I kind of smelled battle around them, the way they walked and talked and moved their hands and their eyes or lifted their heads as they looked at you, and Duane ain't no different, after all, and you say he is one of them, is commanded—I say they all give me the feeling of a pitched battle, of men in hard combat, fighting every minute of their lives."

Colby let Professor La Roche reach for the whiskey bottle now and pour his own drink.

EPILOGUE

"But why should I surrender them to you, Mr. Bledsoe? You've always treated me like the dirt under your feet," Merle Colby said, after examining the peremptory letter from Estelle Dumont La Roche, postmarked Paris. Merle sneered, sniffed, and almost spat upon the letter before handing it back to the lawyer.

The way he kept track of the passage of time was curious; no curiouser, though, than anything else, he supposed, in his rather strange life (everybody's life is much stranger than the next fellow supposes, Eugene had once said to old Doc Cressy). The way Colby calculated the passage of time was by noting each occasion he had for hanging out the flag on the Fourth of July (somehow he shied clear of hanging it out on Decoration Day). But it was four times since Estelle had left our town with Duke and gone abroad to live. And, of course, young Justin was going on five, but it was not the boy's growth and progress but the number of times Colby fetched the flag down from the attic and hung it out the big front upstairs window that was his clock.

"I don't know that I was ever uncivil to you in the street or any other location you can name," Eugene defended himself.

"I've met you many times in the courthouse square, and once during the trial of Jeff Wertheim—you was the prosecuting attorney on that occasion—and you've never spoke to me once.

"You're suing, that's all, suing for my favors." Merle stepped over near his spittoon and showered it with tobacco juice. "The only reason you're here is I've got something you want, and I have half a notion not to give it to you. Your boy told me, that is, Justin"—he studied Eugene's strange expression—"never to give these here letters up to nobody but her. 'And if she don't come for them in time, though, Merle,' he said, 'I will be back in one form or another, don't give them to nobody if it was Christ himself asked for them, you hear? Burn the fuckers.'" He touched the bar.

"Well, would it give you any satisfaction to do so, Mr. Colby?" Eugene asked, but he almost turned his back as he said this. Colby took it as additional proof of his insolence and pride, his snobbery and prejudice, but when Mr. Bledsoe turned again toward him, he saw that the reason for Eugene's turning his back on him was for some other reason; at any rate his face was as discomposed and distorted as if he had had a stroke.

"I will go upstairs and get them, but look here, I'm not sayin' I'll give them to you."

Eugene started to say something in rejoinder, but the younger man had already leaped up the back stairs like some wild monkey. What speed, what noiseless scampering in a man who must be at least forty, Eugene marveled, and who drank and chewed, and God knows what else in the way of dissipation and bad habits. But his eyes were clear, the whites like cream, and the pupils very steely and bright, and he had some kind of pride and honor.

"Well, here they are," Merle said ferociously, having descended and now coming forward with a large packet of letters. "Mrs. Dumont give them back to me for safekeeping until ... " He stopped, and wiped his mouth of tobacco juice.

Mr. Bledsoe sat down precipitately and passed his hand over his face.

James Purdy
(288)

He drew out his handkerchief, which was exceptionally large and snowy and untouched by human effluvia. It might indeed have been a magician's handkerchief.

"Go on, look them over."

Eugene took them as if he were about to handle some kind of explosive he had had no experience with and which might explode on contact. "Why these letters are in . . . his handwriting! They're all his letters . . . to her! I thought you meant they were *her* letters to *him.*"

"I supposed you knowed that, Mr. Bledsoe. I supposed you wouldn't come for letters if they weren't from your boy."

"If they're from him . . . I wouldn't mind keeping them myself." Eugene was immediately sorry he had said this and looked up flushing at the billiard-hall owner.

"You're the lawyer," Merle Colby said. "You tell me who they belong to and I will believe you. Only I know they don't belong to me, I know that much law."

"But how did . . . Justin"—he had said the name at last and the ceiling did not fall upon them—"how did he get back his own letters to her?"

"When they broke off their engagement," Colby replied. "Just a year or so before he was killed."

The color drained from Mr. Bledsoe's face, but he said nothing.

"She gave him back the letters when they were through with one another. When your boy died, I took them to her—to Estelle. Then when she left the country, she give them back to me until . . . well, all she would say was 'until.' "

It was Bledsoe's courtroom stare, his looking at Merle as if he were a hostile witness which drew the ire from the pool-hall keeper. "Now you tell me what the law is, on account of I believe only she should ever set eyes on them. If I give them to you, how do I know what you will do with them?"

"With my own boy's letters?"

"He never wrote them for you to pore over. He didn't love you that good."

Mr. Bledsoe opened his mouth to say something; he grew paler; he was silent.

"If you give them to me, I will, of course, be their guardian." Mr. Bledsoe spoke after a brief silence. "But I can't promise I won't read them."

Mourners Below

(289)

There was an appeal so terrible in that voice that Merle Colby's belligerence, wounded pride, even hatred, dissolved for a moment.

"You can't send them to her, since she won't have them, you know that, being such a stickler for legal procedure. Or you can even go to the courthouse and go through some procedures there, which I can explain to you."

"No," Merle Colby grunted. "I don't want to go in the courthouse, and I don't want nobody to know he give me the letters. Furthermore, I want you to know something: though I burned to read them, I have never touched them since he give them to me, and when he was killed I knowed I would never touch them if I was to be offered ten million dollars to do so. If you read them, that's between you and God Almighty."

"I believe you, Mr. Colby." He put the letters down on the billiard table. "I thank you for it ... from the bottom of my heart." The last phrase was nearly inaudible, and Merle Colby knew Eugene Bledsoe was an ill man when he looked at him then.

"You take the letters. Do with them whatever you wish. I feel I've done my bounden duty by Justin Bledsoe."

"Do you know why he chose you to give the letters to?"

There was a long silence. Colby walked over to the spittoon and made as if to spit, but he had nothing to spit. He walked over to where he had put down his glass before Mr. Bledsoe had entered, but there was nothing in the glass to drink, and he walked over to the green wall and touched it with his finger as if he held a piece of chalk and would write something. But having touched the wall with his fingernail, he returned to the center of the room. He said, "I think I know deep down, yes, sir, but I wouldn't know how to put it in words without making myself sound like an ass. I know you think I'm worse than that, but Justin didn't think so. Justin thought highly of me. And I guess if I was on trial in your courthouse, I would tell the judge or the jury or the court or whoever, *'Justin thought highly of me, and he give me the thing he said was closest to him ... the letters.'*" He walked over to the packet and touched them as one might have touched a person.

"If I take these letters from you, Mr. Colby, I will tell you frankly again that I will keep them as a guardian. But I cannot promise you I won't read them, do you hear?" Mr. Bledsoe's eyes were wet, and his anger at showing his emotion caused his voice to sound furious and threatening, yet also imploring and defeated. Colby heard the latter appeal.

"I want to wash my hands of the affair, Mr. Bledsoe, I'll tell you that now, once and for all. I don't know if Justin, if he is looking down on us, will forgive me or not. I don't think he thought you loved him or understood him, but if you think you did—though your silence over the years has been the wonder of the town and the county and maybe the nation—if you think your conscience can bear it, then I will agree to let you have them, as I said before. I will wash my hands of it all, for I don't by this time know what's right and what's wrong where they are concerned, and after all, though you have denied him by your silence, you are his Dad, you are the one he talked about most of the time unless it was Duane, you impressed him more or most even though he was sad you never loved him."

Colby picked up the packet of letters and handed it to Mr. Bledsoe, who barely had time to accept them to prevent their falling to the floor. He held them against his breast pocket.

"I don't know what you mean by such accusations." Mr. Bledsoe spoke in a hoarse sound, almost a moan, a sound as thin and nerve-disturbing as a claw scraped over a glass wall.

"My silence came from my inability to take loss, you might say. I am not a strong man. Your other charge I cannot answer. If he never loved me, I suppose I am to blame for that. But my silence, as you term it, was the very heart of my grief—and my love." Having picked up the packet, he then, so to speak, picked himself up. "And I thank you for all you've done, Mr. Colby."

"You don't owe me nothing, and you don't need to speak to me on the street when you see me in the future. If it embarrassed you in the past, let it embarrass you for all time to come."

"I would like to speak to you, Mr. Colby. And I would like to show my gratitude, though you have taken away a lot of the purpose of my life in certain words you have spoken this afternoon."

"After all, he—Justin—spoke in anger, too," Merle Colby said, his back to his visitor.

"Mrs. Dumont La Roche will perhaps reconsider taking back the letters." Mr. Bledsoe spoke halfway out the door. "And I doubt I will ever read them."

The door closed softly.

Had he returned unexpectedly he would have been baffled but perhaps gratified to hear the savage cries of weeping coming from the billiard-hall operator as he pressed his face against the cheap green paint of the wall, and presently beat with his two fists against it.

"I have asked your Dad a score of times if he is sick," Mrs. Newsom reported to Duane, "but he just says he is not hungry."

"Well, let him alone then," Duane told her. "Let him lock himself up in there if he has to."

Duane partially opened the sliding door noiselessly and peeked through the aperture.

Eugene Bledsoe sat in stiff, almost military attention before his desk. Between his two outstretched hands lay a packet of letters. The string was still tied about them.

Duane returned to his spying every few minutes. But man and letters remained in the same position as when he had looked in the first time.

But toward nightfall, Duane went and rapped on the door, was told to come in, and entered. The chair had been moved, and the letters had been taken out of their binding ribbon and were stacked about separately, so that each letter formed its own pile, as though they had been read, censored, commented upon, stamped, and were ready perhaps to leave his possession.

"I say." Duane approached the table.

Eugene put his hands protectively over the various piles of correspondence.

"They're private, Duane, very private."

"They're old," Duane ventured to remark.

"Yes, they're not recent, certainly," his father said. "They're from your brother."

"Which one?" Duane spoke thickly.

"From your favorite brother," Eugene said in pathetic harshness.

"I see," Duane said. "Do you know who he wrote them to? . . . Was it you, Father?" he wondered in the dismal silence that followed his first question.

"Your brother seldom wrote me, Duane. They ain't to me."

Duane nodded.

"They were written to Mrs. Dumont—now La Roche."

Duane sat down.

"How did you come by them, Dad?"

James Purdy
(292)

"Oh," the older man responded after a long wait, "yes. . . . Merle Colby had them all this while."

Duane felt that he had suddenly received the full inheritance of all his father's character, and he knew he was Eugene's son more than he was Aileen's, that all the pained refusal to speak, the taciturnity, the bashful surveillance of all his own emotions were to be his legacy forever.

"I understand now why she had the masquerade ball, why you went there, why you gave her the baby boy. I mean I think I understand it. . . . It's all in the letters." He touched some of them with his right hand. "It was your favorite brother's idea, Duane. He sensed he would not come back."

They sat on for what seemed hours, like two dear friends who meet in some afterglow when this life is finished, and when time and human action no longer count.

They would certainly have sat through the night had they not heard Mrs. Newsom ring the supper bell.

"You go in, Duane, and have something. Tell her I couldn't taste a bite."

"No, no, Dad." Duane spoke vehemently and went over to the desk and touched him on the shoulder. "I can't eat if you don't, do you hear? I can't touch anything if you don't at least sit at the table. Can't you just sit down with us even if you don't have no appetite?"

There was another silence, and then Eugene stirred and looked at Duane.

"Oh, I might taste a bite or two, if you feel that way. I think though I will go first to the lavatory and wash my hands. . . . The dust, you know, of old papers . . . "

"What a ways that young fellow has come!" Eugene remarked to Mr. and Mrs. Newsom one evening some years after the birth of Justin Bledsoe II as he stopped by their home, which he called, rather to the couple's disaffection, if not resentment, their "cottage." A few years ago he would have been unwilling to step inside, but now he was a constant visitor.

"I tell you, Mrs. Newsom, I feel like a displaced person in my own house," Eugene remarked.

Mrs. Newsom herself was no longer the supreme housekeeper and do-it-all she had been before the birth of little Justin. She was not able to get on with the midwife who had stayed on as nurse, or with a young woman who now did much of the cooking and cleaning. Prior to giving notice, Mrs. Newsom had said, "There are too many around and about, Mr. Bledsoe. I don't know where to turn or where to lay my hands on my own things."

"I see," Eugene had replied, but even then he was no longer the boss, as he now pointed out to everybody. "I have taken a back seat." He smiled. "My boy is running the show now."

Mrs. Newsom did happen by, though, daily—largely, as anyone must have guessed, to see the new baby.

"I have never seen a more perfect child," was her habitual comment.

The grandfather beamed at any and every mention of him.

At first both Duke and Mrs. La Roche (as Eugene now referred to her, though occasionally he would say Mrs. Dumont) telephoned him from France or England, and always wrote long letters, which interrupted Eugene's Civil War studies with Professor Redpath.

Eugene answered the letters faithfully, for Duane was entirely occupied with his duties as father.

"I never saw such a thing in my life," Eugene confided to Mrs. Newsom. "Never saw a boy who was so obviously meant to be a father, as though that was his real calling. You know he was terribly sore at me when I sort of spoiled things for him to go participate in the Olympics as a skating star. He was a great skater, no question about it, and I hope he'll return to it. But do you know what, Mrs. Newsom? I don't think he'll ever find time for anything but being a father. I've told Duke and Mrs. La Roche all this in my letters." He tapped the envelope.

There was a silence, broken at last by Ab Newsom's knocking the ashes out of his pipe. He seldom spoke, and one did not know whether he merely tolerated Eugene's frequent visits or enjoyed them. At least he never complained of them, though he occasionally gave Eugene's white, manicured hands a look of wonder.

"I think Duane has forgiven me a lot," Eugene went on, letting the sealed envelope rest on his frayed trousers.

"He thought I didn't mourn over my two boys enough. But, Mrs. Newsom, you will bear me out, poor Duane mourned enough for the whole family. The whole nation!" He shook his head and smiled, and jingled the coins in his pants pocket.

James Purdy
(294)